Night Porter

Kevin H. Hilton

To Jean

My Aussie Gold Hunter

Prologue

Through the cloudless night sky over Kielder moorland the full moon's reflected sunlight was making the mist over the moor look like a silvery sea. Peat hags and heather-clad mounds stood proud like little islands.

Though the air temperature was just below freezing, which enabled sound to travel much further, here it was quiet. Until that was, a sudden *whumph* broke that silence with a blast of warm air. It momentarily cleared the mist from a patch of ground between hags. A circular ripple faded into the silvery sea, as the mist closed the gap back up.

In the distance a tawny owl screeched. Moments later a short figure rose from the mist. Helmet and suit reflecting the moonlight brightly like beaded road signage. The figure let out a muffled sigh.

'Are you okay, Nathan?' the voice from the ear-bud sounded more tired and concerned than Nathan felt.

'Yes, Dad…Everything's okay, though this is a *lot* further away than we expected.' His tone was quiet and calm, not at all excited.

This was Nathan Purnell, aged nine, in Northumberland at 2:10 in the morning. He understood his position and surroundings exactly, though he had never physically been on this moor before. This was possible because Nathan had been gifted with a talent for remote-viewing. This is the ability to perceive places which are out of sight. The Garmin GPS device on his wrist only served to confirm the tracer coordinates he heard his father ask him to check. He agreed a rendezvous point and began to make tracks across the wilderness. Behind him he left a circular section of bedsheet, memory-foam mattress, and sections of metal bedframe.

Nathan was not in full possession of the facts concerning his condition. However, he did understand that he was different to other children. Though his father understood more, even he had not been fully informed as to the actual situation.

Some children suffered from nightmares while others sleepwalked, Nathan Purnell, however randomly, sleep-teleported.

Whenever Nathan had asked about his mother, Kelly, his father, Gavin, would simply say she had died when Nathan was still very young. If Nathan pressed for more detail Gavin would only say that it was all very sad and he really didn't want to talk about it.

Details of Kelly's death were not the only thing Gavin Purnell had kept from his son. Gavin had a criminal record, as had Kelly. But illegal activities were all in the past, or so he thought.

He and Kelly had never married, though they had been devoted to one another. Their time together had not been perfect however. They had both wanted children, but Kelly turned out to be infertile. Their doctor suggested they could look at IVF as an option. However, the cost of fertilisation by this proven method would have been too much of a financial burden for them, living on minimum wage. Despite the global *Plandemic* cull's final impact upon the infrastructure and economies, no government funds directly supported repopulation.

Gavin and Kelly were not believers in any god. Nevertheless, in desperation they prayed to God for a solution, *any* solution.

Then one day they were contacted by a clinic which was trialling a new approach to fertilisation. Not only were Gavin and Kelly promised a healthy donor egg, this service would be free. The couple agreed, not wishing to pass up on the opportunity to bring up a child. The specialists they met with made it all sound above board, so they gave their consent. What could go wrong?

After detailed discussion they were told that they had been fully informed of the risks involved in the proposed procedure. They were then asked for their consent. However, no mention had been made concerning the complications with *both* previous trials.

Kelly went for regular check-ups. The clinic staff seemed most supportive. Kelly was promised that when she was full-term she would be brought to the clinic and given the best of care with the birthing.

Nevertheless, things did not go to plan for Kelly either. One night, eight months into the pregnancy, Kelly had gone to bed early. Gavin was watching a repeat of Blue Planet II on Freeview, when terrible sounds came from upstairs. The sounds all mixed together in his mind, a strange *whumph*, a gasping scream and a dull thump, followed by the cry of a baby.

Upstairs in seconds Gavin was horrified by the scene in the bedroom. Crying out in terrified disbelief, in shock he vomited.

To Gavin's mind it was like a scene from an Aliens movie. Kelly lay dead on a wrecked bed. Then down on the floor was premature baby Nathan. His head lifting clear of the remains of womb, next to which were intestines and a section of spine.

The way the premature baby was lifting its head reminded Gavin of what he had read about the Human 2.0 babies resulting from transhumanist experimentation.

He didn't let himself think about that further. Through floods of tears Gavin removed Nathan from the blood and gore, trying desperately to think what to do. It was obvious that his dear Kelly, unconscious and bleeding out, was beyond saving but their baby mustn't die too. Rather than dial the emergency services Gavin phoned the clinic.

A team arrived faster than any ambulance would have responded and the situation was taken in hand.

Being of a rather anxious disposition, Gavin remained in complete shock over the event for some time. He just could not imagine what had happened. It made no sense.

He had accompanied his baby Nathan to the clinic, doing whatever any of the staff said he should do.

A week later, with Nathan reported to be in good health, Gavin was able to take his son home. However, he struggled to put the fateful event behind him.

The clinic had arranged for the house to be cleaned in his absence. There was a new bed and carpet upstairs. No physical evidence of the dreadful event remained. No one would know anything untoward had happened in that bedroom, only Gavin.

Gavin soon found he could not sleep in that room. So even before Kelly's funeral he had decided to make the spare room with its single bed his.

Missing Kelly terribly, Gavin tried to tell himself that he needed to look ahead to the life he would have with his healthy son. He didn't expect for one minute that his involvement with the clinic was to continue.

That expectation changed a couple of weeks later when, to his horror, he heard that *whumph* once again, followed by Nathan crying. Gavin ran to Nathan's room. The cot was in pieces and Nathan was on the floor, on a section of bedding surrounded by pieces of wood. Gavin fell to his knees sobbing. Would this nightmare never end?

Picking up his baby and holding him tight a disturbing thought occurred to Gavin. If one of these *events* happened to Nathan when he was holding him, it would surely kill Gavin too. Then who would Nathan have left to look after him?

After that night Gavin went through a period of looking after his son at arm's length. The clinic team were at a loss what to suggest at first. What seemed to be happening was inexplicable. It was going to be a learning curve for *all* involved.

Gavin had difficulty getting to sleep in the next room, always hyper-alert now, listening out for that sound. So he moved Nathan's cot into his room to watch over him sleeping. Two tiring months passed without an event and Gavin began to hope that the nightmare might be over.

Then one night when he was almost asleep, he heard that *whumph* again. He looked to the cot and saw it falling in on itself. Nathan was not to be seen, or heard. Gavin's heart raced. Where had his son gone? Then he heard muffled sounds coming from downstairs. Nathan was found in the lounge, crawling towards his toys, even though the lights were off.

The next time, some months later, Gavin found Nathan on the pavement outside, thankfully not in the road. He knew then that each *jump* would be further away. But he did not know when the next jump-event would occur because the length of time between seemed a random period.

However, finally concluding that these events only happened to Nathan once he was asleep, Gavin felt safe to hold Nathan close again when awake. Gavin hugged his son often, sometimes weeping.

One thing was certain; the exponential increases in *distance* were going to mean a major threat to Nathan's life.

The clinic worked closely with the Purnells, clearly going more than an extra mile to provide support. A contract of support was drawn up and signed, which required that the clinic and Gavin keep Nathan's problem strictly confidential.

The clinic set up a specialist support team, simply referred to then as *Control*. However, as time went on, Gavin developed the feeling that Control were not keeping him fully informed about his son's condition.

Gavin later had his suspicions confirmed that there was something else Nathan was capable of. As Nathan got older it became apparent that he was also capable of remote-viewing. He displayed abilities for spatial awareness and object recognition in complete darkness or where things were otherwise out of sight.

As Nathan grew up he was seen to be able to walk around, even run around, with his eyes closed. Then as time went on Nathan began to report that he could see places increasingly further away. By nine years of age, from his home in Birmingham, he reported that he could see what people were doing in Sydney, Australia.

This was a big concern for Gavin, and the support team. Each time Nathan had *night-ported* he had always ended up further away. Logically there was assumed to be a link between these jumps and his ability to see further afield. What if he ended up in another country or worse still a sea?!

The research and development arm of the clinic provided Nathan with a customised environment suit and utility belt. With Gavin's permission they also implanted a tracer into Nathan in the flesh between his right index finger and thumb. This was linked to an automatic track and alert system so that a rapid response team could be on hand to extract him from his Reappearance Point, or RP.

Poor Nathan had to sleep in his suit every night. Though it was not as comfy to wear as pyjamas, Nathan knew no different, believing for a while that all children slept this way.

No one knew when the next night-port would occur. It was not intentional on Nathan's part, and he reported no recollection of a dream prior to porting.

In addition to the suit, *Control's* clinic also had Nathan in for a number of sleep-overs, where they scanned his brain activity while he slept. Nevertheless, this study of Nathan's sleep patterns showed nothing unusual.

It was his brain-waves whilst awake which sparked interest, specifically during remote-viewing. However, this activity was noted to cease as he fell asleep.

One night he suddenly vanished from the sleep research unit. His RP was immediately traced to Birmingham's HS2-tram interchange. He remembered waking up thinking he was in the shower but found himself on tram tracks in the rain. Luckily there was no tram coming.

The next night-port, sometime later, took Nathan to Epping Forest, near the edge of London's no-go zone. The rapid response team collected Gavin on their way to get Nathan back. Luckily Nathan was not at the RP long enough to show signs of radiation sickness.

What had been predicted by the sleep researchers was that immediately prior to a night-port Nathan's brain waves would indicate remote-viewing activity. However, on both occasions this proved not to be the case. The team were at a loss to understand why not. There surely had to be something going on in some part of Nathan's young mind to select an RP.

As Nathan got older he was better able to describe his experience of remote-viewing. He explained that it had been confusing for him at first because he could view things *so* clearly that it was like *being there* but without touch, sound or smell. It was also difficult for him to understand why others could not view things the way he could. Not even close, he could differentiate colours in the dark and could even perceive temperature differences.

Sometimes he liked to imagine he would go to distant places he viewed someday, to listen, feel and smell what it was like being there, but not to all of the places.

Some places looked scary, and some people's behaviours frightened him. He didn't like to talk about some of the things he had seen. Some of what he had witnessed had made him less trusting of people.

Nevertheless, it was assumed by the team that this natural curiosity could be a likely trigger for his night-porting.

There was discussion about sending Gavin and Nathan on a world tour to sate some of this curiosity. However, there were those at *Control* who were concerned that such an approach might only make his condition worse. Instead they proposed that what was needed was more survival training.

Ex-military survival expert, Emily Richards, was brought into train Nathan. Gavin thought a woman might have been chosen as a mother-figure, and would go easy on Nathan but she was tough with him. Nevertheless, she taught Nathan that he *could* do what was needed to survive. He just had to stay calm, think positive and not give up.

Between these training sessions the sleep researchers had Nathan trying meditative practices. This was to see if he could learn to port during daytime and thereby gain control of his ability. However, at no point did this approach prove successful.

Because of his frustrations and worry, Nathan sometimes became aggressive, both verbally and physically. He was given opportunities to play with other children to support his socialisation but he did not always get along with other children. It was clear that *Control's* support for Nathan's every need had left him spoiled.

After much discussion with Gavin about Nathan's needs it was agreed that he should go to a private school.

Going to school it was drummed into Nathan by *Control* that he must *'tell no one'*, not even the teachers. During his pre-schooling at the clinic he had been taught how to pretend to be normal, though even the team were not in full agreement as to what *normal* actually was.

It wasn't just that he mustn't be seen using his remote-viewing, Nathan was developing additional differences. He was faster than other children, so had to learn to react and move slower. He was also found to have incredible stamina, including being able to hold his breath for some minutes.

One of the things the clinic had chosen not to show the Purnells was Nathan's MRI scans. Nathan's internal organs differed from human beings.

Gavin and Kelly had been told that a healthy egg had been donated by an anonymous woman. What neither of them had been informed of was that this egg had not been fertilised by Gavin's sperm. They had in fact only been involved as surrogate parents.

Nathan was glad of his warm boots as he jogged through the ground mist across the heather. Pressing onwards to the agreed RV, he watched the progress of his father and the extraction team. They were not coming for him by car this time, but by helicopter.

In his mind he was already sitting in the spare seat next to his father. It was just that for the moment he couldn't quite *be there*.

As he watched the crew he practiced something which he had not mentioned to anyone else. Nathan thought his *secret game* was just a bit of fun. He was teaching himself to lip-read.

1

Three years later

Nathan had become an angry pre-teen. The constant flood of remote-viewing experiences, many of which Nathan would not share with others, especially his anxious father, disturbed him.

Nathan felt like he was fast approaching a crossroads in his life, where he could more easily become a super-villain than super-hero. He had watched all the *origin* movies. The truth was, to be the hero meant waiting around for an opportunity to help others. As the villain however, he could act as and when he wished, to simply take advantage.

He had done what any *normal* youngster with remote-viewing ability might have done. He had let curiosity get the better of him.

Remote-viewing for Nathan was like being the invisible boy or ghost boy. He could not physically touch anything or communicate with anyone but he could go anywhere he desired, unseen.

He had great difficulty resisting the lure of viewing homes of girls he felt attracted to, where he watched them getting ready for bed. He felt both drawn to and ashamed by many of these experiences. He knew girls would be mortified if they discovered that he was watching them. It was like a form of super-stalking. He knew he had to learn to look away, which was not at all easy, especially when he had a massive crush on one in particular.

He had described his remote-viewing to his support team as being something of an effort to do. He suggested that he only used it to check out things of importance. However, that was a lie. He had only said that so they would not put him through even more trials, which he had grown very bored of. In truth remote-viewing was as effortless for him as observing with his eyes.

However, through his voyeurism, Nathan had come to learn things about people which he knew he shouldn't have. Like with the behaviour of the sullen but very pretty girl in the sixth-form, who other children had nick-named Belcher.

Whenever she got excited or laughed, she would start to belch. Years ago, her mother had taken her to their doctor but the doctor had not found the girl to be suffering from any gastric condition but rather some sort of nervous habit. It was ironic to all that the girl's name was Charisma Goodchild.

Nathan had found himself drawn to watching Charisma belching, through his prying gaze. It usually took place in her bedroom. The belching obviously amused or excited her. Going by her facial expressions the louder she belched the better the experience was for her.

Nathan, being unable to hear Charisma, other than at school, had found it intriguing to work out what was going on.

Watching people simultaneously in different places demanded more concentration from Nathan, nevertheless it was still possible for him. By watching Charisma's parent's reactions in parallel to Charisma's behaviour Nathan came to understand something more of her problem.

She would frequently get herself into quite a frenzied state of belching then her mother would shout upstairs, or from the bedroom along the landing, 'Charisma! Stop that!'

Gulp, belch! *Gulp*, belch! *Gulp*, belch!

'Stop that, this instant!!'

With the mood ruined, Charisma would often resort to making another rude noise. For this she would turn over on her bed, onto her front, and do what Nathan at first took to be some yoga exercise. She would raise her backside into the air with her knees slightly parted, then after half a minute or so of relaxing in that position she would lay flat. Very soon after she would be muffling a giggle then repeating the procedure.

Sometimes, as she repeated this procedure, her mother would again shout, 'Charisma!!'

Nathan had to try this out himself a few times before he worked out what she must be doing to rile her mother up. By taking up this position with the backside in the air, relaxing the stomach muscles and rectum, air entered the colon. Lying back down it increased the abdominal pressure and brought about a large fart. Nathan laughed at this discovery, but later learned it was best to have gone to the toilet *before* doing this.

Charisma did not always make farting-noises that way. Sometimes she would simply roll up her sleeve, lick her bicep and then blow wet fart sounds with her lips. This old trick took no working out for Nathan, having done this before. It made him laugh. However, he was left with the question, why was *she* doing this?

He hadn't seen any other girls consistently behave in this manner at home. Both of Charisma's parents were clearly disgusted with her compulsive behaviour and at a loss what to do about it.

However, her behaviour did nothing to quell Nathan's crush on her, even though he thought she would never be interested in a boy years younger than her. She didn't even know who he was. They had never actually spoken before.

Charisma's parents might be disgusted with her but in Nathan's considered opinion there were people with far worse behavioural issues than Charisma Goodchild.

Domestic abuse of one sort or another was far more common than people believed. It was not just a hang-over from the Great Reset Coronavirus lockdowns either, but without giving away his secret there seemed little he could do to help.

Everyone and every place were now within reach of Nathan's remote-viewing. Only his directional focus prevented him suffering a sensory overload of viewing everyone at once.

He would regularly do what he considered to be his radar-sweep. He would check what was going on, close range, in a full three-sixty degree sweep. It was almost second nature, and he liked to think it showed a level of multi-tasking ability which he had heard said normal men couldn't do.

However, remote-viewing led to a deepened self-loathing. Spying upon his support team one day he came to wish that he had never taught himself to lip read.

Nathan witnessed a discussion about how his mother had died, and learned the truth that his father could never bring himself to tell him.

From that moment on Nathan's burden of guilt made him consider himself a natural killer. The more he thought about this, the more he came to believe that there *was* some deep desire in him to kill. He had no idea where this had come from but it was definitely *there*, in his soul.

He worried for a while that he might lose control of this desire; that he might misuse the self-defence training he was receiving, to kill someone at random. Was this to be how he became a super-villain? However, as time passed he convinced himself that, for him, killing would not be random but reasoned.

Out of bitterness over what he felt must be his dark-side Nathan began to distract himself by planning pranks. He had promised his father that he would not let anyone else know about his abilities, so careful planning was crucial. He loved his father. Nevertheless, he considered himself smart enough to know that keeping things secret only really meant never getting caught.

He began to use his sweep to check that the coast was clear of people and of surveillance devices, in order to set up pranks. The intention being always to use his somewhat faster speed to ensure he was away in time to have an alibi.

His approach involved setting-up a number of opportunities in parallel. This was so that he could act as and when one presented itself.

He had come to realise another talent some years ago, which he had also not admitted to, while seeking to cheat with his school tests. Laying loads of crib sheets across his bed and desk at home, to remote-view, he noticed that he didn't need to do this.

Nathan had a photographic memory. This could also be misused. He had learned staff passwords and pin numbers by watching over their shoulders. He knew what was in people's accounts.

While the thought of causing trouble amused him, Nathan could only be bothered if the effort would benefit him in some tangible way.

In one scenario he had planned to act when the spring-water deliveryman arrived. The man had a habit of bringing the water-fountain drums round to the back of the school from the lorry on a trolley. He would leave them sitting outside while he went round to reception with the paperwork to get the back entrance opened.

Water drums in themselves had little value. However, Nathan had acquired some clear odourless emetic off the Internet, plus a small syringe. The plan was to ask for a toilet break from class, in order to have time to get outside. He would lift the dust seal off each drum and inject emetic into each one, through the frangible plastic cap beneath. He would reseal each drum and restack them then make his return to class.

Then it would be a waiting game for things to kick-off. He imagined that this would be quite entertaining. The thought of seeing teachers and pupils doing a five-finger spread after their lunch very much appealed to his pre-teen sense of humour.

As part of his alibi cover, he had also prepared a zip-lock sealed bag of vegetable soup. He had mixed parmesan cheese in with this to more effectively fake his own vomit. He knew it would be absolutely *rank*, especially since the pack was now some days old.

During all of the confusion he hoped that the staffroom would become empty as people went to either the school nurse or the toilets. Nathan then intended to access one or two online bank accounts. This was only plausible since staff, like students, were not allowed to take their mobile devices into lessons with them.

The aim was to transfer money from one staff member's account to another, to spark off an inquiry into a teacher who Nathan disliked.

However, on this day, things did not go to plan.

During a Modern History lesson with Dennis Cotton, Nathan watched as the spring water man headed towards the school.

Dennis was covering the Great Reset, which had brought about their New World Order over a decade ago. He was openly describing how the Reset had not gone to plan, an accepted part of history.

'The initial design of the spiked protein, carried by the Coronavirus, as anticipated, proved not to work effectively enough. It had been designed to hide its symptoms and then deaths by exacerbating the cancers and other major health conditions which the population already suffered from.

'Of course the Privileged were all given the actual vaccine well in advance of the Coronavirus release from Wuhan. These were not the false vaccines and boosters which carried more of the spiked protein toxin for further weakening people's immune system. The longer term aim was to reset and then manage the world population such that it no longer increased exponentially. Many people had misunderstood the plan, believing that the vaccinations would sterilise people. The truth was far more shocking; Global genocide. People could not believe it until they witnessed the final release.

'Initially, *active development* had brought about deaths among the old and infirm. This had been a requirement from bankers to solve their increasingly loss-making pensions and insurance schemes. This development period also further informed the creation of the final super-variant. Final cull quotas were to be assured by the mass weakening with the fake jabs. People who had attempted to second guess this plan were accused of being irresponsible conspiracy theorists. The term *fear-fest* was bandied around in the media by those arguing for *and* those arguing against the vaccinations.

'Only in the aftermath was it admitted that in order to save the world from overpopulation the governments were responsible for this cull. They had all agreed, at a meeting in Davos, to the release of the final stage design of the spiked protein.

'Initially they had all falsely reported this Coronavirus variant as being the Marburg virus. This misinformation was to provide delay in response through confusion. It appeared to explain why the vaccinations and boosters were ineffective against the haemorrhaging.

'*Awakened* scientists, who claimed they could prove the new strain was *not* actually Marburg but rather a chimera-Coronavirus developed in a lab, were promptly silenced.'

'What does chimera mean, Sir?' A lad at the back asked, putting his hand up after calling out his question.

'It means that it was a combination of virus DNA, Oliver. It was claimed that this variant had been weaponised for its role in mass depopulation. However, the first Coronavirus released was also an engineered virus, not natural. It has a patent number. A patent cannot be applied for something naturally occurring.

'The chimera-Coronavirus went on to wipe out more people than the cull quotas agreed to by the world powers. As a result it wrecked infrastructure and economies of many countries, increasing poverty and crime.'

A girl put her hand up 'Sir?'

'Yes Jenny?'

'My dad said the vaccinations were just an experiment in transhumanism. So why did we kill off so many people before the H2Os were fully established?' She referred to those now known to be Human 2.0.

'Your father is correct. There were a number of competing programmes of research and development. What people had injected into them depended on which vaccine they thought they chose, or received. The Transhumanist movement was initially an attempt to solve the problem of healing damaged nerve tissues and extending life expectancy.'

'At a time when the world was already overpopulated, Sir?'

'Yes Jenny. I know it sounds confusing but it was always about market opportunities for big pharmaceutical companies. And yes eugenics was one of those opportunities. Friedrich Nietzsche referred to this as the creation of the Ubermensch, the Superhuman; our H2Os were to be the first real step in that direction.

'These days the New World Order, our one world government, don't mind the truth being known regarding what they had to do to get us to this point, because they now have control. However, to get here required many lies and half-truths to be delivered through news feeds and social media, to basically divide and conquer.'

'So why haven't all survivors benefitted from the H2O programme, Sir?'

'Well Jenny, the rich and Privileged *have* being able to afford the outcomes. The research into the regenerative abilities of organisms, such as hydra and starfish by big pharma, was never intended for a mass market.

'But as I was saying…around the time of the Great Reset the cull quota agreements had become a major part of Agenda 21. Agenda

21's focus had originally been the reduction of climate change and ecological destruction. But as overpopulation increasingly became a key factor, population reduction took precedence above all other sub-agendas. Especially since the *Conference of the Parties*, COP26, could not find real resolution for ecologically destructive world cultures and lifestyles.'

Another student lifted his hand. 'Sir, wasn't it all just mismanaged, because it proved too complex a problem to resolve in any managed way?'

'Yes Mark, and angered by the loss of loved ones, through *that* mismanagement and the cover-ups, many survivors formed an uprising. Groups of *Awakened* extremists, world-wide, then retaliated with dirty-bombings aimed at the *Privileged*. These are believed to have been inspired by the Wuhan Dirty Bombing during the start of the Great Reset. These dirty bombings turned cities like Washington D.C., Canberra and London, into the radioactive wastelands they are now. Even underground bases, like NORAD and its counterpart in the Ural Mountains, were rendered uninhabitable.

'Despite our natural herd immunity or *tolerance* to the spiked proteins, particularly among non-vaccinated and the H2Os, life was changed forever.

The impact upon Humankind's capacity to maintain services and infrastructure created the more decentralised way of life that we experience in towns and cities today.'

'Sir?'

'Yes, Cindy?'

'If surviving members of the NWO admitted that they used fake news and fake jabs, how do we know *this,* that you're telling us, isn't *still* all lies, Sir?'

'Well Cindy, I know it has been said that history is written by the victor of a conflict, but in this case the NWO are not claiming success. They are admitting that they lost control of their plan.'

'My mum says not to believe *any* of this, that it all fucking bollocks, Sir.'

This brought a burst of laughter from the class.

Dennis Cotton gave a stern look of disapproval but didn't want to lose engagement with the subject. 'Well, we are *all* entitled to our opinions. People will believe what they want to believe. Some people believe that the Earth is flat, and that the moon-landings were faked. Yet they also believe in aliens from outer space, like the Magic Door beings, and myths like Bigfoot and *Fantasma da morte.*'

Another burst of laughter suggested these pupils were going to remain sceptics.

'But sir, if we can just believe what we want, doesn't that make history lessons rather pointless? Wouldn't we better off if schools taught life-skills?'

Dennis Cotton felt cornered but before he could give a considered response he was saved from the awkwardness by Nathan.

'Please Mr Cotton, can I go to the toilet?'

'Really Nathan? Can't it wait another twenty minutes?'

'Sorry, Sir.'

'Go on then. Hurry up.'

'Thank you, Sir.'

A couple of lads made groaning and farting noises as Nathan passed them, causing further laughter.

'Okay, settle down the rest of you.'

Nathan tried not to smile as he left the room.

Heading quickly down the corridor, he turned down the stairwell. However, two flights down, he stopped in his tracks.

His remote-view sweep had picked up Charisma, in trouble. She was upstairs in a cubicle of the girl's toilets, visibly sobbing. She sat on the toilet lid with the blade of a scissors from her art class held against her left wrist.

Nathan didn't know when he would get another chance to pull off this prank. It was almost the Christmas holidays. Everything was lined up. But he knew if he went down to the water delivery it could prove too late to get back to Charisma. He turned and sped back up the stairs.

He rushed down the corridor to the toilets, wondering what he was going to be able to do or say once there. He didn't think there was time to get help. It was going to be all down to him.

Bursting into the girl's toilets Nathan blurted 'Don't do it!' in a high voice.

Charisma stopped sobbing. She froze, startled.

'Please put down the scissors, Charisma.'

'Wh-who is that?'

'I'm urr a super-girl.'

'This isn't funny! You sound like a boy to me.'

'*Oh* thanks a lot for that...I'm transitioning, actually.'

'Is this a prank? Have you put a camera in this toilet?'

'No, no. Nothing like that...I don't need a camera, I urr...I have x-ray vision.'

'Asshole.'

'Straight up. Put your hand up inside your jumper and ask me how many fingers you are holding up.' Before she could even say she was ready, Nathan said, 'You're giving me the finger.'

'Lucky guess.'

'And now you've changed to three.'

'How...?'

'Never mind. Would you please just drop the scissors?'

Unnerved now, Charisma dropped them clattering to the tile floor.

'Do you want to talk about it, Charisma?' Nathan was struggling to think what best to say. Keeping the dialogue open seemed the best option.

'No.'

'Something is clearly wrong.'

'Yes, that's why I want to end it!' Charisma began to sob again. 'I hate the person I have become.'

'Then change.'

'I can't.'

'Hey darling, you aren't *seriously* trying to tell a trans-girl that *you* can't change, are you?'

She sighed. 'How can I talk to *you*? I don't recognise your voice. You're just a stranger.'

'I'm told it can be easier talking with a complete stranger, so come on, when did this all start?'

'I guess…It started years ago when Bernie turned up…He's my step-dad.'

'Right.'

'I never liked him. Mum adores him, but he gives me the creeps. It's the way he looks at me. He used to come into my room when I was a kid, to read me bedtime stories, even when I said I didn't want them. Then he started insisting that he had to snuggle under the duvet with me.

'One day I happened to belch and Bernie's leer changed to one of disgust. I knew then I had found my weapon. I made a big thing of belching. It made him angry and that put an end to him coming to my room.'

'Have you told your mother about this?'

'No. She would never believe me.'

'I think you should try.'

'But my behaviour keeps Bernie disgusted.'

'It can't be nice for your mum either though can it?'

'She shouldn't have married Bernie then should she.'

'You need to talk to her. Harming yourself is not the answer.'

'I guess.'

'Promise me.'

Charisma got up and opened the cubicle door to promise in person, but there was no one out there. Nathan was vanishing down the corridor back to class.

Late afternoon at Shetland's Sumburgh Airport, Agent Maeve Corrigan ran across the tarmac from a helicopter to reach her connecting flight. The worsening weather had her keratin-shiny long auburn hair whipping across her face.

A Black Kite stealth troop-carrier waited at the end of the runway. A man stood waiting on its rear ramp. He was not a loadie but an SAS trooper.

'Sergeant,' Maeve said in hurried greeting as she jogged onto the ramp.

'You're late.'

'Tell me about it,' she said with a nod, slowing down.

'I just did...Close her up!' The sergeant barked right behind her, but Maeve didn't jump. He kept close to her as she headed for a vacant seat. 'I know *what* you are, you know.'

'Good for you.'

'Your boss and I go way back. I trust *her*. However, I don't want you making anyone uncomfortable by *reading* us and oversharing, if you get my drift.'

'Well then, Sergeant, you should know two things,' Maeve turned to face him as she took her seat. 'First, I'm a professional, not a party performer. Secondly, I'm a *receiver* not a mind reader. I can only pick up consciously thought words. I don't see people's memories or what they imagine.' She strapped herself in.

The sergeant took a seat facing hers and did the same. 'So Section 13 believe that's going to be enough to help find what we are looking for?'

'So I'm told.'

'Umber.'

'Sergeant?' Maeve frowned.

'The lads call me Beastie.'

'I can see why.'

He smiled, 'But you can call me Ethan.'

That night, in his room, Nathan stared blankly at his homework, he watched over Charisma, lip reading. She had managed to get some alone-time with her mum in the kitchen, while her step-father watched Sky Sports in the lounge. Awkwardly she got round to saying what had been troubling her for such a long time, the reason for her behaviour.

Her mother was upset by the revelation but listened to her daughter. Taking her in her arms, they sobbed together.

It was only the start of their journey but Nathan felt good that he had changed their course from tragedy. He also knew that this felt better than the intended prank would have made him feel.

Homework complete, he went downstairs to spend some quality time with his father.

Gavin was watching the end of a nature programme. 'All done?'

'Yep.'

'*Travels with Trisha* will be on next. Do you want to watch that with me?'

'Sure.' Nathan joined his father on the sofa.

'She's visiting Sweden this week.'

'Great.' Nathan enjoyed watching travel programmes.

Something else Nathan would have liked to have shared with his father was his good deed for the day. However, Nathan knew that would only lead to questions and then trouble. Gavin was a worrier, so they just watched Trisha.

When the programme finished, Gavin made Nathan a mug of hot chocolate and by ten-thirty they were both heading to their rooms.

Nathan went through the routine of having a wash, brushing his teeth, then returning to his room to put on his environment suit. Last to go on were his boots then his helmet.

Lying down he didn't need a sheet over him, but somehow it always felt cosier to have one.

He could have read for a while but instead he set his mobile streaming an album of his favourite band, *The Undone*.

He was asleep even before the fourth track.

In the next room, Gavin could only just hear his son's music, knowing it would all fall quiet at the end of the album.

Whumph.

2

Whumph!

Before opening his eyes Nathan gave his immediate surroundings a sweep. Snow.

Sitting up on the remains of his bedding and opening his eyes he saw a wonderful display of the northern lights dancing overhead. Bands of green topped off with pinks in the upper atmosphere.

He recalled the first night-port to take him to unfamiliar surroundings. He had cried out for his father then, in his confusion. There was still anxiety now but with his training it was easier to deal with by following procedures.

Control spoke before his father was able to connect, telling him his GPS position through his helmet.

'Yeah, that's correct,' Nathan responded having looked to his wrist.

'There is a blizzard coming in, so we cannot give an exact ETA at present. Sorry Nathan.'

With that weather, even with his environment suit, he could go hypothermic in a couple of hours, unless he found or made shelter quickly.

'Where is your RP this time Nathan?' Gavin asked, the GPS reference meaning little to him.

'I seem to have teleported to northern Norway, on the border with Russia, Dad.'

The stealth troop-carrier banked east from Greenland to Svalbard where it banked again

34

to head south over the Barents Sea. It was on a heading that would bring it to a river mouth where the coast of northern Norway met Russia. The meandering Pasvik River formed the border between the two countries, and somewhere along its length was their target.

Before they reached the coast the co-pilot notified Maeve as he had been briefed to do, and patched her into the Black Kite's PA.

'Okay team, we are nearing the recon zone. Let me remind you, we do not know how long this will take. The winding border is over a hundred and twenty miles in length. We will have to cover that distance at near stall speed for me to stand a chance of detecting our target. Hopefully we will not have to make a second run.

'It is a frustration that the information supplied to us was not more specific. As a consequence of this I will require concentration from you all to help me do my job properly.

'I will be attempting to receive inner-voice thoughts. I do not register visual thoughts. So I need you to restrict your thoughts to the visual for the duration, to provide me with a quiet scan of the target area.

'Is that clear?'

'Yes ma'am,' affirmed crew and troopers.

Nathan could see some slightly higher ground to the east, which could offer shelter of deeper snow. However, the river Pasvik would need to be crossed. With the permafrost he hoped that he would find the surface of the river frozen. Nevertheless, it could make for a risky crossing because he wasn't so good at judging thickness of solid materials with his remote-viewing.

As if there was not enough to contend with his sweep picked up a pack of wolves a few miles south of his position. With a north wind blowing they might soon pick up any scent he was carrying from home. His sealed suit was meant to be odourless, but it might carry a trace of something on its surface. At least the filters on his helmet's air ducts ought to remove traces of the toothpaste on his breath. Nevertheless, he picked up speed across the tundra.

Almost an hour into the search, Maeve's body language suddenly changed.

'Plane.'

'Nothing on the radar,' said the co-pilot.

'Seven men, one woman. Not my ride.'

'What?'

'It's him. Our target,' Maeve declared then continued *'They've detected me.'*…'Circle back round, try and get eyes-on. And look for a place to put down.'

Maeve turned to Ethan but didn't need to say more. He nodded. 'Right lads, prepare to head out as soon as we touch down.'

Nathan had expected the tundra to be hard below the snow, but in places it was soft and he could feel the crust crunching. This was another sign of the continued climate change. This thawing of the tundra was even further north than people were being told. This was a worry for all the extra carbon dioxide and methane it would release, adding to the greenhouse effect.

However, the more immediate concern for Nathan was that the softer ground was slowing him down. In addition to which the wolves had now become aware of his presence and were heading his way. He didn't know how the wolves felt about crossing the river but he hoped it might hold them back.

The river was still a mile away and though the wolves were somewhat further away they were faster on their feet than Nathan.

To add to his troubles the flakes of falling snow started to get larger and the snowfall heavier as the storm-front closed in.

Running on, picking the straightest flattest route through the snow covered hags, Nathan tried to decide on the best crossing point of the river to head for. He could see sections without ice but needed to find a fully frozen narrow section. However, the best looking section looked too far away and up river. He had no chance with the wolf pack in that direction.

Continuing on a heading for his next best choice, optical visibility now down to twenty metres, he spotted an aircraft heading his way.

'Plane,' he thought as he looked inside to check out the crew. 'Seven men, one woman. Not my ride.'

He began lip reading, at first presuming it was coincidence them being there, then he knew it wasn't a coincidence, 'They've detected me.'

He wondered if they somehow had access to his tracker, but then as he saw the woman say the words he had just thought, he knew this was *something else*.

He didn't stop his run for the river as the plane passed close by to bank round. He wondered where they had come from so quickly. The woman was speaking English, not Norwegian or Russian. He didn't recognise the aircraft but it had a stealth look about it.

As the plane came in low Nathan saw that the noise of its engines had scared the wolf-pack, stopping them in their tracks. Then as it started heading back towards him they turned tail and ran south. Nathan now took his chance for that better crossing, changing course, heading south east.

The plane was not *optically* visible and the thickening snow and strengthening wind was dulling the sound of the engines. Nevertheless, these people were definitely onto him. He watched as the crew prepared to land and disembark. In this weather they would have to use thermal imaging to try and pick him up, however he knew that his suit had very little heat signature.

'*Control*, I have some air transport coming in for me and about to land. They don't look like our people.' All Nathan could pick up was slight static. The storm had blacked out coms. '*Control*?!'

He just needed to cross the river and dig into cover to get totally out of sight. 'Catch me if you can,' he thought with a laugh.

As the aircraft made a vertical landing nearby, Nathan read the lips of the woman repeating his words. It was weird, it seemed like he had X-Men after him. He knew it couldn't be any bugging device in his suit because she had spoken his *thoughts*.

'Two can play at that game, lady.'

'He seems to have my ability,' said Maeve, 'Definitely, he just repeated what I said to you.'

'Probably best I don't speak anymore then until my ride home arrives.' He watched the woman repeat his thought.

'We were sent here only to make contact with you. What is your name?'

Nathan didn't respond.

Maeve tried again as the rear ramp opened up, letting in swirls of snow. 'We can offer you shelter until your people come. What's your name?'

Telling yourself not to think of anything was always the worst thing you could do. Before he could think of anything else he had thought of what he called himself.

'Night Porter?' repeated Maeve. 'That's what you do for a living? But what's your name?' She led the troopers out into the blizzard trying to get a better fix on where Nathan's thoughts were coming from.

Nathan tried to empty his mind of anything but the river crossing.

Maeve had to keep the dialogue open. 'My name is Maeve…Look, this storm, it's really too dangerous to be out here, Sir.'

'Sir?' Nathan couldn't help thinking.

'Madam then?'

'Ha.' Now Nathan knew this woman could not tell his age or gender. He tried again to focus on the river. It was close now, but he could see that though the people on his trail were much slower than him they did seem to know where he was heading now.

Finally he reached the bank of the Pasvik. However, he did not slow. With a leap of faith he spread his arms and legs and jumped in a dive, to spread his load when he hit the ice. The hard ice almost winded him as he hit, but then he was sliding across.

The layer of snow on the top of the ice created drag however, so he did not slide as far as he would have liked. He shifted into a crawl and kept going. He was very close to the opposite bank when Maeve and the troopers reached the bank he had left.

'Look! Out there,' said one of the troopers.

'Yes. I've got him,' acknowledged Ethan. 'And unless it's a trick of poor visibility, he's a short-arse.'

'I think it's…a kid!' blurted Maeve, catching sight of Nathan nearly at the other side. 'Oh my God!'

'Shit!' exclaimed Nathan as the surface suddenly cracked under him and the current of the river took him underneath the ice sheet.

3

The water pressure closed the vents on Nathan's helmet. His rebreather activated, scrubbing out the carbon-dioxide that would otherwise begin to build up. This compact system would not have lasted for long with an average person. However, *Control* had learned that Nathan could function under poor air quality conditions.

Nevertheless, being trapped under the ice was still a major concern for Nathan. The current was just too strong to get back to the hole he had entered through. He knew he mustn't panic. He had to remain positive and use his training and abilities. At least this accident might be one way to help lose those people tracking him.

On the bank Ethan took charge. 'Head down river,' he signalled. 'There may be a chance they will come back out of an exposed section of water.'

The team moved off, checking ahead with night vision goggles and thermal imaging, which could highlight exposed water. Maeve, keeping up with the team, listened intently for Nathan.

The back of Nathan's helmet scraped the underside of the ice as he swam with the current. He smiled to himself as he saw an exposed section of water ahead, near the bank. He was soon out from under the ice, but as he tried to swim to the bank he realised that he was not going to be quick enough. The current swept him on.

'Look! He's there,' shouted Maeve, just able to make out the figure in the section of exposed water. 'No!!'

As Maeve and the troopers watched Nathan, with fast reactions he grasped the edge of the ice sheet. The current twisted him round feet first and then onto his back. However, as he tried to pull himself back the edge crumbled and he was gone again underneath the ice.

Swimming on he could see that his appearance had given the people on the bank hope. They were now keeping almost level with his progress.

As the Pasvik meandered the current drew Nathan out into the centre of the river. Then at a bend he found himself being taken back to the west bank.

Ahead he could see an exposed section of water coming up but not much beyond that for some distance. He didn't feel he had much of a choice. He would have to try and get out here even if it meant being taken by these people. He decided it was the safest thing to do, and he had to admit he was now curious who these people were.

Nathan swam to the edge in preparation for the exposed section and as he came out he saw one of the troopers come down off the bank and grab him by the arm.

'You're safe now, mate,' Ethan lifted him up to one of his men then climbed back up the bank, gesturing that everyone head back.

'I'm Maeve.' Bending down to look through Nathan's visor, she suggested, 'Let's get you out of this blizzard.'

'We're coming back to the transport, over,' Ethan reported but only got a crackle back.

The team made their way back along the river, with visibility down to less than ten metres and the wind picking up still further. The team knew where their plane was but only by means of their GPS devices, whereas Nathan could remote-view easily even in heavy snowfall. However, he was not intending to let these people know *that* unless they got lost.

'I'll see you get a hot drink and something to eat when we get inside!' Maeve shouted over the storm, but Nathan didn't reply.

'Oh, thanks Mum!' said Ethan.

'I was talking to the boy!' Maeve hoped she had the gender right. She was not so good at discerning age, gender or accent from received thoughts.

Minutes later they were close enough for the coms to work and Ethan gave a sit-rep. Shortly, the thermal imagers picked up the warmth of the transport's ramp lowering. By the time they reached the plane though, most of that warmth had gone. It would of course regenerate when the transport sealed back up. Nevertheless, the team would all be keeping their kit on for some time while they waited out the storm.

It was rather exciting for Nathan boarding the plane. He hadn't been on anything like it before.

'What sort of plane is this?' Nathan asked through his helmet speaker.

'Military,' said Ethan.

'What sort?'

'British.'

Nathan frowned at Ethan wondering if the sergeant was just being awkward. 'I haven't seen this type on TV.'

'Because it's secret.'

'Is it?'

'Well, not any longer, I guess. It's called a Black Kite. Would you like a ride?'

'Sergeant.' Maeve interrupted. 'We are under strict instructions only to introduce ourselves to the contact.'

'*Introduce*? But we have him now. The lad is clearly a Brummie, like me. Let's just get him home.'

'Oakley said under *no* circumstances are we to leave with him. You and I will be heading for Perth after we hand him over to his people.'

'Perth?'

'Yes. It's already signed off with Credenhill.'

'Just you and I?'

'Yes. Just you and I.'

'Well, will I be briefed *properly* this time? Or am I just along for back-up?'

'Both.'

Nathan laughed. 'Do you two always get along so well?'

'I really hope not,' said Maeve with a sigh. 'You can take that helmet off in here I think.'

Nathan nodded and released the seal.

As he took it off Ethan made his overdue introduction, 'I'm Sergeant Best of the SAS.'

'Wow, the SAS.'

'Yeah…Only the best for you.'

'Ha.'

'So how did you get out here?'

Nathan was not about to tell him. 'I urr parachuted in.'

'Parachuted? On your own? I thought you were going to say you pinched a skidoo running away from home and it had run out of fuel or broken down.'

'Mmm, that would have sounded better,' thought Nathan, then he noticed Maeve smile. 'You heard that didn't you?' he thought again.

Maeve nodded. No point trying to hide it if she was going to gain Nathan's trust and get information on the SOVs.

'So why did you get parachuted deep inside the arctic circle?' Ethan pressed.

'It was a um…test.'

'*Test*?'

'Sure. For my next scouts badge.'

'Ha. I suppose this would be the *SAS scouts* would it?'

'I'm not allowed to say.'

'Official secrets and all that?'

'Something *like* that.'

'You aren't a very good liar, kid. Why not come clean, we're on *your* side. Why not tell us your name, at least.'

Nathan was not forthcoming.

'I think maybe I should tell you something about me,' suggested Maeve. 'I work for a section of MI5. We are trying to get further information on a group of Seriously Organised Vigilantes.'

'*Vigilantes*? Why would you think I know anything about vigilantes?'

'We have been told you have links with them.'

'By who? I don't know any vigilantes.'

'Maybe you don't know you know.' Maeve left Nathan with that thought and went to make him the hot chocolate she had promised. She also picked up a muesli bar.

'Thanks,' Nathan reached out for them when Maeve returned. Then he thought 'You can read my mind, so you can see I don't know any vigilantes.'

'I can only pick up thought words, not visual memories,' she replied.

It was clear to Ethan from the jump in dialogue that Maeve and the boy were now consciously connecting. He didn't like that because he felt left out of the loop. 'You must have questions for *us*, kid?'

'So did this person who told you about me also tell you where I would be?'

'Yes.'

'So doesn't this person also know about your vigilantes?'

'We believe they do, but this informer cannot give us all the details.'

'Why ever not?'

'It's something known as meta-interference.'

'I don't understand what that means,' Nathan mumbled through a mouthful of muesli bar before taking a sip from his drink.

'As I understand it, it's when events conspire to prevent a person interfering with the intended course of events along a time-line.'

'*Yeah right*...I don't think *you* are a very good liar either, Maeve.'

Elsewhere, a very different but no less strange course of events were about to come to a head.

Even before the Great Reset, Pieter Dumas had gone *off-grid*. He had chosen his lifestyle change over twelve years ago. Reports of a deadly assassin, referred to as the *Fantasma da morte* had made him fear for his life. As old as he was he still had no wish to die.

Pieter had made his millions in the trafficking of children for the Adrenochrome industry and intended to live to enjoy his ill-gotten gains. So, under a false identity he had a small-holding built in a wilderness area of rainforest in East Asia.

His security system was considered second to none. The surroundings had pressure sensors and laser trips. The house had motion detectors and cameras. Yet still he had worried. He had heard tell of the *Fantasma da morte* killing people inside safe-rooms and bunkers, like a ghost. As a last resort, he had under his pillow a remote for a number of claymore type devices set round the base of his bed.

It was ironic that after all of this effort and expense the roof of his home now leaked in a number of places. No sooner had he patched one hole than another appeared with the next heavy rain.

As he lay on his bed one evening, he listened to the steady dribble of water into the buckets he had placed around the room. The sound almost relaxed him.

It had taken a few years for the fear of being located by the assassin to subside somewhat.

It was still there, but not having heard further reports of the *Fantasma da morte* for some time he was now left with the burning question of *why not*?

He was also plagued by his desperate need for contact with young children. He had tired of the collection of videos he had once recorded of their abuse. Nevertheless, he did not want to access the Dark Net too often in case he was tracked down, even there. Besides, Pieter thought, *watching* did not provide the same thrill as *doing*.

As he lay on his bed while the evening light faded there was an odd scent in the air. He thought that it might be one of the rainforest blooms, though *this* smell was unfamiliar. Some plants did only bloom once a decade he thought. However, he found this smell oddly arousing. Maybe, he thought, it had triggered a distant memory of one of the children.

He was unaware that one bucket had filled to overflowing as he fell asleep. The spill spread across the tiled floor, in the direction of the bed.

If anyone were to examine the security video before it reached its seven day wipe, it would have looked like the weight of the bed had drawn the spill across the room.

It passed the claymores and pooled under the bed. However, what happened next might not have been so easy to explain. As darkness came the liquid gathered itself together and crept up the wall behind the head-board.

Rising to the ceiling it suddenly peeled away from the wall and slopped down onto Pieter. He woke, too late. The stuff, whatever it was, a living nightmare was engulfing his head and shoulders. As he tried to get up the weight of it was holding him down, quickly spreading down his chest and arms. He tried to reach under his pillow for the claymore remote but found his movements were resisted. He could not breathe to scream, but then, off-grid there would be no one to hear him anyway.

In the morning, there was little left of Pieter. His bed contained only his two replacement knee joints and the false hand, which he had once enjoyed tormenting his young victims with.

4

Nathan made sure he did not fall asleep aboard the Black Kite. These people seemed very *odd* coming all this way just for a *chat*. Even if they were from MI5, he didn't want them taking off with him once the storm lifted.

Maeve still made Nathan anxious. Knowing that she could hear his thoughts he worried about the risk of giving away what he needed to keep secret. Another reason to stay awake, he was concerned that she might be able to read his thoughts if he dreamed.

He doubted that *Control* would be happy that he had accepted shelter and boarded this plane. He had been taught how to survive in sub-zero conditions. On the other hand he was sure *Control* would want to know all about these MI5 people when he returned.

Nathan's hunch about Maeve being able to read the thoughts of a dreaming person was correct. She had placed half a crushed sleeping tablet in his hot chocolate.

She now wondered if she should have used a whole one. The half dose had had no effect on the lad.

Later, with the storm likely to rage on well into the next day, Maeve organised a game of cards for the lad with the troopers, to distract him. Then she went and made another hot chocolate this time putting a whole sleeping tablet in. She made herself a coffee before returning with the drinks and offering the chocolate to the lad.

'Here you go, Lone Ranger.' Maeve hoped he would respond with his name to correct her but there was no tricking him.

Nevertheless, Nathan started drinking the chocolate without question.

'Can I get you lads anything?'

With orders of teas and coffees from the troopers Maeve returned to making drinks.

An hour later it was difficult to believe but Nathan was still wide awake.

Years ago, when Gavin had reported that his son was becoming anxious about falling asleep and porting away, the clinic tried to help by providing a sedative. It only helped the first time. They found the same occurred with different forms of sedative. It was like Nathan became immune to their effect.

Maeve also decided there was something very special about this boy, much more than his remote-viewing. If he *was* involved with the SOVs, why had they parachuted him into the icy wilderness of Northern Norway alone? What were they up to?

Gavin Purnell had also not slept a wink. He was always too wired to rest whenever he heard that *whumph* sound. This time the situation was all the worse for finding out Nathan's Reappearance Point was deep inside the Arctic Circle. He had immediately gone to his grab-bag and put extra thermals in with the kit for the trip out.

He was then informed by *Control* he would not be flown out to the RP to collect Nathan. A trusted Russian team would be extracting him. This only added to his worries, Nathan having to deal with strangers.

Gavin had always been a worrier, but it had not stopped him doing things. Some of those things he now looked back on with regret.

To keep his mind occupied Gavin decided to surf the Internet to find out more about where his son had ended up. He seemed to remember from TV that there were polar bears in Norway. However, if Google was to be trusted, they were only on the Norwegian islands of Svalbard these days.

A little later *Control* further disturbed Gavin with the news that though the Russian team were set to extract Nathan the weather was now too dangerous. Nathan would have to find or make shelter. They tried to reassure Gavin that Nathan had received sufficient artic survival training to give him a fighting chance.

Gavin headed for the kitchen for a spot of comfort-eating. It wasn't easy being a single parent at the best of times but these circumstances were proving unbearable. He wished, once again, that Kelly was still with him. She had been so down to earth. He had felt blessed when they had met at the probation centre in Newcastle upon Tyne.

Kelly had been a strong woman. Not in the physical sense, not like the young woman who once beat him up for breaking into her place. Positivity had been Kelly's strength.

As he popped a macaroni and cheese ready-meal in the microwave he wondered if this was life's payback for all his wrong-doings.

The main body of the storm did not pass until the middle of the following day. Even then it was still dark outside. Sunrise in the Arctic Circle wasn't due until March.

'They are coming for me,' Nathan suddenly informed Maeve who was sitting next to him.

She knew this was not a voiced hope, though she could hear nothing yet. She wondered how far this lad could view. She looked out of a window but could see very little. 'It makes sense. The storm is moving off now.'

Minutes later the co-pilot announced, 'We have company coming in from the east. Single contact. Looks to be a chopper, by its speed.'

Nathan noticed that the troopers who had been resting up were suddenly checking their weapons. 'What are they doing?'

'Standard procedure,' explained Ethan. 'We're not expecting trouble.'

Nathan picked up his helmet to see if he could raise *Control*. Sealing it in place he discovered that there was still no reception. Either the storm was still having an effect or the Black Kite was blocking the signal.

He found himself watching his father. Gavin was trying to stay calm because he suspected Nathan would be keeping an eye on him and didn't want to add to his son's distress.

Nathan was periodically looking in on *Control* too. They were clearly still frustrated, having lost contact with him. His tracker was not registering since he had entered the stealth aircraft. However, it was clear that they were wondering if it had failed early.

Nathan had to have a new tracker chip placed in his hand on a regular basis. His body seemed to reject them, breaking them down. He could see they had been discussing whether his tracker had failed prematurely, though it should have been fine for another month.

The routine operation to replace his tracker was quite quick and Nathan always healed without a scar.

He knew that as soon as the helicopter came close enough he would need to signal his position.

Minutes later he could hear the thrum of the approaching rotors. 'I need to go outside.'

Ethan nodded. He could hear the chopper now too. 'Okay, ramp down!' Ethan called to their loadie.

As the ramp came down the troopers pulled their hoods back up over their helmets and zipped up their jackets. Maeve followed suit. She needed to witness the hand-over.

The approaching helicopter could not be seen clearly but looked to the team on the ground like an old Mil Mi-54. It was heading to Nathan's last known GPS coordinates.

With the light of the Black Kite's interior behind him, Nathan began waving his arms.

The Mil altered course and put down about fifty metres away. Four figures rushed out, weapons at the ready. They looked like military to Ethan, the way they carried themselves. The Mil's rotors continued to turn as the Russians came across. They were clearly not intending to socialise. Ethan headed towards them.

Maeve rushed after him. 'Don't make trouble Sergeant.'

'Not intending to.' He didn't like the idea of just handing the lad over to the Russians though. Not with *their* history. They could be anyone. He knew all about their mafia dealings and double crosses. He was glad his Russian was better than conversational. 'Papers, Comrade?' he demanded with a touch of menace.

'Ha!' laughed the man at the lead of the figures. 'Papers, Comrade? Is that your FSB Impression?'

Ethan laughed back. 'Best I could do.'

'It didn't carry the right tone of *boredom*.'

Nathan rushed past Ethan and Maeve and stood by the Russians. Reception of signal from *Control* had confirmed the extraction party. 'Thanks for looking after me through the storm,' he waved.

'The boy seems happy,' the lead Russian said what Maeve knew they were *all* thinking.

Shortly the Mil was airborne and heading away. However, it did not head back east but instead north-west.

Maeve rushed inside and asked the co-pilot to keep track of the Mil's position.

Wasting no time, now that the Russians were out of sight, Ethan and his troopers helped the loadie clear the snow off the Black Kite.

Once free of the snow and the pre-flight checks completed, engines thrusting, the Black Kite lifted off and headed north-west after the

Mil. The transporter hugged the terrain in the hope of keeping off the Mil's radar.

The Mil had turned west when it reached the sea, following the coastline, but as the Black Kite's pilot did the same the co-pilot announced that he had lost the Mil.

'What do you mean gone?' Maeve was concerned.

'Possibly transferring the lad to a boat, or even a sub in one of these fjords,' the co-pilot suggested.

'Right, yes.' Maeve turned to the pilot. 'No sense in holding back now then, we need to get to the last known position asap.'

'Yes ma'am,' the pilot opened up the thrusters.

When the Black Kite came close the co-pilot announced 'They appear to have put down in the next fjord.'

'I'll head in slow' suggested the pilot, 'so we can see what they are up to.'

'Agreed,' Maeve nodded.

The first thing they noticed through their night vision goggles, were a couple of fires on the far side of the fjord.

'Looks like camp fires,' the pilot remarked. 'No wait. I think that's *wreckage.*'

'Take her down closer,' Maeve urged.

As they descended Maeve listened out for thoughts but only picked up those of her own crew.

'Find somewhere to put down.' Maeve turned away from the cockpit. 'Ethan, it looks like they crashed. We're going in.'

As the plane hovered close to the wreckage and smoke, the pilot and co-pilot could see some bodies.

As Maeve prepared to head back out, she found herself wondering, 'Is this why we were not to return with the lad?'

Gina Oakley was not the woman she once was. She couldn't stop blaming herself for all the *Awakened* extremist's retaliation against the NWO. They had hurt many more than the relatively few *guilty* Privileged. Though she saw these events as having been caused by her *jinxing*, she had never managed to develop any conscious control over it.

Over a decade ago, at the start of the Great Reset, Gina had found herself aboard the freighter Damocles. It was being used as a factory ship to produce the Project C-Spray drones involved in targeted culling of criminals in preparation for the Great Reset.

When its reactor went into meltdown, she had suggested that it should be placed somewhere that most people on earth would be happy for it to end up. This ambiguous suggestion turned Wuhan into a 21st Century Chernobyl, because of the What-If reality-drive involved. Gina had no previous experience of that alien technology, but would certainly not wish to use it again.

Many people across the world, bitter about the loss of their loved ones in the cull, wanted extreme payback. Some of these were military personnel and a few of them gained access to nuclear weapons. Sadly the collateral damage of the ensuing dirty-bombings proved as sickening as the cull itself with the death of many more innocents.

When London was attacked Gina was at home in Birmingham. MI5 and MI6 were taken out and Cynthia Cartwright along with many other colleagues died. Gina found herself promoted as new Director General of the British Security Services for her sins, not just MI5's Section 13. The office was situated in the new UK capital of Birmingham.

Gina thought she ought to be thankful that she and her husband Will had survived. Some colleagues from the Devereaux Norton Agency had died previously, in the cull, including her husband's uncle.

When Gina was told that the vaccination she and her husband Will had been given by *Five* had made them *Privileged*, their relationship had suffered. They both felt part of the conspiracy, even if unwittingly so.

Gina's phone rang, still with its Enter the Dragon ring-tone.

'Agent Corrigan.'

'Bad news, Ma'am. The chopper that came for the contact has been brought down. Destroyed.'

'*Destroyed*?'

'Yes.'

'What can you report on the contact?'

'The contact turned out to be a young lad, early teens I'd guess. He was not very talkative. So we didn't get a name, or the truth of what the lad was doing out there. He said he was parachuted there. Nevertheless, our body-cams will have images of him which we can use for facial recognition.

'He left willingly with a group of Russians, but sometime later their chopper was brought down, as I said. On investigation I noticed, in the wreckage of the tail section a circular hole cut in the side of the fuselage. On closer inspection I found a similar mark in the flooring and a curved cut through seating. This put me in mind of reports of children taken by the *Fantasma da morte*.'

'*Sven*?'

'That's what I'm thinking, ma'am.'

'But the last report of Sven was a decade ago.'

'But we *are* still getting reports from children of *Magic Door* experiences when explaining their miraculous return from captors.'

'True.'

The sad fact was that even after the culling which had striven to remove much of the criminal element, there were still many wicked people left to take their place.

'So if it is not Sven then it must be someone using similar technology, I guess linked to the *Magic Door* tech.'

Since Gina had located and visited John Doe, the apparent author of the Hilton Multiverse books he had quit publishing. It had turned out that he had been plagiarising the *real* author who actually existed in a parallel universe.

Dawn Summers, from What-If, had been bringing John the book manuscripts for him to make a living. Since no-one should be any the wiser, John published them in this reality under the actual author's name. Dawn said it was ironic but these multiverse books were selling even better in this reality than their original one.

For someone in another dimension to know what was going on here, Gina had a hunch that Dawn was describing events back to them, like some literary double-agent. Then why not just tell John and cut Kevin out completely? It didn't add up. Nevertheless, Gina had made it clear to John that she did not want him publicising any personal or security service information again, or there would be trouble.

Gina told John that considering the breach of security he had already committed, he would have to make amends. If he wanted to avoid arrest he would have to become her informer. So that next time Dawn gave him a book he was to pass it straight on to her. However, since then Dawn had not given John any more books. Only recently had she started to feed him highlights.

Drawing her thoughts back to the present and the report from Maeve, Gina wondered whether Dawn and her colleague Destiny were somehow involved with this lad. She might know better when she viewed the body-cam recordings of the wreckage for herself. 'Maybe the lad has been returned home by a *Magic Door*.'

'What do you mean, you lost him?' Gavin was distraught that Nathan was not home. He was now being informed that the chopper that was bringing his son home had gone off the radar.

'We are sending in another team to find out what happened.' Emily Richards, as team leader, explained in her rather snooty southern counties accent. 'It could just be engine trouble, causing the crew to put down along the coast to fix it. As soon as we know more I'll let you know.'

Gavin was so horrified at the thought of losing his son he forgot to thank Emily for keeping him informed. He just hung up.

5

Nathan was confused. He knew this had to be some bad dream because he never teleported again so soon. There was a sudden intense explosion of light and heat. He became aware that he was facing upwards, as if the helicopter was in a vertical climb.

He reacted without thought, not following his normal waking procedure. Unbuckling his seatbelt he leaned towards where the aisle should be then he was falling.

Half dazed by the unreal situation he felt like he was flying along a tunnel. There were pieces of metal across this tunnel and he wasn't quick enough to avoid all of them. One hit his head. He realised that he wasn't wearing his helmet. That teeth-rattling collision put him in the path of another bar which struck his knee, sending him into a spin. This wasn't a dream.

There came a sudden tearing pain as his right hand snagged some wire. He screamed out in pain then everything went black as he hit the end of the tunnel.

Disembarking from the Black Kite at Edinburgh Airport to be escorted by airport police to the terminal Ethan followed Maeve on through.

'Where are you going Maeve? The exit is this way,' he pointed to the sign.

'We don't need the exit. We need to pick up our tickets.'

'Bus tickets?'

'*No*. Flight tickets.'

'But I thought you said we were popping up to Perth?'

'Perth W.A.'

'*Australia*?'

'Yes.'

'But why are we going *there* now?'

'That's where the boy will be.'

'*What*? How? We both saw the state of that crash.'

'Don't know. That's where the informer told Oakley that we needed to go next.'

'WA is a *massive* area. This informant better have some finer direction than that.'

'Not really. Just that we hire a 4x4 and head East, keep our ears to the ground and we *will* find him.'

'Sounds like a recipe for a sore head to me.'

Helga Sturmfeld had taken her dog and left for another safe-house at the start of the Great Reset reprisal attacks. Swiss police had raided her Interlaken home but found it cleaned of evidence of Project C-Spray or any of her other links with her Seriously Organised Vigilantes.

Since then she had moved again. Her dog was no longer with her but she had chosen not to have another for the time being. With what she was planning she saw that she might need to keep on the move. Nevertheless, at all times she held onto the reins of the SOVs.

A sit-rep came through from a team she had sent to investigate the Norwegian crash site.

'Frau Sturmfeld, I regret to inform you that there were no survivors.'

'The *boy*?'

'No. There was no trace of the boy. It looks like he must have fallen asleep and ported again.'

'Surely not. He wouldn't be due to teleport again for weeks.'

'Sorry but we found evidence of his boundary clipping plane.'

'Where?'

'In the wreckage of the tail section. We found half of his helmet. He must have gone to sleep without it on.'

'Damn, so no coms. And still no signal from his tracker?'

'We're still not picking up a signal, no. He must be out of range or the signal is getting blocked.'

'I'll have the satellites rerouted to see if that helps. We *must* find him.'

The pain in Nathan's right arm brought him round. His whole body was aching now; His head, his knee, his back, but mostly his hand.

It was dim and dusty where he lay and he was covered in rubble, yet he could see well enough with his remote-viewing. The tunnel had turned out to be a shaft. He was at the bottom of a mine.

As he tried to sit up and brush himself down, he was hit by searing pain in his right hand and wrist. His glove was torn and his thumb dangled limply at an alarming angle. He decided to carefully remove the glove to get a better look. To do this he had to bite back the pain which was so intense he almost gave up the idea of removing the glove, after all, though torn the glove was still providing some support for his injury.

Nevertheless, with the glove removed he could see the wrist was swollen, right up to the cuff of his suit. The snag on the wire had cut right through the web of the glove and his flesh between thumb and forefinger, right to the joint at the back, dislocating the thumb. What was he to do?

'Dad!!'

It was no use crying but he couldn't help himself. He wanted to be home with his father but without his helmet he only had himself and his training to depend upon.

He could see that he had lost blood into the rocks but the bleeding had stopped now. Nevertheless, he needed to clean and dress that wound as a matter of urgency. First he removed his left glove, using his teeth. Then he took the basic first-aid kit from his utility belt.

Using some of his limited water to rinse off the wound he next applied some antiseptic spray, which really stung.

The worst bit came next however, causing him to swear loudly. He pulled on his thumb, realigning the joint and then did his best to single-handedly stitch the wound together, with no local anaesthetic, but plenty more tears and swearing. Finally he bandaged the hand and wrist and placed the arm in a sling. Only then did he take time to investigate where he was with his remote-viewing.

Nathan was in an abandoned gold mine, in Western Australia. There was no ladder out of the mineshaft, and there was no other exit down any of the tunnels leading from the shaft.

Resting his back against the wall below the shaft he felt trapped. There was no obvious way back up the shaft. He couldn't even reach the ceiling.

His support team would be a long time coming but he was confident they would track him down. However, his confidence was shaken by the thought that his tracker implant was in the very hand he had injured. Focusing on the team at *Control* he began lip reading. All too soon it was clear that they had absolutely no idea where he was.

Checking his father next, he saw him looking very anxious. Nathan had to do something. Viewing just outside the mine he could see no one to call to. There was no one for at least a hundred miles, as he did a sweep, just dirt tracks through desert left by gold prospectors.

He had to solve this problem all by himself. To do that he knew he would have to get creative and above all stay positive.

'If the answer is down here, then what have I missed?' The way he was aching he felt like he had hit just about everything.

It was then that he saw a loop of thin rope poking out from under the mound of rubble at the bottom of the shaft. Getting up and pulling at it with his left arm he realised he would have to pull the rubble aside to get the rope out.

Now that he had a focus, if not an immediate solution, he felt better about his situation. He got on with clearing the rubble; stacking it up against the wall opposite.

Eventually Nathan had the coil of rope free. It was quite a length and was attached to a couple of pulleys. He also found a length of scaffold bar. It looked like it had originally been at the top of the shaft but had come down with rock from the walls as he fell, or possibly before.

It wasn't safe to stay at the bottom of the shaft. Nevertheless, as Nathan moved aside he realised it wouldn't exactly be safe *anywhere* down there. That's why there were so many lengths of scaffold around used as pit-props to keep the ceiling up.

Then he had his inspiration. He looked back up the shaft then at the pile of rubble he had formed against the wall. Then he coiled up the rope and went off down one of the tunnels, passing scaffold props as he went. At the far end Nathan viewed the wooden wedge blocks above and below the furthest prop. His idea only stood a chance if he could find sufficient props with wedges facing in the right direction and not too heavily loaded.

He tied one end of his rope around the bottom of a prop then let the coil out as he walked away some distance. Taking up the slack he suddenly yanked on the rope.

Nothing happened.

He tied the remainder of the rope around his waist, took up the slack and then tried to walk away.

Nothing.

So Nathan backed up and then charged down the tunnel back towards the shaft. His knee hurt, but not as much as the rest of him when the rope went tight and pulled him over. He fell on his bad arm and cursed. But as he got back up he noticed the rope was now slack.

Pulling on the rope he heard the scaffold prop scraping on the floor.

'Yes!'

Quickly he went and retrieved the scaffold to test out his idea. He brought it to the bottom of the shaft. It was longer than the length of scaffold which had fallen down the shaft. He put one end up the shaft and the other into the rubble. Propping it against the far corner of the shaft he pulled sideways on it and it jammed solidly.

If this was going to work he would need many more pieces of scaffold, but he could not risk further injury.

Nathan bent down and picked up the pulleys he had left by the rubble. He remembered being taught how pulleys were able to make it possible to do heavier work.

Removing the scaffold pit-prop then taking the pulleys and rope, Nathan headed back down the tunnel. He hoped this would make removal of additional props less likely to cause injury.

Nathan used both scaffolds across the width of the tunnel, wedging against the side walls a safe distance from the first target pit-prop. With only the one arm he rigged one of the pulleys to each of the scaffolds and threaded the rope through. Then he went down the tunnel. Tying one end of the rope to the target prop he retreated to the pulley system and pulled on the rope there.

Not every prop came loose by this means, but where they did, in a couple of places, some of the ceiling came down. Nevertheless, after a time, Nathan had a dozen or so lengths of scaffold from a couple of tunnels stacked at the bottom of the shaft.

Returning to the shaft with his last prop, he put it securely into the rubble at one end. The other end he rested as before into the further corner of the shaft. Then he picked up his next length of scaffold. The idea was to create a zig-zag ladder. This required him to place it on top of the upper end of the first so as to rest it across the shaft into the opposite corner.

Nathan lifted the second length of scaffold above his head, and attempted to scale the incline of the prop from the rubble. This required a major balancing act, and he realised this wasn't going to be as easy as he had imagined. It demanded a complete rethink. Presently it didn't seem possible to complete without the use of both arms. He stepped down to the rubble and slumped back against the wall.

Carlos Montana was a gang leader, involved in kidnapping and extortion, in Mexico. He considered himself a next-gen criminal of the NWO.

When the cull unexpectedly killed many more criminals than innocents, the general public being unaware of Project C-Spray, it had opened up the playing field to those left behind.

At first, the survivors of humankind were very much engaged in the revolution of the Great Reset, establishing a new age; a new norm. However, opportunity for power and credit soon corrupted people as it always had.

Nevertheless, there were rumours that even next-gen criminals were not safe to take advantage of age old opportunities. Something else was out there. Not another virus, but maybe someone playing the field by different rules.

Carlos was growing impatient for the pay-off from his latest acquisition, as were his three men. They were all cooped up in a small house on the edge of town, the closest they had to a safe-house.

He looked across at Maria, the nine year old hostage tied to a chair. She had long since run out of tears. Her streaked face looked as tired as the men felt.

Maria begged once again to be untied so that she could go to the toilet.

This time Carlos conceded and had two of his men escort her to the outhouse. He had learned that children were wily, and would run at the first opportunity, so two men were the minimum escort.

Maria with a man on each side arrived at the tin shack. It smelled disgusting. She didn't want to go in but she needed to. Closing the door there was almost no light inside, at least for a second.

The two men heard the girl gasp. Thinking it must be her reaction to the smell they just snickered.

As the girl had turned, preparing to sit down, the door had suddenly vanished. Before her was her garden at home. She had heard stories of a *magic door* that saved children, but until now had never believed it to be true. She stepped through.

The men outside the outhouse knew Maria would not be able to stay in there long, so thought nothing of it when the toilet was flushed and the girl came back out. They escorted her back inside the house and bound her up again.

Carlos looked at his watch then took up his phone, watching Maria as the call connected.

'Marco, this is Alexi. Time is running out for your little girl. If you don't get our money soon I will be tempted to take another payment option of *instalments*. I will send sweet Maria back to you a piece at a time, eh?' In truth, Carlos never intended to return the girl alive; she had seen their faces.

'You idiot! Do you take me for a fool Alexi?! You think I don't know that you are bluffing?'

'What?! I am serious! My men will have fun with your daughter before they get creative with a blade. So pay up, *now*!'

Maria pulled at her bindings looking fearful. The men found this amusing to watch.

'I have my daughter *here*, Alexi. You let her slip through your fingers.'

'You must have gone insane with grief, Marco. You try to bluff *me*?! Let me help bring you back down to earth. Does this not sound like your precious little Maria?'

Carlos took up a knife from his table and came round to his hostage with an intimidating leer.

As he brought the point of the blade under the girl's chin, causing her to shrink away, the other three men gathered closer.

At that moment Carlos frowned. He thought he caught Maria's voice in the background on the other end of the call. Maybe it was a sister?

In a split second the figure bound to the chair morphed from a little girl into something approximating a giant sea urchin. Long spines, like steel blades extended out, penetrating the men's brains and vital organs.

The phone clattered to the floor but Carlos and his men hung there dead for some moments. Then the spines turned to tentacles which drew the bodies all together. The apparition then turned to liquid which enveloped them for consumption.

Marco's voice could be heard once more. 'The police will trace this call, Alexi...Alexi?'

However, when the police did deem to investigate all they discovered were a pile of clothes and some abandoned weapons by loops of rope over a chair.

6

Next morning, Gavin grew more anxious as the hours slipped by with no further news on Nathan. The thought of his son out there somewhere, quite possibly in trouble and unable to call for help, was causing him to catastrophize. He loved his son so much. He couldn't bear the thought of him in distress, or even worse of losing him.

He tried to distract himself with housework, but as with watching the news he could not focus for long. The news seemed to be even grimmer since this New World *dis*Order came to pass. Some people were still committed to running resistance movements, with their local government offices attempting to track them down.

Leaving the TV on, Gavin began washing dishes which had been left in the sink overnight. Then he dropped a dish while wiping up. This further frustrated him as it wouldn't have happened if he had simply loaded them into his dishwasher.

Picking up the larger pieces of broken plate and putting them in the bin, Gavin heard the front door bell. Leaving the smaller pieces of plate where they lay, he hurried to see who it was.

It was Emily Richards. Though he was more used to speaking with her on the phone, he had met her on a number of occasions in recent years. She was a young and attractive blonde who clearly enjoyed working out at the gym. However, personality-wise, he found her to be cold and abrasive. Though he had never been told what her background was, he suspected she had served in the forces. As well as being in charge of Nathan's survival training she had also been responsible for organising the last couple of his post-port extractions.

Emily knew Gavin was a dreadful worrier. So she had thought it best to come see him personally, to help reassure him that everything possible was being done.

However, for Gavin this personal approach was like that ominous call from police or army officers on TV shows. 'I knew it...He's dead isn't he, Emily?' His eyes welled up.

'We don't know that yet. We still haven't located his whereabouts, Gavin. May I come in?'

Gavin stepped back from the door, his mouth running away with itself. 'He could be adrift in an ocean, or surrounded by lions, or kidnapped by gangsters, or...'

Having closed the front door behind her, Emily turned and slapped Gavin hard across the face, leaving him reeling with shock. 'Snap out of it, Gavin...We are *still* looking for Nathan, using a number of satellites, streaming video through our facial recognition and behavioural motion analysis software. We are also using communications surveillance to listen for any indicators, in all major languages.'

Rubbing his stinging cheek, his voice partly muffled he demanded 'Why isn't Nathan's tracker working?'

'The kitchen's through here, yes?'

'Yeah…' Gavin followed Emily down the hallway. '*Well*?'

'It is possible that the chip has failed, sooner than expected.' Emily spotted the kettle and took it to the sink to fill up.

'What?'

Emily raised her voice over the gush of water. 'Well you know how aggressive Nathan's body is becoming towards foreign matter.'

'Yes. But he had a new implant only a year ago and the techies assured us it had a more resistant coating on it.'

Emily seated the kettle on its pad and switched it on. 'I did say it was a *possibility*. It is *also* possible that Nathan has materialised within a shielded environment.'

'What does that mean?'

'Where do you keep your cups?'

'In the cupboard, behind your head.'

Turning around, something crunched under foot. Looking down Emily saw a fragment of plate, but didn't ask. Looking back up, she opened the cupboard instead.

'*So* what do you mean by *shielded environment*?'

'It could be anything from a deep gorge to someone's basement.'

'But surely if he has appeared in a populated area he would have been in touch by now.'

'Most likely, yes.' Emily started opening draws looking for a teaspoon.

Gavin got her one. 'So I just have to *wait* while you guys look and listen?'

'Pretty much yes, but from the way Nathan has teleported previously, we know two things. He has always ported further each time, so we will prioritise searching further out than a two thousand mile radius. And secondly, the jump always seems to be many times the distance of his previous night-port.'

'You forgot to mention one other thing though, Emily.' Gavin handed her milk from the fridge.

'What's that?'

'Nathan has always had long periods between porting, but not this time. And though it was dark it was not night when he ported, either. So maybe the logic on distance doesn't hold true anymore,' his voice went up an octave.

'You're beginning to catastrophize again, Gavin.'

'Okay, okay.' Gavin nodded with a sigh, trying to hold it together, not fancying another slap. 'So where is the search focusing?'

'Asia and Australasia, presently.' Emily knew they were also searching the surrounding oceans, but made a point of not mentioning this unless asked. She handed Gavin a cup of tea.

'Urr…You put sugar in it.'

'I thought you needed it.'

The Western Brown Snake meandered its way across the sand of the outback. The cool of night was easier to hunt in. It was looking for prey with its heat sensors and the stereo smell provided by its forked tongue. Ready to strike and bite in a split second, its venom deadly. So its prey rarely struggled for long once bitten.

This was only one of Australia's deadly dangerous animals, but something even more dangerous was watching this particular snake. As it moved towards a hole in the ground, the sand beneath it began to move. In a spurt of motion it attempted to back away. However, the sand was shifting too quickly and then it was tumbling into the deep hole. Suddenly its fall was arrested by something that crushed its throat.

It tried to save itself by whipping its tail and turning its head in the hope of biting the warm thing that was constricting it. However, no sooner had it tried this than its head was dashed into a rock, breaking its fangs, lower jaw and skull.

'Yummy.' Nathan did not sound enthused.

To sustain himself so far, he had eaten two scorpions which he had found in the mine, first removing their stingers.

With his drinking flask empty and no source of water down the mine Nathan had also reluctantly drunk his own urine. He concluded that raw scorpion tasted better but only just.

Gutting the snake would have been easier with two hands free. Nathan began by cutting the head off the still writhing dead snake. Next he trod on the tail and pulled a squeezing hand up towards the headless end, to empty its guts. That didn't seem to do much more than expel a little of its stomach content, the remains of a mouse-like creature. So he used his teeth to tear the skin back from the neck then bit down hard on the flesh of the neck. Pulling at the skin he drew it down off the flesh. Moving his teeth further along and pulling off more of the skin, repeating this move he soon had all the skin and scales off.

Next he gripped the tail between his teeth, found the split in the snake's belly and shoved his left thumb inside. He drew it down its length, removing all of the intestine and other organs.

He was then left with the flesh and bones. He didn't like bony fish, and having tried some Western Brown decided that it tasted like bony raw fishy-chicken.

'Ficken eel!' He pulled a face as he chewed. Hungrily taking a second then third mouthful, it was a struggle to bite through the raw meat and bone. He had to admit, however, the snake did taste better than the scorpions.

He was tempted to eat it all as he did not know when he would get to eat again. However, his survival training said to eat little but often, otherwise it would increase his thirst. So he ate the meatiest section and discarded the rest in the rubble at the bottom of the shaft.

He knew the meat would not keep but maybe the smell of it would draw something else down the shaft.

With his hunger relieved slightly, Nathan decided it best to try and get some sleep. He had only had minutes of sleep in the rescue chopper since porting from home. So he was feeling tired again. He thought again of the Russians who had lost their lives attempting to extract him. He wondered if the MI5 woman had known something was going to happen because of the way she had said they were not to fly him home. No, that had to be a coincidence.

Finding himself a flat area of floor he lay there trying to relax. His injured hand still throbbed painfully and the ground was hard. He wished he had the upholstery off the flight seat that sat above the mine.

He knew that once he was out of there he would strip that upholstery which was tied to the seat frame, before heading off in the direction of water. As he used his remote-viewing to work out the quickest way to remove the upholstery he spotted that in the pocket under the seat, beside a life-jacket was a 500ml bottle of water.

That bottle could be a life-saver but would not be enough in itself for the journey ahead. He would need litres of water in the desert above. He had already spotted a dry river bed some miles away. On reaching it he planned to dig into the sand at a bend by a sheltering rocky overhang. Maybe he would find remains of some water below. He had also spotted a tree with some fruit on it in that direction. The fruit looked like quandong. However, if he remembered correctly they would not be juicy, but still, better than nothing.

Having a plan was part of remaining positive. He then began wondering whether for all his efforts to climb out of the shaft, there was now the possibility that he might just port away once he fell asleep. This was also a source of concern though. It was totally unexpected to have ported from the chopper. It should have been too soon for it to happen again. Nevertheless, if he did teleport again now, there was nowhere further than Australia to go. He started to wish he hadn't taken an interest in the SpaceX moon landings.

It proved difficult to sleep on the flight out to Perth via Singapore, because of a wailing baby. However, Maeve was even more disturbed by the aggressive thoughts some passengers had towards the child, especially Ethan.

Nevertheless, he managed to get to sleep before Maeve. She just sat there under a blanket, her seat also reclined. She tried to shut out the thoughts she was receiving so that she could relax. However, in such close proximity to other people it was rather like hoping for sleep during some surreal one-sided conversations party.

Nathan woke a number of times, each time still down the mine. Finally he decided that his body must have rested enough since he could not get back to sleep again.

He just lay there for a while, thinking, trying to solve his single-handed scaffold construction problem. After a while an idea came to him. Getting to his feet he went to the rope, and picked up a rock.

He tied the rock to one end of the rope. Then he tried to throw it up the shaft to get it over the cross support near the top. However, it was very difficult to throw straight up. Besides which, the rock would not go up very far because the higher it went the heavier the trailing rope became.

Nathan tried a bigger rock on the end and tried spinning it on a short length of the rope then releasing it up the shaft. This took some practice, but it wasn't as if he had anything better to do. The rock cracked off the side of the shaft again and again. A number of times it brought some more rubble down. He hoped he wasn't going to cause a cave-in.

Finally he got the rock over a cross support, though not the one he had been hoping for. Still it was better than nothing. With both ends of the rope at the bottom of the shaft he took his knife and cut a five foot length from the free end.

Sitting down he began to untwine the rope using his feet to provide grip. First he removed one of its strings then he untwined that to remove one of its threads.

Next he used the thread to secure a length of scaffold, a quarter of its length in from each end. Then he lifted the prop up and bounced it on its thread to be sure it could take the weight. Then some way up the rope from the free end he tied a knot.

Taking up the tension with the rock end of the rope, Nathan hung the prop from the knot. He positioned the thread so that the prop hung at a bit of an angle. Then he began to lift it up the shaft using the rock end of the rope.

It was still very difficult to do this with only one hand. Nevertheless, using his thighs to hold the rope every so often, it enabled Nathan to use the free end to twist and draw the dangling prop into position. Once he got the lower end of the new prop on top of the upper end of the previous prop he carefully lowered the new prop. It proved very difficult guiding it by the rope to drop the upper end into the diametrically opposed corner of the shaft. This was because the cross support above did not run midway across the shaft, but slightly over to one side.

With the new prop in place Nathan simply lowered the rope knot away from the thread, leaving the prop in place, to then place another prop above it.

Nathan found that the next prop was far more difficult to place above the second because the cross support was to the further side. Nevertheless he managed, at great test to his patience. The third prop seated in the further corner better because of the cross support's position.

The fourth prop did not go up into place as easy as the second had and Nathan realised it was because the angle of the lifting rope was changing as the props got closer to the cross support.

The fifth prop just wouldn't go in and Nathan knew he could only continue with this approach if he could get the rope higher up, over the very top cross support.

He was careful not to knock any of the positioned props loose as he brought the rope back down. However, his first attempt at getting the rope up over the top cross support did bring two of his props crashing back down. He jumped aside of the shaft just in time.

7

Try as he might Nathan could not get the rope up over the highest cross support but he didn't give in. His survival training said always review situations but never give up. He had proven that his construction method had some merit. The problem appeared to be the weight of the rope.

So after a rest from spinning and launching the rock Nathan set to untwining a third of the rope in order to connect its three strings into one long one.

Increasingly having to untangle what he was working with, this was no quick job. It required a lot of rest breaks. It was more tiring than it looked, even for him.

Hours later he had his long lengths of string tied together and after a number of attempts got the rock over the top cross support. This support was still a little way from the top of the shaft but he decided he would tackle that problem when he got that far.

The first problem he found with using a length of string was that a knot in it would not support a prop suspension thread the way the rope knot had. Rethinking his plan, Nathan tied the string to the end of the remaining rope and pulled it up over the top cross support.

Tying another knot in the rope and starting to lift the props again he found he had a new problem. Where he had been able to use tension in the free end of rope to help guide the prop into position there was now less tension. Having untwined a string from the rope the remaining spiral behaved like a spring. The only thing Nathan could do was work more slowly.

Eventually he had a number of props in place but try as he might he could place no more. The props only reached half way up the shaft.

In addition to which he now had a headache. He was dehydrated and with no water he was facing drinking his urine once more. He knew there was a limit to how many times a person could do that before the salts in it simply increased thirst and caused their kidneys shut down. All the more reason he had to get to the bottle in the flight seat above.

Gavin was not long back home, from his job as a delivery driver, when the doorbell rang. It was Emily again. He doubted she had any news on Nathan. He thought she would most likely have phoned if she had.

'Come to give me another slapping?' Gavin joked.

'Maybe later,' there was no sound of humour to her voice. 'You need your grab-bag and passports for both you and Nathan.'

'You've found him!' Gavin raised his arms to hug her, but she batted them aside.

'Not yet…We've intercepted some intel and think he may be in Western Australia.'

'Right…But if someone has spotted him and he hasn't called in, that must mean he's injured or unconscious, right?'

'Will you stop letting your imagination spiral out of control, or you'll be getting that slap sooner than later. I'll explain as you grab your stuff.'

Gavin raced upstairs with Emily hot on his heels.

'We now understand that when Nathan's rescue chopper came down, an MI5 team were first on the scene.'

'MI5?'

'The team we sent out to investigate were watched and then tracked home from a satellite. We accessed the MI5 transmission log, hacking into their system, so we now know that Section 13 were after Nathan.'

'How do these people know about Nathan?'

'They are a special arm of MI5, who we have had run-ins with before. Someone must have informed on us.'

'But I don't understand, Emily.' Gavin stopped to face her as he pulled his grab bag out of his cupboard. 'Why would MI5 be interested in an IVF research team?'

'We think the informer, whoever they are, has told *Thirteen* that Nathan has unusual abilities.'

Gavin's shoulders sagged. 'I thought we could trust you people.'

'Come on, there's no time to lose. *Thirteen* have people on their way to Perth already.'

'But how do *they* know where to go, when *we* don't? Did they speak with Nathan in Norway? And if they did, why did they let him go?'

'We don't know the answers to those questions yet…Have you got everything?'

Gavin checked the top pocket of the pack, confirming the passports were there then made to follow Emily. 'Don't we need visas?'

'They are being taken care of.'

Nathan smiled. He had been watching his father with Emily, they were coming for him. With reference to MI5 agents heading for Perth he checked out a number of aircraft heading his way and finally spotted Ethan and Maeve. He would welcome the help of any of them at this point, but would have preferred to have his father there. However, none of them would be finding him if he couldn't climb out of the mine.

Getting back to his feet he felt a little dizzy this time. His attention had been taken by a length of hinge, down one of the tunnels. He was not sure why but he went and picked it up.

Holding it in his hand it appeared to be from a shed door or a crate lid. It had begun to rust but was still strong. He first imagined using it like a piton in the wall of the shaft. However, as he slammed the narrow end into the wall of the tunnel it did not penetrate far, just chipped some of the wall away.

Then he had another idea. Returning to the spare props lying on the tunnel floor, he slid the hinge strip under a couple of props, stood on them, and then bent the hinge over and round. He decided it was probably a good sign that it did not bend too easily, and smiled again. Maybe this would work.

Examining his handiwork it looked like a strip hook. He lifted a piece of the scaffold with the hook and noted how it slid. It would need friction for what he now had in mind.

Nathan removed his sling, thinking to use that around his improvised hook. It was then that he noticed the bandage round his arm did not look as tight around his wrist. Distracted for the moment he unbound his arm.

He discovered that his wrist was much less swollen than it had been. Far more surprising though was that the torn hand muscle was already knitting together. He knew his cuts healed quickly leaving no scars, but this was something else. The thread he had used to stitch the wound had come away in bits. Looking at his hand it was as if he had only imagined almost tearing his thumb off. He could wiggle his thumb slightly, though it still hurt somewhat.

Before replacing the bandage, Nathan bound the hinge in his sling. Bandaging his hand, this time with fewer layers he placed the wrapped hook at his wrist and then bandaged the strip to his forearm. This was not easy to do with one hand and he had to use his teeth again to tie the end off.

Nathan tested the bent hinge on a length of prop again. With the added friction of a few layers of sling on it, it stopped the slip.

Next he tested the hook out with the intended task. He climbed up the sloped prop into the shaft and put his hook over the next prop. Pulling, testing that both hook and prop would take his weight he gingerly made his way up to another prop. He smiled again. This idea was working.

Returning to the tunnel floor, Nathan used lengths of thread to create harnesses for each remaining prop. Next he tied the free end of the rope around his waist as a makeshift safety line, then placed just two of the props over his shoulder and climbed up the shaft. He felt very tired now but found that if he stopped for a rest every two props up, his energy returned.

Though progress was now a little quicker, like everything else this assembly approach was still difficult. At any moment his weight threatened to collapse it all, but Nathan kept at it.

Having to climb up and down the shaft was going to be draining so Nathan decided to risk taking four props on his next climb. He coped with this but knew he couldn't risk taking more than that.

Eventually, he had put all of the props in place and was now within reach of the top cross support. He rested there for some minutes wondering if he could possibly climb the rest of the way out. However, having come this close he didn't want to risk a change in approach out of impatience for that water just metres away.

Nathan climbed back down and removed the length of rope from the top cross support. Threading it back through the pulleys he went to get more pit-props.

Since the Seriously Organised Vigilantes had played a part in the Great Reset they had become even more like an international paramilitary group. Even though they continued to operate independently of national security services they were now receiving funding from many governments for their covert support.

The chimera-Coronavirus had placed the world's weak and desperate survivors in situations where survival for many of them meant turning to crime. This then escalated from basic looting to more seriously organised criminal activities for some.

The SOVs continued to track the major offenders and extract them for Internet publicised punishments. Nevertheless, Helga Sturmfeld was convinced that a more effective type of vigilante was needed for the NWO. This was the thinking behind the transhumanist genetic engineering experiments which so far had resulted in Nathan.

So much was invested in Nathan it was imperative that he was located and recovered to keep the project on schedule. Nevertheless, there was a fall-back plan which was already well underway.

Nathan was excited. He would soon be out of the mine and be able to get to that bottle of water. He was so tired and thirsty now, as he placed another couple of lengths of scaffold near the bottom of the shaft.

Looking up the shaft he could see with his eyes what he viewed with his mind, the sun was going down. It would be easier to travel in the dark, for him anyway. Nathan had never really known darkness as others had. His world had been permanent day, even though he was visually aware of a night sky. Night just meant it would be cooler.

Turning away from the shaft Nathan reckoned that two more pit-props should be enough.

Though his hook had made climbing the scaffolding easier, it made little difference to the awkwardness of rigging up the rope and pulleys on a prop. He tried to stay patient, not wanting to make any mistakes now.

Finally he had the last prop rigged. He walked back along the tunnel and started to tug once more. That was when the mine caved in.

8

Nathan blinked his dry eyes, coughing on the dust. He had been so lucky that none of the fallen sections of roof had come down on him. His quick reactions and turn of speed had saved him, but he had lost that last prop and one of the pulleys. A good section of rope was now trapped under the heavy rubble too.

Nevertheless, for the time being Nathan pressed on with his scaffold construction as he continued to cough.

The dust was far less as he climbed higher up the shaft putting each new prop in place. He took the opportunity to breathe in the cooling evening air.

Finally the last prop was seated in. He was so very tired now. He knew he only needed one more section of scaffold. However, he found himself wondering whether it would be more of a risk to pull out another prop or to attempt to jump the two metres remaining.

He had never let on at school but he knew that the high-jumps that he had seen others needing a run-up for, he could do from standing.

Visualising the jump, his feet landing on the lip of the shaft, he crouched and kicked-off with all the force he could muster. The scaffold shifted from under him. As he came up to hip height near the edge he realised it was all going wrong. With only one hand and a hook he didn't think he would be able to scrabble on sand to climb out.

The dislodged prop was just about to start knocking others loose on its way down. Nathan grabbed for the edge of the shaft with his left hand and swung his feet up as high as he could to either side. Then once again, with all the force he could muster, he pushed off the edge.

This propelled him upwards and backwards clear of the shaft. He was out. He lay on the sand gasping and sobbing with relief for some moments before getting to his feet and going to the pocket under the flight seat.

He had to use his teeth to unscrew the cap on the bottle but soon was gulping it down. He spared only a little to wash the dust out of each eye before getting the rest down his throat.

He placed the empty bottle in a thigh pocket then set about the task of untying the flight seat cover. He wondered what else of use he could take, deciding to take the remains of his helmet. The front section of it, with the coms, was missing, but if nothing else the shell of the back half might make a good digging tool when he reached that river bed.

In his fifteenth floor Hong Kong office, his colleagues now gone for the evening, Edward Kane worked on into the night. This was the time that he managed his *unofficial* accounts, procuring women and young children for use in satanic rituals. It was his job to ensure that his clients got their product on time with no problems. He was not a believer himself, it was the money that he worshipped above all else.

Crime had become more of a challenge to organise since the cull. Nevertheless, for people with a finger on the pulse and an unhealthy curiosity there were ways and means to develop new serious organised crime opportunities.

Edward got up from his desk and went to check out the mini-bar in the fridge. It was too soon to hit the alcohol, he still had a number of jobs to arrange, so cast his eye over the flavoured spring water bottles. One of the bottles looked like a new flavour. He lifted it out to examine the label.

'Pumpagol?' He had never heard of such a plant. Looking at the picture it appeared to be something from a rainforest. It was a bowl-like plant with thick leaves like those of a succulent sprouting from the rim.

Trusting his secretary's shopping choice Edward unscrewed the top and raised the half litre bottle to his nose. His frown instantly turned to surprise. He had never smelled anything quite like it before. It was wonderful. He took a swig. It tasted even better. The taste was sweeter and stronger than he was used to with other more dilute flavoured waters. He gulped down half the bottle. Cool and delicious. He found himself compelled to finish the bottle right away.

He looked at the other bottles in the fridge door. The others were the usual flavours. He was instantly disappointed but then he noticed there was one other, at the back of a shelf. He took it out. Closing the door he dropped the empty bottle and top into the bin and returned to his desk with the fresh bottle.

Pulling his chair closer to the desk he placed the bottle next to his pad and returned his attention to his Dark Net folder to consider which job to deal with next.

He belched. There was that smell on his breath. He wondered for a moment whether it had been a mistake to drink a whole bottle so quick but then he reached for the second bottle unscrewed the cap and took another couple of gulps.

As he put the bottle back on the desk and looked down at his pad he heard a noise over by the fridge. Something appeared to have got into the bin. As he watched, the lid lifted slightly and two red eyes peered back. He felt the contents of his stomach shift. He wondered if he might be hallucinating, from too many long days, or was he having a reaction to the drink?

Then movement on the desk drew his attention back. The bottle appeared to be melting, tipping towards the pad. Edward grabbed for it to stop it spilling but the bottle squished in his grip as he lifted it. The liquid came out of the top, but with the consistency of a gel.

'What the hell?!'

The bottle dissolved into the gel and covered Edward's hand.

'Urrgh!' He shook his hand but the gel did not fall away.

The bin lid flew off and as Edward looked he saw something bound across the carpet and jump up onto the desk. It was the size of a rat but not a rat.

'Shit!'

He lifted his left hand to fend it off but it grabbed hold, with tentacles before going transparent. Then, along with the gel covering his right hand it spread up his arms under his sleeves.

Edward tried to keep calm. Logic would dictate that this simply could *not* be happening. However, he was anything but calm as the contents of his stomach crept up his throat, blocking his windpipe and covering his voice box. Edward slumped back in his chair. This had to be all in his mind he told himself. It had to pass. He was only imagining that he couldn't breathe, couldn't call out. It couldn't be possible that the gel was coming out of his nostrils like tentacles. The gel in his throat was causing him to gag uncontrollably as it spread out of his mouth over his lips to cover his face. Though it was a clear film it burned and blinded him so he could only feel not see the gel from both hands extend over his shoulders to meet the gel spreading down his neck to his chest.

Edward went into convulsions before the metamorph had totally engulfed him but this made no odds to the final outcome.

When colleagues returned to work in the morning they found no trace of Edward, only his abandoned clothes. Without security cameras in the office there was no recording of the alien assassin digesting its meal or exiting via a *magic door*.

Nathan's idea of using the remains of his helmet to dig with did not prove workable in practice. Even when he was adding pressure with the metal hook still strapped to his wrist, the helmet was too large for the task. It required too much force to do more than scrape at the surface. Nathan removed the sling covering from the hook and found it easier to use that to scrape with, using his left hand to remove loose material from the hole.

After a good twenty minutes at the bend in the riverbed he was down to water. The water was difficult to reach. He pulled a handful of sponge away from inside the seat cover he had brought and used it to soak up the water a bit at a time. He used the sling to create a filter, collecting the water in his empty bottle. After he had quenched his thirst he continued with this process to fill the bottle once more.

Next on his things-to-do list was to get to the quandong tree for something to eat.

On his way he noticed how some rocks retained residual heat from the day longer than others. He never understood how his remote-viewing enabled a sense of temperature, but it did.

Halfway to the quandong tree his regular sweeps with remote-viewing picked up a vehicle in the vicinity. If he ran he might reach the dirt track in time to intercept it, but it would be touch and go. On straight sections of track the vehicle, with four men in it, would speed up, but then slow quickly as rough uneven sections presented themselves.

Nathan used his remote-viewing to select what he hoped to be the fastest route, shifting into a sprint.

Steadily he began to gain confidence that he would reach his predicted intercept point in time. However, the 4x4 suddenly took another track heading away from the hoped for intercept point.

'No!' Nathan slowed to a fast jog but kept track of the vehicle. At best all he could do now was give chase and hope he could catch up whenever they stopped.

As he ran on he looked out for other possible sources of food, since he was now leaving the quandong behind. He had to keep his energy up.

Ethan and Maeve strode out from arrivals and headed to the Hertz desk to pick up the keys to their 4x4. As they placed their carry-on luggage in the boot they saw that their mission kit was already loaded. Ethan looked around to check the coast was clear then opened the packs and checked the content with Maeve. All was as expected.

As Maeve closed the tailgate Ethan asked 'Do you have directions?'

Maeve showed Ethan the map on her smartphone. 'We have two options. We can head up the Brand Highway or the Great Northern Highway. Now, considering how the infrastructure has suffered since the Great Reset the Brand would surely be easier going, along the coastal route. However, the Great Northern to Port Hedland takes us more centrally through W.A. The way I see it, if we get a fix on the lad, keeping more central would possibly make it quicker getting to him, as long as the road conditions are drivable.'

'The Great Northern it is then.' Ethan wasn't too concerned about rougher roads. He held his hand out for the key fob. 'I'll drive first.'

The four men in the 4x4 unwittingly leaving Nathan ever further behind were gold hunters. Since the Great Reset many of the prospector leases had fallen ownerless, attracting the attention of surviving hunters. Gold was still creditable even in the cashless society of the new age.

Monty was driving but his eyes were tiring. He wished that they could have afforded night vision but like most gold hunters they lived on the breadline constantly dreaming of the one big nugget.

Carl sat next to him navigating, though other than the last turnoff he was only acting as *spotter* for Monty in case he missed an approaching rock or hole in the track.

The two on the back seat, Stan and Colt, were dozing between occasional hard shakes from uneven sections of track. It was one such section which saw Stan and Colt crack heads.

'For fuck sake you two!' moaned Colt, 'aren't you watching where you're going?'

'Sorry Colt, the only way was over *that* one,' explained Carl craning round in his seat.

'How much further, Carl?' asked Stan, the old man of the group.

'A few more clicks and we should be making camp.'

'Good. These corrugations are playing merry hell with my kidneys. I need to take a piss.'

Gavin and Emily were both tucking into a meal. Gavin was engrossed in his chosen in-flight entertainment, when the plane shook and shook again.

Gavin turned to Emily, not used to air travel.

'It's just a bit of turbulence.'

There came an announcement 'This is your Captain speaking. We will be experiencing a patch of turbulence for the next few minutes, so please remain in your seats with your seatbelts fastened until the seatbelt sign is switched off, thank you.'

The plane shook so hard that the contents of people's food trays started to dance.

'You might want to get your wine and water down you, by drinking it now, rather than getting it down you by spilling it.' Emily said, draining her mini wine bottle.

Gavin took her advice and followed suit but as they both reached for their water cups the plane unexpectedly banked and climbed. Then more unexpectedly it dropped and a few people screamed, as food and drink lifted off people's trays six inches or so, further unsettling Gavin. Watching the water lift out of the plastic cup his left hand grabbed Emily's right.

'Hell! It's a wonder the wings don't snap off!' He started to catastrophize again as he attempted to catch the water now falling back.

'These planes can take far worse than this,' Emily sounded very matter of fact about the turbulence, not at all concerned. 'Most of the bodywork is made of composite materials these days.'

'Most?!'

'Well yes, it can't all be made of the same material now can it.'

'So which bit isn't?!'

'Oh let me see now, I seem to remember it's the tail section.'

The plane suffered another massive shaking.

'The tail section?!'

'Urr yes. If I remember right it's because they have to balance the weight centred on the wings, it's made of aluminium and held on by superglue.'

'SUPERGLUE?!' he increased his grip on her.

'Calm down. You'll cause other passengers to panic,' she smirked. 'I was joking.'

'With the glue?'

'No the whole thing.'

'What?'

'Yeah. Air travel isn't very safe at all these days, what with all the freak weather caused by climate change.'

'Oh my God!'

'Hey Lady?!' A man across the aisle interrupted. 'Why don't you shut the fuck up!'

She turned to face him not at all concerned by his irritation. 'If you don't enjoy my in-flight entertainment put your ear-buds in.'

Gavin sighed, relaxing a little. 'Emily. You have a nasty sense of humour.'

'I prefer the term wicked.'

Colt, Monty, Stan and Carl had reached the site. Even at night the air was much warmer than the air conditioned interior of the 4x4 they had grown used to on the trip out. Their jumpsuit style clothing went some way towards helping with the more extreme temperatures they faced in the desert. Nevertheless, their expensive N-Viro suits could all have done with renewing. If only they could make that big find. But then if the find was big enough they all liked to think they could quit hunting altogether and settle down some place cooler.

It was Monty's turn to get the food cooking for supper and while he did that the other three set about making camp. But before long the shouting began.

'Stan! You flaming wallaroo!' Colt had a quick temper. 'Carl and I can do this better on our own. Why don't you go sort the dunny.'

Stan shrugged and headed over to the 4x4.

Overhearing this, Monty called to Stan. 'While you're at the ute will you see if you can find the tin opener, the last galah to use it didn't put it back in the cutlery box.'

'Right oh.'

The opener was in with the case of beer bottles, where he'd left it.

Walking over to Monty where he had just got the fire going, Monty pointed at the tinned meat. 'Do you want to open them up for us while I get a brew on?'

That task sounded better than setting up their latrine, a job he seemed to keep getting. 'Yeah, fine.'

Monty handed him a pan to place the contents in.

The tins got trodden on to flatten them afterwards to take up less space in the garbage box. They never threw tins into their surroundings like some people did. Being gold hunters their pet hate was getting a good signal from their detectors only to dig up other people's rubbish.

There was a knack to crushing cans flat under a heel. Usually Stan didn't have a problem, maybe it was the uneven ground, but this time he sprained his ankle. It was the weak ankle he had once damage falling from a ladder. 'Fuck it!'

'What's up?'

'I've twisted my ankle.'

'Your old bones better be okay by tomorrow Stan!' Colt warned, as if that would sort the problem. 'We have a lot of ground to cover.'

Stan sighed. Colt was always shooting his mouth off. The lads may have deferred to Stan for his years of experience metal detecting, since he left the UK before the 20s, but they all knew Colt was the alpha male.

Stan rubbed at his right ankle and was thankful that at least he wasn't trapped and being gassed this time round. He reflected on the fact that he had led a life of poor judgement calls. He had come to Western Australia to make his millions hunting gold. However, so far like the others, he had endured the daily threat of heat exposure, even with an N-Viro suit to only ever find enough each week to get by.

When the brew was ready Monty took the pan of meat off Stan and handed him a mug of coffee.

'Thanks Monty. Did I ever tell you about the time I got trapped in a bunker I found on my property in Northumberland?'

'Oh only about a million times.'

Stan nodded. That was his cue to shut up.

'Did I ever tell you about my interest in pirates, Stan?'

'No.'

'Since I was a kid I was excited by the idea of treasure hunting in the Caribbean. I realised there were two causes of sunken treasure. Storms and pirates. So I started reading about pirates.'

With the camp finally sorted, Colt and Carl came across to the fire and picked up their brews.

'Did you know that Captain Hook, from Peter Pan, was based on a real person?'

'Bollocks,' snorted Colt.

'It's true. J. M. Barrie based Hook on someone called Jim Trudgebend, a short guy who sailed around Indonesia and actually got his hand bitten off by a saltie.'

'Bollocks. I've never heard of this J. M. Barrie, and I watched Peter Pan a number of times as a kid.'

'It's all true. People have even seen the ghost of Trudgebend from time to time. Apparently he used to use the hook to torture information out of people. And when he was done with them he used to hook people through the mouth like fish and tear through their cheeks.'

'Shit!' Carl sounded particularly unnerved, though he was *also* pointing open-mouthed at something.

A strange figure with a hook had appeared by the 4x4.

9

Nathan stood looking at the four surprised faces. He had already decided who to turn to first for help, having been observing them while he closed in.

He turned to Colt. He thought it would stand him in better stead to appear to see him as the natural lead male, if not the wisest. 'Do you have any water sir?'

'Stone the crows! Where the hell did you come from kid?'

'I was involved in an accident.'

Stan hobbled forward with his bad ankle, offering Nathan a billy can. Nathan gulped down the water.

'What's with the hook thing?' Colt gestured with his finger, stepping closer as Stan backed off.

'I hurt my hand but I needed to be able to dig for water so I used a bandage from my first aid kit to create this.'

'Whatever were you doing out here?' Colt was clearly suspicious.

'I'm part of a school trip…Geology class.'

'You sound like a Brit and that doesn't look like a school uniform. More like an N-Viro suit for dirt-biking. You sure you're not just camping out here with your folks, and just winding us up?'

Nathan took a few more gulps then shook his head. 'My family emigrated after the Reset. I go to a private school in Perth. They gave us these environment suits to test out on this trip in the desert.'

'So you're a *Privileged* kid.'

'I guess so.'

'Pfff!'

'Hey,' said Stan. 'The kid can't help how he was brought up...So where are the others and what happened to them?'

'The bus over-turned. I think the road gave way. I don't know where the bus is now though. I've got lost. I've been walking for days.'

'Don't you know you should always stay with the vehicle?'

'We did for a couple of days. We didn't have a phone signal, supplies were running low and no one seemed to be coming. I just thought I could go get help. Do you have a phone I can use?'

'Even 6G doesn't work out here, and we've been getting around to repairing the sat-radio for some time.'

'Oh...Well could you give me a lift to the nearest town then?'

'Nearest town, which ain't a ghost-town, would be hundreds of kilometres away. We can't afford the fuel it would cost us to get you there and then be able to get back here.'

'Why do you need to be here?'

'That's our business.'

'Right, sorry.'

'We're gold hunters.' Stan explained.

'Wow.'

'But until we find enough gold to cover fuel and other expenses we can't leave here.'

'Oh...Well will you find enough tomorrow, do you think?'

106

The men all laughed.

'Wouldn't that be the dream,' said Carl. 'I'd be stoked!'

'It could take weeks,' Stan explained. 'But maybe there's a search party out looking for your group now, maybe even found them.'

'Yeah,' Monty encouraged. 'Maybe they have rescued them already, and they are just out looking for you now.'

'Look why don't you have some of our food and get some rest,' Carl offered Nathan a bowl.

'That's very kind of you. Thanks.'

Colt immediately considered the cost of another mouth to feed. 'Maybe you can help out around here.'

'Yeah, I'd like that.' Nathan showed willing because he could see that civilisation certainly was a long way away. The sooner they found enough gold the sooner he could get home.

'My name's Stan. What's yours?'

'Nathan.' He saw no point in lying now.

'These guys are Colt, Carl and Monty.'

'Hi.'

Emily and Gavin stood outside the arrivals gate at Perth International Airport.

'This way,' Emily pointed across the foyer to the Hertz desk and headed off with Gavin in tow, bringing their luggage trolley.

The woman at the desk seemed pleased that the two of them were coming her way. She probably needed a break from the monotony of small hours business.

It was clear to Emily, the way the woman's gaze focused on Gavin as they got closer, that the woman thought she would be dealing with him.

Emily held out her mobile with the booking confirmation QR code.

'Oh,' was all that the woman said before scanning it and turning to her monitor.

'Do all the Hertz vehicles come with Sat-Trak?' Emily asked, having been informed that the two MI5 officers had taken a Hertz rental.

'Oh yes. That is a standard feature of the Sat-Nav so that we don't lose you…You won't be going off-road will you?'

'Oh I shouldn't think so. I'd like to but the boyfriend,' she jerked her thumb over her shoulder and lowered her voice, 'is a stickler for safety. The journey's been a bit…*tense*.'

The woman nodded sympathetically, 'The Sat-Nav does have a rescue beacon that could be activated if you have a problem, though…' she gave an embarrassed smile, '6G still doesn't reach far towards the centre.'

'Well we'll be staying close to the Great Northern highway over the next week or so, all the way to Katherine.'

'I see. Well everything is in order, and here…' she reached under the desk to the safe-box, '…is your fob. The Hertz app on your phone should connect with the fob and then show you to your car.'

'Thanks.'

'Have a nice trip.'

'It'll be to die for.'

'Ha!'

'Come on Luv. You can have a relaxing shower when we get to the motel.'

Gavin just wanted to find his son but had to admit the idea of a shower was a close second. Nevertheless, unless Emily received further information about Nathan's whereabouts in truth it was going to be a waiting game.

The Toyota in the carpark flashed its lights as they drew close. Gavin expected a top of the range 4x4, since *Control* generally spared no expense but this car looked run of the mill. As long as it was dependable and got them to Nathan in one piece he wasn't worried.

The reason Emily had not hired top of the range was that she did not want them attracting undue attention.

Car packed and trolley parked Emily took the driving seat. She placed her mobile in the dashboard mount, accessed an app and then just seemed to sit there watching the screen.

'What are we waiting for?' Gavin was impatient to get going.

'Just getting a fix on the other Hertz…There they are. Going up the 95.'

'How d'you know it's not someone else?'

'It's the reg I've been told they hired.'

'Right.'

Driving out of Perth in the early hours gave the impression of a ghost city. But then, like everywhere, it had been hit by the Reset-Recession. All too many homes as well as businesses were boarded up.

Near the outskirts Emily pulled into a 24hr Store.

'Ha! Woolworths?' Gavin couldn't believe what he was seeing. 'I thought they all went to the wall last century.'

'Not in Oz.'

'What are we here for?'

'Supplies...I decided not to try organising anything until I knew what terrain we would be heading into,' Emily got out of the car.

'Right,' Gavin followed.

The only light was coming from a collection window. Rather like late-night service at a fuel station, secure shop assistants helped attend to customers shopping requirements. Anything too large to fit through the checkout hatch would need people to come back during the day when the store was open for public access.

Luckily Emily only wanted the basics. If they were in the US that would have included guns but Woolworths would not be providing such supplies. If it came to it, Emily would just go into creative acquisition mode.

Gavin helped carry the bags back towards the car but they were only halfway there when two cars came roaring down the highway. As they passed the carpark, the first vehicle, sporting a very distinctive paint job, sped past the entrance. The second one however, did not. It slammed on the brakes and turned in.

It became obvious to Emily as the vehicle came towards them, ignoring the lane markings, windows down passengers yelling, that they were not here to shop.

Emily looked over her shoulder. Woolworths lights had suddenly gone out. For a 24hr store to close meant only one thing. Trouble.

'Gavin. *Whatever* happens, do exactly what I tell you.'

'What?'

'Did you hear me?'

'Yes.'

The rowdy 4x4 screeched to a halt, cutting Emily and Gavin off from their car. The only reason Emily had parked some distance from the service window was in order that they had another excuse to stretch their legs. She wished she hadn't bothered now, as the other car came back up the highway. It roared into carpark to join the one already there.

She pretended to ignore the car in front of her and attempt to walk around it. She was weary that the driver might suddenly stamp on the accelerator. Instead the doors opened and three men, who had clearly been drinking, got out, just as the other car pulled up.

'Hey doll!'

Gavin sped up to close the gap with Emily, but this draw attention to him.

'Is this fella bothering you, doll?'

'No. He's my boyfriend.'

'Struth doll, you can do way better than that! Look there's no meat on the fella. I think you need some real meat inside you, just so's y'know whatcha missin.'

The other two lads laughed just as the doors to the second car opened up and a further three men spilled out in a similar mood.

Emily thought it smart not to respond and continued towards the car. If they could just get in and get going she was convinced she could lose these rowdy drunks, even with their more powerful engines.

'I'm *talking* to you, *doll*!'

'Enough of that Col!' A large man from the other car chided. 'Can't you *tell*, she's a three-P-sweetie; Prime Pommy Pussie? She needs a more *refined* approach…Let me help you with that shopping, luv.'

'I can manage thank you.'

The man blocked her way and snatched for a bag.

Letting it go, Emily considered the consequences of striking out. The time was not right. She had to make sure Gavin didn't get hurt. He may have had a criminal past but to date she had seen no aggressiveness in his nature.

'There you go,' the man encouraged, but then hurled the shopping away with a jerk of his arm. 'Oops…sorry, luv. Just had one of me Tourette's spasms.'

The men laughed.

This made Gavin's blood boil. 'Okay you've had your fun! Now let us get on our way!'

'No mate, we've only just started. You see we don't reckon you deserve a woman *this* fit. You don't look like you know how to handle her proper…*We* on the other hand…'

Gavin saw the big man grab Emily's wrist and draw her in close. He half expected her to slap the man hard like she did with him but instead she squealed, dropping the other bag.

'Leave her alone!' Gavin dropped his bags and started to lunge forward but someone grabbed him by the elbow and spun him. Then another man punched him hard in the stomach, doubling him over, winded.

'No!!' Emily cried.

Gavin tried to stand, fighting for breath, but only got a punch to his face for his troubles, then the ground came up to meet him.

'Oh dear mate. Not a good look for the Sheilas that…So you can't blame her for deciding to come with us now can'ya?!'

Emily broke free, reaching out for Gavin. Going down on her knees she took Gavin's head in her hands, sobbing.

Gavin found it almost scary how, as Emily's lips reached his right ear, her sobbing momentarily ceased and her calm confident voice said 'Stay here. I'll be back.'

Then Emily was dragged away, kicking and screaming with convincing tears of panic flowing down her face. No one came from the store to help and there were no signs of any police coming.

With a roar of engines and wheel-spin the two cars were off.

Gavin felt useless, like he had just *let* them go. It had all happened so fast. He knew when Emily said *stay* she hadn't meant *on the ground*, so he got up off the tarmac. What was he to do though? She didn't say *call the police*, though he did want to. What if she was simply overconfident and actually needed help?

The rental car had been unlocked but Gavin could not drive after them because Emily still had the keys. He wondered why she hadn't thought to drop the fob along with the shopping.

Trying to pull himself together Gavin collected up the shopping and loaded it into the car. He kept looking back at Woolworths but there was nothing to be seen of the staff.

Getting into the passenger seat and closing the door he pulled down the vanity mirror. His lip was split and bleeding. There was going to be a bruise. He took a tissue from the glove box.

Then he started worrying about Nathan. If this was how Aussies behaved now, Nathan was in more trouble than he'd thought.

Knowing that if Nathan was conscious and watching over him he would be concerned. Gavin guessed that he would probably be projecting himself into the seat next to him, so he turned to the emptiness and with slightly exaggerated pronunciation said 'It's okay Nathan. I'm okay, really. I just wish I knew where you were and that *you* are okay.' His eyes teared up and he used the bloodied tissue to dab at them.

As time passed by, Gavin spotted no other shoppers, no one to speak to at all in fact, as if they all knew to keep off the streets.

Feeling the call of nature and unable to wait any longer he got out and went over to a hedge to urinate. He then returned to the car, to worry some more.

If Emily never came back how was he going to find Nathan? He had a phone of course. So *Control* would surely contact him with information. He considered calling *Control* to report Emily's abduction. But what were *they* going to be able to do across there in England?

There was that Hertz accident alert button of course, but with this situation he thought they would be less than useful. They would probably only be looking to get their vehicle back in one piece, leaving the police to handle the rest.

Almost an hour later one of the 4x4s returned. There were no yelling males this time as the car approached, coming around from behind. Gavin could feel his hairs standing on end. Then, as the car pulled up to his left he realised that it was Emily driving.

Lowering the window he watched in amazement as she got out of the car behaving like she had only been for a drive around the block. However, under the carpark's LED lighting he could clearly see that she was covered in blood.

'Oh my God, Emily. What did they do?'

'Oh you don't want to know…Really.'

'Tell me.' His blood was starting to boil again with thoughts of what she must have gone through. They should report this.

'Well they took me to a farm, and pulled a stupid prank. They chucked all this kangaroo blood over me then just let me go.'

'*Really*?'

Emily could see he was thinking about another question, so she passed the Toyota keys over. 'Follow me out of town.'

'What?'

'Did you hear what I said?'

'Yes.'

As Emily turned her back on Gavin he shifted over to the driving seat and got the engine started.

Fifteen minutes later with the last of the city lights behind them, Emily pulled off the road and Gavin followed suit. Then he watched as she used some rag, which she had found in the door-shelf, to clean the car. The way she did this, it looked to Gavin like she had done this sort of thing before; steering wheel, gear shift, handles and anything she might have touched, in the back seat or front. Then Gavin watched her go round to the back, remove some heavy package wrapped in a blanket. She placed it in their car. Next, taking her travel bag out of the Toyota, she went back behind the other vehicle.

Freshened up she returned, carrying her bag and another bundle. She placed them both in the back.

Closing the tail-gate she came round to the driver side. 'Right…Budge over.'

Gavin shuffled aside as Emily got in. He continued to watch as she went about her business. She took her phone opened a message from *Control*, smiled, clicked on a link and placed the phone back in its dashboard cradle.

The screen lit up again with the hacked sat-trak app. First it showed a motel in Reedy as their destination. Next their current position followed by directions. Emily started the engine.

As they pulled away Gavin realised that he was still trembling from the whole experience, as if he had been chilled to the bone. Emily, on the other hand, appeared quite calm and collected, like this was just another day at the office. He began to wonder what she wasn't telling him.

'So what *was* that package you put in the back?'

'The dirty clothes.'

'I meant the…Oh never mind.' He decided he *didn't* want to know.

Five minutes further along the highway, Gavin spotted a glow up ahead. As they drew closer it became clear what it was.

'That farm, look…It's on fire.'

'Oh yeah…*Fancy* that.'

'Well…Aren't we going to stop?'

'Does this rental *look* like a fire engine?'

As they drove on past the drive leading down to the farm, by the light of the raging flames, Gavin recognised the distinctive paintwork of the 4x4.

10

Nathan woke early. He had slept through his father's journey from the airport and the incident at Woolworths. However, he lay where he'd been invited to spend the night, by the camp fire across from Stan, and began searching for his father. It wasn't as simple as thinking of his father and being there. He wished that he had observed their arrival so that he could at least identify their vehicle. As time passed and Stan could be heard getting up, Nathan became frustrated that he had still not located his father and Emily.

Nathan turned to watch Stan wincing from the pain in his ankle.

'You awake too lad?'

'Yeah.'

'Sleep okay?'

'Yeah.'

Nathan had removed the bandaging and hook from his right arm before wrapping himself in the blanket that Stan had offered him. He thought it probably helped him sleep better.

'I reckon I could use your help today. I'll show you how to use a detector and then maybe we'll get out on the quad, once the lads have it down off the trailer. I'll need to keep off my foot as much as I can.'

'Right.'

'But first we need to eat. Well second actually. First off I need to go for a dump.'

With Stan's ankle damaged it had fallen to Monty to dig the dunny before bed, for which they were all grateful.

After a mixture of dehydrated and tinned food to sustain them, and day sacks with water and snacks they all headed off to their agreed patches.

Nathan sat behind Stan on the quad as they drove to the top of what was commonly referred to as a jump-up; a hill. From there Stan described how to read the terrain.

'It all looks like dry ground but in the wet season we can get flash floods and they can wash a lot of stuff through. So you need to use your imagination and see where the water would run. Look for features where the water would hit bends and leave behind heavy deposits like gold.

'You can see a lot from a good quality satellite survey map, but it's always best to get to grips with it physically. The terrain changes a bit each time there's a flash flood, and in this century floods haven't always come in the wet season.

'So look down here, where this dry creek bed is coming towards this jump-up and then veers away there. It will be worth us checking out that bend.'

'Great. Let's go!' Nathan was excited by the prospect and not just as a means to an end.

Down from the jump-up and round to the creek on the quad Nathan was given the detector and day sack to carry.

'Be careful not to damage that detector Lad.'

'I won't…I mean I won't damage it.'

'Good.'

Once they were where Stan wanted them, he showed Nathan how to move the detector's coil from side to side a couple of centimetres off the ground. It needed to be in a steady pattern that missed no ground as he moved forward making the most of each swing without too much exertion. This was something that would need to be kept up for hours.

Stan watched Nathan have a go. At first he had tried it with his right arm but his hand still ached too much so he swapped to his left and got into the rhythm of it.

'Yes that's good. Now let's find something.' Stan suggested, reaching into his pocket and pulling out an old dollar with the Queens head on it. He tossed it onto the ground.

Taking the detector back off Nathan he switched it on and explained that it provided both auditory and visual feedback. The headphones were noise-cancelling, to avoid distractions, so that the variety of whistles could be more clearly interpreted. When the subtle differences were learned it was possible to get a sense of what lay below. The screen situated by the handle visualised the computer interpretation of that signal to help confirm the metal, size and depth.

'Put the headphones on and pass the coil over the dollar whilst watching the screen.'

Nathan nodded and did as he was told. He laughed at the excited squeal from the machine and the strong scan on the screen.

Stan lifted one of Nathan's headphones enough to say 'Now bury it and try that again.' Letting go of the headphone he handed Nathan the plastic trowel.

Nathan did as he was told and noted the difference in sound and scan. He nodded.

'Well dig it back up then.'

Smiling, Nathan retrieved Stan's coin.

Putting the coin back in his pocket Stan hobbled over to the elbow of the flat bottomed gulley and motioned for Nathan to lift his head phones. 'Right. Start here and work round there, and don't forget to swing up the bank as you go. Then on the way back cover the ground adjacent. I'll sit and watch. If you pick up anything that you're unsure about I'll come across to take a look.'

Nathan nodded and set to it. He found it an absorbing process. Soon he realised he had forgotten about being lost in the desert and needing to get home. His focus was on finding a real gold nugget. But he didn't pick up anything in the next sixty seconds, or the next. Over twenty minutes went by and then his whole body language suddenly changed.

Nathan took the headphones off and put down the detector then started digging with the trowel. Peering into the hole it was as if he expected to see the nugget.

'Use the detector to scan the dirt you have dug out to see if it is still in the hole, Nathan.'

It was still in. He dug deeper and then checked again. It still was.

'The deeper it is the bigger the nugget could be,' explained Stan.

The next check confirmed it was out.

'Use the trowel or your hand to hold a sample over the coil to check.'

Nathan did as he was told and soon he had it. It would have been nothing to write home about for Stan but Stan could see the gleam in Nathan's face, his first nugget. Nathan looked like he had caught the gold bug. The sliver of gold was put in a collection canister, the hole in the ground was filled in and Nathan was back to detecting with renewed vigour.

With that spot checked over they moved up the creek to another where Nathan found a more decent nugget, a few grams in weight. Before lunch break he found another one, though slightly smaller.

'Not bad for a newbie's morning's work. Now don't forget you need to keep drinking in this heat. I can see you are almost *too* focused on what you are doing. It is all too easy to die of heat exposure out here.'

Stan led Nathan to sit with him in partial shade of a bush to eat lunch.

After a while Stan broke the silence. 'So whereabouts were you from originally?'

'Birmingham.'

'I thought so,' Stan nodded. 'I used to live up in Northumberland, but moved here some time ago. I was lured by the dream of gold hunting. But I think I'm getting too old for it all now. There is so much luck involved, at times I feel like it's no better than a gambling addiction.'

'So why not quit?'

'And do what?'

'I don't know. Does nothing else interest you?'

'What do *you* want to be when you leave school?'

'An explorer maybe.'

'Where is left to explore?'

'Under the sea maybe. My dad has always been interested in underwater stuff.'

'Yes but are you? You need to do what is right for you. Don't lead your life trying to please others.'

'But I think I *want* to help people.'

'Well that's a good goal. But remember you need to help yourself before you can help others…Shall we get back to hunting nuggets? The gold won't find itself.'

'Sure.'

That afternoon they headed back down the creek, past where they had left the quad and eventually came across a patch where Nathan ended up finding four good little nuggets.

Finally Stan called it a day, mainly because their water had run out, and they headed back to camp.

Later when they had all eaten, Colt insisted all their finds be totalled up on the digital weighing machine. He praised Nathan for the part he had played. 'Good work. If we all keep going like this each day we might be able to afford that trip back to town sometime next week.'

'Next *week*?!' Nathan was suddenly down-hearted. He'd had such a great day, but the reality of this news took the wind out of his sails. There had to be something he could do with his powers to change this situation.

As he stared at the tiny heap of gold left on the digital balance he began to notice something. With the sun down and the air temperature dropping he was seeing a thermal difference between the air, ground and gold. The gold was losing heat to the air quicker than the ground, making it stand out. There were faint plumes above each nugget like ghostly flags as the gold took heat from its surroundings and shed it off.

With a 360 degree scan spiralling outwards from camp he spotted a few spots on the ground which needed checking out.

'I'm going for a walk,' he announced.

'Are you now?' Colt looked at him quizzically.

'Yeah. I won't be long.'

'Take a torch,' Stan insisted.

'I was going to.' He didn't dare say he didn't need one.

Minutes later, some distance from camp, he had the first of the cooler objects in his palm. It was gold alright, just lying there on the surface. Not a big nugget but still it was gold, and so was the next and the next. The more he scanned the more he found. He got to the point where he started dismissing the smaller pieces as he sped from one to the next in the dark.

Walking back to camp with a small but weighty mass in his pocket it occurred to him that he couldn't say 'Look what I just found.' How was he going to explain finding what he now had in his pocket without people learning about his talent?

As he remembered to turn his torch back on, a solution came to him. He was in a far better mood when he returned to camp.

Gavin was feeling irritable. He had felt that way all day. A day spent *waiting out* as Emily called it, off-road in an area of hot dry scrub between

Cue and Reedy. If they *had* to stop, why couldn't she have chosen somewhere nicer like the island they crossed at Lake Austin?

Part of his mood was due to feeling foolish. Emily's mention at the airport of a shower at the motel had somehow got his hopes up. Seeing a motel on the sat-trak made it seem all the more real. However, they never arrived. The trace on the sat-trak wasn't the motel of course, but MI5's Hertz rental parked outside it.

Driving until after sunrise, Emily had got them so far but then pulled off the road and parked up, out of sight. He thought at first she was too tired, after last night's ordeal. However, when he offered to drive on she simply said 'No, we have to *wait out*, here.'

'Waiting for what?' he had asked.

'*Thirteen's* next move.'

'What?'

'*Thirteen* appear to have some lead on Nathan. We need to wait 'til they make a move, so we can follow them, from a safe distance.'

'Safe distance? I don't get it. Why can't we at least get closer than *this*, even if we stay in a different motel?'

'Because it's *Thirteen*, okay?'

Gavin pulled an exaggerated confused-stroke-irritated face and shook his head at her.

'*Thirteen* use people with *talents*.'

'Well I wouldn't exactly expect them to employ idiots.'

'I think they have some of *them* too, but these *others* can each do extraordinary things.'

'Like what? Book into motels and *actually* get to take showers?'

'Track people down.'

'Oh.'

'If we interrupt them before they have a trace on Nathan, things could get more complicated. So we are *waiting out* 'til they *move out*.'

The hours passed. They ate, they drank, they stretched their legs, they napped, they snacked and they tried to stay patient.

Gavin returned to his worrying over Nathan while Emily decided to search local radio channels. There was very little available and what there was, not only sounded amateur it came with free waves of static.

'So tell me, Emily. How long will we be able to keep *waiting out* until we have to come up with another plan?'

'A few days, with the supplies we have.'

'Shouldn't we have a plan *before* then?'

11

Nathan played it cool and hoped no one spotted the slight bulging which he now had, split up between two pockets in his suit. For his plan to work he needed to be back out with Stan and for Stan's ankle still to be bad enough for him to continue to rest up away from him.

Stan took him out to a patch which had looked promising from the jump-up but was further out from camp.

Arriving before mid-morning and parking up in the shade of a rocky outcrop, Stan briefed Nathan on the patch to detect first.

He put the day-sack on his back first then took the detector. Nestling his arm into the brace as he gripped the handle, Nathan was off with a smile. This would be the day he turned things around, he promised himself.

Every so often, whether he got a signal or not, he went through the motions of digging a hole, taking gold from a pocket and putting it into the finds canister. As he filled each hole back in he would glance back to Stan who was none the wiser. Sometimes he'd be watching and Nathan would give him a thumbs-up. He also threw in a couple of thumbs-down for credibility's sake.

At one point there was no response from Stan. He just lay there on the rock next to the quad. Nathan walked back to him concerned that something might be wrong. Maybe heat exposure, even lying in the shade, if his N-Viro suit had packed up.

Nathan shook his shoulder.

'Eh what's up? What have you found?'

'I thought something had happened to you.'

'No sorry. I nodded off. So how are you doing?'

'Fine.' Nathan showed him the contents of his canister so far.

'That's better than fine lad.'

'Well I best get back to it.'

'I wish this ankle were better, I'd be right there with you.'

'No worries.' Nathan returned to where he had got to and continued his sweeps of the ground.

By lunch time he could see that Stan was asleep again and rather than disturb him he stayed out where he was and ate his food under the shade of a bush.

As he ate he tried searching for his father again. Unable to locate his father however, it occurred to Nathan to check up on Charisma. He soon wished he hadn't though. His snooping led to him witnessing something he would never forget and he almost lost his lunch.

He was surprised to find that Bernie was still living at the house after Charisma had opened up to her mum about the reason for her disturbing behaviour.

What Nathan did not know was that Bernie had first tried pleading with Helen that he had been misunderstood. When that got him nowhere he begged that he could at least be given the chance to find somewhere else to live before moving out. Because Helen still loved him despite his behaviour towards Charisma she agreed that he could stay but he had to sleep in the spare room.

Bernie was angry with Charisma for coming between him and Helen. However, as he turned his focus to finding a new place to live, his imagination had taken a turn for the darker.

It had occurred to Bernie that this could be a new chapter in his life and that maybe it was time to make some of his darker fantasies a reality.

Unknown to Nathan, Charisma or Helen, instead of using his time to find a place to live he had a new agenda. He checked out a number of abandoned buildings, of which there were many these days. However, he soon learned it was safer to avoid anywhere with signs of activity.

Finally he found a place out in an area of old green-belt, a disused static caravan at the corner of a field. He had to break into it but within a couple of days he had the lock fixed and made a number of other mods to secure the place, preparing it for what he had in mind.

Telling Helen he was having great difficulty finding a place close to work and affordable, he had asked for a couple more weeks. She agreed.

This particular evening he was so pleased with himself. That bitter-sweet anger he had felt towards Charisma had finally turned to something else. He had abducted an American girl who he came across begging on the street. Telling her he would take care of her he had taken her to the static caravan, where, after drugging her he had left her bound up like a fly in a spider's web.

Now, as Nathan checked on him, Bernie lay under his duvet smiling. He was imagining what the girl's discomfort and terror would be like when she woke, to find herself tied up, all alone in the dark, miles from anywhere.

As Nathan watched Charisma outside the spare room listening at the door, he still knew none of what Bernie had been up to other than what Charisma had spoken of that day at school.

Without warning Charisma burst into Bernie's room, confusing his thoughts.

'What do you want, Charisma?'

Nathan moved his viewpoint across the bedroom so that he could better lip-read what was said.

Closing the door behind her and moving over to the bedside Charisma explained 'I don't want you staying here a minute longer. While I'm sorry that Mum has been so hurt by this, it's all *your* fault.'

'*My* fault? If *you* had continued to keep your thoughts to yourself, instead of making such accusations, we would have still been a happy family.'

'Oh *really*?'

'You've always been a trouble-maker. I tried so hard with you when I got together with your mum. You were jealous.'

'*Jealous*?'

'Yes. Jealous of your mother. I saw the way you looked at me.'

'What? The *disgust*?'

'You wanted me and your immature mind thought you could suck me in.'

'*Suck you in*? You have no idea…'

That was when Bernie made his mistake. His left hand shot out from under the duvet and grabbed Charisma's wrist.

Charisma didn't back off, or even cry out however.

To Bernie's *and* Nathan's surprise Charisma's right hand turned and gripped Bernie's wrist in turn, and then seemed to melt over it. Her whole right arm was flowing over his left.

In fear and disbelief Bernie tried to pull away. He couldn't. He was being sucked in. He drew a breath to call out but her left hand slapped over his mouth and nose blocking out any sound, as her left arm flowed over his head. The morphing mass penetrated nostrils and throat, choking him as it slid on down to his stomach.

Nathan wondered if he was having some bizarre dream, as even Charisma's clothes turned to gloop along with her body slipping under the duvet to engulf the struggling man.

Nathan shifted his viewpoint to check where Helen was. That was when he found her in the kitchen with Charisma. There were two Charismas, except the one upstairs wasn't human.

Nathan could do nothing to warn them about what was going on upstairs. And all things considered they were unlikely to be checking on Bernie before going to bed themselves. Would *they* be the next victims of this *thing*?

Maeve was flicking through Tik Tok clips trying to block out the words she was picking up from Ethan in the room next door. The clips were mainly a mixture of the latest freakiest freak weather from around the world and silly clips of people and pets. The words from next door were mainly expletives, occasionally voiced in greater frustration. Maeve assumed that Ethan was playing some shoot'em up on his TV.

She decided that when the temperature dropped a little more they should get out for a bit. Though it was more common for people to stay indoors these days, she didn't want them becoming a focus of any curiosity for their inactivity. The potential for curiosity was heightened by the fact that they were not sharing a room but Maeve had no intention of that happening.

Eventually, with no update from the office regarding the eyes and ears of GCHQ searching for the lad, Maeve went and knocked on Ethan's door.

There was no grudging delayed response to interruption. The door opened quickly instead, to reveal Ethan looking like he was itching to go.

'News?'

'Afraid not…I assume you've been playing a video game.'

Ethan nodded. 'The latest Call of Duty.'

'Don't you get tired of all the killing?'

Ethan seemed to consider that for a moment. 'Not that I've noticed, no.'

'Well I'm tired of listening to it, so let's get some exercise.'

'You up for a run?'

'A run? In *this* heat? No. There *is* a gym in Reedy though. I thought we could go for a workout.'

'*Or* we could just workout in my room.'

'Oh *no*.'

'What?'

'And have the place smelling like a gym?'

'Wouldn't bother me after years of sharing quarters with other soldiers. Mind you, none were as good looking as you.'

'Stop.'

'I'm just saying.'

'I'm not interested.'

'I get it. We are just here to do a job...You're not my type anyway.'

'*Oh*? And what's your *type*?'

Maeve noticed Ethan's internal monologue suddenly stop. Maybe he was visualising.

'Let's check out *your* gym then Maeve.'

'It's not *my* gym.'

Ten minutes later they located the gym but it was closed.

With a tilt of his head Ethan said 'The bar over there looks open.'

'Oh I don't think so.' Maeve considered the state of it. '*The Seedy Reedy*?'

'Looks open to me *and* it looks like they may have a sense of humour.' He started crossing the road.

'I'm not drinking on duty.'

'Just the one.'

'I'll have a diet cola.'

'You *do* know that stuff'll kill you quicker than a beer, don't you?'

'You sure about that?'

As they entered the bar it fell silent, except to Maeve who heard all the comments from the five men. It was clear that they didn't get many female visitors dropping in.

'I'm going to head back.'

'Oh come on Maeve, loosen up.'

A couple of the men stifled a laugh. 'Yeah, come on darlin,' one piped up.

'I'll have a Fosters and diet cola for the missus.' Ethan thought it wise to make it clear Maeve was taken.

'Sorry mate. No Fosters,' the barman shook his head. 'The road-train didn't get through this week. We only have our local brew.'

'Fine. I'll have a pint of that then.'

'Oh and the road-train was meant to be bringing the spares for the chiller, so the cola will be as warm as the beer.'

'Oh what the hell,' Maeve sighed. 'Make it two beers then.'

All the men cheered.

There was nowhere private to sit and chat, so they both sat on stools by the bar which had an air-con fan above it.

'Where you folks from?' asked one of the men.

'England.'

'Thought so. I know a guy who came across from the UK some years back, a gold hunter by the name of Stan Gillespie. D'you know him?'

'No, sorry, can't say I do.'

'Oh…Really? I thought with so few of you left over there since the Reset and then the bombing…'

'The *bombing*? That was just London.'

'Well yeah, but with it being such a small island to start with, I'd have thought it wasn't like when they did Canberra here and no one noticed.'

The man's friends all laughed.

'Have you heard of any other Brits in the area?' Maeve asked.

'Not recently. Though there was that lad,' the man turned to the others, 'what was he called?'

'Norris I think.'

'No it was Neil.'

'Was it hell! It was Nevil.'

'Anyway,' the first man returned his attention to their visitors, 'the lad was just passing through. Said he wanted to see the place before it became totally uninhabitable. Can you believe that? Miserable sod. He headed north on his bike and we never saw him again…So what brings you folks here?'

'Well,' Ethan considered his response for a long moment, 'We thought we'd just come and see the place…you know…before it became totally uninhabitable.'

That evening, after they had eaten, colt called for the weigh-up and they all gathered round the digital balance. Stan was looking excited, waiting to see the look on the others faces when they saw what Nathan had dug up.

Monty went first, emptying his canister on the plate to nods of approval. Then it was Carl, who had done okay but not quite as well as Monty. Nevertheless the balance was showing a fair few grams; a good days work.

'Right Stan,' Colt prompted.

'No, you go first.'

'Why? Every little helps. If you and the lad didn't do so well today you know we take it as it goes.'

'Okay, Nathan. Show'em what you got.'

Nathan stepped forward and the others gasped, even before any gold hit the plate. His canister was clearly full.

As he tipped it out carefully some of the nuggets spilled over the edge and Stan scooped them back up and on. But Nathan wasn't finished there. He reached into his pocket and placed a few more nuggets onto the pile. Now they weren't talking grams anymore. Everyone suddenly shared in the excitement of talking ounces.

Then Nathan reached into another pocket and pulled out a nugget larger than his gloved thumb which he actually had found with the detector.

'Struth lad! You're a natural!' Carl cheered.

Not waiting for Colt to add *his* finds to the pile Nathan happily announced 'Now we can afford to head into town tomorrow.'

There was an odd gleam in Colt's eyes. 'Town? No we can't go *yet*.'

'But surely with the nuggets *you* have, plus the gold from yesterday, there'll be more than enough now.'

'What?...' Colt looked amused. 'How much do you think gold is worth?'

'Urr well I…'

'You did good lad but we still need more than this before we can afford to go back to town.'

'Do we?' Stan didn't sound so sure.

'Yeah. Absolutely. And with the lad's help over the next couple of days…'

'Couple of days?!' Nathan was not pleased. He was suddenly cross with himself for ever making contact with these people. If he had simply carried on in the direction of the nearest town, he could have covered maybe a hundred kilometres a night, and be almost there by now.

'Tell you what,' Colt suggested, 'We'll all come with you tomorrow to cover more of this *miracle* patch.'

Nathan managed to keep in the expletive which was bursting to come out. 'I'm going for a walk!'

Emily was growing frustrated by all the waiting too. She was patient but would still rather be getting on with the job at hand. Everything hinged on *Thirteen's* intel.

Her biggest concern was that Gavin would start asking difficult questions at some point, having the time to think too much.

'What do you think is going to happen once we find Nathan, Emily?'

'I don't know what you mean? We check he's okay and get on the first plane back home.'

'Sure but what are *Control* getting out of this, really?'

'They are providing both of you support because of the birth incident. You know this, Gavin.'

'Yes but for how much longer?'

'As long as it takes, I guess?'

'Until his next jump you mean, when he will surely die, unless *Control* work out a way to prevent his porting.'

'Hey, don't think like that.'

'How do I *not* think like *that*? He's my son. He's teleported to the other side of the world. There's nowhere *further* to go!'

'Okay, but...we are only here because *Thirteen* have come here looking for someone who may be Nathan. Maybe it isn't. *Control* are still checking for reports of him elsewhere, in case this is a false lead.'

'Right. So if they find a way for Nathan to control his jumps, will they just say problem solved, have a nice life? *Really*?'

'We'll have to wait and see, won't we?'

There was something about Emily's answer that niggled at Gavin.

Back in camp and rolled up once again in his borrowed blanket, Nathan watched the flicker of the fire. He had covered quite some distance again hunting nuggets before the ground temperature had evened out. He hoped this time it would be enough to satisfy Colt. However, he still had to figure out a way of concealing his heat vision trick. That much-needed inspiration was not forthcoming though.

If they found nothing he could say he must have found it all the day before, but that tack wouldn't get them to town.

Attempting to put it out of his mind for a while he tried searching once again for his father. He drew a blank. He wasn't staying at any of the towns he focused on. He did however, locate the two MI5 agents. They just seemed to be staying put, waiting. Clearly they still had no idea where he was. He tried talking to Maeve with his inner voice, as he had done aboard the Black Kite but she couldn't hear his thoughts. Maybe the distance was too great.

He decided to check out Charisma's house again. He found Charisma and her mother still alive, thankfully, but they were still unaware anything had happened to Bernie.

That *thing* Nathan had observed had gone now, unless it had *replaced* Charisma or her mother. Bernie's bed was empty, except, when Nathan looked more closely he spotted something in the depression on his pillow. It looked like a number of fillings.

12

Destiny was going about his constant string of tasks. As a Time-Slave he knew all that lay ahead of him but had no choice in the matter. Just like his partner Dawn they did what they did, keeping time on track, like mind-controlled passengers inside metamorphs. Whether what they did seemed heroic or pointless there was always a reason why these things were made to happen.

Destiny saw the portal open in the air before him as he stood under the What-If reality drive. He stepped through into a static caravan.

At the back of the caravan, on a double bed, bound down, was a girl. Destiny walked across and removed her gag, seeing what was coming and playing his part.

'You bastard!'

'I'm here to rescue you.'

'Like fuck you are, you fucking sicko!'

'No really…I'm not the person who abducted you.'

'No, you're working together. You're just trying to get into my panties, you filthy shit!'

Destiny ignored her rantings. She looked either traumatised or excited, he wasn't sure which. While he continued to undo her bindings she kept bad mouthing him, as he knew she would.

'My boyfriend is going to fucking do you over asshole!'

'I don't think so.'

'No?! That's 'cos you're sick in the fucking head.' She jabbed the index finger of her freed hand against her temple a few times for emphasis.

As Destiny freed her other hand she began slapping at him with as much force as she could muster. He stepped back, letting her remove the remainder of her bindings unassisted.

She hopped off the bed and grabbed up her shoes off the floor where Bernie had chucked them. Slipping her feet into them quickly she warned 'You better start running for it, you bastard, because we'll be coming for you. No going to the police, we'll get our own payback. You're *dead meat*!'

For good measure she thrust a knee between Destiny's legs but oddly it was like impacting a sack of rice. He just frowned.

Her heart racing, she rushed out of the door and found herself where she thought she wanted to be, at her boyfriend's parent's house, not her own.

'What the fuck?!' What was the static caravan doing in the garden of her boyfriend's parents? Were they involved? 'NO!!'

Confused she turned, unsure whether to run away. Not wanting to go home. However, behind her there was nothing but herbaceous border and a fence. No door. No static caravan. What was going on?

It had been an unnerving few days. Her parents hadn't wanted her staying out late with her new boyfriend but she had snuck out through her bedroom window, only something very strange happened as she ran across the back yard. Before she could dodge aside she had run through a door that had opened up in thin air.

She instantly found herself somewhere else entirely. She had gone from Birmingham Alabama in the United States in the nineteen seventies to Birmingham in the Midlands of the United Kingdom in the twenty thirties. It took a while to work this out but the lack of phone booths to ring her boyfriend from was her first clue. People here seemed to all be talking into rectangles. She almost got knocked over twice because the vehicles here were so quiet. Then out of desperation, having seen what the date was, sixty years in the future, she tried begging but no one had any cash on them. She watched people shop with cards.

Now thankfully she was back in Alabama. She ran to the back door of her boyfriend's house and tried to open the door. It was locked. She hammered on it, which was a little unusual.

A man came to the door. It looked to her like the father, but not quite. She wondered if it was an uncle, maybe. Nevertheless, the man seemed quite taken aback on seeing her.

'Sharon?...It *can't* be…and you're *still* a kid.'

'What the fuck are you talking about? I've never met you before.'

'It's me, Danny. You've been missing for thirty years!'

'What?'

'Yes the Steinstiens all moved back to Israel twenty odd years ago, your parents and your seven brothers.'

Nathan now had an idea of how to pull off this ruse a second time. He was back at the patch, surrounded this time by the whole team. Each man taking a separate plot around his own new plot, they were clearly all expecting to find easy pickings.

However, most of that gold was still in Nathan's pockets. He had been wishing there were some way to plant the nuggets ahead of them but they would notice his footprints, on ground he wasn't supposed to have been over yet.

The solution had finally occurred to him. Using his remote-viewing he took every opportunity, when no one was looking in his direction, to throw nuggets onto the other plots. He was blessed with strength and accuracy to get most of the nuggets out where he intended by the end of the morning, with no one any the wiser, even Stan.

Nathan was pleased with himself. Throwing nuggets felt like a game compared to the effort of having to dig loads of holes to *pretend* to have found another nugget.

Nevertheless, he still dug a number of holes both for pretend finds and for a couple of actual finds which were much more exciting.

Emily checked her mobile once again for any movement of *Thirteen's* Hertz rental. The vehicle was still parked at the motel. So they had to be there waiting also, unless they had suspected they were being tracked and abandoned the vehicle, taking another, or simply had removed the tracker.

Emily decided they had to go and check out what the situation was.

'Okay Gavin we are heading out.'

'Finally! If they are on the move that means they must know where Nathan is now, right?'

'No.'

'What?'

'They are not on the move. I just think we need to check out that they are *actually* there at the motel.'

'And we couldn't have done that *before* now?'

'I told you. This is a risk but maybe it is time we took it. Water is getting low anyway.'

'Hey, I'm not suggesting we stay a minute longer. Obviously we'll be careful not to get spotted, right?'

'We can try.'

There was no waiting for supper, or even the drive back to camp this time. When Colt called it a day he excitedly got the balance out of the 4x4 and they had their weigh-in.

However, though the day's total was greater than yesterday it wasn't four times greater. It wasn't quite twice as much.

'That's odd,' Colt was clearly disappointed. 'I expected much more with all four detectors to work this patch.'

'Well we all know some days don't turn out as good as others,' Stan suggested.

'True,' Carl agreed, 'but I tell you something else I thought odd, these nuggets needed hardly any digging down to, like they were lying on the surface.'

'Yeah I noticed that too,' Monty agreed.

'How about you, Nathan?' Colt asked starting to feel there was something suspicious going on again.

'Yeah some of them were close to the surface.'

'But Stan said you had been digging them up yesterday.'

'Some, yeah.'

'Right well our hunting has certainly taken a turn for the better since you came along. You're like our lucky charm.'

'Yeah,' the others agreed.

'Let's hope your luck holds out after you drop me off at town tomorrow then.'

'Hold on lad. You can't honestly think we'd let you go until this whole patch has been swept, or Stan's ankle has healed?'

'What?! You promised!'

'Be reasonable lad. We've never had it this good.'

'Let the lad be, Colt,' Stan defended. 'You know he needs to let his folks know where he is.' He hobbled to the side of the vehicle. 'Come on Nathan. Let's all go get some tucker.'

Stowing the detectors and day sacks they all climbed aboard the 4x4 and headed back to camp.

Colt said very little as he drove them back. He was clearly stewing over the thought of losing Nathan.

Ethan knocked on Maeve's door. She opened it quickly and turning her back on Ethan went back over to the window. 'Come in and close the door.'

'Do you fancy going back to the bar?'

'I think *they've* found us,' Maeve announced, peering back out from the side of the net curtains.

'Who? The guys from the *bar*?' There was a hint of ridicule in Ethan's response.

'No…I'm not sure…Maybe SOVs.'

'*Really*?'

'Yes. I picked them up, saying *That's it there*, then reading our number plate.'

'Maybe it was just a police check?'

'Why? We are staying at this motel. It is definitely someone interested in *that* vehicle and we know how good the SOVs are at getting hold of information.'

'If they are that good, wouldn't they have known we were here since we arrived? And why don't *they* know where the lad is by now?'

'I'm guessing they believe we will know before them, which means something has gone wrong.'

'Wouldn't that also mean they know something about Gina's informant?'

'Possibly.'

Nathan felt like he was being held captive. This brought him to the decision that after supper, when he said he was going for a walk he would *not* be coming back.

However, it became clear that Colt had other ideas. After supper, Colt went to the back of the 4x4 and from under the equipment pulled out an old double-barrelled shotgun under the pretext that it needed cleaning.

Deciding that it would be odd after two walks in a row not to go off again, Nathan declared 'Just off for another walk.'

'Not tonight lad. You're staying put til I know you are *with* us.'

'Steady on Colt,' Stan came to Nathan's defence, 'you can't *kidnap* the lad. He's got a family to get back to.'

'Who said anything about *kidnapping*? This is *borrowing*. There's no ransom being asked for here.'

'No, it's more like slavery,' Nathan argued.

'Slavery! Ha! You've been *enjoying* yourself.'

'I admit, it has been fun but that was because I thought we were just finding enough to get into town.'

'He's right Colt. You know he is.' Monty added his support.

'No!...Think about it, we could get so rich with the lad on the team that we might not need to come out here again next year, or *ever*, maybe.'

'You're getting greedy!' Nathan felt himself getting crosser.

'You don't know what it's like being out here all the time, no bars no women. You've only been here a couple of days, so far.'

'Well I'm not staying any longer. I'm off.'

'I don't think you want to do that,' Colt could be seen taking the safety off the shotgun, 'because you won't get very far.'

'What the hell do you think you're doing Colt?!' Stan was up and hobbling towards him intent on taking the shotgun off him before he did something stupid.

Colt turned the shotgun on Stan. Stan's ankle gave way and with that sudden movement and cry of pain the shotgun went off in Colt's hands.

'NO!!' Nathan was shocked that Colt had actually gone and pulled the trigger. He had thought it was all show.

Monty ran at Colt, to take the gun off him before anyone else was hurt, but that was a mistake.

Turning like a madman Colt emptied the second barrel into Monty's chest, hurling him off his feet, dead before he hit the ground.

Carl was surprised by this sudden turn of events but confident that Colt wouldn't shoot him. It occurred to Carl as he saw Colt reach into his pocket for two more cartridges this meant a bigger share of the gold now.

Cracking open the shotgun, Colt was aware that Nathan was coming towards him, almost a blur. He lifted the barrels in an attempt to strike the lad down but it was like trying to swipe at a train. The shotgun was knocked from his grip and then he was hit hard under the nose. Game over. Colt collapsed dead.

Nathan's right hand was all healed now. There had been no discomfort as he delivered the palm-heel strike. He then turned his attention to Carl. He had drawn a knife, though he looked uncertain how to proceed. 'Well lad, seems like it's just you and me now.'

'I don't think so.'

Carl thought about having all the gold to himself and the rest of the miracle patch still to detect. However, it was sure to be complicated with having to keep an eye on Nathan the whole time. 'No, maybe you're right lad.'

Carl lunged at Nathan, the blade coming up in a powerful motion towards the lad's chest, but he was again surprised at how fast Nathan could move.

Nathan side-stepped, drew Carl forwards, off balance and round. Almost second nature to Nathan somehow. He removed the knife by applying pressure at the base of thumb and index finger. Then almost without thought releasing his grip on Carl he drew the primary edge of the blade across the man's throat.

Spluttering blood as he collapsed beside Colt, Carl's last sight was of Nathan calmly wiping the knife handle clean of prints on Colt's N-Viro suit.

It had all happened so fast that even Nathan didn't know that he had been capable of such cold-blooded killing. He had thought a number of times that in a difficult situation he could probably kill, but this had come surprisingly easy.

He wondered for a moment if there had been a solution which would not have involved the killing, but he told himself there were more important concerns. He checked all the bodies for signs of life. All were dead, except Stan. Stan's breathing was shallow, he had been hit in the left arm and side with the shot, but he was still in the land of the living.

Lifting him up Nathan placed him on the back seat of the 4x4. Stan urgently needed a hospital. Luckily there was one in the nearest town, unfortunately it was a long way away and

Nathan was not confident he could get him there in time.

Nathan decided to leave the quad and detached the trailer to reduce the drain on fuel. He took the keys from Colt's body and got into the driving seat, adjusting its position.

Engine started, doors all closed, lights on, Nathan hoped he'd paid enough attention to how people drove.

13

In the early hours Maeve and Ethan left the motel. Ethan had disabled the tracker while Maeve had pawed over the map. She had determined a route off highway 95 which might lose their tail.

As they turned east onto Reedy Road and started with its heavy corrugations, Ethan suggested that he drive. However, Maeve was keen to just keep going.

Ethan kept checking the road behind them. On the highway he had seen no tailing lights, but then whoever it was could be driving using night-vision. He wished *Thirteen* had provided Maeve with night-vision goggles. Now on the dirt road all they could see behind in the red glow of their tail-lights was the cloud of dust Maeve was kicking up behind.

As the faint glimmer of sun began to tint the sky ahead of them, Nathan warned 'You might want to slow a tad more. Maeve. Early morning and evening a lot of animals, like kangaroos, turn suicidal here and…'

Turning to Ethan, Maeve declared 'I *am* keeping a lookout…'

'Lookout!'

A herd of cattle appeared as if out of nowhere. It wasn't quite a stampede but they were moving too fast to avoid. Maeve slammed on the brakes and swerved but hit a cow then a bull hit Maeve's door smashing her window.

As the Toyota came off the road onto the sand verge it tilted and then as two cows and the bull shoved against it in their rush to get past, it went over on its side.

'Great,' Ethan praised Maeve's driving as she came to rest on top of him.

'What the hell was that? It came out of nowhere.'

'Either it was cattle or we've just had our first shared hallucination.' Ethan shook glass off his left sleeve. 'Nope. Feels pretty real.'

Ethan tried to reach for the sunroof button. Watching him struggle for a moment, Maeve tried to get off him. She reached the ignition and turned it off first then pressed the button opening the sunroof. She used the opening to climb out, treading on Ethan's hip then slipping and putting a foot in Ethan's crotch.

'Sorry.'

'Urgh…Not as sorry as me.'

Ethan clambered out with a groan then surveyed the damage in the brightening light.

'It all happened so fast, Ethan.'

'I'd did try to warn you.'

'Yes but…'

'I think we can get the car back the right way up, as long as it doesn't go on its roof. Oh and it looks like this tyre is flat,' Ethan pointed at the driver-side front wheel as he came round the underside, 'probably punctured by a horn.'

Minutes later, without rope or a lever, careful rocking had the car on its roof.

Nathan's driving wasn't proving any less stressful. The corrugations were dreadful. He thought the vibrations might actually shake the old 4x4 apart.

As the sun began to rise Nathan heard Stan coming round, groaning. They were still a long way off what should be smoother going on the highway.

Stan was clearly suffering a lot of pain. 'Stop…Stop!'

Nathan pulled over, got out and went round to the rear passenger-side door.

'Nathan lad, you've got to tell Colt to stop. I can't go any further.'

Nathan hadn't considered having to explain to Stan what had happened, even though that whole minute and a half was on constant replay in his mind.

'You need to drink something.' Nathan got him some water. He knew a person should not eat before an operation but he was pretty sure he needed to keep him hydrated.

After Nathan got half a cup into him he thought it would be a good time to put one of the spare jerry-cans of fuel into the tank. He went round to the back and dragged one out.

After the top up was done, he returned to Stan to try getting him to drink a little more.

By this time Stan had realised the others were not with them. 'What's happening lad?'

'You've been shot. You need a hospital.'

'I know that…But who's driving?'

'Me.'

'Where are the others?'

'They have stayed behind.'

'Colt let *you* drive me to hospital?'

'Well I didn't exactly give him much choice.'

'Ha! You pinched the car. I didn't think you had it in you lad.'

'Me neither.'

'When did you learn to drive?'

'Oh…a couple of hours ago.'

Emily pulled off the road suddenly and looked more closely at the satellite image she was using to keep track of the agents from *Thirteen*.

'What is it?' Gavin craned for a look.

'Shit…I think they've gone and crashed.'

'What?'

'See. Cattle herd.'

Together they watched as the sun rose and two figures climbed out of the vehicle.

'Well at least they're alive,' Gavin saw the lives of the agents and that of his son as being interconnected.

'Yes…What are they doing? Oh that's good, *that's* good, go on, yes, yes…*Fuck*!'

'What does that mean?'

'*Seriously*?...They are not going to get that back on the road now. Not without a tow-truck equipped with a crane.'

'So what now?'

'There's only one thing for it I guess.'

'Which is?'

'We're now on our honeymoon and on an outback adventure.'

'What?'

'Are you any good at acting, Gavin?'

'Not really, no.'

'Best let me do most of the talking then. I'll be motor-mouth Emily.'

'*Okay*?'

Emily got them out of the spinifex and back onto the corrugations. 'I'm glad we got more supplies at Reedy. We might be sharing more than car space...Should have got a rental with a roof rack.'

An hour later with the sun up over the horizon, making sunglasses a necessity for driving, Emily slowed as she came to the overturned Toyota.

'My goodness,' she called through Gavin's open window, 'Are you okay? Do you need help?'

She stopped the car and both she and Gavin got out.

'Are we glad to see you!' Ethan sounded desperate.

'Oh and you're British too. What a small world, eh?' It was clear to Emily that these two were also acting.

'We didn't think we'd see *anyone* down here, did we dear?'

'You're a godsend, to be sure.' Maeve's accent sounded thicker than usual.

'We didn't expect to see anyone either. Certainly not with an upside down SUV, eh? We're on our honeymoon you see, wanted to head into the Red Centre. I always wanted to come out here. I used to watch everything Australian. You know, Neighbours, Home and Away, Crocodile Dundee, and Wolf Creek. It's a beautiful country and everyone's so friendly.'

'Have you got rescue coming?' Gavin enquired.

'No. We've got absolutely no signal.'

Gavin smiled. 'We've...'

'...Got no signal either,' Emily quickly finished for Gavin, pretending she had an ordinary mobile in her hand. 'We have room in our car to get you out of here though. However, I don't know how much of your luggage we'll be able to bring, sorry.'

'That's very kind of you, taking time out of your honeymoon to rescue us.' Ethan sounded sincerely grateful, almost emotional with relief.

'Well can't just leave you here can we?...Ha! The guilt would put a right old dampener on the honeymoon, oh and then having to lie to friends and family when we got back home about what a wonderful time we had. Never daring to mention that we'd abandoned two fellow Brits in the desert to a fate of heat exposure and starvation.'

Maeve's expression turned to one of disbelief but not at what Emily was saying. Maeve realised that Ethan was actually eyeing Emily up.

'So how did the accident happen?' Emily asked with a smile for Ethan.

'Don't know.' Ethan turned to look at Maeve. 'I woke up to find she'd turned the car right over.'

'You make it sound like it was all *my* fault, so you do.'

'Well I *was* the passenger.'

'I'm amazed that you can sleep with all that vibration. I was just trying to find out if a faster speed made things any easier driving over the corrugations, when I lost control.'

'Yes, aren't they a pain.' Emily chipped in, turning to look back at Ethan. 'They keep making me need the loo. I'm glad I don't have to drive on this stuff for a living, not like those Outback Truckers. Have you seen the length of some of those road-trains? It's no wonder the rule of the road is pull off to the side if you see one coming. And the dust they kick up. You better have your windows closed, eh? Don't you find that dust gets simply everywhere? The other day I actually found some in my pot of multi-vitamins. I mean…'

'Okay!' Maeve suddenly didn't sound so Irish. 'Let's *all* cut the crap!'

Ethan turned to her with a look of surprise.

'Acting is getting us nowhere…He's the father. The lad is called Nathan, and she, I believe to be an SOV.'

Ethan threw Emily a glance of daggers.

'*What*?' Emily sounded flabbergasted at the absurdity.

Gavin turned to Emily to ask what she *should* have, 'What's an SOV?'

The groaning from the back seat started up again. Stan was coming round once more.

'Stop. Please stop!'

'We're nearly there, Stan.'

'You said *that* the last couple of times lad. I need to rest.'

'I need to get you to the hospital, at Bonney Downs. You can rest there.'

'I'm not going to make it *there*, Nathan. Let me die here in peace. Just pull off the road. Please…'

Nathan pulled over and switched the engine off. He helped Stan drink some more water. Checking him over, he noted that the bleeding had stopped. That was surely a good sign, he hoped.

'You're not like other boys are you, Nathan?'

'What do you mean?'

'There's something about you.'

'Like what?'

'You're smarter...*tougher*.'

'Maybe you've only met stupid weak lads.'

'No. I think your one of those water-babies.'

'A *water-baby*?'

'Uh huh...A H2O...That injury you arrived at camp with, I notice it has left no scar.'

'So?'

'I don't heal like that.'

Nathan held the water to Stan's lips again. 'Well maybe that's just because *you're* stupid and weak.'

'*What*?' Stan spluttered on the water. 'Are you trying to choke me to death?'

Emily now back behind the wheel with Maeve next to her and the two men in the back seat, they headed back to Reedy.

Maeve started with the questions. 'So since you have not found Nathan, I assume that he has not been in a position to contact Gavin yet.'

'Correct. However, we have been satellite scanning Australia for him.'

'So have we. All we have seen so far are ranchers and gold prospectors. But how did you know to come here?'

'We picked up one of *Thirteen's* communications then followed *you*.'

'So you *hacked* into the MI5 servers?'

158

'Hardly. We *are* on the same side these days.'

'*What*?'

'Who do you think funds us?'

'Not MI5 that's for sure.' Maeve blustered though did start to wonder.

'No. Think bigger. Who funds the security services?'

'Governments.'

'Banks.'

'Pfff.' Maeve shook her head in denial. 'As I understand it *Five* are tasked with investigating any SOV related leads, to find out what you are up to.'

'Well that sounds like the dog chasing its tail doesn't it. I'm pretty sure that the ones at the top are not giving any of us the whole picture, even though they *preach* open transparency these days. There are still many separate agendas in play.'

'Right, and I guess your agenda is to give nothing away,' Ethan put in.

'Certainly there *are* things I know that I have not been told *Five* have high enough clearance for. I know your *Section Thirteen* is considered special and separate to the main arm for *Five*. However, *we* are like the New World Order's *black-ops* section now. It's not for everyone to know about. However, *you* clearly know things we are not party to about Nathan, because of your *informer* and that's why we followed you to W.A. So why don't you tell us about your informer?'

'We can't,' said Maeve a little too quickly.

'Or won't?'

Gavin couldn't hold his tongue any longer. 'The IVF centre is not a clinic after all, *is it* Emily?! Nathan is just some kind of military *experiment* to you people?!'

'I guess so Gavin...Human 3.0. Except they've created something with Nathan that they don't understand at all. How does somebody teleport? I mean that's fantasy, surely. Where does the energy required for an ability like that come from? And why *can't* he control it by now?'

'Because it only happens when he's asleep!'

'Night Porter...Oh I get it now.' Maeve thought back to what she had got out of Nathan in Norway.

'But Gavin,' Emily pushed further. 'In all the time you have looked after your son you would have expected him to have developed some idea as to how he was doing it. Plus what else he might be able to do, beyond remote-viewing?'

'Hang on.' Ethan piped up. 'So what you're saying is the tip-off we got, to come look for the lad here was to find someone who can remote-view *and* teleport but can't get home?'

'Yes. That sums it up.' Emily nodded. 'What *I* don't get is why your *informer* couldn't have saved us *all* a lot of time, and saved Nathan from whatever trouble he is in. They just needed to be more specific as to where he is presently...And...*And* how do they know anyway? Does *Thirteen* have a *Precog* working for them?'

'Possibly,' Maeve agreed. She didn't see any reason not to be open with Gavin and Emily now. They clearly seemed to be no threat to

Nathan listening to their ongoing inner voices. 'As I understand it, our informer, whoever they are, calls the problem *meta-interference*.'

'And what's *that*?' Gavin didn't particularly like any of what he was hearing.

'Basically, *time* interfering with *your* attempts to interfere with what *is* going to happen.'

'So fate then.'

'Well a more *physical* experience of fate I suppose, yes.'

'So what is Nathan's *fate*?'

Emily was aware that all eyes were now on her, as the alleged SOV. 'Well, considering what we've just heard, I'm guessing that while certain people have plans for the lad, I rather believe that *time* will tell.'

14

Just before re-joining the Great Northern Highway a call came through on Emily's mobile with a *ding*. All eyes turned to the screen on its dash-mounting, the sat-nav now obscured by the incoming call screen which simply said *Control*.

Rather than take the call on speaker phone, Emily pulled over immediately, took the mobile out of its mount and went outside.

Ethan turned to Gavin but Maeve focused on Emily's internal monologue.

'Who's *Control*, Gavin?'

'They are the IVF clinic. Or what I *thought* was a clinic. Ever since the incident which killed my wife, Kelly, these people seemed to have done everything to look after Nathan and to some extent me. But now I'm thinking it has all been about protecting their…their *creation*.'

'Are we talking genetic engineering?'

'I guess so.'

'So they somehow found a way of creating people who could teleport?'

'It seems that way but to be honest they seem as confused as me as to what is happening.'

'So how did your wife die?'

'I've never told Nathan this, in case he thinks it's his fault, but he was born premature, teleporting out of his mother.'

'Even as a baby?'

Gavin nodded, his eyes tearing up.

'But *surely* that would have made birthing easier.'

'Except that when Nathan teleports he takes with him everything within a spherical volume of his body. He removes it all in the blink of an eye. He's got through loads of beds. If he is stretched out then the sphere is bigger than if he is curled up. The sphere has increased as he has grown taller. Nowadays he could leave a hole in the floor and any wall close by. Luckily the rooms in our house are high-ceilinged because he sleeps in the middle of his room on top of a bunk bed.'

Thinking back to what must have happened to Kelly, Ethan queried, 'So, what you are saying is that Nathan disembowelled his mother?'

'Yes.'

'*Shit.*'

'Even now that image stays with me. And now I know *these* people did this.' Gavin pointed accusingly out of the car at Emily.

'What do you know about Emily?' Maeve asked without turning to look past the seat.

'She has been teaching Nathan survival and self-defence. She heads up the retrieval team.'

'Does he *never* teleport back home?'

'No. It only happens when he's asleep. Usually shortly after dropping off…and each time he goes significantly further than before.'

'Is it to places he knows?' asked Ethan.

'I think so. However, he does not need to have been there.'

'What do you mean? He just needs to see the place on TV?'

'No, although that *could* be part of it I suppose. Nathan's remote-viewing enables him to see what is happening in places that he has never been to. He can even look inside things to see what's hidden in there, that sort of thing.'

'That explains a few things.' Maeve nodded.

'So my worry is, if he is still alive, where will he go next, and when? He has been taking an interest in that SpaceX Moon Base.'

'Oh…That's not good.' Ethan agreed.

'Emily's coming back in.' Maeve announced.

They turned to watch but she hadn't moved. Then Emily concluded the call with *Control*, disconnected and turned towards the car, noticing their eyes were on her.

Opening the door Emily explained, 'Good news. The latest satellite feed has been analysed for aircraft seat wreckage and some remains have been found next to an old gold mine.'

'*Where*?' Gavin craned forward as Emily replaced the mobile in the mount and pulled up a map from the link she had been sent by *Control*.

'North-east of our position. So…I think we need to head up the highway to Newman, right away…I've organised for a team to fly down to the mine from Port Hedland to check it out.'

'When will we hear?' Gavin's mind was racing. Would his son be there? Would he be hurt or worse? Or would they find that he has left?

'It will take a few hours, but hopefully we'll hear something before we reach Newman.'

'And how far away is *that*?'

'Just under 500km.'

'How long will that take?' the exasperation with the sheer size of Australia clear in Gavin's voice.

'If I get my foot down, maybe five hours.'

'*Five*?!'

Nathan pulled over yet again, not because Stan had requested a stop but because Stan's breathing could be seen to be getting shallower. It had proved very useful being able to remote-view while looking in a different direction.

This time when Ethan attempted to rouse Stan for another drink however, he wouldn't come round. He had fallen unconscious. At least the fact that he was breathing meant his heart would still be beating. The heat coming off him looked a little higher than normal. Maybe it was infection rather than hyperthermia, Nathan considered what he'd been taught, but either way it was not a good sign.

Nathan couldn't give Stan any more water by mouth when he was unconscious, in case he choked, and there were no sterile saline kits to attempt rehydration by drip.

Nathan closed the door and opened up the back of the 4x4. The only thing he could do now was drive even faster than he had been. However, going faster burned more fuel. He used the last spare jerry can to top up the tank.

As he returned the empty can he spotted a long tube and a funnel. He considered getting this into Stan's stomach to get water into him. He lifted one end of the tube to his nose. It smelled oily, like most things in the back. Regardless of that fact he decided that the tube was too thick. Stan would just as likely choke on the tube.

Memory of a Bear Grylls solution to the problem hadn't quite connected at that point. So, closing the tail gate, Nathan went back to the driving seat and set off, picking up speed as he hit the corrugations.

His remote-viewing allowed him to check well ahead for animals likely to come across the road. When he had been driving in the dark without lights animals didn't get hypnotised by headlights, nevertheless, a few had stopped in the road to listen so then Nathan had used the horn.

However, he had found that some cattle couldn't care less about a blaring horn, day or night. At one point had had to swerve and go off road, hurling Stan's limp form up in the air. At least he hadn't ended up in the foot-well.

He was desperate for Stan to survive this. Stan had been kind to Nathan. He felt he owed the old man but at the same time he tried to tell himself not to feel guilty if Stan didn't make it. Emily had often said 'Remember, we can only do our best.'

Nathan searched once again for his dad and Emily, as he sped north. He hoped his dad was okay. He decided that he would be, with Emily. He considered Emily a tough woman, not quite *mum* material maybe, but certainly *bad-ass auntie*.

Ethan leaned against his seatbelt to put his head between the front seats. He didn't like the way that Emily was not opening up much about the SOVs, having *claimed* that they were now on the same side.

'So what can you tell us about the SOVs that *isn't* above our clearance?'

'Well let's see…They have been consistently underestimated…When the Chilterns base was destroyed by terrorists, people had not realised that by then we were already an international organisation.'

'I know the history. My biological mother was the founder.'

'Oh, so you're *that* Ethan…Ethan Best.'

'The one and only.'

'I'm sorry you're mother died in the blast, I hear she was a good woman.'

'I beg to differ, and as a point of fact she died *before* the blast.'

'What do you mean?'

'I don't like vigilantes, thinking that they are beyond the law; using vigilantism as an excuse for their psychopathic tendencies. I killed her, and fed her to her pigs.'

'You did *what*?'

Maeve and Gavin were also shocked by this revelation.

'The base was getting rid of its tortured victims by means of the pigs. I treated mother to the same.'

'But you must only have been a kid back then.'

'I was.'

'Sounds like *you* are a bit of a psycho too then.'

167

'Yes. Only difference is, nowadays, I only do what the British army orders me too.'

'Army? I thought you were MI5.'

'I'm on secondment...We're straying off the subject. Tell us about some of the SOV projects.'

'Well there was Project C-Spray...'

'I know all about the removal of criminals in the lead up to the Great Reset *and* its premature end. Tell us about some of the *present day* projects.'

A message came through on the mobile, curtailing the interrogation. Emily pulled off the road and took the call outside once more.

'You seem to be giving her a hard time, Ethan.'

'Do you have a problem with that Maeve?'

'It's *my* job to ask about the SOVs.'

'Yeah well...There's something about that woman that gets under my skin.'

'Does she remind you of your mother?' asked Gavin.

'*Fuck off*!'

'I don't think that's Ethan's issue, Gavin.' Maeve didn't want any of them getting on bad terms when they still had to find Nathan. 'I have to say, it *has* been interesting listening between the lines though, with Emily, if you get my drift.'

Gavin didn't, but he was used to not fully understanding things now.

Shortly Emily returned to the car. Opening the door she didn't get in before Ethan had another go.

'What's with taking the call outside, where Gavin can't hear?'

Gavin hadn't considered that, but rather thought it had been to keep Ethan and Maeve out of the picture.

'I prefer it that way. This is *my* retrieval mission.'

'So what's the news?!' Gavin urged impatiently.

'Nathan's suspected RP was checked out. It was definitely him.'

'Is he okay?!'

'He wasn't there. There were boot tracks leading away. These were traced quite some distance to a camp. There appears to have been some sort of altercation there though, because…'

'Oh God, no…!'

'They found three men there, all dead.'

The sun was setting as Nathan entered Bonney Downs at speed. He didn't care that he soon picked up a police tail. He slowed but not to within legal limits, only down to what *he* considered safer limits.

The local police kept close behind, all the way to their small hospital, lights and siren blaring.

Nathan bumped over the sleeping policemen and skidded to a halt outside the A&E. Before the police had a chance to catch him Nathan bailed out of the driving seat. Leaving the door open he shoved aside A&E's automatic door which was too slow for him, shattering it.

'Help! I need help! I have a man with a gunshot in critical condition!'

The medical personnel were quick to respond having no other emergency. They followed Nathan outside where two advancing police officers attempted to restrain him in vain.

'He's in here! Quick!' Nathan opened the tail gate.

He had finally remembered some Bear Grylls, a solution for rehydration. He had lowered the smaller section of back seat so that Stan could be laid out more comfortably.

As nurses and police looked inside they were first greeted with Stan's rather grey face and bluish tinted lips. Nathan quickly pulled a jerry can and holdall off Stan, revealing more of the scene.

Everyone gasped, except for the senior police officer. 'What the *fuck* lad?'

Stan had his trousers and pants down round his ankles, with a long tube sticking out of his rectum. It led up to an empty 1.5L water bottle, screwed into the tube and secured to the rear of the front passenger headrest by means of some wire.

The senior policeman's hand gripped Nathan's right shoulder. 'Looks cactus to me.'

'What?'

'Dead.'

15

Ethan now at the wheel, Emily sat in the back with Gavin airing his worries.

'I think somebody must have kidnapped Nathan if he wasn't at the camp. They must have found out about his abilities and thought they could get a stack of credit for him then got into a fight over him.'

'Stop catastrophizing will you!'

'Why else would people get killed when he turned up?'

'We don't know yet.'

'Oh you're not thinking…Nathan wouldn't have killed them just to steal their car.'

'I'm certainly not thinking that, no.'

'He can't drive anyway…Can he?'

'That hasn't been in his training yet, no. Listen, Nathan wouldn't need to kill to steal anything. His first concern, as always, will be to call *Control*. They can't have had a working radio or he would have been in touch. We just need to hang on 'til we hear more from the search team.' Emily gestured with the mobile in her hand. 'They are following the tracks of the vehicle which left the camp. Until then it doesn't help to guess. Especially the way *you* do it.'

It was dark outside now, as Nathan sat in an interview room facing the same senior officer who had brought him to the police station.

'The sooner we get this done the sooner we can get on lad.'

'But I *want* my phone call.'

'I told you that you can call your parents after we complete this statement.'

'But I haven't done anything *wrong*!'

'What, apart from joy-riding through town, malicious damage to hospital property, and not to mention killing a man by shoving a tube of something up his arse!'

'It was water and I was trying to get him to hospital. Why would I do that if I *had* killed him? Anyway, he's *not* dead.'

'I think that's for the coroner to decide.'

Nathan shook his head in frustration.

'Name?' The policeman asked for the third time, still with no luck.

'If you'd just let me make my call, things would get sorted real quick and then you probably wouldn't have to do *this* paperwork.'

'Oh...So you're *Privileged* are you?'

'Yes.'

'Oh that changes everything *Brit Boy*.'

'It does?'

'Yeah, sure. I was going to give you a rough time because I thought you were just some outback beatnik, but now I know you're one of the *Privileged* I'll happily make this even *harder* for you.'

'*Thanks*.'

The policeman noticed Nathan's expression begin to change to smile. 'You think I'm joking do you? You people make me sick.'

'It's not that...'

They both heard the sound of an approaching helicopter.

Emily received another call but this time, seeing as she was not driving, she didn't ask Ethan to stop.

'Emily…Go ahead…That's good…Well how far is that from Newman?...Right. Okay, get straight down there when you're done. We'll be there as soon as we can…Yes. Heading there right now…Oh, and the kit?...What's the delay?...*Great*…No, no…Yes.'

Gavin picked up on the disappointed tone at the end there but other than that Emily's call had sounded promising. 'Well?...'

'We have him!'

Nathan was glad to be out of the police station, thanks to the team from the helicopter. He had been returned to the hospital to see Stan, who didn't look at all well but no longer had that look of knocking on death's door. Connected to a drip and monitors Stan looked like he would be laid up for a while.

'I'm so glad to see you pulled through, Stan.'

'All thanks to you, lad. You're some kind of amazing, you know,' he croaked through split lips, 'driving all that way *and* looking after me.'

'What are mates for? I did what I could. *Now*, I haven't told the cops it's Colt's car, or what happened back there. Someone else is dealing with all that for me, it turns out.'

'Your folks?'

'No, someone *else*. Look, you rest up good. I have to go shortly. Just remember this, I've put the gold under the driver's seat. The car is in the police pound and they have been told not to interfere with the vehicle.'

'*Told*?'

'Yeah. It should all be there when you get out. Just promise me one thing.'

'Anything.'

'Get that gold sold but don't go looking to share it with the others. They're surrounded by all the gold they'll ever need. Go do something that involves putting your feet up.'

Stan thought about what Nathan was saying *without* saying it. If he mustn't to go back to camp it would hardly be to ensure that the others die out there. That didn't sound like the Nathan he had come to know. So something must have happened after he was shot. They must all be dead. He decided he didn't want to know details. 'You know, doing something new sounds like sage advice lad.'

'Nathan, we need to go.'

Nathan and Stan looked at the man striding into the ward.

'Okay. I'll be right there.'

'Have a good life lad. I've got a *feeling* about you.'

'I hope you're right.' As Nathan reached the door he looked back and waved then turned to quiz his escort. 'Are you taking me to see my dad now?'

'Yes.'

'So you know where he is?'

'Yes. Heading up to Newman.'

'Great.' A map would have made the search a bit easier, but by the time Nathan boarded the helicopter he had found Gavin.

His father looked like he had been in a fight. He had others with him. While he was not surprised to see Emily there, he *was* surprised to discover the two MI5 agents had joined them.

He had been told this would not be a long flight, nevertheless, buckling into his seat at the back, Nathan vowed not to fall asleep this time. So to keep his mind occupied he viewed the pilot at the controls. He wondered how much more difficult than a car it would be to learn to fly a helicopter.

Not all children passing through a magic door were destined to go home.

As this scruffy looking prepubescent Asian girl stepped out onto a deserted street one night, she did so with purpose.

She was on the streets for a few days, begging for food. She resorted to searching through bins when she didn't get any, before someone from a charity came to her rescue.

She was first taken to a hostel, cleaned up and fed. Then she was asked her name and questioned about her circumstances.

Yoake didn't like being touched but was clearly grateful for the help she was receiving. Now that she was cleaned up it was noticed that there was a much more pleasant smell about her.

Yoake was informed of a schooling program she could enrol in. Within the week Yoake was moved from the hostel to a state-run boarding school. It was explained that the school offered lots of opportunities to girls and boys to prepare for their future. Sometimes this involved going away for extra educational experiences.

On this evening Yoake was invited to come and meet some very important people. Following the head teacher and school nurse she was led into a tunnel. The tunnel went under the school some distance before coming to a corridor with rooms off it. She was shown into one of the rooms. It was a lounge but no one else was in there.

The head teacher asked Yoake if she would like anything to drink. Yoake nodded, anything would be fine.

The head teacher said they would be back shortly then she and the nurse left.

The nurse returned with a cup of what looked like blackcurrant juice. Yoake drank it down.

A little later the head teacher returned with the nurse. 'The visitors are all here now, Yoake. This is a major opportunity for you. How do you feel?'

'Very...*relaxed.*'

'*Good.*'

'We have a change of clothes for you.'

Yoake questioned nothing as the nurse helped her out of her uniform and into a gown with an upside-down pentagram on it.

She obediently followed them down the corridor and into a room at the end. It was not very large but looked like some sort of council chamber. There were a great many people there though, all dressed in dark gowns with hoods up, seated but silent. She recognised a couple of faces, people from the charity, but Yoake said nothing.

She was led to a table and told to get onto it and lie down, which she did. The nurse adjusted Yoake's prone form then took a seat.

Next, a tall figure, a man who Yoake had not seen before began to speak, but not in any explanation of this event. Instead he seemed to be commanding the congregation. They all joined him in his Latin chanting. It sounded like a prayer or a *calling* upon their God.

Yoake lay there as the tall man stepped up behind her, lifting a large dagger above his head. Yoake smiled oddly before the prayer reached its peak and the blade came down.

As the blade penetrated what appeared to be Yoake's robe and flesh, she exploded.

The congregation gasped as one. This had never happened before. There on the altar was the child's robe, looking like it had somehow been inside her. Now it glistened with gore. What's more, the congregation had each been struck in the face with a piece of their sacrifice to Satan.

As each person lifted a hand to wipe away the chunk of Yaoke it smeared then spread. It was still alive.

The sweet smelling air of the chamber filled with the sound of screams becoming muffled.

At that same moment, Nathan was sitting patiently in the closest thing Newman's airstrip had to a waiting lounge. The helicopter had been refuelled and its crew now sat with

Nathan and his retrieval team in the air-con cooled room.

It had been explained to him that when Emily and his father arrived they would all be flying up to Port Hedland to get on a boat. It was not thought safe to attempt any long haul flights.

He had made no mention of the two agents traveling with Emily and his dad. He would wait to see what happened when they arrived. They would probably be left with the car to return to Perth.

From where he sat, checking on his dad's progress, he also checked out his immediate surroundings.

Next to the lounge was a general office. There were a couple of employees in there busy at their terminals managing what looked like cargo shipments due in and out. One of the shipments Nathan saw was food and drink destined for a gold, silver and copper mine at Telfer, owned by a Chinese company.

Behind the office was a maintenance hangar with what looked like a very messy workshop in one corner. Everything from unwashed mugs to duct tape and superglue were strewn across the benches. The floor was little better with tools dotted around. It looked like every job had only been half finished.

Beyond the airstrip and down the road a way was the town. Like many towns it now had a number of disused buildings. However, the population remained large enough to allow Newman to function as a town should.

Nathan watched as finally Ethan drove his dad and the other two into town, Emily directing him to the airfield.

Still Nathan said nothing, but as the Toyota headlights drew into the entrance to the airfield people stirred in the lounge. Nathan took that as his cue and went outside.

Ethan pulled into one of the floodlit parking bays at the side of the maintenance hangar and even before he had switched off Nathan was coming round the side of the building.

Gavin threw open the car door and leaped out, grabbing Nathan in a tight hug before swinging him round, sobbing.

There were smiles all round as the other three got out of the car. Then they all headed back to the cool of the lounge to sort out the details of what would happen next.

Emily turned to Ethan as they headed inside. 'I guess we will be saying goodbye.'

'What do you mean?'

'Well I expect you'll be needed back home asap.'

'I thought we would *all* be going back to the UK with Nathan.'

Emily shook her head. 'Nathan is coming on a cruise.'

'A *cruise*?' Maeve questioned.

'Sure. Nathan is a safety risk on a plane, obviously.'

'Of course.'

'So we are heading up to Port Hedland now by chopper.' Emily turned to the pilot, 'Have you agreed the flight plan with air traffic control already?'

'Yes.'

Gavin butted in, 'Ethan, if Nathan and I are flying out can I have the keys to the car? I left my mobile in there.'

'Sure,' Ethan handed Gavin the keys then returned his attention to Emily. 'You still haven't told us anything useful about present SOV projects.'

Maeve cut in, '*Thirteen* will need to confirm what you claim about working on the same side. Who in *Five* would confirm that?'

'I don't know who in *Five* would be authorised to do that, more likely someone in Joint Security Services. I can probably get you a name.'

'That would help.'

Emily turned to Ethan. 'So are we friends now?'

'Don't push it.'

'Ah you'll miss me really.' Emily turned to Maeve. 'If I get you the JSS name, will you tell me who your informer is?'

'I doubt it. I don't think Gina Oakley is likely to tell anyone.'

'Well, even though my lot found the lad, *Thirteen* did have a hand in that.'

Ethan couldn't to listen to Emily any more. He left Maeve with her and went outside. He returned a few minutes later to find Maeve was still talking shop with Emily. This irritated him. They'd had all that time in the car to do that.

'Maeve. You got a minute?'

'I'll leave you to find a motel and prepare your return to Perth,' Emily jumped on the chance to curtail Maeve's continued probing, then turned to her team who were waiting on her giving the green light. 'Okay, let's get going. Where are Nathan and Gavin?'

Out of earshot, leading Maeve quickly round to the car, Ethan said 'They're gone.'

'What's gone?'

'Nathan and Gavin.'

'What do you mean they're gone? They're probably just waiting in the helicopter.'

'No. I checked. There's no one there.'

'Did you try ringing Gavin's mobile, or calling for them?'

'No. I had thought to get you to try your *Maeve's-dropping* thing first, so that they don't know that we've spotted they're gone.'

Maeve focussed on nearby internal voices but only picked up on a few thoughts from the SOVs.

'Why would they go, when they are just about to be taken home? It doesn't make sense.'

'I'm guessing Gavin wasn't too keen on going back with Emily.'

'Dear me, you really do have it in for that woman, don't you Ethan.'

'There's just something off about her.'

'Like you thought there was something off about me when we met? Maybe you've just got a problem with women…Listen, I've had hours to pick up on her internal monologues and she checks out as trustworthy. She only seems to want what's best for Nathan.'

'Speak of the devil.'

Emily came round corner. 'Have you seen Nathan and Gavin? We need to make a move, the sooner we can get Nathan into one of the SpaceX suits that I've organised up at Port Hedland, the safer he'll be.'

'They're gone.'

'Gone? What do you mean *gone*? Are you saying kidnapped?'

'No not *kidnapped*!' Ethan's tone suggesting stupidity. 'Run *off* somewhere.'

'*Okay*, yeah, well maybe they have just gone to the bathroom, *durr…*'

'Nope.'

'Well did you *think* to check the chopper?'

'He did, and they're not there.' Maeve shook her head.

'Well what did they say to you before they *disappeared*?' Now Emily began to sound suspicious of the agents.

'Gavin asked for the keys to the car. He needed to get his mobile.'

'The car is still locked.' Maeve added.

'Well if they were looking to run off, wouldn't they have taken the car?' Emily suggested as she referred to one of her phone apps, looking for Gavin's mobile.

'A car with a *tracker*?'

'Good point. Oh, and I see that Gavin's mobile is *in* the car, so your assumption is gaining credibility. This'll be Gavin going off on one of his catastrophizing fantasies again.' Emily sighed, replacing her mobile in her pocket. 'Okay well we better all start looking for them then, hadn't we.'

'Have you got the spare car keys, Emily?' asked Ethan.

'Urr well…They're in the glove box.'

'*Oh brilliant.*'

'*Look* we'll just get the chopper up to help with the search.' Emily was getting irritated by Ethan's attitude.

At that moment the pilot came round the corner. 'You're not going to believe this Ms Richards…'

'What now?!'

'Some asshole appears to have jammed most of the flight controls, with superglue.'

16

Gavin had had hours to plan their escape but knew it would not work without his son's abilities and quick wit. The only thing that would almost certainly guarantee failure was if Nathan needed convincing, since time would be of the essence.

When Gavin swept his son up in his arms and finally fought back his sobs of relief he said 'We *have* to get away from these people.' Nathan asked no questions, just nodded over his dad's shoulder. 'I'll explain later, Nathan. Just follow me.'

Gavin led Nathan into the lounge where the others were gathering. It seemed important to do nothing to arouse suspicion. This plan would only work if they didn't see it coming.

They listened to Emily as she explained that they would be getting a boat home from Port Hedland then Gavin managed to get the keys off Ethan.

As they got around the side of the hangar Nathan rushed to get into the Toyota.

'No. We need to leave it behind. It has a tracker in it, which is why I'm leaving my phone inside. We are only taking the keys so that they cannot follow.'

'Right, but what about spare keys?'

'Damn. I hadn't thought about that.'

'It's okay Dad. I can see them in the glove compartment.'

'Good.'

'Won't they just use other vehicles though?'

'I'm just hoping to cause enough delay with confusion to enable us to put some distance between us and them.'

'Right.'

'Oh and Dad, try not to think in words, just imagine images.'

'*Images*? What do you mean?'

'I'm pretty sure that Maeve can hear inner voices.'

'Is that right? How did you work that out?'

'I'll tell you later. We need to go.'

'Okay, you to lead us off this airfield but without having to go past security at the front gate.'

'Okay,' Nathan pointed into the dark beyond the floodlights. 'Head in that direction for a few hundred metres until you reach the fence. If you keep straight you won't run into anything before you reach it.'

'Why not just take my hand and we'll run together?'

'I have to do something first then I'll catch you up.'

'No. We *must* stick together now.'

'We will *after* I disable the chopper.'

'What?'

'Go Dad.'

They parted at a jog.

Nathan went into the workshop which he had viewed was empty and grabbed the tube of superglue, then raced to the unattended helicopter. A minute later he was racing across the airfield, trying not to laugh.

There turned out to be no barbed wire on the airfield fencing, luckily. It was just tall enough to keep the kangaroos out. Father and son climbed over it at a concrete post then Nathan led them towards a dry creek.

They headed along the creek towards the lights of the town with Nathan's occasional hushed warnings of 'Rock…Log…Bush.'

Towed along blindly, Gavin's only physical clue as to where the obstacles lay was in the left or right movement of Nathan's guiding hand.

Nathan's ability meant they could move fast with knowledge of people's whereabouts.

They passed under a floodway and drew closer to the edge of town. Shortly after that Nathan was leading Gavin out of the creek through some bushes and into the yard of a derelict house.

'We are going to need to find food and water, Nathan.'

'I guessed that, but what has got you so spooked this time?'

'While I was travelling with Emily and those two agents I found out that they want to *experiment* on you.'

'The *agents*?'

'No the Seriously Organised Vigilantes.'

'Who are *they*?'

'Emily's people.'

'*Control*?'

'Yes. They are *not* a clinic. They are some major project team of the SOV's.'

'The *who*? Oh the *vigilantes*…But why?'

'It's another transhumanism experiment, looking to create a better human than the H2Os. So when your mother and I thought we were getting IVF treatment it turns out we were both being used as surrogates.'

'*Surrogates*?'

'Yes, like foster parents. Neither of us are your biological parents.'

'Then *who* is?'

'I don't *know*. Emily never said. Maybe she doesn't know either. Or she knows that she mustn't say. She mentioned something about *Black Ops*.'

'But that sounds *military*.'

'I know. I don't want you involved with them any longer. I'm worried enough for your safety without any thought of you being turned into some sort of *soldier*.'

'So who can we turn to for help?'

'I really don't know. I'm sorry, Nathan. Ethan didn't seem to care for Emily much, so maybe the agents could help. Though they seemed to be at odds Emily said that they are actually on the same side, which seemed to be news to the agents.'

'So it's us versus the world then.'

'Looks that way…I'm hoping your survival training is going to enable you to keep us both alive.'

'We are going to have to live off the land and that's going to be some challenge here in Western Australia. We are going to have to forage and scavenge. This house here seems as good a place as any to start.'

The wind-battered back door was half off its hinges which screeched as Nathan opened it and took a step inside.

'You might want to stay outside, Dad.'

'*No*. We stick together now.'

'Suit yourself but there *are* two snakes in here.'

'Oh right…well take care…and *be quick*.'

It helped that Nathan knew what he wanted before he entered the musty dark interior. His first port of call was the kitchen sink. He tried both taps but there was no water to refill the bottle he still carried, so he was back out to the veranda in less than a minute with a stick and an old curtain.

'This is for you,' Nathan handed his father the stick.

'*Okay…*' he sounded unsure why.

'You need to walk with it, maybe with a limp.'

'A limp?'

'Yes. They might start looking for us by satellite. We need to change the way we move. If we keep slow we may look like we belong here. If we move fast it will look suspicious.'

'Yes I see.'

Nathan shook out the curtain, giving off a cloud of dust.

'So what do we want *that* for?' Gavin turned away coughing as Nathan took out his pocket knife.

'I need to cover my environment suit.' He cut a strip off a long edge then cut a slot in the middle. Pulling it over his head he used the strip to tie the makeshift tabard at his waist. 'Okay…There's something else this way.'

As Gavin followed Nathan round the side of the house and onto the unlit street he asked in a hushed voice 'Did Emily teach you how to do this?'

'Some of it but it is basic escape and evasion. I picked up a lot of that from TV.'

The water in the next house proved to be shut off too, even after Nathan located the stop-cock. It was still open so the main must have been stopped further down into town. Nevertheless, another reason for checking out this house was to access something he had viewed *under* it.

As Nathan scanned their surroundings he checked under-floor cavities as well as interiors. Newman had been and still was largely an aborigine town. Many of the abandoned properties were stripped of everything useful to aid the survival of those who remained after the cull. Except that some of them had left secret stashes.

'You can come in with me. No snakes in this one.'

'Glad to hear it.' Gavin followed him in through the missing front door. The floor was covered with sand.

The floor-boarding squeaked as Nathan reach the middle of the kitchen but the sand did not trickle through. He scraped at the sand with his right foot and revealed carpet. He then scraped outward to find the edge of the carpet.

'What are you doing?'

'It's a surprise.' Nathan crouched down over to one side, brushing at the sand with his hand and lifting an edge of the hidden carpet. He realised that the kitchen table and two chairs were on top of the carpet. He stood up and moved the chairs out of the way.

'Help me with this.'

'With what?' Gavin couldn't see a thing.

'We need to shift this kitchen table aside.' He placed his father's hands to one end then went to the other end. 'Right, move the table to your left.'

With the table out of the way Nathan told his father to stay to one side as he took the edge of the carpet and began to pull. However, the more he lifted the more difficult it became with the weight of the sand and he had to get his father to help him pull.

'What on earth are we doing?' Gavin was keen that they either get out of town before sun-up or find a place to hide. Surely Nathan couldn't be thinking that they hide down in a dark cellar?

'I'm after something hidden under the floor.'

With the carpet aside far enough to enable access, Nathan took his pocket knife out and selected the wood saw. He used the teeth of the saw to help lift the end of a board. The board did not run right to the edge of the kitchen. It had been cut to two metres in length. Nathan soon had it up and to one side which enabled him to remove the next two boards without using the saw blade. Folding the saw away then pocketing the knife, Nathan reached down into the cavity and pulled on a handle.

Gavin could hear some big metallic box being pulled out. 'What is it?'

'Let's see,' he said, giving nothing away.

This box had been hidden since before the Great Reset. There was no lock on the box just two latches. Springing the latches and then opening the lid there were a few bundles of bank notes, worthless in the single credit economy of the New World Order. There were also a few boxes of ammunition which made it clear what the long object, wrapped in cloth, would be. Nathan lifted out the weapon and the rounds for it.

Unwrapping the weapon Nathan found it had remained clean. He inspected the barrel and hoped it would be safe enough to use, though it was not loaded yet.

Wrapping the boxes up in the cloth for easier carrying and slinging the rifle across his back Nathan led his father outside into the pre-dawn light.

'My *God* Nathan, that's a gun!'

'A hunting rifle.'

'D-d'you know how to use a rifle?'

'Not yet, no.'

Gavin groaned. He would rather be taking control of their situation but Nathan clearly seemed to know more about what they was doing.

'We can use this when we get back out of town, to catch food, Dad.'

'I don't want either of us getting hurt.'

'I'll make sure you are behind me.'

Moving closer into town, Nathan reminding Gavin to slow down and to use his stick, they came to an abandoned house with taps which worked. Nathan found a plastic bottle which he washed out before filling along with his own.

As the town woke and the focus turned to finding food, Nathan had to make a few detours to avoid people out and about.

Finally Nathan brought them to the rear of a fuel station. Lifting bin lids, turning away to gag from two of them, he came across a bin with a little out of date food. The bagged loaves were mouldy but then he found some packs of biscuits.

Huddling down between the bins Nathan opened one of the packs and tried a biscuit. It was hard and stale but edible. He offered the opened packet to his father.

Gavin wasn't happy. Was this to be their future? Eating scraps out of bins? He took a biscuit but didn't take a bite right away, watching his son crunch his mouthful. 'What's it like?'

'Dry but *keepdownable*.'

'Huh.' Gavin snapped off a piece and before long, as his stomach rumbled for more, he continued to munch without complaint.

Suddenly Nathan announced, 'I have an idea Dad, but we have to move *now*.'

'What are we doing?'

'I've just been checking out a possible ride out of here.'

'Okay. Are we stealing a car?'

Nathan shook his head as he gathered up his stuff.

He took them round to the truck park to the north side of the fuel station. There were two road trains parked there. The closest one had a driver still asleep at the back of his cab. The truck on the far side had no driver. The driver for that one had spent the night elsewhere.

On the passenger seat of the unoccupied cab Nathan had viewed a delivery manifest which mentioned Katherine, a city to the north east of their position. Nathan had reasoned that heading east would provide greater opportunity to access food and water in the wild. He wasn't sure which direction the occupied truck was headed but the one bound for Katherine would do fine.

The forward section of the chosen road train had a freight container. The lock on it could not be opened but they would not want to be sealed into a container anyway. The two flatbeds behind that carried pallets, covered with tarpaulins to keep the dust off the cargo.

Choosing the middle flatbed, having the most internal space under the tarpaulin, Nathan and Gavin climbed on. Nathan loosened a rope just enough to lift an edge so that they could climb under.

Placing the rifle and its rounds under the tarpaulin first Nathan was about to crawl under when he stopped.

'What's the matter?'

'We don't know how long we will be under here before we jump off, so let's go to the loo now.' They didn't risk going to the washroom in the fuel station. Instead they went in the bushes nearby.

Soon they had themselves on the flatbed under the tarpaulin. Shuffling along they positioned themselves as comfortably as possible between two pallets of shrink-wrapped farm machinery. It was dark and stuffy under the tarpaulin but they hoped that once they were on the move there would be sufficient flow of air to stop them cooking.

An hour later the neighbouring truck pulled away and they began to wonder if they had chosen the wrong road train. Then half an hour later their trucker turned up. It was a woman. She spent ten minutes checking her vehicle over before heading off, which resulted in her tightening up the tarpaulin and trapping her stowaways.

17

Emily was making it clear that she was livid as Ethan drove the three of them around Newton in a car on loan from one of the airport staff. The helicopter crew were in two other cars on loan.

'I swear Gavin isn't fit to be a father!'

Ethan laughed, considering her comment to be rather ironic.

'Nathan's life depends on him getting the SpaceX suit ASAP! Gavin running off with his son like this could…' Emily sighed, loudly. 'Gavin just doesn't think! He's always panicking and catastrophizing!'

'Anything Maeve?' Ethan ignored Emily's rant.

'Not yet Ethan, no.'

Emily looked at the satellite feed on her phone once more but she saw nothing out of the ordinary. There were a number of vehicles on the move. The town's two police cars had joined the search checking different sections. After examining the town plan, Emily made a judgement call that they should focus on the section marked as still having access to mains water. The runaways would be needing water.

'Well it seems to me that the lad definitely doesn't want to be found. I wonder what Gavin has said to him?' Maeve pondered openly.

'I'm wondering the same thing,' Emily nodded. 'Nathan's first priority has always been self-preservation and second to make contact with *Control*. But *Control* have picked up nothing. If only we could have placed a tracker on him.'

'I didn't expect them to run off either, though in hindsight Gavin did seem a bit disturbed by you at times, Emily.'

'*So* it's not just me,' Ethan chortled.

'Thanks.'

'I reckon they have gone to ground.' Ethan said as he turned the car left heading back into town towards a fuel station.

'I agree,' said Emily. 'Nathan will probably be looking to travel at night, keeping out of the sun during the day. I think we are going to have to organise a house to house search next,' she suggested as they passed a road train with a woman driver leaving town.

A major international organised crime syndicate in Riyadh were in mid-meeting when an unexpected noise was heard, just outside the boardroom. It sounded like someone whistling for a dog, followed by the sound of wet sacks being dropped outside of the boardroom doors.

The report on profits from human trafficking stopped. However, since the meeting was being held in a secure penthouse suite above a commercial holdings tower, there was no real sense of threat. There just seemed to be no rational explanation for such a sound.

The double doors burst inward. 'Hello Boys…Oh and *Girls*.'

What appeared to be a woman dressed in motorcycle gear stood there holding a weapon that looked like a prop off a sci-fi film set. Behind her were what looked like large chunks of security guard.

'Who are you?!' demanded the chair of the meeting, showing no fear of the intruder. 'How did you get in here?'

The figure returned her weapon to the rear holster over her shoulder then unclipped and removed her helmet, shaking out her head of red hair. The sweet smell of pheromone immediately pervaded the room. It was experienced as attractive by all, which made the intruder seem even less of a threat.

'We're Dawn. We gained entry by what some call a *Magic Door.*'

'*Magic door*? We have no time for *fools.*' The old man snapped from the other end of the boardroom. Drawing a weapon from the underside of the table he aimed it down its length. The two figures at the end by the doors quickly shuffled their chairs aside and not a moment too soon. The old man fired but the round did nothing against Dawn's body armour.

'Oh dear me. *So* predictable. Chest shot? *Really*? And when we had removed our helmet for you too.'

This time the old man went for a head-shot but Dawn knew what was coming and moved aside.

'Missed u...' The third round penetrated Dawn's forehead and left a mess on the wall behind.

The people in the room were shocked then relieved only to become further shocked as Dawn's head reformed.

She turned to the mess on the wall, which was already gathering itself together. They all saw it turn into something with wings, fly off the wall and into her hair. As Dawn reabsorbed her expelled content, sounds of disgust issued from her captive audience.

Dawn returned her attention to the syndicate with sarcasm. '*What*? Have you never seen a metamorph before? Well, don't worry. There will be no need for counselling sessions after this, *I promise*.' Dawn drew her weapon and explained. 'This is a thought controlled weapon. It's really quite versatile. And *we're* here today to shake things up a bit.'

'Who are you working for?!'

'We're a Time-Slave.'

'You're gramma is appalling.'

'Not at all. *We* are a colony, not a single being. But before I continue I should apologise for not being hungry today. I've been overeating of late you see. So this will have to be handled…*differently*.'

'You are *quite* mad. You're not making any sense.'

'That's *right*. I guess *you* would say yours will be senseless deaths, though I'm sure many would argue there *is* good reason, considering all your lists of crimes.'

'I have alerted security! You will never get out of here alive.'

'Ha! You Humans are *so* overconfident.' Dawn pulled the trigger and bright blue forks of lightening spread out from the muzzle of her weapon.

The energy did not burn. Instead it shook everyone so vigorously they haemorrhaged all over. Their skin split, inside and out and their cries of alarm sounded like gargling. Some attempted to get up and leave. They only succeeded in collapsing onto the boardroom table or the floor, while the rest simply bled out, trembling uncontrollably in their seats.

'If it were up to *us* we'd have fed you to the polar bears. But I see *that* happens to your replacements.'

In a flash Dawn stepped through a portal and was gone just as security came down the corridor.

After only twenty minutes both Gavin and Nathan began to think that hitching a lift on a flatbed travelling along corrugated roads was not such a good idea. It was proving incredibly uncomfortable.

Where they had their backs against shrink wrap for comfort it had seemed fine at first 'til the sweat built up. However, worse than that was the lack of cushioning from the floor of the flat-bed. They had to keep moving to reduce soreness. It occurred to them both this was probably what it must be like for people being trafficked.

With their scavenged belongings constantly shifting about, they agreed to take it in turns to try and rest, but rest wasn't possible.

Before long Gavin needed a toilet break but he had no idea when the next stop would be. In desperation he shuffled round to the edge of the tarpaulin that Nathan had loosened. He wanted to see if he could crawl out and pee over the side. He was soon back with the disturbing news, 'Nathan, we've been sealed in.'

'Yeah, I know.'

'Why didn't you say something?'

'To what end, Dad? You worry enough as it is.'

'So what now?'

'I think we are about to find out.'

The truck could be felt slowing.

'Are we at another town?'

'No. The woman in the cab is pulling over to check for us.'

'How…?'

'She got a radio message from the police I think. I guess they are looking for us.'

'Are you telling me you can remote-hear as well as view?'

'No. I haven't told anyone but I've learned to lip read.'

'What else haven't you told me?'

'Urr…A few things…maybe.'

They came to a halt and heard the cab door open, followed by footsteps. 'Okay I know you're in there!' The woman yelled beating the side of the freight container and listening.

Gavin almost replied but Nathan smothered it with his hand.

Then the woman remembered something and came to the side of their flat-bed. Muttering under her breath she began loosening the rope at the side.

Bright sunlight poured in as she lifted the tarpaulin up right beside Gavin and Nathan.

'Right oh…Out!'

Looking sheepish, father and son got off the flat-bed.

'Struth! What the merry hell you got there young'un?'

'Hunting rifle.'

'Looks like it. The cops down at Newman just told me I might have a couple of bloody freeloaders aboard. I just told them I didn't think so but I'd check. So it seems they was right.'

'Sorry for any inconvenience,' Gavin apologised. 'We just had to get away from there. Our lives are at risk.'

'You're the one who's unbalanced, right, and needs his meds urgently?'

'*No*. That's not true,' Nathan pleaded.

'They want to deport us back to the UK,' Gavin tried to explain, 'but it's not safe for us there. Criminals are out to kill us and we can no longer trust the police, because they have been infiltrated. Government agents arrived in Newman last night looking for us.'

'Sounds a bit far-fetched to me.'

'It's them who're lying,' Nathan pleaded again, 'So that we'll get held for them to pick up, then we're done for.'

'Well your dad looks…*on the edge* to me.'

'He's just worried you'll take us back.'

'I'm certainly *not* taking you back. I have a tight schedule to keep. I *could* drop you off at Port Hedland on my way through though.' She started tightening up the ropes again. 'Riding up front with me.'

'Thanks.'

'No worries. I don't trust cops anyway.'

'So you're *not* turning us in?' Gavin needed confirmation.

'Not unless you do something *stupid*.'

'Thank you *so* much.' Relief poured out of Gavin.

'You're both Poms right?'

'Yes.'

'I'm Enid, from Darwin.'

'Pleased to meet you Enid, I'm Gavin and my son is Nathan. Do you mind if I take a leak before we head off.'

'Go ahead, *treat* yourself. Just don't piss on me tyres.'

Nathan laughed out loud.

Once they were in the cool of the cab, with belongings stowed, Enid reported back to the police that she hadn't found any *unwanted* passengers. Then they were off again.

After hours of house to house searching and Maeve picking up nothing, the three of them went back to the police station. Maeve asked the police if any cars had left the town that morning. It became apparent that while those cars which had left town had been searched, two road trains had left unchecked. Those two drivers were asked to look over their vehicles.

The first one was heading down to Perth the second across to Queensland via Katherine. Emily wanted satellite coverage of the trucks but *Control's* satellite could not gain coverage across that distance at the same time. Emily made a judgement call to check the Perth-bound road train, reasoning that being the closest city Gavin would likely want to head that way.

The Perth-bound vehicle checked out as clean. That meant a high probability of Gavin and Nathan being on the other. However, Enid, had by then reported that she did not have any stowaways.

'I'm pretty sure she is lying. Stupid cow. And after we *told* her this was a medical emergency too!'

'Gavin must have come up with some convincing story then,' suggested Ethan.

'Yeah…Okay, so, I've been repositioning the satellite to track this Enid woman…Right, I have her vehicle now. She is way up past something labelled on here as Auski GT…?'

'Ghost Town. Used to be a tourist camp back in the day,' clarified the aboriginal police officer liaising with them.

'Right and she's now heading for Port Hedland and Highway 1. Can we contact the police there and request a vehicle search?'

The aboriginal police officer nodded and went to his desk to put wheels in motion.

'So what now, Emily?' asked Maeve.

'Well if they *are* with Enid I could catch up with them once the chopper arrives with the Nathan's space kit.'

'*You*? What about *us*?' Ethan wanted to know.

'Well, you've been a help here for sure but I guess your mission is over one way or another. You should head home. You could catch a flight back to Perth from Port Hedland. You're welcome to a lift, unless you'd rather drive back in that rental?'

'You're not getting rid of us *that* easy.'

'*What*? I thought you'd be glad to see the back of me. And surely *Thirteen* need you both assigned to something more pressing?'

'Not that I've been informed of.' Maeve was keen to stay involved. Sure that there was more to this case.

'Well you're welcome to tag along then if you want to treat it as a jolly.'

'It won't be a *jolly*, trust me,' Ethan growled.

'You are *so* easy to wind up.'

18

Nathan had been keeping Port Hedland in view as they closed in on the city.

'I think you should drop Dad and I off *before* we get to the city limits, Enid,' he warned, having remote-viewed two police vehicles heading out towards them.

'But I thought you were heading east?'

'We are.'

'But I don't have a delivery at Port Hedland. I'm heading straight through.'

'He's just concerned that you don't get in any trouble if there are any police checks,' Gavin added. 'We'll sort another ride when we can.'

'Right oh. If you're sure…I'll drop you off at the welcome sign.'

'No, no, really. Here's fine,' Nathan insisted watching the police cars already well past the city's welcome sign.

Enid frowned and looked at Gavin. 'Your son seems to be inheriting your nerves, mate.'

'Possibly with good reason…We can make it from here, thanks,' Gavin wondered whether Enid had any intention of letting them off as she just continued on driving. However, she was just looking for a good spot to drop them, by an area of bush.

'Thanks, Enid. We really appreciate what you have done for us,' Gavin said as he and Nathan climbed down from the cab.

'You take care now. And here, take a couple of these bottles of water,' she offered, reaching round to the map pocket behind her seat.

'Thanks for everything, Enid.'

'No worries.'

Seconds after Gavin closed the cab door, Enid left them in a cloud of dust and diesel fumes.

'I take it there's trouble up ahead, Nathan?'

'Yep. Two police vehicles heading our way. Come on let's get out into the bush.' Nathan led his father quickly to the other side of the highway and into the mixture of bushes, viewing well ahead for a path through.

Fifteen minutes later Nathan viewed the police pass Enid's road train and wondered whether he was just being paranoid. Nevertheless, a few minutes later, both police vehicles stopped on the highway parallel with their position.

Nathan stopped and drew his father down to a crouch.

'What is it?'

'The police are looking this way with binoculars.'

'What?'

'Like they know we are here.'

Gavin looked up into the sky, 'Oh, I think they must be using a satellite again.'

Nathan looked up. He could see nothing until he scanned with his remote-viewing. 'You're right, I've got it.'

'That's it then.' Gavin stood up.

'No. *Wait.* I have an idea.' Nathan pulled down on Gavin's arm.

Emily gave the sergeant orders over the police radio, watching via the satellite view on her mobile. With Ethan and Maeve standing behind her, she was relieved that Gavin and Nathan were now within reach. She barely registered the sound of the helicopter from Port Hedland making its approach to Newman airfield.

Banking the aircraft round, the pilot was told to set down near the other helicopter. With rotors winding down and the pilot shutting the electrics off the co-pilot jumped out to sort the refuelling. The pilot then opened his door and jumped down with a splash into a wide puddle. It looked as if another helicopter had been washed down there recently. He thought no more of it. He certainly never noticed the discarded tube of superglue floating in the water as he headed to the airfield office.

The co-pilot walked across to the man he spotted in the cockpit of the grounded helicopter, to ask about the fuel. The man was busy scraping at the controls on the dashboard looking particularly frustrated.

Meanwhile the rippling in the puddle from the slowing rotors seemed to rise in height rather than drop. Then the tube of glue moved below the pilot's door.

On Highway 1, the sergeant had pulled over along with the second police vehicle just as instructed by Emily. The officers then stood on their vehicles looking out across the bush, as directed.

'I think I see one of them,' a corporal announced, lowering his binoculars to point then losing sight. 'Male in his forties, I'd guess, looked to be armed, with a rifle.'

'Right.' The sergeant removed his side arm and jumped down, which seemed to be the cue for the other three to remove theirs and follow.

Emily's voice could be heard on the radio but was ignored.

'I don't think he will shoot. You can put your weapons away, and someone needs to stay with the vehicles.'

The sergeant hated being told how to do his job by some *suit*, especially some *foreign* suit. The men marched into the bush, catching glimpses of the male with the rifle on his back. Gavin now appeared to be heading slowly towards them, to give himself up peacefully the police sergeant hoped.

'Hey! The lad is coming around you!' Emily warned.

The police officers neither saw nor heard Nathan as he sped around the back of them, hidden by bushes, heading for the highway. The men remained focused on the man with the rifle, preparing themselves to make their arrest.

'He's going to your vehicles, damn it!'

Another voice was heard over the sergeant's radio. 'Emily, just tell them to shout out that we have the kid's space suit.'

'Ssh!'

The sergeant shook his head. 'Flaming galahs.'

Gavin kept coming towards the police, though it occurred to the sergeant that he seemed to be moving particularly slowly.

Then they all heard the sound of an engine back at the highway. It wasn't passing traffic. They all turned to see the rear police car pull onto the highway do a U-turn then head east in the wrong lane.

The sergeant turned back to see Gavin now running east as fast as his legs could carry him.

'Did you leave your keys in the ignition again, John?!' The sergeant bellowed at one of his constables.

'Sorry…'

The sergeant threw his own keys to his senior constable. 'Get after the boy…You two with me.' He ran off after Gavin with the two constables right behind him.

It was only as he ran the sergeant realised that the voice at the other end of his radio had finally fallen silent. He started to think that maybe he should have paid more attention to that woman after all. They had clearly been *played*.

One of the constables pulled ahead. He was clearly fitter than Gavin. The sergeant grew hopeful that the situation would soon be in hand. However, as the gap slowly closed they all became aware of a cloud of dust ahead.

The stolen police car was now driving down a farm track to make a pick up. Slowing down, it made another U-turn, kicking up more dust. As the dust cleared in the breeze they saw the passenger door swing open.

Gavin was barely in before Nathan put the pedal to the metal.

'Shit!' The sergeant came to a halt, gasping. He turned to see whether his other car was going to be able to head it off, back at the highway. His car just sat there. His senior constable had his hands held up and out in a gesture of hopeless apology.

The sergeant lifted his radio to his mouth, still trying to catch his breath. 'Don't tell me you dropped my keys along the way, Denny?'

'No Sir. The driver side tyre has been slashed.'

'Bastard!'

Emily hadn't wasted further time with the bungling Port Hedland police, once Ethan prompted that her helicopter may have arrived. Together the trio drove back to the airfield.

They met the pilot in the airfield office in something of a rush. He listened to Emily's clipped explanation as they strode out across to the landing pad.

He was going to have to chase down a police vehicle on Highway 1. He smiled. That was going to be a first for him. But only if the Port Hedland police reinforcements didn't apprehend Gavin and Nathan before the helicopter arrived on the scene.

As they came to the aircraft the co-pilot came towards them with an odd look on his face.

'What is it?' asked the pilot.

'I just finished refuelling and went to do the pre-flights…'

'And…?'

'Someone here seems to have gone and superglued the controls.'

'What?'

'*No*! Not again!' Emily yelled.

'How is that possible?' asked Maeve.

There was a long moment of stunned disbelief before a penny dropped for Ethan.

'Oh *she* knows,' he said accusingly.

'What are you talking about?' Emily turned on him.

'Nathan is able to teleport *any time* he likes. You've been keeping that a secret.' Ethan shoved Emily's shoulder hard with his frustration.

'*What*?! You're *insane*!' She shoved him right back.

No more accusations, Ethan took a swing at Emily. She blocked it and followed through with a kick to his groin, which Ethan blocked. Then stepping forward, making Emily step back and closer to the aircraft, Ethan swept her forward foot away. Emily used the momentum imparted to her foot to execute a spinning reverse kick to the head. However, Ethan had anticipated that and dropped when he had seen Emily was not put off balance. He blocked and twisted the incoming leg putting Emily to the ground, where there was no longer any trace of a puddle.

As Emily went down, she twisted to break her fall with her arms, bringing her other foot up and finally making hard contact with Ethan's head. It seemed to have no effect however, as he came down on top of her grabbing her wrists. Then the two were rolling around on the ground like it was all some re-enactment of a playground skirmish.

The pilot and co-pilot could not believe what they were seeing. Then Maeve who was already dismayed by the behaviour started groaning 'Oh no. You *have* to be kidding me…'

Emily managed to get on top of Ethan using his weight and hers to help pin one of his arms behind his back. Her angry face drew closer and closer to his as he failed to push her aside with one arm. She started to smile at his struggling then it happened. Maeve had heard it coming but still watched as Emily kissed Ethan.

Emily relaxed slightly and Ethan took his chance shifting her aside and getting on top of her, where he kissed her back.

Maeve groaned again and turned away, back to the office. 'Get a room!'

Nathan had no intention of stopping to let his father drive. He had the driving seat pulled forward to better reach the pedals, just as he had done with Colt's 4x4. The real problem was going to be Port Hedland. The only way east meant going through the city and he could see that the police were already forming a road block on both sides of the highway.

'Did Emily teach you how to steal and drive cars?'

'No Dad.'

'So…?'

'I guess I pick a lot of stuff up by watching. I'm glad too, or I would never have saved old Stan when Colt shot him.'

'You didn't tell me what happened there.'

'No because you'll get upset.'

'What, more upset than with the mess we are now in?'

'Maybe.'

'You're worrying me, Nathan.'

'Sorry. I met up with these gold hunters, hoping they would have a radio for me to contact Control. They hadn't. When I asked to be taken to the nearest town they said they could not afford the trip until they had found enough gold. So then I was stuck with them trying to help find enough. I used my powers.'

'Your powers?'

'Yes. I can see temperature differences. Where gold was at the surface it caused little plumes in the air, just after sundown, as the air cooled.'

'Wow.'

'So I went out at night gathering nuggets which I pretended to find the following day, thereby keeping my remote-viewing a secret.'

'Clever lad.'

'Only, they got greedy. Colt didn't want me to leave but Stan wanted to take me to town, so Colt shot him.'

'*Shot* him?'

'*Yeah.* He went mad. He shot Monty too.' Nathan fell silent.

'So what happened?' Gavin pushed.

'I…put Stan in Colt's car and drove away.'

'Hold on. How did you get away from this madman?'

'You don't want to know.'

'I *need* to know.'

212

Nathan sighed. 'It all happened so quick…I just *reacted*…'

'What did you do, Nathan?'

'I killed Colt. Then Carl turned on me with a knife and I killed him too.'

'Oh Nathan…But it's okay. It was self-defence.'

'*Was it*?'

'Sure it was.'

'But Dad, I *enjoyed* it.'

19

Surprised by his unexpected feelings, fighting a desire for something more, Ethan got up off Emily.

Brushing down his trousers, he turned around to see that both pilot and co-pilot, like Maeve, had made themselves scarce. 'Sorry about that, Emily. That was unprofessional of me.'

'Well at least we know what *our* problem is.'

'*Do* we?' It sounded like Emily had somehow hit a nerve.

'Ur right…well, I'm going to check on how the police roadblock is coming along at Port Hedland.' Emily strutted off to the office without looking back.

'*Fine*.' Ethan turned on his heel and went to the maintenance workshop in the hangar next door. He suddenly thought it was about time to see what could help him break into their rental car.

In the office Emily found that Maeve was ahead of her, already talking to the police at Port Hedland, on speakerphone. The sergeant in charge of the Highway 1 roadblock was aware of his colleague's fiasco and could be heard promising the same was not going to happen with him.

Emily took out her mobile and checked the satellite view for the stolen police car. She suspected it would not be far away from the city now.

'Damn it!'

'What's up?' Maeve asked, turning away from the desk phone.

'They're not there…on the 1.'

'What?'

'We've lost them!' She dragged the satellite view around one way then another on the screen. 'I shouldn't have been pissing about with Ethan.'

'No.'

To avoid the roadblock out of sight some way up ahead, Nathan took a right off the Great Northern Highway onto Hamilton Road. His intention was to skirt around South Hedland and reconnect with the highway further east.

'You're going faster than the speed limit,' Gavin warned.'

'It's okay Dad. We're in a police car.'

'Where are you going now?'

Nathan pulled into a Caltex fuel station. 'We're going to need a full tank.'

'But I don't have a card. Emily was dealing with everything.'

Nathan pulled up in such a way that a pump obscured view of him from the cashier in the shop. 'Just act natural and fill her up, Dad.'

'Natural? What do you mean, natural?'

'You're a plain clothes officer.'

'As I told Emily, I'm not good at acting.'

'Well I can't do it…Okay just imagine that you're filling up the car at home. I'll sort the payment out.'

'How?'

'You'll see…My last idea worked didn't it.'

Gavin got out and was pleasantly surprised to see that 'pay at kiosk' enabled him to start filling up.

Possibly because he was nervous the pump seemed to take forever but eventually started to click off. He returned the nozzle to its hanger then opened the passenger door and bent down.

'So what now?'

'Just get in.'

Closing the door, Gavin looked over his shoulder as Nathan sped off the forecourt. Struggling to connect his seat belt he spotted two assistants at the window staring out in surprise.

'You can't do that, Nathan.'

'Just did…Police can do anything.'

Gavin started to feel his criminal past was coming back to haunt him, and began to stew with worry.

Nathan took the Forest Circular onto Murdoch Drive which got them onto Buttweld Road. Nathan laughed out loud.

'It's not funny, Nathan. We're in enough trouble for taking the car, in addition to your under-aged driving, *without* a licence, and now we've stolen fuel too.'

'I was laughing at the road name, Dad.'

'Oh.'

'*Besides*…you forgot one *misdemeanour*.'

'What's that.'

'*Serial killer.*'

'What?'

'The two people I murdered.'

'Oh…Right…I think it has to be three to make it serial.'

'I'll see what I can do.'
'Don't joke like that, Nathan.'

Emily sat in the back of the rental, using Ethan's phone to speak with the Port Hedland police as he drove the three of them north. She surveyed her satellite feed with growing consternation and not just because of the speed they were travelling at.

Cloud was coming in thick and fast from the north-west. It was getting so thick that at times it was even interfering with the infrared spectrum of the eye-in-the-sky.

The police had reported a no-show from the roadblock at the west side of the city. Then they relayed a report that an unidentified plain clothed officer had apparently stolen fuel from a station in South Hedland.

Emily immediately twigged that this must have been Gavin filling up the stolen car. This suggested that the Purnells were attempting to bypass the city. They would not have stolen fuel if they were going to ground, unless it was bluff tactics. However, she could spot the police car in the labyrinth of roads.

The officer on the phone was clearly frustrated by failure to apprehend, and wanting someone to blame, 'Do you think they may have hacked into your satellite, the way they are avoiding capture?'

'Anything is possible Captain,' Emily offered no further explanation. 'Ah…Found them! They are back on the Great North Highway, heading west towards Pardoo.'

'Right.'

Now that they knew where the Purnells were, Emily thought it best to check the weather. 'Oh great!'

A massive cyclone was building over the Indian Ocean.

The problem with travelling anywhere at speed was that all too soon you caught up with slower traffic. On a single lane road this could be a problem but the highway had an overtaking lane. However, Nathan noticed that the slower vehicle ahead, a Hilux, was driving erratically, shifting from one lane to the other and back.

Ahead of the erratic driver was a bridge. They were approaching the De Grey River. Nathan didn't want the driver getting onto the bridge before them but couldn't close the gap fast enough. He put on the lights and the siren and flashed further warnings with the headlights.

However, as the gap closed in something of a rush, the possible drunk driver showed no sign of awareness of their approach. Then Nathan realised it was all too late to get past, as the car in front came onto the bridge.

Nathan slammed on the brakes, but so did the car in front, slewing the Hilux and blocking any way around it. Nathan swerved worried he might collide with the Hilux or the bridge. The police car went into a sideways skid and ended up beside the Hilux, as if in a diagonal parking lot.

Nathan was momentarily distracted by his relief over avoiding a crash, and so was Gavin. Their relief was short lived however, as they realised that the scruffy man, now peering in at the window, was pointing a gun at Gavin.

'Tell your boy to get out of the car, real slow and come around to me.'

'Hey, come on now, put the gun away. There's no need for this…' Gavin pleaded.

'No I think there *is* a need see. Look lively lad.'

Nathan didn't want his father getting hurt. He found himself wondering if he could be fast enough to kill the man before he could pull the trigger.

Slowly he got out of the police car and came round the front. He saw the man reach into a back pocket with his free hand and surprisingly pull out a pair of cuffs.

'Put one of these on your right wrist kid, and the other down there on the roo-bars,' he pointed at the front of his Hilux, 'then I'll deal with your dad.'

'Who are you? A cop?'

'Pfff no…A bounty hunter. However, I have been listening in to some interesting chatter on the police frequency though.'

'We can explain.'

'*Good*. I can do with some in-car entertainment as I head on up to Broome, with Silent Jim,' he gestured with his head and Nathan noted the aboriginal man cuffed to the back seat.

'You're not taking us back to Port Hedland?'

'Time is money and I'm hoping you are too. They can come fetch you from there if you're *that* important.'

Noting that Nathan was now secured to the bars, the bounty hunter shifted aside, gesturing for Gavin to get out. He soon had him in the back with Jim then retrieved Nathan, gun still in hand, and secured him next to Gavin. He had a self-satisfied smirk on his face as he closed the door.

The bounty hunter reversed the police car off the bridge and onto the sand at the side of the highway. Then he returned and soon had his Hilux driving straight and smooth on course for Broome.

'Do I detect a British accent?' Gavin asked hopefully.

'Yeah, served in the Special Air Service, until the Great Reset,' he bragged yet with a hint of cynicism. 'The name's Disney.'

Between a gap in the cloud Emily spotted the stolen police car, abandoned by the De Grey River. She reasoned that it was unlikely to have run out of fuel, so maybe there had been engine trouble. She looked for signs of the Purnells in the vicinity but only noted a couple of saltwater crocodiles at the river's edge.

By the time Ethan got them to Port Hedland it was late and the stolen police car had been retrieved. It was reported by the police Captain to Maeve, as an MI5 officer, that only one set of footprints were found leading from the car to the highway and bridge. There were also skid marks at the end of the bridge matching the police tyres. The captain suggested that whoever had been driving may have suddenly thought to head along the river instead of continuing on the highway.

The captain's conclusions didn't make sense to Maeve, or Emily and Ethan. They thought it was more likely that the Purnells had taken an opportunity to swap cars there, possibly hijacking one on the bridge. This made some sense as a means of reducing traceability. But that would then mean that the Purnells were adding kidnapping to their growing list of felonies.

Since Maeve had taken opportunity to rest on the drive up, after a quick snack and refuel, they headed east with Maeve at the wheel. This was however, against police advice to stay in town. A bad cyclone was in-coming and folk were already battening down the hatches in preparation.

Disney had listened to the whole story of the Purnells desperate need to avoid deportation. He was inclined to believe it, however, it lacked substance. After mulling it over he decided to probe further.

'So you are saying the British Government want you dead because of what you both know and you can't tell me or it would put my life in danger too?'

'Yes.' Gavin thought he was getting through to this man.

'That's very considerate of you, but what if I tell you I don't give a toss about the British Government after what they did. It's *why* I'm over here in this God-forsaken land.'

'Well I still can't divulge the information.'

'It could be *worth* something.'

'People get *disappeared* for knowing this stuff.'

Nathan suppressed a smile. He was starting to believe that his father was finally learning how to act after all.

'I know *all* about people vanishing. A buddy of mine, Big Ben McGregor was in MI5 and *he* got disappeared. He could take care of himself too. Ex-SAS like me. I helped his sister Marion try and find out what happened. The closest anyone got was finding his bike in a multi-storey carpark in Cambridge.'

'Well isn't that all the more reason to keep clear of us?'

'Don't worry about that. I'll be dropping you *all* off with the Broome constabulary.'

'But you could just let us go.' Nathan pleaded. 'The police don't know you have us.'

'Sorry kid. We live in a shit world with shit lessons. And the biggest shit lesson, the *dead otter* level lesson, is to look after *yourself*.'

'What if we are not worth any money?' Gavin noticed Silent Jim nod, as if he was finally on the right track with Disney.

'Well…I'll tell you what. When I take Jimmy into the cop-shop I'll make a somewhat *vague* inquiry and if they're not biting I'll drop you off at Sally One-Shoe's.'

'Oh thank you Mr Disney.' Nathan felt there was now light at the end of the tunnel.

'Is Sally's place a motel?' Gavin asked, unsure, 'Or just a bar?'

Silent Jim suddenly started howling with laughter.

'No mate,' Disney explained. 'Sal is the local human trafficker.'

222

By the time Maeve got to the De Grey River, the wind was picking up. So with the headlights on full beam to light the end of the bridge all that could be found were a faint trace of skid marks. Even then the trio had to scuff through the orange layer of constantly shifting sand to see signs of rubber.

After a quick discussion it was decided to keep heading east on the highway in the hope of picking the trail back up.

Maeve intended to listen out for clues along the way. While it might seem obvious that the Purnells could stop at any settlement along the way, they might not risk it if they had abducted someone. It was more likely that when needing a break they would pull off the highway into the bush, out of sight.

Shortly after crossing the De Grey they saw their first flash of lightening behind them, but heard no thunder. It was still some way off. Emily checked the weather but chose not to share the report with the other two unless asked.

It bugged Gavin that a Brit could have become quite so uncaring towards fellow Brits.

'So what got you so bitter, Disney? Surely it couldn't have just been the disappearance of your mate Ben McDougal?'

'McGregor…No. I guess it was down to a lot of things. Mostly it was when my wife April was shot by police in Hereford, back in 23. She was a local organiser of *Stand in the Park*. The police claimed their action was taken under the then new prevention of terrorism measures. That was bollocks of course. I was involved with *real* counter terrorism in the SAS. This was simply some political hit, killing April and two of her friends, as was happening in other parts of the UK. All of it to ensure a smoother transition to the New World Order.'

'So you upped and left, there and then?'

'No, not immediately…I tried to organise an enquiry but I got a prompt from *above* to drop it. *Then* I was approached by some people claiming to be members of the Awakened Anti-NWO. I didn't want anything to do with them though. Some extremists were involved in the dirty bombing of London. The country was turning to shit and if I stayed in the army I would be helping dish out a lot more of it. So I left and came here. In hindsight I had only gone and swapped one hell for another.'

'That's terrible. I know what it's like to lose a loved one. Nathan's mother died when he was born and I found out recently that she had been part of some medical experiment.'

'Life has become all about credit for the next meal ticket; an existence but only just, in an unjust sort of way. The less you care, the easier it gets. Just don't set your expectations too high.'

'Best you white fellas all slash your wrists now before it's too late.' Jim laughed cynically. He couldn't stand listening to anymore. His people had been suffering oppression at the hands of political systems for generations.

'Ah sorry Jim, no time for that, we are almost there,' Disney announced as they came to the junction on Highway 1 and turned left into Broome.

The car interior fell silent as they reached Roebuck then passed the deserted edge of town on to the slightly livelier centre. Each of Disney's passengers were now paying close attention to their passing surroundings, no doubt preparing for any opportunity to make a break for it.

Finally Disney pulled into the police station car park. He got out of the car and came round to Silent Jim's door. Opening it without a word he took his cuff keys and swapped the cuff which held Jim to the handle above the window, to his own wrist. Jim didn't need telling that it was time to follow Disney inside the station, once again.

Looking back into the car Disney chucked the keys to Gavin. 'I'm only going to be gone a few minutes. I suggest you see yourselves out.'

'What? You're letting us go? Why?'

'Couple of reasons I guess. I've been feeling like April says it's the right thing to do. The second, and surely just coincidence, but young Nathan there…well, he has a look of my mate Ben.'

20

Ethan slowed down a little, even though the rain had caught up with them.

'What are you slowing up for?' Emily peered into the darkness from the front passenger seat, wondering if Ethan and seen something.

'I want to be sure we can get to the next fuel station while we still have some fuel.'

'We can't be *that* low already.'

'You'd think, wouldn't you, but I *have* been hammering it, trying to keep ahead of the storm.'

'Well if you *don't* judge it right the conditions will get too difficult to drive in.'

'*Oh* you know…that *never* occurred to me.'

'I was just saying.'

Ethan sighed. 'Anything useful on that phone yet?'

'I told you…I have no signal.'

'But at some point you'll get signal back.'

'And *at some point* I'll tell you if there's anything worth knowing.'

'People!' Maeve was getting increasingly irritated. 'I don't know what's worse…Listening to you two bicker, or knowing you want to make out.'

'That was only *one* time,' Ethan insisted.

'It was a joke,' Emily added.

'Uh…*yeah*.'

Gavin depended on Nathan again to take the lead as they left Disney's Hilux and the police carpark.

Nathan headed south, towards an area of abandoned properties on the edge of town. The trouble with that plan was that the storm had arrived. As they ran down the empty main street Nathan remote-viewed in the direction of the storm and what he saw was not good. Not good at all. It was nothing short of a supercell cyclone, over the Indian Ocean still but it wouldn't be staying there. The strong gusts buffeting them both now as they ran were nothing compared to what was to come.

Bins blew over and rubbish raced across the street then a flying branch hit Gavin hard and fast on the right side of his head. He went down on hands and knees, dazed.

Nathan saw him go down and turned back into the wind. 'Dad!'

Gavin lifted a hand to his head then tried to look at it in the flickering street light. There was blood.

Nathan tried to help his father up. At that point, out of nowhere, came a large sheet of chipboard, stripped off some abandoned property down the street. Nathan saw it coming but couldn't get his dad moving. He turned his back into it as it hit, sheltering Gavin. However, the force of the blow flattened them both.

By the time they got their wits about them they noticed a police car had pulled up next to them.

'What are you idiots doing out in this. You should be at home.'

'Sorry officer,' Gavin apologised weakly.

227

'Looks like you're hurt.'

'I'll tell you something else they look like…' a second officer dashed out of the car, '…the pair we've been told to watch out for!'

Before Nathan could think what to do, they were both being cuffed and put in the back of the vehicle.

Gavin went quietly, though his head was ringing. Nathan tried to protest that this was a mistake but stayed with his father.

As they returned to the station, Nathan saw Disney driving away. They made no attempt to resist arrest as they were rushed inside, out of the wind.

The minimal night-shift was all too busy dealing with storm related issues to be particularly attentive. So there was only a very basic booking process before the Purnells were led to the cells. They were both checked for weapons and had their belts removed.

'What about my Dad's head injury?' Nathan protested as his belt was taken off him. 'I have a first aid kit on that belt I could treat him.'

'*Someone* will take a look at him when they get a chance.'

'But I could do it *now*! It won't take a minute or two.'

The police officer didn't seem interested. 'What you can *do*…is go in this cell.' The officer unlocked the door then Nathan's cuffs.

Nathan was ushered inside then the door was locked after him.

'No, no! We need to stick together!' Gavin was directed to the cell next door.

'There's only one bunk in each, mate. Settle down. You're *only* next door.'

'You don't understand!'

'You got me there,' the officer locked him in. 'What a couple of whinging Poms! So *selfish*. There's people out there we're trying to deal with, far worse off than you!'

The officer walked away.

'Sorry Nathan!' Gavin called through the bars in the door.

'No. It's my fault Dad. I should have seen what was coming.'

'Don't blame yourself. My head has almost stopped bleeding now.'

Nathan sat on his bunk and listened to the howling wind. A thought occurred to him but he didn't want to share it with his anxious father. When the storm hit proper, it might destroy the police station. Then maybe they could make their escape from the wreckage. The cyclone would be calm in the centre, *if* the centre passed over them, and might offer opportunity to get away before the winds hit in the opposite direction.

However, these cells looked very strong, so maybe Nathan needed to sleep on it. He had tried not to fall asleep in the car, next to his father. However, he wasn't going to be able to keep awake forever.

Nathan tried to pull the bunk into the middle of the cell but it was firmly bolted to the wall. All he succeeded in doing was pulling the mattress off. He decided to put the mattress on the floor to lie on.

'Love you Dad!' he called as he lay down and closed his eyes.

'Love you too Nathan,' he heard his father call back.

Maeve's mobile vibrated as they drew closer to habitation, she barely noticed it over the combination of corrugations and the buffeting of the wind. She checked it out, the sudden glow in the car giving its arrival away.

'At least one of us has got signal,' Emily looked round hopeful for good news.

'It's a missed call *and* a text…from the Port Hedland police…The Purnells have turned up at Broome and are being detained there for us.'

'That's not too far away,' Ethan confirmed.

'Thank goodness,' said Emily, 'We'll be able to get Nathan into a space suit, and give Gavin a bollocking.'

'*Really, Emily*? You think that will help?' Maeve wasn't convinced.

'It's better than no space suit.'

'I meant you having a go at Gavin.'

'Oh…He needs to think before he flies off the handle. Why would he think that I want to do anything but help his son?'

'I don't know,' Ethan chipped in, 'Maybe because you people like abusing others.'

'*Us people*? All I've done is teach the lad how to survive this…this *curse* he has.'

'That the SOV *experimentation* gave him.'

'What *are* you saying? You would rather I didn't teach him how to survive? I didn't have a hand in their transhumanist experiment. I was brought in when it was realised Nathan had a problem.'

'Fair enough.'

'*Fair enough*? Is that your idea of an apology.'

'Okay, okay. *Sorry.*'

'Right, now that's out of the way,' Maeve put in, 'we need to consider what we are going to do once we have Nathan suited up and both of them out of police custody.'

'Find a sturdy looking motel, and get something good to eat?' Emily suggested.

'Not sure we have time for a stop-over. While you two've been bickering, I've been checking out this storm and it looks *very* bad. The supercell could easily flatten the area. I think we need to head south or east as soon as possible. Maybe keep going all the way to Alice Springs.'

'Okay, I'll sort the fuel while you two get the Purnells.' Ethan offered.

However, a little later, as they came to a junction and turned left for Broome, the light from the fuel station at Roebuck Plains came into view. So did headlights from a number of vehicles queuing for fuel.

'Looks like we may have arrived just in time for an evacuation,' said Emily with concern. 'Probably families who don't have access to a shelter.'

'The Purnells aren't going anywhere,' Ethan suggested, 'so we best join that queue now before they run out of fuel.'

'I agree,' Maeve nodded. 'According to Google we have another thirty-five klicks to go.'

Stress of a different nature was taking place to the north of the cyclone, in Bengal. As the wind caused the jungle canopy to sway, three men below picked their way carefully through the

231

undergrowth, by torch light. One man was armed with a rifle while the other two carried machetes. All three of them had empty packs on their backs, ready for what lay ahead. They were all following their ears towards the sound of the animal in pain.

A tiger lay by an untouched leg of deer, its own foreleg caught in a wire snare. It had clearly been struggling for some hours and was now tired and bleeding.

Catching the scent of approaching humans its pained calls turned to angry roars. Its heart began to beat faster losing more blood from its leg as the flicker of torch beams drew nearer.

As the men appeared before the big cat, just out of reach it gave its loudest roar, but they did not back away, instead they laughed.

The man with the rifle commented on the high price the Chinese would pay for those snarling teeth, and how much they would get for the pelt and organs.

The more endangered a species became the more it was worth killing. The man raised the butt of the rifle to his shoulder with a smile as his colleagues illuminated the target with their torches. Standing its ground the tiger had no idea that it was making an easy target for a heart shot.

The rifle disintegrated as a suppressed round passed through the man's left hand before shattering the stock. All three men were confused but not for long as four figures clad in black emerged from the jungle, laser-sighted automatic weapons up.

The three poachers turned to run but a leg shot took the first man down causing the other two to freeze, lifting their hands in surrender.

One of the four figures took a sidearm and shot the tiger with a dart. Then, while the tranquiliser put the big cat to sleep the three poachers were disarmed and tied securely to three of the surrounding trees, then their questioning began.

The poachers were asked who was boss and who their buyers were. At first they said nothing until it was pointed out that they would not last long if left in this jungle. Reluctantly the man with the injured hand admitted that he was the boss and that they always sold to the highest bidder, but he wasn't saying where.

It was pointed out to him that just as the poachers had used the deer leg to bait the tiger, *Tiger Team* had used the unfortunate tiger to bait the poachers. A number of video cameras had been installed to record the whole episode. If the poachers provided enough detail on their trade they might just get early release.

The poachers were unsure at first what was being suggested here. The lead figure in black enquired after the condition of the animal. The tiger was going to be okay. This one would not need to be air-lifted out. The vet had tended to the cat's wound with some stitches and an anti-biotic jab and warned that it would be coming round in ten minutes or so. Then it became clear to the poachers that this discussion was not about early release from *jail*. The uninjured man blurted out a name.

Suggesting that the men needed to spill much more; people, places, times and even passwords, the four figures disappeared back into the jungle.

The tiger was groggy at first. The lolling tongue retracted, the nose twitched its whiskers. The head lifted slightly, its eyes unfocussed initially. Bit by bit it came to its senses and realised it was surrounded by humans and fear set in, sharpening its wits.

The tiger staggered to its feet and snarled. The humans began jabbering like monkeys did. It remembered how hungry it was because now it could smell fresh blood.

The jabbering rose in pitch just before the first of the screams began, accompanied by pleading that in time turned to additional screaming, before eventual silence.

At first light the tiger was gone. *Tiger Team* returned but only to retrieve their cameras, leaving the remains of the poachers for the tigers. The video would be edited before being posted online for their sponsors.

Since the Great Reset approaches to sponsorship had changed. Television around the world still had its charities begging for money to save endangered animals, or to stop cruelty to animals. However, now it was possible to sponsor *protection teams*, via the Dark Net. These were in actual fact hit squads who dealt with the root cause of such problems. Such sponsorship was not limited purely to the protection of animals. It was also widely available for child protection.

Maeve flashed her MI5 badge as she reached the desk at Broome police station.

'Maeve Corrigan, British Intelligence. Here to take the Purnells back into custody.'

'Ah yeah…' was all the desk sergeant had to say, at first.

Maeve picked up some of the unsaid and was immediately alarmed but tried not to show it. 'What's up, Sergeant?'

He led Maeve and her two colleagues along to the cells. 'Well, turns out one of them has escaped. With the weather blowing a hoolie out there you'd think they'd both want to stay out of it.' He swung a cell door open and they all peered in.

Gavin was in a sorry state, his shoulders heaving with great sobs, his right wrist cuffed to the remains of a bunk. The hole in the floor was so big it was through to the basement and also through to the neighbouring cell.

'The kid used some sort of explosive device to escape through the janitor's room, but left his half-wit father behind.'

21

As Ethan attempted to get some sense out of Gavin, the women both made calls to their offices.

Control were very disappointed to hear that Nathan had ported away before he could be given a space suit. It was agreed to get an immediate search underway of all SpaceX buildings on the moon. There was still hope, but they wouldn't be sending Emily up there after him, she was to return to the UK. However, Emily explained that her return would have to be after weathering out the storm.

Maeve spoke with Gina Oakley who did not sound so disappointed or surprised by the news. In fact she had new information to share from her anonymous informer.

'It turns out that you are not there to save Nathan but rather to uncover an SOV project which needs to be closed down immediately.'

'But Ma'am, Emily told Ethan and I that *Five* are now working for the same *masters* as the SOVs.'

'Well *I* don't see it that way. Not all SOV projects could possibly be considered above board. So park that for now. What I want you to do *first* is find an ex-associate of mine called Disney, who my informant has told me is in the vicinity.'

'Then what?'

'When you find him, tell him from me that it's safe to come home now, *if* he helps you and

Ethan. It's also important that you tell him that I now know he wasn't involved in the Awakened extremists London Dirty Bombing.'

'*Okay*...But what am I asking this Disney to help with?'

'My informant couldn't say, sorry.'

'Well I think he *should* bloody well say sorry. This isn't some mystery tour over here. We've got really dangerous weather conditions to contend with.'

'I do appreciate that Maeve, that's why you've got Ethan with you.' Gina hung up.

Maeve just looked at the phone wondering for a moment if she had been cut off by a downed line, but there was still a dialling tone.

She turned to the desk sergeant and asked 'Do you know of someone local going by the name of Disney?'

'Ah yeah, real rough piece of work, a bounty hunter. He's got a place down by Taylors Lagoon.'

'On the *coast*?' That was worrying, Maeve thought, she would rather be heading away from the weather.

'Ah nah, it's further inland.'

'Right...So could you possibly provide me with clear directions, please?'

'Struth lady, who do you think we are? Triple-A?'

'*Look*, we're *all* a bit overwhelmed right now, but the sooner you get me those directions the sooner we'll be out of your hair.'

'Fair dinkum,' the desk sergeant turned to his computer, brought up a map, printed it out, made some notes on it and handed it over. 'There y'go.'

'Oh and does this Disney character have a mobile number?'

With a sigh the sergeant took the map back from Maeve, checked his computer, scribbled the number next to where Disney lived and handed it back. 'Anything else, *Ma'am*?'

'I hope not.'

Maeve found Gavin with Ethan and Emily in an interview room.

'We've got to go,' she urged.

'He's almost catatonic Maeve,' Ethan reported. 'Clearly traumatised. I couldn't get a thing out of him.'

'Let me try. I have a *way* with him,' said Emily stepping forward raising her hand for a good slap.

Maeve was faster and caught Emily by the shoulder. 'I don't think that's a good idea. Just get him in the car. It's my turn to drive.'

'You sure?'

'Of course I'm sure. You and Ethan have been doing the lion's share.'

'No I mean, you sure you want to? I mean Ethan did say it was your fault the other rental ended up on its roof.'

'That was a freak accident.'

'Well I'm just saying, because the weather is getting freakier and we've only got the one car left now.'

'Just get Gavin in the car. We're wasting time.' As Maeve took the lead she reached for her mobile to tell Disney they were coming by and that she had a message from Gina. However, she thought better of it and returned the phone to her pocket. She didn't want to spook this Disney if Gina said he was important

238

to the change in mission. She had no idea how he would react to the news, or them turning up unannounced come to that.

'We need to refill our water supply,' Emily prompted as they reached the Toyota.

'Right well get onto it,' Maeve helped Ethan get Gavin strapped into the back seat.

'So what happens after we reach Disney?' Ethan enquired.

'I'm guess he has shelter for us.'

'And after the storm passes?'

'From what Gina said, it seemed to suggest that heading away from the storm something important would develop.'

'Was that her super-intuition talking, or her informer?'

'The latter.'

'I'd have preferred the former.'

'Right!' Emily dashed out with two full carrier bags, clearly carrying more than water. 'Open the boot Ethan!'

'What have you got there, Emily?'

'Good reason to get a move on.'

'Meaning?' Maeve asked, but heard the answer before Emily came clean.

'I've looted the police kitchen.'

Maeve picked up speed as she left the station but could not keep it up or any smooth direction. Town debris was coming from all directions. Maeve had to keep swerving and changing speed. All of them helped keep a lookout in the still dim morning light, all except Gavin who just stared blankly but no longer sobbed.

'Shit! That almost had us,' Maeve moaned as a gust from between buildings almost put the Toyota into a telegraph pole.

'This wreckage should reduce once we're out of Dodge,' Ethan offered.

Suddenly Maeve screeched to a halt, their path blocked by a fallen tree. Maeve changed into reverse gear.

'Hang on,' Ethan suggested. 'It's a dead tree and not too thick.'

'You suggesting I try driving through it?'

'No. Look the roots are gone. I reckon we can swing it round to the side.'

No one argued and three of them got out. The lack of branches reduced the drag and together they got it aside, saving them looking for an alternative route.

Getting back in the car, Maeve had to put the de-mister on to combat the damp from their rain soaked clothing.

As they passed back through Roebuck there was no longer a queue for fuel at the filling station. The lights were off at the kiosk, as was its roof.

By the time they were back onto Highway 1 at the junction there was much less debris, though the wind was no less forceful.

Ethan turned to Gavin. 'Bet you're glad we're out of there. One less thing for you to worry about.'

No response.

Emily tried. 'I have people searching buildings on the moon, Gavin. It's only a question of time before we find Nathan.'

Still nothing.

'Who's to say he hasn't gone and turned up in Europe or even back home,' Maeve tried.

Nothing.

Maeve had been hoping for some internal monologue from Gavin, to give some clue how to draw him back to the real world, but there wasn't a word.

Gavin was traumatised by one image going over and over in his mind, of Nathan tumbling through space. Dying.

Disney had had a few near misses with panicked kangaroos and cattle crossing in front of him, hoping to escape what was coming. Finally he reached his old ranch. Hitting the remote on the dashboard the garage door in the large mound opened up, letting him drive straight into his bunker.

He didn't close the door after him though. There were a few things he wanted from the house first. He dashed out, selecting the key he needed as he ran.

It was like a scene from Supermarket Sweep. He had a stolen trolley under his stairs which he wheeled into the kitchen-diner, to raid his fridge-freezer and larder. Then, as almost a second thought, he dashed upstairs to grab a number of things there before exiting the house. Back out into the rain the trolley did not move as smoothly across the soaking yard, nevertheless he got to the shelter of the garage and closed the heavy steel door down.

Switching the lights on he then dealt with the security panel to allow him through another armoured door and into the bunker proper.

The heart of the bunker was down a stairwell. The bunker had been built to survive more than wildfires and cyclones. Grabbing a load off the trolley, Disney headed down.

Arriving in the main living area he was at first confused because he did not remember leaving the lights on when he was down there last. The lights became the least of his concerns though as he saw a man sitting there in Disney's favourite chair.

'What the hell?! How did you get in here?! Who are you?!' Disney dropped what he was carrying on a table and strode towards the intruder.

As he crossed the room Disney checked the man for possible weapons. The intruded made no attempt to defend himself. In fact he showed not the slightest concern over Disney's angry advance. He simply raised a hand to suggest that Disney stop.

'You better answer me or things are going to get very painful for you mate.'

'I just came to tell you that it is time you left, Mr Disney.'

'Left?! I only just got back!'

'Nevertheless, you cannot stay.' The man's calm matter-of-fact tone irritated Disney intensely.

'Who the *fuck* do you think you are?!'

'My name…is Destiny.'

Even though Ethan's laughter was taken by the wind as he inspected the damage to the front of the Toyota, Maeve could clearly see his amusement.

'It's not funny…Sergeant!'

Ethan barely needed to be facing Maeve to get her response, never mind lip-read it. 'And after Emily warned you! It's lucky there's only one headlight out! Just hope feathers haven't got into the air intakes!'

Soaked once again, though not cold, they joined Emily and Gavin back in the car, where they could have a lower volume discussion.

'I veered to miss the first emu, just didn't expect a second.'

'There's almost always the mate close behind.'

'They look so light too…But that was like hitting a forty kilo Christmas turkey.'

'Yeah thanks for that, Maeve' Emily chipped in. 'You'll have lost me my deposit for sure.' She didn't sound worried, just glad they were able to keep going.

'How about you let me drive now?' Ethan suggested.

'Certainly not.' Maeve pulled away trying to remain more cautious.

'By the way, while you two were out taking a shower, a message came through from *Control*.' Emily passed her mobile back to Ethan with the message on screen. 'Do you want to try telling Gavin, or shall I give it a go?'

'You've known him for longer than me. Besides, he already hates you.' He handed it back.

'Thanks.'

'I'm not sure talking about him in front of him will be helping. What's it say?' Maeve had not caught the words.

243

'Gavin...I don't know if you can hear me...' Emily looked back to where he sat staring into Maeve's head-rest, '...but *Control* have told us that SpaceX reported finding no sign of Nathan on the moon...But we shouldn't give up. *Control* are continuing with a satellite and communications search of Earth...I'm sure he will turn up...' She didn't sound it.

'Do you *really* think SpaceX searched their moon base properly, Emily? Think about it...' Ethan put in.

'What are you getting at?'

'Well, the lad might still be on the moon...If you were stationed there and you knew that supply ships are stuffed to the gunnels and working conditions cramped, how believable would a stowaway really be?'

'Well...Not impossible...Surely.'

'*Control* might as well have told the truth that Nathan teleported in. It sounds just as credible. Those people are so busy up there, that I bet they lied about the search just to deal with the stupid request and get back to work.'

'I see your point, but Nathan would soon make himself known to someone.'

'If he could, sure.'

'We are in agreement that there is *still* hope though?'

'For now.'

'Look, up ahead.' Maeve pointed through the rain at airborne debris.

'Someone is losing their farmstead,' Ethan stated the obvious.

'Well we are in no position to help,' Emily knew there would be thousands of people across the north now suffering similar fates.

Nevertheless, Maeve turned off the highway and headed down the track towards the plume.

'Shouldn't we just keep going, to meet this Disney guy, Maeve, before the storm gets any worse?'

'That *is* his place.'

22

Disney rushed up into the garage, chased by smoke and flames. He slammed the heavy security door shut to starve the fire of additional oxygen. Then stood there for some moments trying to make sense of what had just happened and what he should do now.

He could ignore Destiny's suggestion and wait out the cyclone in his garage, but it might make more sense to head south right away. There was no telling what state the roads would be in after the full force of the storm had passed.

He put the contents of the trolley into the back of the Hilux. Next he filled up with fuel from a store of half a dozen jerry-cans, putting the left over cans in the back before closing the tailgate. Punching the remote once again to open the garage door the wind howled around the garage as he reversed out. Destiny hadn't come out of the bunker after him, and Disney wasn't about to chance going back in to rescue him.

'Serve the stupid bastard right,' he cursed his intruder.

Having second thoughts about leaving his place, Disney paused in the yard watching the destruction of his home. It felt like Mother Nature was telling him it was time to move on too. He saw a section of roof decide to leave home, shortly followed by an assortment of his lighter-weight belongings.

'This isn't even the worst of it,' Disney shook his head as the front door to the house burst in and another section of roof from the back took flying lessons.

He had a mate down in Alice Springs. He decided it made sense to head that way. He took out his mobile to call him but saw there was no signal.

'Network's down. What a surprise.'

As he put away his mobile he noticed a light in his rear-view mirror. A vehicle with one headlight out was coming down his track.

'Who the hell is this now?' He didn't get out to greet his next uninvited visitors, he just watched as they swung round in the yard and pulled up driver's window to driver's window.

The woman at the wheel lowered her window, exposing her pretty face to the lashing rain and yelled with a pleasant Irish accent 'Are you Disney?!'

He lowered his window. 'What of it?!' He had had enough of strangers for one day.

'I'm Maeve Corrigan. MI5!'

Disney's attention went from the flashed ID to the passenger behind Maeve, whose gaunt face rested against the window.

'Look lady I don't know anything about your passengers, they were just a couple of hitch-hikers caught out in the storm! I took pity on them!'

Maeve shook her head. 'I have a message from Gina Oakley for you!'

'Gina?!'

Maeve nodded. 'She said it's safe to come home now, *if* you help us. She knows you didn't have any part in the London Dirty Bombing!'

Disney seemed to go on hold for a moment as he assimilated this piece of information, then came back with 'what do you need?!'

'To get to Alice Springs!'

'Funny! I was just headed there myself! You better follow me!'

As he closed his window and pulled away, tailed by the single headlight, he grumbled 'This isn't *just* about needing to be led to Alice Springs if it involves Gina Oakley.'

The volume of the aggressive rap music had been turned up loud enough to drown out the sound of baby Otto crying, in the basement. For the parents, Dagma and Walt, this had the benefit of preventing the neighbours hearing anything. Fortunately for Otto, this also meant that his parents didn't hear the front and rear entry of four black-clad figures.

Dagma and Walt were shocked by the sudden appearance of these figures, with their body armour and helmet cams. Walt made to stand up but the muzzle of a Heckler and Koch MP7 ensured that he stayed put on the sofa with his wife.

No move was made to turn the sound down as might have been expected of the police. But as two of the masked figures turned away to search the house Walt noticed the uniforms did not say Polizei.

Shortly Otto was located in the dark, damp and dirty basement on a urine soaked rug. Switching the light on to reduce the dazzle of the trooper's torch light, Otto's situation and condition was recorded and assessed.

Removal of his filthy clothing revealed evidence of multiple bruising and cigarette burns at different stages of healing. A more thorough examination would follow. For now the trooper wrapped Otto in a blanket and exited the house with him to the unmarked SOV van waiting at the back of the property.

The camera's still recording, for posting to the Dark Net later, Dagma and Walt were made to get up from their sofa. They were marched at gunpoint down to the scene of their crimes.

The couple soon found themselves being armed with a cheese-grater each and were told that only the survivor would receive medical attention.

As the penny dropped, what was going down, Walt was first to lash out, grazing his wife's face. However, she was more tactical, being no beginner at brutality herself and kicked her husband between the legs. As he went down to his knees she rasped the grater across his neck. However, because of the amount of steroid-induced muscle there, she did not reach the jugular immediately. And so the fight to the death was on.

In the end, the blood soaked floor was littered with tattoo gratings and hair. Male bulk had won out. Walt swayed before the SOVs bleeding from every exposed area of flesh, half his scalp gone. With a nod a trooper stepped forward with a syringe and administered what Walt hoped would at least be a pain-killer. However, it was a blood-thinner.

On the way to Disney's the water crossing the floodways had been getting deeper. Now beyond Willare the floodways were looking decidedly dangerous. By the time they reached Ellendale Lake Station, the lake had swamped the highway. The choppy water lashed at the side of the vehicles.

Disney drove through the floodwater cautiously and a good job he did because checking his rear view mirror he noticed the Toyota had come to a stop some way behind. He waited for it to catch up.

When its passengers got out and started putting packs on and carrying kit, Disney concluded that their engine had got waterlogged. He changed gear and steadily reversed to meet them.

The one he had known as Gavin seemed listless and needed to be led by the other male. This male carried the biggest pack and Disney had a hunch he had had some military training by the way he held himself.

However, as Disney watched them abandon their vehicle he noticed something odd.

The rear left hand passenger door opened against the howling wind and rain, then the unidentified male shoved Gavin up and in. 'I hope you have room for four passengers and their kit, mate!'

'See what you can pack in the back!' Disney didn't get to ask what was on his mind as Ethan went to the tailgate, removed his pack and loaded it in, then turned to help the other two stow their kit.

Disney's attention turned to Gavin. 'You okay mate?'

Gavin said nothing, just sat there not even buckling himself in. He looked in desperate need of mental health support, like some cases of PTSD Disney had seen.

'Where's your boy, still in the car?'

The front passenger door and right rear passenger door both opened at the same time. The wind roared right through the interior. Something like paper was glimpsed as it was sucked outside and away across the lake. Disney couldn't think what it was. He hoped it was loose rubbish and not something of value.

'Hi. I'm Ethan,' he stuck out a hand as soon as he had his door closed.

Disney noted the firm grip. 'Where's Nathan, Ethan?'

Ethan wasn't sure how much to say, so as the two women clambered aboard he simply said 'Gone.'

'Deported?'

Emily closed the door after her and the interior became somewhat quieter.

'Yeah…He ported…So I guess they opened up to you when you gave them a lift into Broome.'

'Yes, though it sounded to me like they were lying.'

'Ha yeah, well it would wouldn't it. I'm still trying to get my head around it.'

'But what I don't get is why you lot didn't go with him?'

'What?' Ethan looked confused and wondered what exactly Gavin had told Disney. 'We can't.'

'Because you haven't finished your mission yet?'

Ethan continued to frown.

'Sorry to be a *pain*,' the voice from directly behind Disney urged, 'but can we possibly talk *as you drive*?'

'Right oh.' Disney pulled away through the water.

'That's Emily,' Ethan smiled, completing the introductions.

'Hi Emily...So what am I supposed to be helping MI5 with down in Alice Springs? Bit out of your jurisdiction isn't it?'

Maeve responded, leaning forward between the front seats. 'We haven't been fully briefed yet.'

'Gina keeping things close to her chest once again?'

'You could say that. So far the mission has been rather, let's say *unusual*.'

'Except that the unusual often *is* usual where Gina is involved. I had a bizarre experience at my ranch before you lot turned up.'

'Oh?'

'I'd only just got home and was getting stuff into my bunker to wait out the storm when I discovered some guy already in there.'

'By the looks of what was happening to your house can you blame him?'

'Well if you put it like that no, but what bugged me was that he had managed to get in there despite my security system. And...when he saw me *he* told *me* to get out.'

'So you did what he said?' Maeve couldn't believe that.

252

'Well not before I tried to get hold of him and find out how he got in there. For someone so calm this intruder could move very fast. I couldn't lay a finger on him. I don't know what aftershave he used but he smelled like a candy store. Anyway as I chased him around the bunker, a few things got knocked over, it must have shorted something out. A fire started. That's when I noticed something else weird. The automatic fire extinguishing system should have responded at the first whiff of smoke. I could hear the system pumping but nothing was coming out. It was like the nozzles had all been blocked.'

'With superglue?' Maeve offered.

'*Superglue*?'

'Never mind.'

'Maybe the intruder went into the next room, I didn't go looking. The flames spread all too quickly and there was no way I was going to get them under control. I had to get out of there...I never saw him come out.'

'Did he tell you his name?'

'Yeah, he did actually...Destiny.'

'*Destiny*? Gina has spoken of someone called Destiny,' Ethan suddenly felt Disney's description of the intruder's speed and smell was starting to add up.

'Who was he?'

'If I'm right, the truth is going to be difficult to accept.'

'Try me. We have a long journey ahead of us still.'

'Well it won't be a case of who *was* Destiny, but rather what is Destiny?...Destiny is a...um metamorph colony.'

'A *metawhaty*?'

'An alien colony of single-celled shape-shifters, which use portals to jump between time and space to do as they are bid. Destiny and Dawn are Time-Slaves, according to Gina.'

'Ha, ha ha.' You almost had me going there.

'Me too,' Emily laughed along.

Maeve sat quietly registering the internal voices, the hairs on her arms standing up.

'I'm being serious. Extra-terrestrials are *real*.'

'You're a funny guy Ethan. I had you down for ex-forces not stand-up.'

'I'm Regiment, like you Disney, except I'm still on active duty.'

'Hereford?'

'Yep.'

'So seconded to *Five*?'

'For the time being.'

'So let me get this straight. This trip is some sort of X-files adventure, *but for real*. There are aliens in Australia?'

'We don't know what we are dealing with yet,' said Maeve, 'but *you* would appear to have had a *close encounter*.'

'*Shit*. Maybe we would be better off turning around and heading back into the cyclone.'

'Seems to me, we're caught between a Spock and a harm place,' Emily's attempt at humour went unnoticed.

Half an hour later it was Gavin who broke the silence. 'Need a piss.'

Ethan was reluctant to offer help, and as they all tried to keep an eye on Gavin without watching, Ethan knew he had made the right decision to stay in the car. The gusting wind whipped the stream of urine up and added it to the rain already soaking Gavin.

Disney was tempted to drive away as Gavin made to get back aboard, the women huddling together to give Gavin even more seat room.

However, it was Ethan who cursed, as he looked at an update on his phone. 'Bollocks.'

'What is it?' asked Emily.

'The bridge at Fitzroy is down.'

'Can we go another way?' Maeve looked to Disney for local knowledge.

'Well there's the old crossing the other side of town but I would think that if the new bridge has been brought down the old one is likely already gone.'

'The report doesn't say anything about the old one,' Ethan sounded exasperated.

'There's a sign down there a way.' Maeve pointed ahead of them.

When they got to the sign and slowed right down to read it, it said Wunaamin Miliwundi National Resilience Centre.

'Just the ticket,' said Maeve. 'We could do with a resilience boost right now.'

'That's one of the Coronavirus Internment Camps,' Disney explained. 'It will have been abandoned years ago.'

'Wait,' Emily looked for something on her mobile. 'Wunaamin Miliwundi is ringing a bell with me.'

'Probably heard it mentioned as a national park area. The Wunaamin Miliwundi Ranges.' Disney suggested.

'No, no. This is something to do with one of *our* projects. Not one that I'm involved in but it's worth seeing whether we can get shelter there from this storm.'

'What do you think, Maeve?' Disney looked to her for a decision, 'Sound like a familiar MI5 project?'

'No. Emily is from a…*different* section. Let's check it out. I'm not sure there's going to be anything left of Fitzroy.'

Disney turned down the track. The sections between the many long deep puddles looked well-travelled and hard ground, not rutted mud. However, the Hilux had to ride over the top of lots of small bushes blown in their path, so it was slow going.

The track went on for some miles before it opened out onto a scene of destruction. Great swirls of construction materials were being lifted up and dropped above rows of exposed concrete foundations.

'Great,' Maeve sighed.

'Welcome to the Australian Outback,' Disney announced as the wind shoved at the Hilux for emphasis.

Emily opened her door.

'Where are you going?'

She didn't get chance to reply as the wind slammed the door shut as soon as she was out.

Through the blur of the frantic windscreen wipers they watched as Emily went across to the nearest of two ponds. She was almost blown in by a gust that seemed to throw a bush after her for good measure. She fell down on hands and knees just at the right moment to avoid the unseen projectile.

Disney saw Ethan's left hand go to the door handle in readiness to rescue her. 'You're colleague prone to suicidal acts?'

'I don't know.' Ethan tried to work out what Emily thought she was doing.

She crawled across to a big rock at the nearest corner. Then through the sheets of rain she appeared to be poking at something then waiting before leaning in for a closer look.

To everyone's amazement the water in the nearest pond was seen to start dropping fast. As if the rock had been some sort of sluice control. However, what was revealed was a ramp. As all but the continuing rain was pumped away, the ramp was seen to lead to an armoured door which began to open.

Emily excitedly waved Disney to drive down and in, as she ran down into the shelter of the hidden underground car park.

No sooner was the Hilux in behind her than the doors were closing. Looking around there were a number of other vehicles including trucks and quads but nobody was there waiting.

That all changed as a lift door opened and four armed troopers sprang out followed by a Chinese woman in a white lab coat.

'You have no authority here Miss Richards. Why have you brought these people with you?'

'To escape the storm,' she pointed upwards. 'Maybe you have *missed* what's going in above your heads.'

'There's no need to be facetious. You need to leave *immediately*.'

'No. We need to stay until the cyclone passes *then* we'll be on our way.'

'You do not have high enough clearance to enter this facility.'

'Listen, do you want me to have to explain to Miss Sturmfeld why I chose to beat ten bells of shit out of one of her *lab assistants*, in order not to die in the outback?'

Looking at the puddle spreading around Emily's feet, she had second thoughts. 'Wait here.'

The woman in the white coat returned to the lift and was gone some minutes. When she returned she was accompanied by four more troopers.

'Listen!' Emily snapped, 'you can bring your whole *fucking* security detail up here for all I care, it won't change the fact that it's a greater threat to life outside!'

'You can stay,' said the woman.

'Oh…'

'My name is Nadine. I will accompany two of you at a time, under guard, to your temporary quarters. You are to leave your belongings in your vehicle, including all electronic devices. You will each be searched before getting into the lift.'

'What about Gavin here?' Ethan asked.

'Yes, he will be searched too.'

'No. What I mean is, he suffered a blow to the head and we've been unable to provide any real medical attention.'

'We will be able to see to him below. Gavin can accompany Emily.'

As they were escorted below, Maeve shared Ethan's internal wonderings about what the hell this place was. She monitored everyone she could, to better understand what was going on

258

here. However, as she was led away next, with Disney, Ethan gave her a nod. He began a constant internal reporting of what he was seeing to keep Maeve informed the best he could.

23

The rooms Maeve and the others had been confined to were not quite hotel standard but then they weren't exactly jail cells either. They just started to feel that way after a couple of days.

Maeve agreed with Ethan's internal voice, though could not let him know this, that the cyclone could take a few days to pass. They just had to sit it out.

Though Maeve picked up on the fact that Disney had been located three doors down from her, no one else knew where any of the others were situated.

Ethan had tried yelling and thumping the walls but not even a guard came to investigate. Meals were provided three times a day. Though accompanied by guards they couldn't complain about the charitable hospitality. Their rooms had an en-suite bathroom and TV screens so that they could all keep up to date on the news and weather. The north of Australia was declared to be in a state of emergency, which might be why by day three they had still not been released.

On day four of detainment Maeve picked up on the name *Nathan*. She thought it was probably from Gavin but couldn't be certain. She hoped maybe the attention Gavin had been promised was getting somewhere with his depressive silence.

What had actually happened was that Helga Sturmfeld had arrived and taken the decision to try talking with Gavin. She had been informed that his present mental condition suggested he might be open to a different approach.

'Gavin, I don't know if you remember me. We met a long time ago. I've come to tell you that Nathan was located back in the UK a few days ago.'

She was not sure he was taking in any of what she was saying, accepting that this may all need to be repeated to him a number of times as he came out of his condition.

'We decided that rather than risk losing Nathan to space it was going to be best to take a major step with him. We tried a new laser surgery technique. We have disabled the part of his brain which seems to be linked to his teleportation. It would seem that in doing this there were consequences though.'

Gavin's eyes still seemed rather blank, as if all she was saying was *blah blah blah*.

'The problem is that Nathan sadly now seems to have lost all memory of you. He will need you to help him get that back, if that is at all possible.'

Gavin's expression remained unchanged.

'On the flight over…now that the cyclone has blown out…I told him all about you and showed him pictures too, to try to prompt recollection. I'm so sorry this has happened and hope you will forgive me for taking these measures.'

Still there was little response. So she decided to have Nathan brought in. Finally Gavin's eyes lit up at the sight of his son and they hugged. Gavin was not immediately conscious of any difference in Nathan.

A number of malnourished bears desperately held to the bars of their cages hoping for food, or better yet freedom to find food. Before them, their Chinese captor prepared something in a stewing pot. It wouldn't be long now before he did his rounds again with the big needle, harvesting the contents of their gall bladders.

Except on this day his routine was disturbed by the approach of a van. He wasn't expecting a delivery and certainly wasn't expecting *Bear Team* troopers.

He went straight for his shotgun, but their Tasers were faster.

When he regained consciousness it was he who now lay behind bars. These were not bars of a police jail though. These were cage bars. His bears were gone but their faeces were not. Some of which he had been lying in.

Then he noticed movement and turned to see one of the black clad figures. He shouted at them, that they had no right to put him in a cage and steal his animals. He also promised that they would soon very much regret their mistake, because he *knew* people.

Other figures appear on hearing the shouting and he was asked who these *people* he *knew* were?

Suddenly his threats sounded empty as he seemed to forget any names.

To help him remember, the cage door was opened. He shuffled aside, expecting to be pulled out and roughed up, but large rocks were thrown in with him, then the cage was locked again.

As they dragged him across the yard he decided he was going to be okay. Anyone who makes something heavier to drag had to be a complete idiot.

However, he didn't have much time to reflect on this, or remember valuable names as two of the figures hurled his cage into the cesspit. There it began to sink, his protests caught on video camera.

When Nathan ported away from his cell at the Broome police station, but before he decided to open his eyes, he knew he was lost.

He hadn't felt this lost since the first time he remembered waking, as a young child, out somewhere unfamiliar. Even the sounds were unusual. The good news was this wasn't the moon. The bad news was it wasn't any planet in *his* solar system.

Nathan's mind was full of questions. How had it been possible for him to teleport to somewhere that his remote-viewing had not yet reached? How could he have jumped so far beyond what might have been expected? How was he going to get home when he no longer knew in which direction home lay? And how was he going to manage to survive on an *alien* world?

He suddenly remembered watching the *Prometheus* and *Alien Covenant* films on *Sky*, even though he had known he wasn't old enough. They had scared him then, and they scared him even more now. How would he judge whether anything was safe to touch never mind consume?

Sitting up he found himself in a field of what looked like samphire but he didn't venture to put any in his mouth to taste. He became aware of a pulsing to the light. Looking up into the blue sky then he saw them, two suns spinning around one another.

'Freaky.'

A near fluorescent pink four-winged insect or bird creature, possibly disturbed by his voice, flit past him. Looking along its direction of travel then standing up on the remains of his cell's mattress and floor, Nathan spotted sea.

Across the sea was an island with a couple of hills on it. Beginning his remote-viewing sweeps, extending outward, he soon identified that the land he was on was also an island.

Stepping off the circle of concrete floor he decided to head to the beach, scanning around for movement.

In the days ahead, he discovered that this planet was peppered with islands. He also discovered that not only was he not alone, he shared the planet with two other humans. He just had to investigate and headed in their direction. By some further coincidence these humans, a man and a woman actually appeared to speak English. They lived on a barge called *Obsession*.

On day five Emily was surprised to see Helga appear at her door, with no guards.

'Miss Sturmfeld?'

'Come, my dear. I have something to show you.'

Emily followed the head of the SOVs out of her room. 'I was told this facility was beyond my clearance.'

'It was. However, I have decided to raise your clearance level. I need your help with something which has now become even more important than your previous assignment.'

'I don't understand. Are you saying I'm no longer assigned to Nathan?'

'Nathan became a major opportunity for us when, unlike those babies we *lost*, *he* survived porting from *his* mother. Nevertheless, the challenge of finding out how he was *able* to teleport would now appear to be lost to us.'

'Are you saying you have given up looking for Nathan?'

'I'm saying that our focus now has to move to plan B.'

'Right…A different approach.'

'Exactly…In our fight against criminals, I knew early on that this day may sadly come and that we should somehow bank what we had.'

'*Bank*? I don't follow.'

'With the ability to control teleportation and remote-viewing, Nathan would have been able to identify and kill a violent criminal in seconds. Or longer, if need be.'

Emily knew Nathan was looked upon as a weapon, but now something else occurred to her. 'Are you saying you are looking to make *other* vigilantes redundant?'

'Not redundant so much as better *supported*. Anyone with remote-viewing could inform a team where to go better than any satellite system that we presently have. And having that same person able to teleport would of course have meant a near instant response time.'

'Sure but he's just a kid.'

'A growing kid.' Helga opened a door and led Emily down another corridor.

They could both hear what sounded like a school sports hall.

'They will be playing a game of five aside football I expect.'

'*They*?' Emily followed Helga to a balcony.

However, as Helga got sight of the activity below, enthusiasm turned to disappointment. She clapped her hands crossly and shouted 'Stop this at once!'

Emily was far more than disappointed. 'What the *Fuck*?!'

Nathan found some of the fruit which he had seen the couple eating. It could be found growing on large spineless cacti-like plants at the top edge of beaches. It tasted like nothing he had tasted before, neither sweet nor tart. He supposed it was okay but wouldn't want to eat a lot of it. Nevertheless, these fruits did keep him hydrated.

Other things he saw the couple eat seemed to involve a period of cooking, but without his survival belt he had no immediate means of making fire. Nothing seemed dry enough to make an ember with and what he saw the couple burn on their barge stove seemed to rely on natural oils from the plants.

On occasions he watched the couple catch flying fish creatures in nets off the side of the barge. He thought these looked like the insect bird he had seen on his first day there. These were gutted and stewed.

Out of desperation, as Nathan crossed between islands he caught one of these with a quick snatch of a hand. Biting into it he heard the creature's pitiful squeal and decided that the taste of its raw flesh was pure punishment. He used the remainder of that swim to the neighbouring beach to rinse his mouth out.

The sea was not as salty as seas on Earth and there was an oily sheen on the surface which seemed both beautiful and polluted at the same time. There were no tides to the sea because this planet had no moon. The sea ought to have been stagnant from a lack of tidal current yet somehow life had found a way of creating a means of movement.

There was air movement, from thermal changes, which caused ripples but he hadn't witnessed any storms anywhere on the planet. It didn't rain so much as become very humid and misty, as the suns went down, the mist condensing on the cooler surfaces of plants and rocks.

The nights were quite cool but his environment suit plus the curtain he still wore were able to keep him warm enough. Although he had found it difficult to sleep the first couple of nights because of the flying fish insects singing, he got used to it.

The only predators he saw lived in the sea and did not come out onto land. Whenever he crossed between islands, sometimes having to swim quite some distance, he would check that none of these predators were close by before he set off. He had only watched them eating smaller creatures but didn't fancy taking any chances.

He was glad of the boots he continued to wear as the rocks on the beach had rough edged, possibly from thermal cracking and a lack of wave action. The sand, he decided, might be the result of creatures eating coralline organisms like the parrotfish on earth which consumed the polyps and excreted sand.

Some rocks were a conglomerate of beautiful crystals, which Nathan was, at times, tempted to try and knock loose and collect. However, Nathan remained focussed on making his way to where the couple were still moored. He hoped they would not move off before he got to them. He still had quite a journey ahead of him.

The seven year-old clones stopped hitting one another and looked up at the balcony.

'Do you know who I am?'

'Yes Miss Sturmfeld.' Their chorus of responses suggested neither shame nor obedience, only recognition.

'Where is Miss Tomkins?'

'Gone to the toilet Miss.'

It sounded like a recital to Emily. She was still trying to get her head around what she was seeing.

'Come on. Best we get down there.' Helga beckoned Emily to follow. 'When we proved we could clone Nathan successfully I put plans in place for a larger number to be created.'

'I see,' Emily followed Helga back down the corridor to a staircase.

'They were provided programming in terms of history and morals on top of general education. But the problem was always their socialisation. They really needed to receive parental guidance and to be able to mix with ordinary children. But we couldn't risk that because they had to remain secret. As a result they are somewhat *unstable*, prone to random acts of violence, as you saw, even against one another.'

'So they are sociopathic, as opposed to psychopathic, then?'

'I'm afraid so. It was proposed that we try other forms of media programming, and more team oriented activities. But team sports seem to lead to frustrations. They are so equally matched that it is nearly impossible for them to score points other than by chance and that frustration leads to outbursts of violence. I'm hoping that you may come up with a solution.'

'I hope so too.'

As they got to the bottom of the stairs Helga saw the PE Instructor. 'Miss Tomkins. You left the boys unsupervised.'

'Yes, sorry Miss Sturmfeld. I think one of them managed to spike my drink or food or something. I have a funny tummy again. Those Gnats are too fast and crafty by half.'

'Well they have been trained that way since they were four.' Helga turned to Emily. 'Like their eleven year-old sibling they have all been regularly training in assassin techniques which will make them effective vigilantes.'

Before Emily could respond to this the three of them arrived in the sports hall and were immediately confronted by the clones.

'We want to go out into the outside world, but *she* says we are not allowed out yet, that only *you* can let us go.'

'Well I don't believe you are ready for that step yet,' Helga asserted.

'Yes we *are*!'

Emily sensed a tantrum coming.

Maeve lay on her bed tuning in to any internal monologues within the facility, as she had the previous days of detainment.

She only had the TV on for headlines. The local headlines were not good. Broome and Port Hedland among other places looked like they had been blown away by a bomb blast.

There came a knock on the door then the sound of a key-card being inserted, just like there had been when a meal arrived. However, this was not mealtime.

Nadine entered. Behind her, standing in the corridor either side of the door, Maeve could just make out shoulders of Nadine's armed escort.

'It is time for you all to go, Miss Corrigan.'

'Oh, at last,' Maeve got off the bed, and with no belongings of her own to bring with her she headed past Nadine to the door.

She looked both relaxed and relieved to be exiting her room. This made it all the more surprising, as she came level with the guards that she burst into action. The previous night, appearing to be asleep face down, she had unscrewed a strip of metal from the back of her bedframe in preparation for such a situation.

Twisting to the left first she planted the strip of metal in the neck of one guard causing blood to spray over her from his jugular. Spinning to the right she hammered her elbow into the windpipe of the second guard. The blow was so forceful it crashed his helmeted head off the wall and left him chocking on crushed cartilage.

Maeve had picked up on Nadine's internal voice minutes before. She had been given a kill ordered and intended to carry it out.

She was reaching under her white coat for her Glock as Maeve turned. However, Maeve was faster. Kicking out and up, the ball of her left foot caught Nadine under the chin. The whiplash could be heard snapping the neck and she was dead before she hit the floor.

Maeve, checked for a pulse, none. Then tearing open the white coat she removed the Glock, also taking Nadine's two spare clips and security pass from around her oddly angled limp neck.

Turning her attention back to the guards they were still alive but would not be for long. One was bleeding out, the other suffocating. Maeve quickly removed their weapons and security passes as she had done with Nadine.

With the detainment rooms likely under CCTV surveillance it came as no surprise to hear more SOV guards approaching fast. She knew she did not have long if she was going to set her plan in motion.

Maeve went straight to Disney's room, Nadine's security pass in one hand an MP7 in the other.

24

Disney was immediately on alert on hearing the key-card at the door with no prior knock. It had followed the sound of a scuffle further down the corridor. He had been out of the Regiment for some years now but his training never really left him. It had been second nature for a long time and been a life-saver on a number of occasions.

Nevertheless, he had not expected to see Maeve there, throwing him an MP7.

He caught the weapon and released the safety as he sped to back her up. 'What's going on?'

'We've got to get Ethan, Emily and Gavin, hopefully in that order and try getting out of here. There is a kill order on us.'

Disney noticed the blood on Maeve and looking down the corridor spotted the two dying guards. 'I'm not surprised, if you've been beating up the hosts.'

Maeve handed him two spare magazines and a security pass. 'Here comes more trouble.'

Using the door frame for cover, Maeve dropped to a crouch, with Disney taking the higher firing position. The firefight lasted only seconds before four guards soon lay dead in the open corridor.

'You get their weapons and passes, I'll try for Ethan,' Maeve commanded as she got up, flexing and rubbing at her right shoulder where a round had winged her.

'You okay?'

'Just a graze...Let's go.' A few steps away she started calling, 'Ethan?!'

She remembered that Ethan had self-reported his attempts to attract attention which she had been unable to hear. She spotted a fire-door leading to another corridor.

'Through here,' she pushed on the door just as Disney reached her. He had the additional weapons slung over his shoulders and magazines shoved down his trousers. 'Ethan?!'

'Maeve?' A muffled response came from a few doors further along.

Reaching the door Maeve inserted Nadine's pass but the door remained locked.

'Shit. They've already deactivated her pass.' Maeve tried the spare she had taken from a guard. 'Bollocks. Disney hand me another pass.'

'Here y'go.'

'No good. Give me a newer one!'

'What?'

'One you've just taken.'

'Oh.'

This one worked and Ethan was there, ready.

'Right, Disney has your weapons.'

'What's the plan, Boss?' Ethan asked taking possession of two MP7's and spare clips.

'We're on the third floor. We need to find Emily and Gavin and get the hell up and out of here.'

'We shouldn't chance the lift though, Maeve, but I didn't notice stairs when I was brought here. I think we're going to need to take out their security control room.'

'Agreed,' Disney confirmed.

Sounds of an approach could be heard.

'Right well I have no idea where that is. Looks like Emily and Gavin will have to wait out for extraction 'til we take control, if we can. I have no clue how big this place is.'

'But Emily might…Emily!' Ethan yelled.

There was no response from Emily or Gavin in that corridor, and Maeve was picking up nothing.

At that moment further troopers arrived. More than four this time, from both ends of the corridor.

'Stay between Disney and me,' Ethan told Maeve.

'Get another door open if you can,' Disney suggested.

Maeve wasn't keen. 'We can't afford to get pinned down in a room.'

'Just for cover.'

As Ethan took out two troopers with head-shots Maeve got a door open. Ducking back behind a fire-door to escape Ethan's sharp shooting one of the troopers got hit in the back as Ethan shot through the hinge gap, then stepped sideways into the cover of the open doorway.

Disney shot out the lights in their corridor to shroud them in darkness. Then firing paused as rounds needed to be conserved.

The one remaining trooper in their intended direction of travel peered round their fire-door to check out the situation. He received a round through his left goggle.

'Right...On me.' Ethan dashed for the cleared end of the corridor.

As Disney brought up the rear he saw the other fire-door swinging open and opened fire, running backwards. This was not an idea firing technique, nevertheless a trooper fell away, the door closing again.

As the threesome passed through the door, Disney took up a defensive position. He pulled one dead trooper on top of another to take enemy rounds like sandbags, dropping behind them.

Ethan and Maeve grabbed more clips and passes.

'Emily?!' This time it was Maeve calling but there was still no response. 'Okay, go.'

They jogged down the corridor to a junction. Taking up position either side of the corridor they checked out both directions.

More troopers sounded to be headed towards them from the left. 'Trouble's in this direction. On me.' Ethan headed into it.

Half way down the corridor they reached a stairwell the clattering of boots they had heard was coming up.

'You thinking what I'm thinking, Ethan?' Maeve glanced round the corner.

'Security control is in the basement?' Disney offered.

'Makes sense to me,' Ethan nodded and descended the steps quietly, two at a time, confident in the advantage of their higher ground.

The advancing troopers were close, almost upon them. They stopped on the half-landing hidden by the central column which might have contained a lift or ventilation shaft.

Disney continued to guard the rear as Ethan and Maeve brought their weapons to bear round the corner. They gave no warning, immediately opening fire. This time Ethan was crouched and Maeve standing behind him.

The six advancing troopers had upped their game. They were kitted out with gas masks and preparing to use gas grenades. This did not stop the two streams of rounds penetrating collars and goggles, starting with the troopers at the rear to prevent retreat.

It was over in seconds, but not for Disney. Two troopers from the firefight back in the corridor had now caught up with them and came charging down the stairs.

Disney swung his MP7 round low and hard catching the troopers across the legs and bringing them down sprawling over the landing. Disney wasn't finished with them though. Taking his Glock he grabbed the nearest by the back of the neck lifting him just high enough to witness what came next.

Disney aimed the Glock at the face of the second trooper, it was a young woman. He pulled the trigger, without a seconds thought.
Then he placed the Glock against the temple of the head he had in his vice-like grip.

'Now…If you want to live a little longer than your buddy, you will take us to this facility's security control centre.'

'Disney!' Maeve had turned in time to also witness the cold blooded killing.

'If we want to get out of here alive, we can't afford to be squeamish.'

'He's not wrong, Maeve.' Ethan agreed before turning his attention back to the massacre on the steps below. He picked his way through the bodies removing three undamaged masks and a number of grenades.

Disney took a pair of cuffs off the live trooper and cuffed him then prodded him forward, taking what was on offer from Ethan as they passed.

Maeve sighed then followed, also taking mask and grenades from Ethan, and kitting up.

There were no further attacks however and the trooper, wishing to remain alive, took them to the control centre. He knew they would not be able to get in. The lock on the door was pin coded not a key-card lock.

'What's the code?' Disney asked, placing the Glock at the base of the young man's neck.

'I don't know.'

Disney pushed the weapon hard, grazing skin.

'I don't know! I don't know!'

'I don't think he knows,' Maeve said calmly. 'Let me try something.'

The trooper flinched wondering what *she* might do to him but Maeve pushed past and hammered on the door.

'Open up! Government Agents!'

The four of them heard the laughter from within, bringing a smile to the trooper's face.

Maeve tried again. 'What's the password?!'

'Go fuck yourself!' was the clear response.

Nevertheless, it was the unspoken response that Maeve was listening for.

With a nod to Ethan and Disney she took a gas grenade. They copied though were frowning behind their masks.

Maeve typed in a code, the door buzzed, she kicked it wide and as gunfire spat out she threw her grenade, followed by those of the other two.

As the smoke billowed out and the gunfire was replaced by the sound of coughing, Disney asked 'How did you work that out?'

'Would you believe a lucky guess?'

Ethan laughed.

Even before the ventilation system had all the gas removed, Maeve, Ethan and Disney had the two occupants, like the still living trooper, disarmed and cuffed face down on the floor.

The door was closed. If they had intended to remain in the centre for long they would have sought to change the key code but time was of the essence.

Maeve helped the young woman to her feet. 'We want to get out of here, and I'm sure you want us gone too. So let's work towards a win-win outcome, okay?'

The woman nodded.

'Right...We need to get to Emily Richards and Gavin Purnell, who came here with us.'

'I'm not sure that's going to be possible.'

'Don't lie to me. You have had all of us under surveillance since we arrived.'

'That's not what I mean. *You* are the least of our worries right now.'

'Look!' called Ethan, pointing at a screen on the other side of the room, 'There's Emily now.'

As she passed close to a camera it was clear that her nose was bleeding and she had a cut and swollen lip. She had two troopers on her heels.

'Where is that?' Maeve urged the woman.

'That corridor leads past here.'

'Ethan.'

He didn't waste a second. No sooner was he in the corridor than he spotted her.

Running towards her it all happened so fast. He began to raise his MP7, she began to raise a hand, and he threw his Glock for her to catch. Then as the Glock was still in mid-air he double-tapped the troopers coming up behind her.

The Glock hit Emily in the chest and bounced off to the side.

'What did you do that for, you *idiot*!'

'You were meant to catch it!'

'I was raising my hand to say *hold fire*!'

'What?'

Emily turned to look down at the two bodies. There was nothing to be done for them now.

'They were on *our* side!'

'How was *I* to know?!'

'I guess the fact that they had a clear shot at my back and were *not* firing!'

'Well, since you put it like that…'

'Where are the others?'

'We haven't located Gavin yet, but Maeve and Disney are in the control centre.'

Emily rubbed at her chest, picked up the Glock, stepped back took an MP7 and spare clips off one of the dead troopers then followed Ethan.

As the two of them entered the control room and closed the door, Maeve announced 'I've located Gavin. We just need to go get him and get out of here.'

'We can't,' Emily shook her head.

'Why not?'

'There is something we absolutely *must* to do first.'

'What?'

'We have to kill *all* of the children.'

25

Maeve stared at Emily in disbelief. 'What do you mean, *kill all of the children*?'

'Seven year-old clones of Nathan. Only these are nothing like him. These are complete sociopaths, very fast and strong for their age. They killed Helga Sturmfeld, right in front of me. Then turned on me and their PE instructor. Sturmfeld told me she had had them all training as assassins.'

'*Really*?'

'Nathan's genes are not all human.'

'That's the problem we have been trying to deal with,' said the restrained woman beside Maeve, her lips oddly still like she was practicing ventriloquism.

'Can't we just lock them down? I really don't think I could kill a child.'

'I could,' offered Disney coldly.

'Me too,' Ethan nodded.

'How many are there?' asked Maeve.

'Ten,' Emily said with certainty.

'Ha. *I wish*,' said the cuffed woman again looking like she had something wrong with her lips. 'Try one hundred and one.'

'A hundred and one?!' Maeve's heart sank. '*Nightmare*.'

'A hundred and one abominations,' Ethan tried to make light of their situation.

'So, *again*, why can't we lock them down?' Maeve turned to the security personnel for answers.

'They've been to their dormitories and told the others,' said a man on the floor, also oddly keeping his lips as still as he could. 'They'll be preparing to fight it out now with any non-clone.'

'But why didn't you lock their dormitories down, for heaven's sake?!'

'I tried that but they have Miss Sturmfeld's pass, and *that* cannot be over-ridden.'

'So we need to find which one of them has that and get it back.'

'I guess so.'

'Get up, all of you.' Maeve waited for them to get to their feet. 'The way I see it we all want to get out of this alive and to do that we need to work together. Agreed?'

The security staff and trooper nodded.

'Okay then. Get their cuffs off.'

Disney and Ethan did so but didn't stop keeping an eye on them.

'Is there any abort plan for this cloning programme?'

The man lifted a hand to cover his mouth. 'Not the programme, as such...But the facility can be set to self-destruct.'

'What's with the hand covering the mouth and these ventriloquism acts?'

'We have reason to believe that along with the clones ability to *remote-view* they have learned to lip-read.'

'Hell.'

'No. Hell will be if they ever learn to teleport.'

Maeve covered *her* mouth now. 'Okay, so the self-destruct...I guess that is on a timer and is set from here?'

'Yes and no.'

'Don't talk in riddles, we haven't time.'

'The self-destruct can be *primed* from here but the timer is set from a key-pad outside.'

'The one in the false rock?' asked Emily from behind her hand.

'Yes, once everyone who needs to be out is out. That way there is no need to beat the clock in getting out, hopefully avoiding any stress-induced mistakes, and gives a full ten minutes to get beyond the blast radius.'

'What if we get out and just lock the clones in for a better supported team to sort out?' Maeve asked hopefully.

The security man shook his head. 'The clones will work out how to get out before that could be organised. Their problem solving skills are through the roof, not to mention their ability to kill. It has been like being with a ticking time-bomb working in this facility. I told Miss Sturmfeld my concerns on a number of occasions. *She* should have listened. I cannot stress enough how unlike human seven year-olds they are, and the older one is even brighter.'

'The *older* one?'

'Yes. The one Miss Sturmfeld put in with Gavin. He is eleven.'

'Shit!' Emily didn't think much for Gavin's chances now. She looked to the screen where Gavin was seen lying on his bed watching the TV but could see no sign of the older clone. 'We need to get to him now.'

'I agree *but first* set that primer,' Maeve ordered the woman next to her. 'I need to give a sit-rep to the UK. Where are my belongings, still in the Hilux?'

'No. Everyone's phones were brought down here and put in separate shielded zip-lock bags to prevent tracing. They're in the locker over here,' the man stepped across and opened it for them. 'However, you won't get a signal down here. You'll need to use this terminal here.'

'Okay, thanks,' Maeve got straight down to reporting to Gina.

Ethan raised another question. 'What if we *don't* make it to the outer key-pad? Shouldn't we have a back-up timer?'

'There isn't that option, sorry,' said the woman still setting the self-destruct primer.

'Umber!' Ethan cursed, knowing how crucial it now was that none of the clones escaped.

Shortly the woman turned to address everyone in the room. 'We cannot afford to let any of the clones learn the code.'

'Obviously,' agreed Maeve as she sent the sit-rep.

The woman recited the sixteen digit code like a credit card number, still with a hand over her mouth.

'Right then, lead the way to Gavin's room, please,' Maeve prompted the two security staff and trooper to head out first. She and Emily followed with Ethan and Disney bringing up the rear.

Ethan closed the control room door as he was last out. He was glad that no one had spoken the key-code for it. He hoped that none of the clones had ever *remote-viewed* the code being punched in.

When they reached the stairs they fully expected to be ambushed. Going up in a hurry the SOVs looked back at Ethan, Disney and Maeve taking care to be quiet.

The woman waved for them to hurry. 'There's no point trying to quiet. They will be watching us right now. Imagine being surrounded by their out-of-body ghosts and you won't be far wrong.'

'Shit.' The more Disney heard the less he liked.

They heard screams from adults as they passed the catering and entertainment level but the anticipated stairwell ambush did not happen. However, as they all exited back onto the accommodation level they could hear bursts of gunfire from multiple weapons then it went quiet. They did not go to check the outcome but pressed on for Gavin's room.

Turning a corner, the man from security control stopped in his tracks and tried to jump back but collided with those following. He struggle to get back but was not quick enough. A throwing star caught him in the chest and he collapsed aside dead.

'Poison-tipped shuriken!' the trooper warned, tucking in close to the wall and opening up with his MP7 on full-auto, joined by Ethan.

The sounds of children squealing with the pain of rounds tearing through their bodies was nothing less than sickening but it simply had to be ignored.

Disney took a gas grenade and pulled the pin ready to throw it round the corner, but the woman from security control grabbed Disney's arm and yelled over the gunfire, 'Put the pin back in or you'll be giving them yet another advantage!'

'What?!' Disney replaced the pin staring at the woman for an explanation.

She leaned in close to his ear, 'They can function without breathing for a significant time. They are immune to this gas and many other toxins, including what's on the throwing stars. And don't forget, the fog of gas will obstruct our view not theirs!'

'Fuck, lady, what have you people done here?!'

'I've been asking myself the same question for some years, but this isn't the sort of job you get to *leave!*'

The trooper took a shuriken between the eyes and fell forward to the floor. Maeve quickly took position on the floor using his body for cover.

'I'm out!' Yelled Ethan, pulling back to get another clip in as Emily took his place dropping to a crouch where the trooper had been. Disney took the position above her.

As Ethan loaded a fresh clip he noticed clones coming up from the rear dressed similarly like little ninjas.

They moved so fast he could barely respond in time. 'Behind us!'

Disney turned one-eighty and dropped to a lower firing position opening up. They were cornered. He moved his head just in time but felt a shuriken skim his hair.

'Clear!' yelled Emily immediately taking position on the other side of the corner, then opening up again with her MP7.

Maeve scrambled up off the floor, almost stumbling over the dead trooper. Something hit her heel. She looked down to see a shuriken embedded in the tread of her boot. She scuffed it loose and took up a new firing position, then yelling to Ethan and Disney, 'Move!'

Disney followed by Ethan retreated round the corner. As they started laying down fire again, Maeve turned to the woman from security control. 'Which room is Gavin's?!'

'D18. I'll show you. It's just down here!'

'We're moving!' Maeve announced.

'We'll cover!' Ethan replied, 'Shout when you have a new safe position!'

Maeve charged after the woman from security control who wasn't wasting any time.

However, as the woman forged ahead through the litter of dead bodies, two rose up from playing dead. One of them cut her leg with a shuriken before she realised she had walked into a trap.

As the woman collapsed, Maeve opened up on the two clones. Then with tears in her eyes, almost gagging, she proceeded to deliver head shots to each body she reached, hoping that was enough.

Reaching the woman's body Maeve removed the lanyard from round her neck. Then, placing a fresh clip into her Glock, she continued with the head shots beyond Gavin's room until the corridor was definitely clear. Next she checked to see if any of the clones had Helga's security pass. They didn't.

The firing back at the corner stopped.

'Watch for any playing dead there!' she called back, 'and check for Helga's security pass!'

Slipping the key-card into the lock for B18 she pushed the door wide, staying in the corridor, to one side of the doorframe, she saw what looked like Gavin giving Nathan a piggy-back.

The older clone had his legs wrapped around Gavin's waist and an arm around his neck. Gavin looked both confused and embarrassed. The clone held what looked like a flattened paper cup in his free hand.

'I've come to get you both out of this place,' Maeve was winging it. This was clearly going to be a tricky situation to resolve.

Gavin tried to say something but the clone's grip on his neck was too tight. Gavin looked unsteady on his feet.

'No you haven't! I've seen what you have done to some of my brothers.'

'*They* were out of control,' Maeve tried to reason.

The sound of a series of single shots came from down the corridor as Ethan, Emily and Disney secured the area.

'And *you're* not?' the clone scoffed.

'You're *older*. You are better able to reason. You want out of this place don't you? To see the real world up there?'

'We've *seen* the real world. We just haven't got our hands on it yet.'

'Well, if we work together...'

'You'll never win!' the clone said with a smile.

As Emily, Ethan and Disney reached the door and Maeve took a step inside the room, the clone drew the scored edge of the paper cup across Gavin's neck.

'No!' Maeve rushed forward as the paper cut deep. Gavin's expression went from confused to hopeless, as blood began pumping over the still smiling boy's arm.

The clone lowered his feet to the floor in an instant, preparing to pounce on Maeve as Gavin fell away, but a round from Ethan took him between the eyes. The clone followed Gavin to the floor.

Maeve reached Gavin. Kneeling down on the floor, she raised his head to better seal the wound but there was nothing more any of them could do.

'What's...happening,' Gavin's eyes were rolling. 'Where's Nathan?'

'It's okay Gavin. Everything is going to be okay. You're going to see Nathan right now. Just you rest. You'll see him soon.'

The others hung back, not wanting to crowd Gavin as he bled out.

Disney stepped back into the corridor to check for movement.

Maeve felt the last of the pulse go. Then after a moment's silence tried to lift Gavin's limp form.

'What are you doing?' asked Emily.

'We have to take him with us.'

'I don't think we *can*, Maeve.' Ethan reasoned. 'It's going to be difficult enough trying to get out of here alive without attempting to extract Gavin...Sorry mate,' he added for Gavin's sake.

Reluctantly Maeve nodded.

The five of them moved out heading for the way out.

Maeve turned to Disney, 'I want you to know, whatever happens, I'm sorry I got you into this mess.'

'Naa. Best fun I've had in years. Anyway, I'm doing this for Gina.'

'Thanks.'

Passing through a fire-door they could hear a child crying.

As Maeve turned a corner she saw a clone in what looked like a hospital gown sitting in the corridor with his back against the wall. His little hands were rubbing at his eyes.

'What's wrong?' Maeve asked as she cautiously closed in, looking out for any others that might be hiding nearby.

'The *others* hate me.'

'Why?'

'They say I'm *different*. I've tried to be like them.'

'Well I'm glad you're *not*.'

'*Are you*?' The clone seemed to cheer up somewhat.

'Sure. Maybe you'd like to come with us?'

'*Really*?' the clone blinked back tears and broke into a smile.

It occurred to Maeve that they might be able to use this boy's *remote-viewing* to scan for any clone ambushes and more importantly to tell them which of the clones had Helga's security pass. She offered a friendly hand.

'No!' Emily warned as the clone leaned forward to take the offered hand, reaching behind his back for the shuriken pressed against the wall.

Emily raised her weapon but was too late. The clone clawed the teeth of his poisoned weapon over Maeve's exposed wrist before the round from Emily's weapon entered his head.

Maeve came down hard on her backside, struggling against the neurotoxin to catch her last breath. 'God…'

'Come on Emily, we've got to go,' Ethan urged.

'Coming,' Emily bent down and took the working security pass off Maeve.

Reaching the lift Ethan turned to Emily again. 'You know more about this place than either Disney or I, so is there a stairs we can take instead of risking the lift?'

'Not that I know of.'

'*Alright* then.' Ethan pressed the button and stepped back.

All three of them raised their weapons in preparation for a lift full of ninjas. As the door opened it appeared to be empty. They checked there were no clones hiding on the ceiling then they entered.

Disney hit the garage button and the doors closed. The lift began to rise, but only went half a floor up before it stopped. Disney tried the button again but nothing happened.

'They've got into the control room.' Emily stated the obvious.

The sound of childish laughter came through the speakers in the lift. The three of them raised their weapons to the ceiling thinking it might have come from there.

'Through the hatch it is then.' Ethan jumped, pushing the hinged tile up and back. Three MP7s pointed at the exit but no heads appeared.

Slinging his weapon over his shoulder, Ethan gripped the edge of the hatch and with a helping hand from Disney climbed up and out.

Checking that the lift shaft was clear first, Ethan helped Emily up next then Disney.

With Ethan taking the lead the three of them went up the ladder, half expecting the lift to start back up and come after them.

Shortly they reached the garage level and Ethan opened the cover for the manual crank and started opening the lift doors. Below him on the ladder both Emily and Disney took aim at the widening gap between the doors.

Seeing or hearing nothing untoward, as soon as the gap was wide enough to climb through, Ethan stopped cranking and climbed into the garage. From a crouched position, ready to jump back through the gap, Ethan looked around. Still no movement or sound of breathing he turned and helped Emily out of the shaft then Disney.

'Looks like we made it,' said Disney heading across the garage to his Hilux.

'Sure does,' Emily was relieved, but knew the time to celebrate was not yet. Maybe once they had the garage door closed behind them, the self-destruct code in the exterior key-pad, and were high-tailing it out of there.

Emily hoped the security pass she had in her hand was going to work. She did not relish the idea of having to go looking for Helga's missing pass.

As she lifted the pass, metres from the door lock she heard a thump and turned around.

Disney lay on the floor beside his car, a shuriken protruding from the back of his skull. There was no sign where it had come from.

Emily felt fear gripping her then it was Ethan, grabbing her and launching her the rest of the way towards the lock.

He lifted the pass to the scanner.

It didn't work.

Then came the laughter from the shadows. Not one young voice but many.

Then a single taunting voice from the shadows said, 'looking for this?'

More childish laughter followed.

Ethan didn't want to give up but things now looked pretty hopeless. There was no cover. They were cornered.

They both opened up with their weapons hoping to cause a clone or two to move and reveal themselves. However, *they* were too smart for that and too well hidden.

'I'm out!' Announced Emily.

'Out, or out out?!'

'Out out!'

Ethan's MP7 clicked on an empty chamber. He patted himself down for a spare clip. 'Me too.'

The clones started to appear, edging forward, throwing stars in hand. There were dozens of them, excited for the kill.

Ethan and Emily's Glocks had both been emptied earlier ensuring that downed clones were definitely dead.

'Any ideas, Ethan? Now would be a good time.'

'*Yeah*…Only the one.'

'What?'

He kissed her full on the lips.

'Ah, see…You *do* love me.'

'Oh fuck off,' he smiled with his eyes.

26

Adam and Penelope were out foraging with the *Obsession* moored some metres out in a bay, its sticky-nets up to catch *fliers*.

Adam was gathering *fuel-fruit* from the upper edge of the beach. It was less effort to gather than digging up *coal-bulbs*. Though the fruit did not last as long as the bulbs their oils did make them burn hotter. In fact it was *fuel-fruit* oil which powered the *Obsession*.

Penelope was collecting veg. Some of it was more suited for dessert like the rainbow crusts which grew in damp crevices under rocks, which she had named *sweet-lichen*. But today she was after the rarer *frog-spawn*, a protein rich seed-head on one type of spineless cacti, which grew just beyond the beach. It could be eaten uncooked but was a little less bitter if boiled for ten minutes.

Between them, Adam and Penelope had agreed names for many things around their planet *Maroon*; A planet which was still strange to them and largely unexplored, since being left there by Time-Slaves.

Penelope looked back towards Adam. She liked to keep tabs on him. He had a habit of wandering off and after all this time she still didn't fully trust this world. They still came across new things from time to time. However, they had never yet come across any really dangerous predator. Even the *sea-discus* which fed on the *fliers*, a kind of electric ray, showed no interest in humans.

From Adam she glanced toward their barge then something unusual caught her eye, something out at sea splashing. It looked much larger than a *sea-discus* and it was heading towards their bay. For a moment it almost looked like a person swimming, but Penelope dismissed the idea. She and Adam were the only ones on the planet and besides, whatever this was it was surely far too fast to be a person.

'Adam?!' she moved to the edge of the beach pointing. 'There's some strange animal swimming into the bay!'

Adam stopped what he was doing and looked out to sea. He also thought it looked like an extremely fast swimmer. He had never seen anything like it.

Penelope came to join Adam, who had now ventured down to the water's edge. They watched as the animal stopped swimming stood up. It was a boy. He waded towards them, wiping the water from his face.

In a Brummie accent he began 'Sorry to disturb you both…'

'Have you come to take us home at last, Destiny?' Adam wasn't shocked by what he was seeing or hearing, after all that he had seen over the years.

'Sorry, what?'

'Oh, is that *you* Dawn?'

'I don't understand. I'm Nathan. Nathan Purnell.' He offered an elbow. He had never shaken hands with anyone, having grown up post-plandemic.

Adam and Penelope frowned at his offered elbow, which he lowered with a shrug.

'We thought you were one of the metamorph Time-Slaves who marooned us here,' said Penelope.

'Especially since you seem to have taken the form of a younger version of a close friend of mine,' added Adam.

'Urr…*Not* Ben McGregor?'

'Yes, *Ben*. Do you know him, or maybe his son *Robbie*?'

'No but someone else recently compared me to Ben, a guy going by the name of Disney.'

'Yes, *Disney*. Ben used to talk about him; an SAS colleague.'

'Disney helped my father and I…Before we got arrested and I ended up here.'

'Through a portal?' Penelope ventured.

'I urr…guess you could call it that.'

'Time-Slaves then,' Penelope nodded like she knew all about it. 'I was trapped in a chest freezer and the bottom fell through dumping me here.'

Nathan wondered if this woman had simply gone stir-crazy doing time here.

'I don't remember much about how I got here,' Adam put in. 'I remember being on a camping trip with a hypnotherapist called Candice, on Skye, and then coming round on a beach lying on a mass of sopping wet peat. How about you?'

'Oh, a large chunk of cell floor and a section of mattress.'

'Right,' Adam nodded, that made just as much sense. 'So were you told to come and find us?'

'*Told* to? No.'

'So you've come across us purely by chance?'

'Not…exactly.' Nathan paused wondering whether he should open up to this couple. What could go wrong? They didn't seem a threat. 'I have been watching you for some days.'

'Oh…well you should have introduced yourself sooner then, dear,' Penelope chuckled at the thought of Nathan being shy. Shyness was not something she had ever suffered from, previously having been a TV presenter in the US.

'I couldn't get here any sooner. I was a long way away.'

'But you…'

'I have what is called *remote-viewing*. I can see everywhere on this planet, from here.'

'I don't understand.'

'If you close your eyes and imagine a place you have been. I can do that with my eyes open but what *I'm* seeing is the actual place and time, not my imagination. I don't even need to have visited there yet.'

'*Wow*. So what is happening back home? I'd love to know.'

'So would I. I can't see it anymore. Do you know which direction earth is? Maybe I could try focussing.'

'Sorry lad, the stars are all different here.'

'Yes I'd noticed, especially the twin suns.'

'Yes they are quite something aren't they? They are slowly tumbling as well as spinning. When they align with our planet's orbit that is as close as we get to a winter here.'

'It's very strange that I have appeared here. I had expected to end up on the moon. I don't understand how I could end up somewhere that I have never even *remote-viewed* before.'

'Time-Slaves. *Definitely*.' Penelope insisted.

'I don't know any *Time-Slaves*. Why would they do this to me?'

'They do what time has them do,' Adam's explanation was unhelpful.

'So every time I teleport when I'm asleep, it happens because it's *time*?'

'I guess.'

'That sucks. I'd rather find there's a reason behind it all so that I can learn how to control it.'

'If you learn to control it maybe you could take us back home,' suggested Penelope.

'Like I said, I don't know where home is anymore. I always knew where to go before, but this is *too* far.'

'Look, what did you say your name was again?'

'Nathan.'

'Okay, *Nathan*, I'm Penelope, this is Adam, we'd be happy for you to join us for dinner. Wouldn't we, Adam.'

'Absolutely. We'd love to learn more about your adventures. You're our first visitor in over a decade.'

'Thanks. I certainly have nowhere else to be, right now.'

'Okay then, you can help Penelope forage for food and I'll join you shortly. I've almost finished collecting *fuel-fruit*. Then I just need to check for *fliers* in the *sticky-nets*.'

Nathan nodded and followed Penelope up off the beach to a basket she had left there.

Penelope showed Nathan how to spot which plants were ripe and some that were of more use as a herbal remedy than a staple foodstuff. He didn't like to point out to her that he had learned most of the food plants from watching her already.

Aboard the barge as the suns went down he watched again as the couple prepared and cooked the food.

'It will be interesting to try these foods cooked,' Nathan admitted.

'Oh dear, of course you wouldn't have been able to make a fire,' Penelope realised. 'We have a couple of lighters here.'

'The police took my survival kit off me when I was arrested so I lost my striker and I couldn't find anything dry enough to rub together here.'

'I know, right.' Adam nodded. 'You'd think with it being so warm things would dry out, but there seems to be an oiliness to everything.'

'Even the sea.'

'Ha yeah.'

Nathan took a deep breath in through his nose and smiled. 'The cooking certainly smells good.'

'So you can't smell with your *remote-viewing* then, Nathan?' asked Penelope.

'No, nor hear. I did learn to lip-read some years ago though, which is why I knew you both spoke English.'

'You sound like you are from Birmingham,' Adam guessed.

'Yes.'

'I'm from Bristol, and Penelope is from Los Angeles. I used to be in the house renovation trade. In fact Ben McGregor became an employee of mine after his head injury.'

'Head injury?'

'Yes. He had himself a dreadful accident, got amnesia and developed object recognition issues. It was quite a challenge for him, so sad, when he had been something of a hero prior to that. Still, he kept going. True SAS spirit I guess. I do wonder about him at times, how he got on after my alien abduction. He was having trouble with his wife. I've just thought, Nathan, I haven't asked you what year you are from. I've just *assumed* that you are from *our* time.'

'It is twenty thirty-three back home.'

'So you are from the past then?'

'The *past*?'

'Yes. Maybe it's just that my clock is out, what with the different length days and years here, but I had reckoned this must be around the twenty forties.'

'Well I have never experienced any difference in time when I have night ported before.'

'Night ported?'

'Yes, that's what I call it because it only happens, as I said, when I'm asleep.'

'Of course…So what was happening back home before you were brought here?'

'Well I'm not sure how far back I need to go, but you know about the plandemic right?'

'The what?'

'The global cull, for the New World Order. The release of the American patented

Coronavirus from China to start off the depopulation programme.'

'Oh my god!' Penelope was shocked. 'I knew about the virus before I came here. Some countries and States were going into lockdowns, but I never thought for a moment...you're saying it was released intentionally?'

Adam just stared in disbelief.

'Absolutely. We get taught all about it in history lessons.'

'Are you being serious?' Adam was struggling with this news.

'Yes. We have one world government now. But it is struggling to keep control because the final virus design killed many more people than had been agreed.'

'*Agreed*?...By *who*?'

'By the governments. The cull left many countries without workable infrastructure. Oh and then of course came the nuclear terrorism.'

'Oh *God*, Nathan! Don't tell us anymore!' Penelope's eyes were watering.

'Well I reckon you got the better deal being stranded on this beautiful planet. I don't think you'd like it back home now.'

Penelope distracted herself by serving up but couldn't get the images out of her head of this New World Order Nathan had described.

Once they were sat at the table Penelope decided to mention something from her last days on Earth. 'Before I fell here, I was investigating Adrenochrome, a drug. I think I must have asked too many questions and got too close to the truth. Men came to get rid of me.'

'*Really*? I've never heard of Adrenochrome.'

'It was being extracted from children. Then there was rumour of someone, or something, attacking these Adrenochrome networks. They went by the name of *Fantasma da morte*. I've had plenty of time to think about this and I reckon it was Time-Slaves, because the children mentioned people with a magic door saving them, which sounds a lot like the portal *I* experienced.'

Nathan frowned, unsure about the logic of this. 'Why would they save the children for a world about to go into a viral cull?'

'Who knows,' Adam held his hands up. 'It's the chaos of life and death. You know, I had often wondered whether I had been marooned here as *punishment* for not solving the murder of my girlfriend Toyah. But now having heard what has happened on Earth since, I'm starting to wonder whether this has been to save me from further trauma.'

'Maybe,' Penelope agreed. 'I always thought of this as a second chance for me. I would have died in that freezer. I prayed to be saved and ended up here, with you.'

'Well some people do claim that prayer can make things happen, somehow,' Adam agreed.

As they finished the meal off with some *sweet-lichen*, Penelope said 'While I do the dishes, Adam, why don't you make up that spare bunk for Nathan.'

'Good idea. It won't take long and it will be far more comfortable than sleeping rough, I promise you.'

'No, honestly Adam, I couldn't.'

'Don't be silly lad, you're our guest.'

'You don't understand. You would be risking me sinking your barge.'

'*What?*'

'I destroyed a helicopter that I fell asleep on.'

'A *helicopter*?'

'Yes. It is too dangerous to be near me when I sleep in case I teleport, taking stuff around me as I go. There used to be long periods between events, but lately these periods have become much shorter. So I must sleep outside.'

'Maybe I can help you build a camp.'

'Does it rain here?'

'Not very often…There's just the mist.'

'Yes I've got used to that. This environment suit keeps my body-temperature stable.'

'Well can I get you anything to take with you? Like a torch?'

'Thanks, but I don't need a torch. The *remote-viewing* has always been like seeing things in daylight. In fact, it is often safer and easier for me to travel at night.'

'Fascinating.'

'How about food?' Penelope asked.

'I don't suppose you have a spare belt I could use do you?'

'I think I do, somewhere,' Adam scanned around trying to think where he might have put it.

'It would also be great if you could spare a water-bottle, a knife, a lighter and any other survival related items.'

'Right, well, let's see what we can do,' Adam got up from the table and began searching draws.

Nathan helped Penelope clear the table.

'Thank you dear. I do hope you don't go too soon, it has been wonderful having a visitor.'

'Even though I upset you?'

'Well that wasn't your fault. I asked the question. When I was investigating things for my own show I unearthed some *horrible* truths that needed reporting. It goes with the territory. I'll be fine.'

'How about this then?!' Adam called, sounding quite pleased with himself.

'Oh that looks great,' Nathan was surprised by what Adam had managed to pull together. 'Are you sure you can spare all this.'

'Sure. Take it. I'd hate to think I could have helped but hadn't.'

'Thanks…Well I look forward to seeing you in the morning and maybe in return for your gift and hospitality I can start to draw you a map of your world, unless you already have one?'

'No, no we don't. Could you *actually* do that?'

'Yes. No problem. I can even put notes of what can be found on islands of interest.'

'Oh Nathan,' Penelope sounded very excited by the idea, 'that would be absolutely fantastic!'

That night as Adam and Penelope lay in bed discussing what else they should ask someone with *remote-viewing* they heard an unusual sound.

Whumph.

Nathan woke feeling very weak. His tummy felt heavy. Was it something he had eaten? He lay there taking in his surroundings, pretending to be still asleep as he always did. Watching and listening *before* reacting.

A heavy-set woman, who looked all muscle rather than fat, dressed like some sort of Maori warrior princess, stood quietly looking down at him.

The air around them was thick and humid, and was filled with unfamiliar sounds and scents. The scent of this woman was pleasant which somehow reassured Nathan. He tried to get up, every muscle strained. His limbs felt weighed down.

'Welcome to Krewlornia.'

27

Nathan felt exhausted. He had never felt this way before, not even after the battery of tests *Control* had him do from time to time.

'Who are you?' He asked the woman.

'Ata.'

'I am…'

'Nathan Purnell. I know. You have been expected.'

'*Expected*?'

'Yes. Come. Let me help you up. You have a difficult time ahead. People are coming for us as we speak.'

'Yes, I see.' Struggling to his feet, it felt like he was carrying two extra people on his back. 'Why am I so heavy?'

'Krewlornia is three of Earth's gravities.'

'*Oh no*, I can't be doing with this. Let me go to sleep. Maybe I can port somewhere better.'

'No you don't…Before the others arrive I must tell you *this*: from now on *whatever* I do or say I will be…*acting*…in your interest. Do you understand, Nathan?'

'Sort of,' he thought this Ata very strange.

'So what *am* I telling you?'

'From now on *whatever* you do or say…You will be…*acting*…in *my* interest.'

'Good…They come.'

The deep crunch of undergrowth could now be heard with their approach. There were four men and two women, similarly clad to Ata, and carrying spears in addition to bow and arrows.

None of them were more than a head taller than Nathan. He considered that they might not be much older than him either.

There was no sense of threat as they came out of the dumpy trees into the clearing where Nathan and Ata waited. They were clearly there to escort them. However, that raised a question in Nathan's mind. If Ata was with him, why was an escort required?

A woman at the back barked an order which Nathan only understood by tone and started to follow Ata.

Each step was an effort but Nathan tried not to think about it. He tried instead to focus on what was going on around him.

At one point he tripped on a root. Suddenly he was falling to the ground very fast. He broke his fall on hands and knees. It felt like he had just jumped from a high wall.

They all stopped and turned at the sound of his stumble. One of the men behind Nathan said something and the others laughed, except for Ata and the lead woman. The woman was not amused. She admonished the man and they all fell silent and continued.

'What did he say?' Nathan asked Ata.

'He compared you to a stumbling baby.'

'Oh.'

'Can these people not speak English?'

'No. Only the languages of Krewlornina, of which there are quite a number but very few of the Harlash know them all.'

'So how come *you* speak my language.'

'Many of the Harlash develop a talent; a kind of magic.'

'Why would you magically be able to speak a language from another world?'

'You misunderstand. My talent enables me to speak all languages.'

'Oh…Arrgh!' Suddenly Nathan's exposed hand was on fire where it had brushed against a thick leaf.

'You touched a fire-nettle. The pain will pass.'

'Ooo…Not soon enough.' Nathan was suddenly wary of touching anything but noticed the Harlash showed no concern. 'How come they are not getting stung?'

'They will all have suffered its poison when they were children. Just the once. They are now immune.'

'I don't understand.'

'All you need to understand is that everyone and everything on Krewlornia has a natural desire to hurt or kill everything else. Harlash bodies and minds are quick to learn and as such build up resistance to much of it…Or die.'

'Or *die*?!'

'Yes. Harlash are not immortal.'

They arrived at a riverside where a boat was tethered and guarded by another woman.

Aboard the boat the party set off down river all the way to a large lake and headed across to a wooded island with a castle.

'What is that place, Ata?'

'Curumwal.'

They passed a cloud of large colourful butterflies. Forgetting himself he allowed one on alight on the hand which he gripped the side of the boat with. It stung him.

'Ouch! Now I have pain in both hands!' Nathan noticed the others were turning their heads away trying to suppress they laugher over his fussing like a child. He decided he must learn to suffer in silence. He turned to Ata, 'I can see that they are amused by my discomfort.'

'Yes. Harlash enjoy the pain and misfortune of others because it reminds them of their past sufferings as children.'

'So they are a bad people.'

'Some are worse than others.' Ata nodded. 'They have a saying here which translates as *Suffering is Living.*'

'Hell…I can't wait to say goodbye.'

'Poor Nathan. You have so much to learn.'

The rest of the trip Nathan remained silent, *remote-viewing* the castle, assuming that was where he was being taken. It was clear that on Krewlornia things were not equal. Men were subservient. Men carried out the manual labour while the women managed, though managing seemed to require quite a lot of talking and taking it easy. Except for one woman who he witnessed giving birth.

The birth was not a pleasant sight. He had viewed them happening on Earth. These seemed little different beyond the extra cradling to ensure that the baby was not dropped. At least it didn't involve a traumatic birth like his own would have been.

Passing through an armoured gate like a canal lock the boat was moored at a dock and once again Nathan had to get to his feet. He felt even more tired than he had when he woke.

Ata helped him off the boat and up the flight of stairs into the castle.

He was taken to a room where two men removed the curtain he still wore and then his environment suit. There was some puzzling over the zips which they had never seen the like of before.

Nathan wished that Ata had stayed with him to translate as he tried to tell them he did not wish to get undressed. They talked to him and to each other but again their words were only understood by a combination of tone and action.

They washed him and dried him at all times taking care that his frail body did not fall to the stone floor. Then they dressed him in a leather skirt like their own and tied sandals to his feet.

Next he was led to a hall where Ata waited and food was served.

The food tasted different; strong tasting but good. By the end of the meal his arms ached from lifting the cutlery to his mouth. His hands still hurt from the stings though not as much.

'I think I need to go and lie down now.' Nathan told Ata.

She shook her head. 'That is not possible yet. You have to work now.'

'*Work*?'

'Don't worry. It will not be heavy labour, and I have been ordered to teach and supervise this work.'

'What sort of work?'

'In the kitchens, today, scrubbing the floor.'

'Scrubbing…?'

The task proved to be mentally, physically and emotionally challenging because he could hear the kitchen staff laughing at his struggling. Not only did he have to find the energy to scrub the flagstones he had to concentrate on Ata teaching him the language of Curumwal.

In addition to the word for *come* which he had already picked up, he learned *bucket, brush, water, stone* and *floor*, very quickly. The lesson never seemed to stop as he went on to learn *table, stool, boy, man* and *lady*.

'I'm exhausted Ata,' he complained.

'You must learn to take energy from your braelic,' Ata beat against her chest.

'My heart?'

'No. Next to your heart you have a liver like organ which provides you energy that it converts from dark energy all around.'

'You're suggesting that I am to draw energy from *evil*?'

'No. Energy of any kind is neither good nor evil, though what you choose to do with it may be.'

Nathan didn't remember anything called a braelic in his biology lessons. Surely it was just some folk-belief among these people. They did not appear technologically advanced enough to know much about the sciences. Alternatively they could be physically different and believe him to be one of them.

Nathan tried to focus on this imaginary organ and whether focusing worked simply as a distraction he didn't know but it seemed to help, just a bit. Nevertheless, as time went on his muscles began to tremble and the brush began to feel more and more like a railway sleeper. He dropped the brush and it snapped to the floor so fast that it looked more like it had been caught in a magnetic field than a fall under gravity.

Nathan tried taking a break by distracting Ata with questions. 'What do you normally do?'

'What do you mean, *normally*?'

'Well I'm guessing you don't spend your time training *expected* visitors.'

'No. I do all sorts of things, whatever I am told to.'

'You look like a warrior but you do not carry a spear.'

'You do not need a spear to be a warrior. Harlash with spears, depending on type of spear, could be castle guards, warriors, or royal guards.'

'Is the Queen a good one?'

'Define *good*.'

'Well is she looking to take other people's lands from them or simply look after her own land?'

'She has eyes on certain other territories yes but no more than others have eyes on hers.'

'So is there a war here?'

'Not a war as such but foreigners would typically be killed for their trespass.'

'So why am I still alive?'

'That remains to be seen.' Ata pointed at the floor. 'I think you need to keep going, Nathan. I know it is hard for you but it is for the best.'

'*Define* best,' he threw back at her, irritated by having no choice in the matter.

'You need to build your strength up, to adapt.'

Ata sounded even tougher than Emily as a teacher. 'No, what I *need* is somewhere to *sleep*.'

313

'Patience.'

'Why do I get the feeling you know more about me than my language?'

'As I said you can think of it as my *talent*.'

'What other talents do you have?'

'It is not considered polite to ask such questions of people. Some have no talent at all.'

'Oh. But what other talents *do* people have?'

'There are many. Some can purify water, light fires, and lure prey towards them. Other, rarer, talents include the ability to move objects by will power, to heal…'

'Can any *remote-view*?'

'A few.'

'How about teleport?'

'No.'

'Read minds?'

'No.'

'Fly?'

'No.'

'How about shoot lasers out of their eyes?'

'No. These people have no concept of such things as *lasers*.'

'Right…I'm getting the sense from the way you talk of *these people*, the Harlash, that you are not from here.'

'True.'

'Yet they have welcomed you in rather than kill you as a foreigner?'

'Yes. It is part of my *atonement*.'

'Atonement for what?'

'I do not wish to say at this time. And you are slacking again,' Ata gestured back to the flagstones.

Nathan ceased with the questions but returned to viewing the island people, in particular the Queen.

The Queen was dressed unlike any of her subjects, as Nathan might have expected. Her clothes were very ornate. They appeared to be made of some scaly skin which glittered like multi-coloured sequins. The drape of the fabric under the Krewlornian gravity was very revealing of her form and she looked as much a warrior as those who guarded her, despite her age. Though no taller than anyone else there was a flowing quality to the way she moved.

As Nathan watched while he scrubbed, the Queen gave orders for something. He could not read their lips yet until he had gained their language but in short order people arrived in the throne-room. Males and females, young and old, they began to gather in a broken ring of eight, holding hands, standing in the hall below the steps to the throne waiting.

Once they had all gathered the Queen descended to join them. Taking hands to either side of the break she made the ring whole. Their lips began to move in a rhythmic chant. It was not clear to Nathan at this point but the purpose of the chanting was to open their minds and enable their energy to be tapped into and directed by the Queen as *Minister*. As they all stared at the floor of the hall a vapour began to appear over the flagstones.

The vapour became an iridescent cloud which deepened then parted in the middle to reveal a birds-eye-view of a scene.

Nathan was so distracted by all this that his hand stopped scrubbing. It was like watching a film about witches. It looked like these people somehow had *magic* rather than super-powers.

'Nathan.'

'Sorry, Ata,' he swapped hands for the scrubbing once again and then continued.

The view through the iridescent cloud was like a portal. Nathan did not recognise anyone in view but then he didn't expect to. He tried to put his *remote-viewing* through the portal but he could not. Then the scene was just an image and then it was fading.

The Queen seemed visibly disappointed and dismissed the ring of people, then as if having second thoughts appeared to bark another order.

As Nathan watched two of the royal guards made their way down to the kitchen, where they spoke to Ata.

Ata's tone sounded imploring. Nathan wondered what was wrong. Were they going to take her away? As they approached it became apparent that is was *him* these women had come for.

Ata made to come along with him but was clearly told to stay where she was.

'Where are they taking me, Ata?'

'To meet Queen Xervren of Curumwal.'

'But you must come,' he insisted as he was led by the arm towards the door, all eyes of the kitchen staff on him. 'I will need you there to translate for me.'

'I already told them that. Sorry.'

Nathan had become so exhausted that he was dragged through the castle, his sandals scuffing along the flagstones. However, as they approached the throne room, the guards considered it prudent to take an arm each and lift Nathan up to stop the annoying sound.

Once through the great doors of the Queen's hall and before the steps to the throne, Nathan was put back on his feet. He trembled with his weariness, which may have looked like fear.

The Queen ordered her guards back to their posts at the side of the hall.

It struck Nathan that while this woman's tone was confidently commanding it had a kindly softness to it. He relaxed.

Nevertheless, his exhausted body persisted in trembling as Queen Xervren looked him over.

She spoke to him but she might as well have been talking to herself, for all it had meant to Nathan.

'I am Nathan Purnell,' even his voice was a quiver. 'I apologise for appearing on your land, though I understand I was *expected*.'

The Queen seemed amused by the sound of his Brummie accented English. She turned aside and called for something.

Shortly a maid with a tray arrived.

The Queen said something else and the tray was offered to Nathan. On it was a single small ceramic cup. He took it and looked inside.

The liquid was orange and as he lifted it shakily to his mouth it smelled of something that he didn't recognise but hadn't expected to.

With the Queen and her maid watching he took a sip. It was bitter and he pulled a face.

The Queen smiled and made some urging sound, so he swallowed the rest, replacing the cup to the tray.

As he did so his trembling muscles went into spasm and his knees gave way. His tongue started to swell and his saliva glands went into overdrive. He clutched at his tummy as he doubled over onto the floor in pain and began vomiting.

The Queen and her maid did little more than offer mocking sounds of sympathy.

Nathan had clearly been poisoned.

28

Xervren had slept well for the first time in ages. She woke with a smile remembering the previous day's capture and poisoning. Things were finally coming together for her.

Shuffling to the end of her bed and parting the net curtain of her insect tent she crossed her room to her dresser. Taking a round pot of scented oil and a hair brush from her table she returned to her bed and sat at the end.

Drawing the curtains further aside she poured a little oil into her hands. She put the pot at her feet, then began running her fingers through her long curly dark hair. She could have had a nubile young male or two doing this for her, as other queens might, but she felt she was past all that now. She enjoyed her own company and independence, knowing that way there was no risk of letting slip any of her secret plans.

With her hair oiled and smelling of sweet blossoms and fruits she began to brush her hair. There was no rush, starting from the bottom and working her way up she found the pull and the rhythmic motion relaxing.

As she brushed, her attention settled on a bag beside the table and she remembered what it contained. Placing the brush on the bed she went and picked up the leather bag and returned.

Undoing the cord which secured the bag she reached inside and drew out some woven material which was of little interest. She dropped it to the floor, not noticing that it tipped over the pot of oil.

Reaching back in she drew out a shiny material which was like nothing on Krewlornia. It was thin and yet tough. It had dozens of little teeth along split seams. She noticed a piece of jewellery or something at the end of each of these split seams. She made to pull one off but it slid and as it did so it joined the teeth behind it. This fascinated her. Where the teeth closed the seam became tightly joined and if she slid the device the other way the seam opened back up again. Krewlornia had no means of manufacturing the likes of a zip fastener.

Placing Nathan's environment suit on the bed beside her, she reached back into the bag and pulled out a bottle. It was translucent and contained clear liquid. She tried to get the top off but it was too tight to pull off, till she noticed that it twisted. Twisting the cap off, she smelled the contents. There was no smell to it, and not expecting it to be a poison she tasted some. It seemed to be water with no apparent magical property. She placed that on top of the jumpsuit and reached back into the bag.

The next item she did recognise. It was a metal knife. She tested the edge with her thumb. It was nowhere near as sharp as any of their ceramic blades. Maybe it was a toy, or training weapon, she thought.

Next out of the bag was a curious metal slab. As she inspected it closely it had a top to it which neither pulled off nor twisted. One third of the top was like an inset corner. She thought to push down on the corner. With a click the other part of the top flipped up and a flame whooshed out.

In her shock she dropped the alien device but not before it had set fire to her hair. She batted at the flames with her hands but the residue of oil there had them alight too. Then the sacking and oil on the floor were alight and the netting over the bed.

Queen Xervren called for help but by the time the guards came in from the corridor the room was filling with smoke.

One guard rushed to the window to let the smoke out, but this only served to feed the flames.

The other guard wanted to bat at the flames which engulfed the Queen but froze for a moment worried that this might later be taken as an assault. She turned instead and ran to the coat hooks and grabbed a thick leather long-coat. Turning back round she saw the Queen writhing on the floor, her lace night-clothes alight. She covered her and began gently tamping down on the twisting body.

Lifting the coat after a while, to check that the Queen was now okay, the oil caught again with the air. So the guard covered her Queen once again.

When the fire *was* out, the Queen's hair, eye-brows and eye-lashes were gone and her body was blotched with a number of severe burns. She was taken to a nearby guest-room where the royal physician treated her burns with a selection of salves and leaves, bound in place by bandages.

As if to add insult to injury, on top of the ashes in the Queen's bedroom, untouched, lay what was to become considered as Nathan's *magic* suit.

Nathan's stomach was still a little sore when he woke but nowhere near as sore as his arms. He didn't understand why the Queen would want to harm him just for appearing on her land, especially when Ata had said his arrival had been expected. It wasn't like he had been a threat to the Queen. However, maybe he was *now* since he felt he had a score to settle.

Scanning through the castle he saw no sign of the Queen at first. He saw someone wrapped in bandages being guarded and wondered whether this was another victim of the Queen's sadistic amusement. Then he saw there had been a fire in a nearby room and noticed his environment suit on top of the ashes and his lighter, gifted him by Adam, on the floor.

His attention was drawn back to the room he occupied as Ata arrived.

'*So*...you are awake now. You have been allowed a lie-in this morning only because there has been some kind of attack on the Queen.'

'Did they catch them?'

'No.'

'Good. She deserved it.'

'Nathan! Shh!'

'No one can understand what I'm saying.'

'The Harlash are quick learners. The more you speak English the quicker they will pick it up. And you spoke all too much in the kitchens, which is where you must go now.'

'I don't feel hungry.'

'Good…because you have more scrubbing to do.'

'You're *kidding* right?'

'No. Come on.'

'But my arms are aching.'

'I told you yesterday, did I not, that you had a difficult time ahead.'

Nathan made to pull the sheet over him and ignore Ata but even that hurt his arm and back muscles.

'Don't even think about it.'

'But I'm *exhausted*!'

'You have to *work* through it.'

'*Work* through it? I need physio!'

'Yes well, they don't have that sort of thing here. Come on.'

Grudgingly Nathan complied, creeping after Ata, back to the kitchen, where the brush and bucket of astringent water waited.

As he scrubbed, Nathan kept watch over Queen Xervren. She slept fitfully until mid-afternoon, with the royal physician helping her keep hydrated with cups of water. She coughed and spluttered trying to drink through cracked burned lips.

Nathan was surprised, considering that he expected to be blamed for this incident that the Queen had not yet ordered him executed. Nevertheless, he did not feel sorry for the condition she was in. As far as Nathan was concerned fate had seen to it that she'd gotten her comeuppance.

However, it later occurred to him that she might only be waiting until she could recover enough to *watch* him being executed. He then spent some time considering how best to escape.

Escape would not be easy. He was still too frail to run away and had much to learn about the world outside the castle never mind inside.

That left the option of evasion. He then used his remote-viewing to look for a good place to hide within the castle. He knew it would have to be somewhere that he could access easily enough yet not an immediately obvious place to look for him.

The only place he could find was a room in a tower which was filled with old heavy looking furniture. The door was probably locked but even had he acquired the key there was an old wardrobe immediately inside the doorway which he would not be able to shift. However, the wardrobe and possibly locked door would work in his favour if he were able to scale the tower wall and climb in through the window. Something else beyond his present physical capacity. Besides, on inspection, the window looked like it would need to be jimmied open.

'There, that's the whole floor done, Ata.'

'Good work, Nathan. You can get a change of water and follow me to the soil closets.'

'*What*? I have to water the gardens now? *Really*?'

'No not the gardens today. You have toilets to clean.'

'*Toilets*?!'

There was no audience with the Queen for Nathan for a couple of days, just his relentless duties to carry out under Ata's supervision.

Every day was so tiring and dragged dreadfully. He had no watch to check time. By remote-viewing on Earth he had always been able to find clocks to check.

On Krewlornia the length of a day was close to thirty hours and a year's orbit around the sun was two and a half Earth years. But there was no word for year in any of the Harlash languages, or any understanding of what a year meant. This was because Krewlornia orbited without any tilt, so never had any seasons, just different temperate zones. Nathan learned this and other things from Ata.

Her language lessons were being soaked up quicker than Nathan had expected. In addition to which, by the third day, helping Ata unload a supply boat Nathan realised that his muscles were no longer aching.

However, his muscles were starting to get bigger, like he was on some body-building crash course. This seemed odd since he had never filled out like this with the exercises Emily made him do. It had to be the effect of the higher gravity he concluded.

Then one evening in the kitchen, when he was trusted to do dishes without dropping them two of the Queen's guards came for him. Once again Ata suggested it would be best if she accompany Nathan as he still was not yet fluent in Curumwalish. Once again she was told to stay behind.

Nathan had hoped the Queen had decided to call it quits but now expected the worst.

This time he was not dragged to the throne-room but walked with the guards, wishing he could run in the opposite direction. However, he knew he was still not fit enough to make his escape.

In the hall, the heavy doors closed behind them. The Queen descended the stairs looking to Nathan for any reaction to the sight of her. She saw no surprise in his face, seeing her very short hair and now unblemished skin.

Xervren dismissed her guards then looked over Nathan's body. His muscles were filling out but he still looked like a weakling in her eyes. Nevertheless, at least his trembling had ceased.

Nathen had no idea what was going through her mind. She did not attempt to speak to him this time so could make no judgement on tone of voice. Then she called out a name and the young woman with the tray appeared.

Nathan's mind went into overdrive. The Queen must wish to finish him off properly this time. He could not run because he was not fast enough. He could not fight the guards. Even one would have been too much to handle.

He could delay the impending poisoning by spilling the liquid, but that would probably only work the once.

Nathan accepted in that moment that he was about to die so there was another option.

Xervren commanded him to take the cup from the tray.

'I'd rather drink my own urine, my Royal Baldness.'

Xervren gestured to the maid who took the cup then pushed it upon him.

With a reluctant sign Nathan took the cup.

Xervren urged him to drink.

Nathan lifted the cup and pretended to sip then pulled a face as he had done before. This time when she commanded again that he drink he threw the contents into her open mouth.

To his surprise, though some of the liquid splashed over her face that which went into her mouth she swallowed, instead of spitting it out. She smiled and wiped her face then ordered the maid away.

Xervren looked at Nathan in a different light now. She continued to smile, but not in a good way, Nathan thought.

She could have ordered the guards to run him through with their spears, or simply throttled him with her bare hands. But Nathan realised that the Queen was playing a different game that he had yet to understand.

The maid reappeared with another cup on the tray.

'What's the matter with you people? I don't want any!'

As the young woman came close Nathan knocked the tray and cup from her grip and picked up the tray as a potential shield.

It was at that point that he felt a pin prick in his neck. Lifting a hand to check he pulled away a thorn. Looking back at the Queen he saw her holding a small blowpipe, then his knees buckled.

This time when he came round he was not in his bed but still in the throne-room. The Queen was kneeling beside him, lifting his head with a smile.

He couldn't move a muscle. He just watched as Xervren took another cup from her maid and poured its contents into his mouth.

Nathan attempted to cough it out but he wasn't completely successful. His head began to spin and his hearing began to echo.

Suddenly he thought he was on the toilet floor at his school. One of his teachers was holding him and Charisma was there looking at him with amusement. He tried to talk but the sound didn't seem to make any sense. Then it was getting dark but neither Charisma nor the teacher thought to switch on the lights.

When Nathan woke he was in his bed. Ata was on the other bed, the other side of the room.

'I have to kill the Queen, Ata,' he croaked. 'She is a madwoman.'

'Maybe you need to get to know her better.'

'Yeah right. Does that go for humour where you are from?...She keeps trying to poison me!'

'Do you know how tribes in the Amazon treat *their* young? Stinging them with insects and spiders, tying them down to ant-hills?'

'No. But it sounds like they need shooting. That is extreme domestic abuse and should be stopped.'

'That is their culture.'

'That is *no* excuse.'

'Without this treatment to toughen the young up, to build up their resistance to toxins, it leads to an unpleasant life. When these tribal people reach adulthood their Shaman takes on the role of poisoning them. In some cases these toxins create out of body experiences, where the ceremony focuses on bonding with an animal totem.'

'You seem to know more about Earth history than *me*, Ata.'

'Some.'

'So what are you saying? The Queen is preparing me to live with your people?'

'Not *my* people, *her* people.'

29

As a result of what Ata had told Nathan but also how Emily had trained him to deal with a variety of situations, Nathan's attitude changed. He knew that until he night ported away from this dark and dangerous world he had to find a way of surviving it. Emily had taught him to try and make good come out of bad and to turn life's challenges into opportunities. Above all he needed to remain positive.

In the weeks that followed he did not resist the Queen's poisonings which began to include stings and bites of animals as well as her toxic concoctions. He remembered a saying, what doesn't kill you makes you stronger, however, it didn't say you had to like it.

Nathan noticed that the Queen became less amused once he accepted her all her torments. Nathan did wonder then why she still insisted in overseeing this treatment which surely could have been passed onto someone else to carry out.

In that time Nathan's command of the Curumwalish language became almost fluent. However, he soon came to learn that whilst he could get away with talking English, which was ignored as his gibbering, asking the Queen questions in Curumwalish was not wise. A few jabs from spearheads of royal guards soon made the point that he should really only speak when spoken to.

Nathan took to addressing the Queen with English slurs like *Bitch* and *Cow* with a polite smile and gracious tone to hide their meaning. He was prepared to lie if anyone ever asked him to translate. He just hoped that no one would ask Ata. He had come to trust Ata and see her as his guardian while he remained on Krewlornia.

They continued to share the same room but never the same bed. In Curumwal at least he considered still too young for that sort of thing. However, Ata *had* cuddled him when he told her how much he was missing his father. When she did this Nathan smelled her comforting scent and wondered if it was just natural, because he had never seen her putting any on. And come to think of it he hadn't noticed any of the others smelling like her.

He also noticed that she still had difficulty talking about certain topics even though they had grown close. A number of questions he had about her remained unanswered and he came to accept that the time was not right or maybe never would be.

Then one day royal guards came for Ata while they were out in the fields helping harvest seeds. She was gone some time and Nathan continued with his task and indulged in a little gossip with friends who he had now made among the servants, like Garowak.

Later he wished that he had viewed where she was taken to, because when he did scan to check on her she was not in their room, or in the kitchen or the throne room. He thought she might have had to leave the castle on some errand for the Queen.

That evening after the seeds were in and Nathan had eaten, he was expecting to be told he could go to his room when royal guards turned up for him.

Nathan groaned. He hated it when he had to go get poisoned before his food had had time to digest. It never made any sense to him. It always made more mess, which some poor servant then had to clean up once he was taken away to his room.

Nevertheless, this time the guards led him a different way. This was not up to the throne-room but down to the dungeon, where he had never been before, physically.

In the torch-lit dungeon below stood the Queen and shockingly, bound to a rack, was Ata.

'No!' Nathan tried to run to her even before they reached the dungeon, but his arms were grabbed firmly by the guards. Bursting through the open doorway Nathan's immediate thought was this must be his fault. The Queen must have been demanding a translation from Ata of *Bitch*, *Cow* and other common phases Nathan had begun to use with Xervren.

Ata was in a dreadful state. She looked pained and worn out from torture. Her neck and torso were braced to a bench which was split in the middle with a big screw so that the bench could stretch her. Her arms and legs were bound to large wheels which not only stretched her limbs but bent them against their joints.

At the Queen's command for another tweak of the rack the torturer made a number of adjustments and Ata released a drawn out scream which put Nathan's teeth on edge.

'Stop this! Stop this at once!' He implored in his best Curumwalish.

'She refuses to tell us who she is.' Xervren dismissed his demand.

'She is Ata. You *know* that!'

'I know that she *isn't*. Tell me, Nathan. Who *is* she?'

'She is *Ata*!'

The Queen ordered more tightening.

'She's Ata! She's Ata!' cried Nathan over the screaming.

'What has she told you about herself?'

Nathan tried desperately to think. 'Not a lot actually but she is a *good* person.'

'This is where you are *mistaken*!'

Nathan remembered the first thing Ata had ever told him about acting in his interest and although at times it had been a case of tough love she *had* stood by him.

'What has she told you?!'

'I urr…Well let's see…'

'Don't stall. You cannot save this *demon*.'

The rack was separated further. Ata's form already looked impossibly stretched. She screamed 'He knows nothing! I told him nothing!!'

'Nathan!' Xervren snapped.

'She has said…she is not from Curumwal.'

'I *know* that!'

'She…Urr…Know's about my homeworld.'

'Oh I bet she does.'

'She…She…*I don't know*.'

Xervren turned her attention to Ata. 'If you do not tell me your real name and own up to your crime the boy will be forced to watch more.'

'Okay, okay. Just let him go,' Ata croaked.

'There will be *no* bargaining!'

'My name…My name is…' Ata struggled with the brace around her neck.

'Loosen its neck brace,' Xervren ordered.

The torturer did so.

'Speak the truth!'

'I cannot…It is the meta-interference.'

'No more excuses,' Xervren stepped forwards drawing a little ceramic blade from her waist band. She drew it down the length of Ata's buckled left leg, only lifting the blade only to skip over the bindings.

Ata took a sharp breath, wincing at the pain as her blood began to flow. 'My name is…'

'She cannot say!' Nathan believed Ata must be prevented from answering somehow. This might explain why she had been unable to answer many of *his* questions. 'Someone has cast a *spell* on her so that she cannot answer!'

'Rubbish. It has cast a *glamour* on *you* with that sweet smell!...But I know who this thing is and what it did!'

'So why are you doing this to her?!'

'I want to hear it admit the crime…In your presence. So you will know it to be evil and grow to respect *me* more.' Xervren ran the blade up the other leg bringing a second stream of blood trickling down to the flagstones and running between the cracks.

'I will never respect you if you cannot stop hurting her! You're killing her!' Nathan cried.

However, Xervren was clearly enjoying this and would not be stopped. She added to the flow of blood with further cuts, this time to Ata's arms.

'This demon stole my *only* child!'

'That *can't* be true! Ata wouldn't do that. She *has* no children.'

'It took my child to give to someone *else*.'

'Why would she do that? It makes no sense.'

'Because the demon has not *told* you that it switches babies. It gave me one from your planet. But though the child looked like my Xaviol, I knew she was not.'

'I don't believe you. It is *you* who is wicked!'

'It is the truth.'

'Where I'm from some babies die.'

'No. Not like this!'

'How do you know?'

'One of my talents is seeing the aura around people. I can tell from the colours and patterns the clan and bloodline of every Harlash. This switched baby had only the weakest of aura and could not survive on our world. She lasted only days.'

Desperate to explain this some other way as he watched the blood flow out of Ata, hoping that he could somehow save her, Nathan suggested, 'Was this weak aura not just a sign of Xaviol becoming ill?'

'No it was *not* that she was ill! I can tell sickness from changes in an aura. And *you* Nathan have a deformed aura, and I *know* why. Dark magic was used on your birth world. You see, I can view remotely like you too and by using my prayer-circles. I was able to find my Xaviol. However, I was unable to bring *her* home to Curumwal.'

'Meta-interference,' Ata gasped.

'Nonsense!' Xervren plunged the knife into Ata's chest.

'No!' Nathan pleaded.

'Instead,' Xervren continued to explain, 'By prayer-circle it was foretold that I would one day bring a child of Xaviol here and like a lure it would return this demon to me.'

'Wait. Are you saying that my mother was Xaviol?'

'Yes Nathan.'

'But that...that means *you* are...my Grandmother!'

'Yes Nathan. You were the first survivor of three attempts to bring a child of Xaviol here by prayer-circle, porting you out. It took far more practice than expected.'

'Then it was *you* who killed my mother!' Nathan struggled against the guards restraining grip almost getting loose with his newly developed strength. He so badly wanted to kill Xervren for murdering his mother. 'You punish Ata and yet it is *you* who killed your own daughter!'

'No...The three women who died were only vessels. Your mother, Xaviol, is still out there. I'm sure of it. However, I have been unable to find her again. I believe another of these evil demons has *moved* her.'

'I don't care about that! You and your prayer-circle killed my birth mother with your sick need for vengeance!'

'It is no matter. She was of little value. You are home now, where you belong.'

'Well I'm leaving as soon as I can teleport away!'

'Don't be a stupid child. No one can teleport on their own. Individuals can *move* things but it takes being part of a prayer-circle to make it

336

possible to *teleport* objects. However, it proved very difficult to teleport people very far without adding *amplifiers* to the prayer-circle. To bring you here I had to form the largest prayer-circle in Krewlornian history. That meant fighting many battles to capture *amplifier* talents from other lands.'

'You are a bitter woman! Ata has been punished enough! Let her go now, please!'

'This is my *atonement*, Nathan.' Ata gasped weakly.

'Tell me what she says is not true, Ata!' tears streamed down Nathan's face.

'It is *all* true. I am a *Time-Slave*.'

'*There*, you see, she is just a Time-Slave!' Nathan turned to Xervren. 'That means she was *not* to blame! She could only do what time bade her! I've heard of these people. What they do is through no choice of their own, good or bad.'

'*Everyone* has a choice!'

'So *choose* to forgive Ata! Please!'

'The demon is not called Ata! She must be destroyed.'

Xervren reached for a pot on a table and splashed the contents over Ata's tortured, bloody form. Ata writhed against her biting bonds as the fluid seared her wounds.

Then Xervren turned and took a torch from the wall and thrust it onto Ata's chest. Ata and the rack went up in flames. There came the most blood curdling screams from Ata *and* Nathan as he fought to get free and save his friend, knowing it was hopeless.

Through his tear filled eyes he saw Ata's form suddenly relax, turning to fizzing brown gloop that flowed from the rack to continue burning as a shallow pool on the flagstones below. Not a trace of bone.

'Its name,' Xervren announced, 'was Dawn.'

30

Nathan couldn't sleep that night. Ata's screams echoed round his head. The experience had traumatised him. The Queen was a sick evil woman but what if what she said was true, and she *was* his Grandmother.

If his biological mother was from Curumwal, then that would certainly explain how he was developing to cope with this 3G world and the *talents* that he had. Having already learned that he was an SOV genetic experiment, he now wanted to find this Xaviol too. However, there was not much chance of that if Xervren couldn't find her and Ata, or Dawn, was now gone.

His remote-viewing stretched beyond the Earth-sized moon to the planets but not further than Krewlornia's solar system. He couldn't even see where Adam and Penelope were.

Nathan thought about Earth's SpaceX programme, working towards interplanetary travel. It was actually people of a radio-silent world who had managed to achieve interstellar travel first, through prayer.

Nevertheless, if his Grandmother was right and he was not leaving Krewlornia he would never see his father again. He hoped he was okay.

'I love you Dad.'

The blood between the flagstones under the rack had not simply pooled there. It had seeped under the flags then spread, even before the remains of Dawn had been burned alive. Now it moved out of sight up through the castle walls out of the dungeon to Nathan's room. There was no hurry.

Nathan did not want to get up. It took his friend, Garowak, to come calling on him to remind him that he still had duties to fulfil.

Grudgingly, Nathan got out of his bed and went downstairs with Garowak.

Once he was gone, the blood of Ata came out of the cracks in the wall and crept up the wooden legs of Ata's empty bed. Shortly it had engulfed the bed, covers and all and began to digest these plant-based materials.

At the end of the day Nathan returned to his room. He immediately lay on his bed and pulled his cover over his still sandaled legs. He was just getting his head comfy on his pillow when he was freaked out to see Ata's bed suddenly change form into a girl.

'What the *Hell*?!' he blustered, sitting up straight.

'Do not be alarmed.'

'Ata?' he didn't recognise the sight or sound of this magic-girl.

'Do not call us *that* name. Think of us as Alvorecer. However, we must not be seen. We had to sacrifice much of our colony in atonement for the switching of baby princess Xaviol.'

'What? I don't understand what you are saying.'

'Our colony has been released of its duties as a *Time-Slave*. We are now to serve and protect you.'

'Well unless you can get me back to Earth I don't see how you can help.'

'Oh there are many ways. For instance we can disguise you.' Alvorecer reached out for Nathan's hand and started to spread over it. He was aware of its enticing smell, reminding him of Ata.

'Yuk! No!' He drew his hand away. 'I've seen something like you before. It engulfed and ate someone!'

'Relax.'

'*No way*!'

'Metamorphs cannot digest Harlash. You do not *taste* nice. And don't believe what you hear about getting contaminated by our touch, we *can* actually choose who we infect.'

'Right,' Nathan didn't sound at all convinced.

'There's no rush. We've got your back. We'll just be over here, pretending to be a bed.'

'I won't be able to sleep knowing you are in here. It would be like knowing there's a zeshlec creeping around in here.'

'Oh that's just *mean*…You were fine sleeping in the same room when we were Ata.'

'Yeah *well*, that was because I had no idea you were a metamorph.'

'That's discrimination.'

'Sure. But you are a deadly dangerous animal.'

'No no, a deadly dangerous *colony*.'

Nathan pulled the cover off and made for the door. Alvorecer was already morphing back into the bed.

'Where are you going Nathan?' asked a mouth in the pillow.

'Out.'

341

'Where?'

'Out and about. Don't wait up.' He slammed the door, and a shiver went down his muscled back. Feeling safer in the corridor he thought to go and see if he could scale the outside of the tower with the storage room in. At least he felt fit enough to climb things these days.

However, as he stepped out into the courtyard the guard at the door stopped him.

'Where do you think you're going?' she accosted him.

'For a walk. I can't sleep.'

'Go back to your room.'

He wondered if it was common knowledge now that he was the Queen's Grandson. Didn't that make him royal by association? 'Do you *know* who I am?'

'Nathan.'

'*Prince* Nathan.'

'Go to bed *Prince*,' the guard chuckled.

He considered running for it. It might be a bit of fun. However, the guard shouldn't leave her post, and after what Nathan saw the Queen do to Ata he wouldn't wish that on anyone. 'Okay.'

As he went back inside he turned the other way and headed for the stairs instead. He went to Xervren's chamber where he viewed her preparing to go to bed.

Two guards stood outside her door. They watched Nathan approach.

'I have come to see the Queen.'

'She has made no such command.'

'Yeah I know. I'm *asking* to see the Queen.'

'She is sleeping, Nathan.'

'No she's *not*.'

'Go to bed, Nathan.'

'Grandma!'

The other side of the door, Xervren had heard Nathan's requests. She had no interest in seeing him. His concerns were of no concern to her. However, there was something novel about hearing a grandchild call out to her without royal title, even if that child was only a boy. Xervren opened the door.

'Ah Grandma.'

'What is it, Nathan?'

'I want to go home.'

Xervren tutted. 'You *are* home.'

'Back to Earth.'

'*Impossible.*'

'You have no need for me here.'

'What makes you think that?'

'You said the only reason I was brought here was to lure Ata into capture.'

'That was certainly the immediate reason, but I haven't been using my valuable time poisoning you just to send you back to that filthy moon-world.'

'I want to go back to my Dad!'

'He was only your guardian. His duty is done.'

'I love my Dad and I want to see him again.'

Xervren stared at Nathan for some moments but he just stared right back at her.

'I will sleep on it…And send for you in the morning…Now return to your room.'

It felt like a partial win to Nathan, better than no win. He turned and headed back along the corridor.

By the time he reached the stairs Xervren had closed the door and was climbing into bed.

However, he went quickly up the stairs to the battlements.

The battlements were guarded but by using his remote-viewing he was able to evade being spotted as he climbed up onto the roof.

There he lay back against the tiles and looked up at the stars. The Milky Way here was a lot brighter than from Earth, if it were even the same galaxy. That brightness probably meant that Krewlornia's system was closer to the galactic core. Some of it was even visible during daylight hours.

Nathan then looked at the moon which the Harlash called Jewel. It reminded him of a prehistoric Earth. It had clouds and oceans. There was life on it, but no Harlash. Things looked more elegant there because of the significantly lower gravity.

Their sun, when it rose was bigger than Earth's star, Sol, but not as bright. Still it was not good to stare at it. *Remote-viewing* was okay though. He could view the sun-spot flares without damage that way.

In the morning he returned to his room to collect his servant's belt. He saw that Alvorecer was still a bed.

The pillow formed lips again. 'Where have you been all night?'

'Oh *sorry*, were you worried *sick*?' Nathan had no idea if the metamorph understood sarcasm.

'It is my duty as your future guardian to look out for you, Nathan.'

'Don't bother. I have a Dad.' Nathan picked up his belt, turned and left.

He went straight to the mess hall for some breakfast, after which he waited for someone to give him orders since he no longer had Ata to supervise him. However, no one seemed to call on him. He wondered if they were unsure about him now since technically he was the only prince in the castle.

Two royal guards eventually came for him and escorted him to the throne-room where the Queen waited.

Before Nathan could ask, Xervren gave him her response. 'I have considered your *demand*, and the answer is *no*.'

'Why? I want to see my Dad!'

'There is nothing left for you there.'

'Are you not listening to me? *Dad* is there and I need to go back to him.'

'*I* need you to begin your training as a warrior. You are old enough and *should* be fit enough now to make a start. It will be tough for a boy of course but you do have royal blood so you should survive.'

'*No*! I want to see Dad!'

Xervren gave an exasperated sigh. 'Very well,' she stood clapped her hands together. 'Bring the *Distant Worlds Prayer-Circle*!'

Sitting back on her throne she addressed Nathan once more. 'Come sit at my feet and I will explain something of prayer-circles. I'm not sure you had such things on that moon-world.'

'There are churches where people go to pray,' Nathan told her as he ascended the steps.

'But can they make things happen?'

'Some people believe they can, life curing illnesses.'

'*Really*? Then maybe there is some universal reason to this...I am the *Minister* of the circles in Curumwal. That means I am able to assemble prayer-circles for different tasks and most importantly have the talent to guide the magic they create by my thoughts.'

'*Really*? So you pray for something to happen and it really does happen?'

'Yes, as I mentioned before. This is how you were brought here. However, new and more challenging tasks require circle-development and practice.'

'Circle-development? I don't understand.'

'Like team-building. You need the *right* people with the *right* talents in order to create something which is greater than the sum of its parts.'

People of different ages began to enter the throne-room and gather at the foot of the throne steps.

'From here you should be able to see inside the circle, though I'm sure you would prefer to watch with your remote-viewing.' Xervren rose from her throne and descended to the circle of eight before her.

Just like when Nathan had viewed this previously, nothing started to happen until Xervren closed the circle and the chanting began. The words sounded like some foreign or ancient language of Krewlornia, certainly not Curumwalish. It had a sinister sound to it as if the words did not want to be chanted.

The vapour came and then the mist, thickening only to part from the centre outward to reveal a view of a room Nathan did not recognise.

However, into view came Nathan. Nathan saw himself clearly, looking younger, but he could not remember this room. His father came into view. He looked confused or unwell. Young Nathan pounced onto him and Gavin began giving him a piggy back ride.

'This is a trick!' Nathan called. 'It is a lie! I never did that. I have never been in that room.'

'You misunderstand, Nathan. This is not a view into the past,' Xervren lied.

'What do you mean?'

'These people who brought you up, created many of you.'

'No! This must be some parallel universe.'

'It is *your* universe. I have known this for some time. In tracking the aura of our bloodline it was because there so many places like this one where there were multiple replicas of you created by their dark magic, that it made your moon-world stand out like a beacon.'

'But…but…It cannot be!'

'And yet…*It is*…These are the *evil* people you are so keen to return to.'

The scene within the circle continued to unfold as Xervren knew it would.

'There's Maeve,' Nathan muttered as he watched her arrive at the door.

She started talking. He could not hear but by lip-reading understood more of what was going on.

'I've come to get you both out of this place,' Maeve said.

Without remote-viewing through the portal it was not possible for Nathan to read everyone's lips, especially when Xervren was Ministering the view point. Luckily for Nathan Xervren shifted the view to better watch Gavin and the clone.

Gavin was trying to say something but the clone's grip on his neck was too tight. Gavin looked unsteady on his feet.

'No you haven't!' responded the clone. 'I've seen what you have done to some of my brothers.'

'Is this suggesting they *cloned* me?' Nathan wondered aloud.

'Evil magic for certain. No good will come of it.' Xervren warned, knowing what was coming next.

'And *you're* not?' the clone scoffed at some statement.

Maeve's response was missed.

'We've *seen* the real world. We just haven't got our hands on it yet,' the clone looked so defiant.

There was another pause then 'You'll never win!' and then with a smile the clone drew the scored edge of a paper cup he was holding across Gavin's neck.

'No!' Nathan cried. 'It's not real! It's *not* real. It's a cruel trick!'

'Sorry Nathan. What we see is *true*. These prayer-circles cannot lie.'

'Dad!' Nathan screamed jumping from the steps into the circle hoping to pass through the portal to his father's side.

However, the gravity slammed him to the floor. Where his reactions on Earth would have made the jump feel like relaxed slow-mo, here it was dangerously quick.

As he jumped he saw his father collapsing, gushing blood from a deep wound to his throat, Maeve rushing to his aid in vain.

Nathan landed badly, hit his head and knees on the floor and winded himself. When he gathered his wits the scene had gone. Blood dripped from forehead but luckily nothing appeared broken.

'We have to go back and save him!'

'It is not possible, Nathan.'

'We have to try! *Please*?!'

'The past is the past. We cannot change it.'

'We *must* find a way. *Please*?'

'Don't you *think*, if it *were* possible, I would have brought back my baby Xaviol?'

Nathan thought about that for a moment. That did make sense. 'I suppose…' Nathan began to weep for his dad.

Xervren had no intention of telling Nathan about the number of failures in trying to retrieve her daughter, despite being able to track back through time with the right talent in the circle.

Xervren dismissed the prayer-circle and left Nathan to cry on the floor. She felt an odd urge to comfort him and paused on the steps for a moment. However, she couldn't be seen to offer comfort to anyone, it would surely lose her respect, especially comforting a *boy*. So she turned and headed on up to her throne.

Nathan felt deep sadness gripping him but knew from what Emily had taught him about survival he had to pull himself together. Rubbing his bloody head he told himself he had to find something to focus on.

If Xervren had not *Night-Ported* him with her prayer-circle, his mum would still be alive and his dad would never have been killed like that.

Nathan did not think to consider that *actually* if it wasn't for Xervren an earlier version of Nathen Purnell would have lived instead of him, to different parents.

He began to focus on his growing desire to kill Xervren and decided that clearly the way to do that was with Alvorecer's help.

31

Alvorecer watched as Nathan staggered into the bedroom.

'What happened to you?' Alvorecer knew but it seemed a good way to get Nathan to talk.

Nathan's hand went to the scab forming on head as he looked across to the mouth in the pillow. 'I tried to jump through one of Xervren's prayer-circle portals to save Dad. I couldn't and now he's *dead*!'

'I'm sorry to hear that, Nathan. But you know you have no control over another person's *remote-view*. You might as well have tried to jump into a TV screen.'

'I know that *now*. I just thought that was how she had *Night-Ported* me, through such a portal.'

'Well she did, but there was a little more to it than that. The prayer-circles boost her powers. She depends upon the Ministering of a prayer-circle to *remote-view* like you do naturally. *You* are a talent to be reckoned with, Nathan.'

'I don't feel like it right now.'

'You have much to learn and practice.'

'Xervren wants me to start training as a warrior.'

'All training is good.'

'Especially if it helps me learn how to kill her. I want you to help me too.'

'If you want to get back to Earth we cannot kill Xervren. She is the only Minister of the prayer-circle which you need to create the Earth-Krewlornia portal.'

'But Curumwal isn't the only land to use prayer-circles is it?'

'No, Nathan. But only Xervren has the experience to carry out what you need to achieve.'

In his frustration, Nathan punched the talking pillow.

It reformed its mouth. 'Oh very mature.'

Alvorecer was wiser than Nathan expected any bed to sound. So he adjusted his plan, to one of preparation for some future opportunity where he could kill his Grandmother *and* get home. He decided to accept Alvorecer and learn what they could do working together.

'So what was it you thought you could do for me, Alvorecer?'

The bed morphed back into the girl with the brown hair and big brown eyes. 'If you are ready to try again, hold out your hand.'

Nathan extended his right hand and Alvorecer its left. As they made contact the metamorph began to spread up Nathan's arm. It made his skin crawl. He shivered and something in his head was screaming *don't*.

'Wait wait!'

'Trust in me.' Alvorecer stopped just above the elbow looking deep into his eyes.

For Nathan this was a bad choice of words. It reminded him of an old Disney animation of Jungle Book. Ka the snake used to say this phrase as he tried to mesmerise those he wished to eat. Thinking of Disney films led Nathan to consider another character.

'You're just like *Venom*!'

'What an insult! I'm nothing of the sort!' Alvorecer clearly knew who Nathan referred to. 'Venom is from a different reality time-line.'

'But you are *both* metamorph shape-shifting aliens.'

'That's as maybe, but Venom did not come from Tormidier. Besides, the author created us before having any knowledge of *Venom*.'

'Wait, *what*?...Author creator?...You mean *God*?'

'No...God is time and space, everything and everybody everywhere, in all time-lines and in all realities. Authors script those time-lines for these realities, within God's version of a subconscious if you like. However, there is no conscious mind, no conscious intent to do good *or* bad, just an energy ensuring that life happens, as per the scripts.'

'I urr...Are you saying our future is being *written* here? Like a book?'

'Or a film script, yes.'

Nathan laughed. 'But that's absurd...You *believe* that there is someone making all these bad things happen to us...for *entertainment*?'

'I kinda *know*.'

'So you are saying that there's some nasty-minded *shit* out there, who would happily have my parents killed and give me a miserable life?'

'Yes, that about sums it up. He probably knows how it looks and if he has any decency maybe he tells close friends and relatives what and absolute *arsehole* he is.'

Nathan laughed again, however he was seething underneath. 'Well if I ever get my hands on him he's *dead*!'

'That's not possible. Others have tried. God has most authors resident within separate realities, otherwise it would bring about the apocalypse all the sooner.'

'What do you mean *apocalypse*?'

'If there is no co-author, coincidental author, or new author willing to take up where the original author left off through decision or death, then that universe collapses. The authors own universes are subject to these same laws. So they are only authoring because their own life-story sets them writing the life-stories of others. What they write and what is written of them is all from that interconnected creative subconscious of God.'

'But these authors would have to live for thousands or millions of years. They must be immortals.'

'No. It's all about back story. *History* and in fact *detail* of the world around you are an illusion. The author only has to write sufficient for the living memory of those involved in the framework God had already created. Coming to terms with this can be a challenge and can make people quite cynical. For some, their own life-story starts to feel contrived in the way that too many things appear to happen without good reason.'

Nathan shook his head, frowning, still not convinced. 'So how many authors are there?'

'*Everyone* is a potential author by their own imaginations, and everyone is a support character in some author's story.'

'So you are saying that we are all playing out what someone else is imagining through *God's* subconscious and there's not a thing we can do about it?'

'Mostly…But that's not to say there are no connections to these authors.'

'What do you mean?'

'You're father ended up with a connection to *our* Author, following a government experiment with transhumanism. He began to experience some prophetic dreams…*Sleep-Reading.*'

'Dad never told me any of this.'

'Not Gavin…Ben.'

'Ben who?'

'Ben McGregor.'

'Oh, so Ben *really is* my biological father?'

'Yes.'

'Where is he?'

'Destiny, another *Time-Slave*, took him to help your mother.'

'Xaviol?'

'Yes, though Ben knows her as Zoe. Oh and neither of them know anything about you because Helga Sturmfeld had you and your clones created secretly.'

'So where *are* my biological parents now?'

'They were taken to the Poldarnel planetoid, close to the asteroid belt around Trappist-1, in a different reality.'

'I thought you said you couldn't get access to other realities?'

'*We* can't but *Time-Slaves* can, when required to do so by *Time*, via the What-If reality engine.'

'How do I know that *you* are not just making all of this up?'

'I have nothing to gain by lying to you. I am trying to build trust.'

355

'Emily taught me…'

'Yes I know…*Never trust…Always manage your risks and expectations*.'

'That's right…How do you *know* these things?'

'I still have memories from when my colony was a *Time-Slave*. Dawn was from New Washington in the USA and…'

'*New* Washington?'

'Yes, a different universe, again, where metamorphs were being used as a biological weapon. They were used to wipe out inhabitants of planets so that the Star Cancer horde could then easily take their resources.'

Nathan just stared, trying to take all of this in.

'In fact, the Harlash have no knowledge of *their* origin. Krewlornia was set up by the Huddnu, living out near the galactic rim, as a secret weapons development site, in their war against the Jenfro, which they lost. Harlash are genetically engineered bio-weapons.'

'So I'm someone else's *weapon*?'

'Yes.'

'I have no intention of being anyone's weapon.'

'That's what your mother used to say, and yet *Time-Slaves* and even the Seriously Organised Vigilantes had her doing work for them as the *Fantasma de morte*.'

'*Fantasma da morte* was my mother?'

'Yes that was what locals first called her for her activities in South America. Later it came to be considered an international myth.'

'She was able to achieve attacks which seemed unexplainable, thanks to extraterrestrial technology, port-weapons supplied by Destiny. Zoe couldn't help herself. She had to do what she would do.'

'You make it sound like we are *all* slaves of Time.'

'In a way yes. Freedom is an illusion which keeps most people happier. The difference for a *Time-Slave* is that they *know* everything that is coming and cannot avoid even the part they play in it. They cannot stop themselves from doing bad things if that's what *God* requires on a time-line.'

'That's *terrible*.'

'So to finish answering your earlier question, when Dawn was infected by my colony her soul was maintained for our impersonation of her human identity. As Dawn we made contact with your father and others. Now, even though Dawn's soul has been released to the fire in the dungeon, much of the *Time-Slave* memory remains with *us*.'

'Okay, hang on…This is *a lot* to take in. Let's go back a step then…So will *I* be able to make a connection with *our* Author, like Ben, to get their help in making things happen for me…*Us*?'

'I know it is possible, yes. This is how prayer works. If enough people share the same prayers, or a *Minister* guides an effective *prayer-circle* things can *certainly* be encouraged to happen.'

'This is good!' Nathan was suddenly sounding much more positive following this new insight.

'It's not all good though…Bad things can be made to happen because of prayer too.'

'Okay…Well, does that depend on how the author is feeling?'

'It can do. The authors, like every one of us, are just parts of the *order* and *chaos* that *is* God. The universal subconscious that keeps the infinity of time-lines rolling is driven by creativity at all levels from evolution and natural disasters to art work and innovation.

'Every idea imagined, even dreamed, and even if it comes to nothing within the originator's reality, does happen in some other universe. Every book or film is an experienced reality somewhere by its very creation.'

'So wait…Are you telling me that the Marvel Multiverse, DC Comics characters, and even horror films are actually real somewhere?'

'Yes *everything*, somewhere.'

'*Oh* I don't know about that.' Nathan returned to doubting, his shoulders slumping. It was difficult to maintain his earlier gain in positivity once things began to sound less than credible.

'Whatever you can imagine Nathan, really is reality somewhere, even if it requires different physics or circumstances. That's why, if you *don't* want to end up feeling like some *arsehole of an author*, responsible for the fate of their characters, it's better for your soul not to imagine any *bad* things at all. Only pray for *good* things to happen.'

Nathan slumped down heavily on his bed. 'I don't know what to say…So that means all the bad things I've thought of in the past, like planning on making people at my school sick by putting an emetic in the water…That *has* happened in a parallel universe, even though I never actually did it in *mine*.'

'Certainly, yes. You didn't do it because *you* decided not to. In another reality at that fork it went down the negative time-line for the other *you* deciding that you *would* do it.'

'This is all *too* much Alvorecer…Isn't it all a bit *chicken and egg* though? If everything we do is in our written time-line then that would have to include what we imagine or pray for too.'

'Indeed.'

'So via this universal subconscious that is God our choices of what to imagine or pray for are already a done deal, good or bad?'

'Absolutely…But if you don't seek to better yourself, by imagining and doing better things, the illusion of your freedom will be experienced more as a hell than a heaven.'

Distracted, his mind racing around in circles trying to come to grips with what Alvorecer had just explained Nathan just sat there staring blankly.

Alvorecer saw this as its opportunity to engulfing him. Nathan only acknowledged that he was covered in metamorph when his brain registered that the girl was gone.

'Hey! Get off me!'

'Calm down Nathan,' said tiny synchronised mouths close to each ear drum. 'I told you we can't eat Harlash.'

'So what *do* you eat?'

'Most animal or plant materials…We cannot consume minerals. In fact if you don't mind, I haven't eaten in a while, I'll just have this leather skirt.'

'What?! No!'

'Oops…Too late.'

'You idiot!'

'You don't need clothes anymore anyway, you have us.'

As Nathan watched the dissolved skirt was replaced by an exact replica, the original belt-buckle falling to the floor.'

'So you can imitate metal and I guess stone, you just can't eat it.'

'Yes but we don't have to eat something to be able to replicate it however, we just have to have a clear shared idea of what it is we are replicating. So if you described something to us, like different clothes you wanted, unless we had experience of them we might not get it right first time. Luckily for you we understand English and have Dawn's memories from Earth, which should help us work together.'

'So now that you have covered me could you disguise me as say a royal guard?' Nathan was getting ideas.

'As long as she was the same height and not smaller in build to you,' Alvorecer morphed into one of the guards, uniform skirt, breast plating and all.

'Neat.' Nathan's voice was a give-away though.

'I can do something about the voice too.'

Nathan felt Alvorecer invading his mouth. 'Stop it! What do you think you are doing?!'

'Be patient. I'm just going to coat your vocal cords.'

'No no...wait *wait*.' The last two words sounded just like one of the royal guards. 'Crikey...This is amazing.'

'I know, right.'

'So I could go anywhere I want now.'

'Within reason...We still have limitations. While I can armour your flesh against blades and some projectiles, we can still be hurt or even killed by energy, from fire or microwaves to electricity or blaster bolts.'

'Well of course.'

'What are you thinking?'

'Don't you know?'

'I cannot read your mind, yet.'

'Yet?'

'Yes. I am aware of your brain activity through your skull. In time it is not beyond reason that in addition to my knowledge of you and second-guessing your wishes it may be possible to come close to reading your mind. I could start to recognise connections between your brain activity patterns and physical actions as the language of your intentions.'

'Right, but only if my thoughts *directly* connect to actions.'

'Or words spoken.'

'How long would that take?'

'I don't know. Years I guess.'

'So how do I tell you what disguise I need.'

'As you did with this one...by speech.'

'That could be awkward.'

'Well I *can* register a whisper.'

'Okay then.' Nathan whispered. 'Make me look like Xervren.'

32

Nathan knew he had to keep Alvorecer secret. If Xervren found out about the metamorph she would want to kill it, again. So rather than arouse suspicions he thought it best to behave as normal as he could, whilst still covered in the colony of morphocytes.

Nevertheless, he was amazed at what Alvorecer could simulate the appearance as well as feel of; Metal and ceramic, leather and fabric too. The impression of water and blood was still just morphocytes not a chemical change. But Alvorecer explained that there were limitations to this simulation. It could not create electro-magnetic fields, so could not replicate functioning electrical technology.

After finishing his duties out in the fields, Nathan was keen to learn more about what he might be able to do with the help of his metamorph companion.

'Is it possible for you to help me climb walls?'

'Certainly…It is possible to penetrate many types of surface in the way that roots or glue can. And for those very smooth surfaces, like glass, we can produce suckers.'

'Fantastic!'

'However…Certain conditions we cannot cope so well with. If it also requires lifting additional weight, such as yourself, this will depend on the degree of gravity, the angle of the surface and the quality of the surface. If the surface is greasy or crumbly, or has repellent properties then we have a problem.'

'I'll bear that in mind. I want to try climbing one of the towers.'

'Why?'

'For fun.'

'Seems like a waste of our energy. We haven't eaten much today.'

'Okay, let's go after we've eaten.' Nathan headed for the mess.

In the mess as he took an empty bowl and joined the queue to get served a woman came across to him. She identified herself as Maralat, one of the combat instructors. She had been ordered to begin his training in the morning, so he would not be working in the fields anymore.

She did not sit with him to explain further. Instead she walked back to the separate area for women, above the main floor.

Nathan finished getting his bowl of stew. He took a couple of what, on Krewlornia, passed for bread rolls and some fruit, placing them on his wooden tray. Then he looked for a seat out of the way, so that no one would see him try to feed Alvorecer.

That was when he spotted Garowak. He saw him too, smiled and waved. As Nathan headed towards his friend he whispered through barely moving lips 'Sorry Alvorecer. I was looking to feed you some of this.'

'No problem,' said the voice in his ears. 'We will slide off and go eat something then meet you back in our room.'

'*No don't.* People will notice.'

'No they won't. We will leave part of the colony behind so that you still appear clothed.'

Nathan smiled, unsure about this, as he sat down with his tray across from his friend. The separation felt like sweat was pouring off him as most of Alvorecer soaked into the flagstones and was gone. As promised it had left him with a skirt and belt.

Nathan marvelled that these morphocytes were able to change their volume so substantially; to be able to appear as a bed, a girl, or clothing and still manage to separate. He wondered if this meant that the colony could produce multiple entities.

Garowak didn't seem to notice a thing in the poor light of the hall.

In case he had though, Nathan thought it best to distract him with conversation. 'I haven't seen you in the fields this last couple of days.'

'No. I have been put on training to be a warrior.'

'*Really*? So have I, with Maralat.'

'Yes. I heard you would be joining us. There are only nine recruits this year. It will be tough. Some of us won't make it.'

'Not pass?'

'Pass *away*.'

'*Die*?'

'It is a *great honour* to the family for youngsters, including those of the less-useful sex, to be selected for warrior training. So there is no failure now, even in death.'

Nathan wondered whether this was what Xervren had intended all along. For him to die in training, despite telling him she had invested too much of her time to lose him. This could just be some face-saving ruse so that he was seen to die with honour, not simply have the Queen do as he bid and let him leave for his own agenda.

He had no intention of dying however, and was certain that Alvorecer would see to that. This reminded him, he had wanted to start practicing what he could do with Alvorecer.

Nathan tried to make his excuses and leave. 'Sorry, Garowak, I have to go and catch up on some sleep. The days on your world are longer than on mine.'

'What do you mean, on your world?'

'I thought you knew. I thought everyone knew. I was brought here from another world.'

'You mean from another land.'

'I mean another world orbiting another sun. Xervren brought me here by prayer-circle.'

'I heard you were brought from another land and that's why you had to learn Curumwalish. And you were weak because you had been prevented from exercising.'

'No. That's not it at all. My world is the size of your moon and the gravity is a third of yours. I have had to become accustomed to all this. And I still tire easily, that's why I still need extra sleep when I can get it.'

'I best let you go then. But one last question Nathan.'

'Yes?'

'If what you say is really true, why did I see you being brought in from across the lake the day you arrived?'

'Because I appeared in a jungle.'

'But why did you not appear within the prayer-circle?'

'I had assumed that it was because Xervren was not in full control of what she was doing. She made many attempts to bring me here since I was a baby. But perhaps the truth is different.'

'Like you choose to imagine that you are from another world but you were actually brought from a land that you'd rather forget.'

'No…I was taken from my father and now he's dead. I think Xervren only brought me here as a *lure*.'

'I don't understand.'

'She told me I was brought here because a soothsayer had foretold that my arrival would bring Ata, the woman I arrived with.'

'Your supervisor, who left?'

'She didn't *leave*, Garowak. The Queen had her tortured to death.'

'What? Why?'

'She claimed that Ata was the woman who had *switched* her baby Xaviol many years ago.'

'We know this story. But many believed it was the grief speaking. Many also think she has convinced herself that you are her grandchild because she was never able to conceive another child as heir.'

Nathan knew he couldn't tell Garowak too much more without running into some awkward questions, so simply said 'If the Queen needed to concoct a story about finding an heir, then why not choose a girl?'

'This is what everyone is wondering. People believe the Queen's grief is finally driving her mad.'

'Maybe you are right.' Nathan stood up, faking a yawn. 'Sorry, I really do need to get my head down.'

'See you tomorrow then.'

'For sure.' Nathan turned and left.

When he arrived at his bedroom, it seemed to be empty. He wondered if Alvorecer had not yet finished eating and decided to lie on his bed while he waited for her to return.

He felt something sliding up his legs. He made to shoot off the bed but stumbled. Before he could get up Alvorecer enveloped him.

'*Don't* do that! It's *creepy*!' Nathan rubbed at an elbow.

'Sorry Nathan. We told you we would wait hear for you.'

'You could have said something first. I didn't know you were in here.'

'Apologies…Do you still want to climb that tower?'

'Yes.'

What Nathan had expected was to walk out into the courtyard with Alvorecer providing camouflage. He had been right about the camouflage however he took on a stony pattern and texture. He was further surprised by what happened next.

The first odd sensation was that he was wearing a sort of wetsuit exoskeleton which could control his limbs. He was made to climb up the bedroom wall and across the ceiling. Above the door they reached down for the handle with an extra length of arm coming out of his right hand. Then getting out into the corridor and closing the door behind them they kept to the ceiling. They worked their way out of the castle, via the battlements rather than the courtyard. The door from the closest tower onto the battlements was not guarded, though the battlements were patrolled.

Over the battlements they went onto the outer wall. Nathan became very aware of how high up they were. Though he was not scared of heights, he knew that a fall from there, even under 1G, would likely kill him.

'Where to now then, Nathan?' Alvorecer asked, releasing a hand from the surface of the stonework so that he could point.

Feeling the left hand come loose was unnerving for Nathan, but the other hand held as firm as his toes and knees to the stone. 'Urr…That way…That big tower with the windows.'

It was best to keep to the shadows even with Alvorecer's camouflage because light could still cast shadow with their form. However, this castle wall was in shade so it was less of a concern.

Nathan was surprised at just how fast Alvorecer could move him across this vertical surface under 3Gs. With further direction Nathan soon arrived at the window to the room full of old furniture.

The window was hinged. Testing it by pulling on the glass Alvorecer found it was locked but Nathan already knew this because he could see the latch inside.

'This has been fun Alvorecer, but unless you can reach through glass and lift that latch we won't be able to get in.'

'Will this do?' Alvorecer poured some of its colony against the window frame, penetrated the gap reached the latch and lifted it, swinging the window open.

'Fantastic.'

They went inside. The room was cluttered.

'I know there's not a lot of space in here for a hideaway but with some rearranging it could work.'

'We could also consume some of it.'

'Consume?'

'Like the bed next to yours.'

'Oh, I see…When you left to go and eat did you go and consume some furniture then?'

'No. I much prefer meat. Though the meat here is not as sweet as on Earth. I found a few kablad to eat.' Alvorecer referred to the six legged rat-like animals which were always scavenging around the castle.

'Mmm nice.'

'The food has been better on other worlds.'

'So how many worlds has your colony visited?'

'As a *Time-Slave* we visited many.'

'So out of all the things you have eaten what tasted the best?'

'Humans.'

33

Warrior training with Maralat did not start with weapons training as Nathan was expecting but instead began with basic physical training. Days were spent stretching and exercising, in the courtyard along with a number of previously trained warriors. However, once these trained warriors had prepared themselves for the day they went about their duties. For the trainees the exercising continued, with running up and down slopes. Then it shifted up a gear to running with a pack which each day increased in weight. This all improved stamina as well as muscle tone.

Next came days of learning how to fall and get straight back up again. This involved falling from standing then from running. Then it involved jumping from steps of different heights. It might have looked like mucking about had it not been for the body-slams the 3G handed out. Of course Nathan's previous experiences of how brutal 3G falls could be ensured that he took this training seriously.

As recovering from falls became second nature Maralat had them work in pairs using long and short staffs but not to learn attack moves. First they had to learn how to take blows to different parts of their bodies with minimal damage. Needless to say the recruits were all pretty bruised by the end of the first day, on top of bruises many of them had already accumulated from bad falls in the days previous.

Even though Harlash healed three times faster than Humans, this did not make them complacent over injuries. Though they were all taught how to tend their injuries, none were looking forward to further beatings, even if they were taking it in turns to dish it out. What made matters worse was that the boys who were seen to be taking it easy on those they were paired up with were then beaten more severely by Maralat. This treatment had been received by a number of boys paired up with Nathan. They were worried about being too hard on the *Queen's Grandson*. They had heard it said that Nathan was a weakling who could barely scrub a floor when he had arrived. However, Maralat told them in no uncertain terms not to treat Nathan any different.

Days later, when Maralat decided the boys were building up a tolerance to the pain she moved them on to defensive blocking of blows.

Nathan didn't exactly enjoy the training but he did appreciate the value of it. He had thought that Alvorecer would have shielded him more. However, in its wisdom the metamorph deemed it necessary that Nathan get the same experience in case they were ever apart. This was not to say that Alvorecer would not intervene in some way if it thought Nathan's life were in serious danger.

The day came when weapons training began and they were given leather armour to protect their chests and forearms. In addition to the staffs they had to learn how to use long and short blades carrying a shield. They also had to learn to fight without a shield using one or two blades. The weapons-training was extensive and thorough dealing with blow-pipes, throwing blades and rope weapons. Eventually the training became observational, learning how best to use the environment and items in it as effective weapons.

Nathan was amazed as time went on how much there was to being a warrior. Emily had taught him defensive actions of unarmed combat, plus escape, evasion and survival techniques, but Maralat's training was something else entirely. It was like learning how to be a 3G Ninja.

Every time Nathan felt the end of training would be near there seemed to be more to learn, like the elusive summit of a round peaked mountain.

Despite having no concept of a year on Krewlornia the Curumwalish did have what approximated to a week, referred to as a *face*. Krewlornia's moon, unlike Earth's moon, revolved in its orbit, though quite slowly. Having no hidden side, every five days the moon would present a large crater, like a startled mouth, near two eye-like land-masses in its ocean.

Warrior training took many *faces* to complete. The first sign that the end might truly be near, after learning to work in squads, was being taught rules of engagement.

Because resources on Krewlornia were considered precious and not to be wasted, the victor of a battle was expected to take the dead from both sides, as food.

Learning that the Harlash, or at least the Curumwalish, were cannibals had Nathan wondering whether he had already been fed Harlash flesh.

Another less disturbing fact concerned the treatment of an enemy. Unless an enemy had a known value to being kept alive they were to be dispatched immediately. No valueless prisoners were to be taken. Because the Harlash could recover from even severe injuries the rule was to always ensure the head of the enemy was removed. The trainee warriors had to learn to do this on dummies while chanting *remove the head*. However, they would never truly know what it felt like to remove a living head until they did this in action.

Thinking about having to do this for real Nathan experienced that sense of excitement he had had when he killed Colt and Carl in the outback. He had not needed to remove their heads to be certain of their deaths however.

It occurred to Nathan that in English translation there was an acronym for this rule: ARTHUR. Always Remove The Head Unless Required.

On the final day of training Maralat praised the trainees. She told them that she was glad to see that while accidents had happened during training none of them had died this time.

Nathan asked 'So where do we go now?' He was hoping to get away from the castle for a while. He had come to know Krewlornia by *remote-viewing*, there were many beautiful places, but he had yet to hear and smell those places.

'Tomorrow, you will all return to your homes and duties until called upon.'

'But Maralat, I thought this training was all about becoming a guard or forming part of a patrol group.'

'Ha. You have quite an imagination, Nathan. I'm sorry if this training has deluded you into feeling more feminine. Males will always be for heavy lifting and of course sex. Males are too stupid and lazy to serve as anything more than reserve warriors in times of attack.'

'But that's not fair. Men and Women should be considered equals.'

'Ha. Enough joking, Nathan. The Queen has said she that wants to see you as soon as I am done with you.'

Nathan had not been to see his grandmother since his training had begun. However, he was aware that she had come to watch progress from time to time.

The guards at the throne room door were expecting Nathan and they let him pass without comment.

He noticed a table in the hall with a number of cups on but said nothing turning instead to Xervren he said 'You wanted to see me Grandma.'

'Yes, Nathan. Now that you have completed your warrior training, I have a mission for you.'

'You *do*?' Nathan felt a burst of excitement, maybe he would be travelling after all.

'I require you to pick three of the male warriors you trained with, to accompany you on this mission. You are to lead them to a number of villages to bring back boys I have chosen for prayer-circle training.'

'Oh. I would have thought you would have sent some of yours guards, as you did to collect me.'

'Are you suggesting that you do not accept my *order*?'

'No, no. I'm happy to go Grandma. Just surprised is all.'

'Good. It is important to me that people of the villages see my Grandson now.'

Nathan thought she sounded almost proud of him. Maybe she was softening.

'But first you must experience the Resilience Ceremony.' Xervern pointed down to the table. 'The table has been prepared with a selection of poisons. You must choose and drink three of them.'

'*Three*?' Nathan revised his view of her. She wasn't softening, she was going *insane*.

Xervren clapped her hands and four maids came into the hall. Two had baskets which Nathan recognised from the times he had been stung and bitten by their contents. The other two brought branches of fire-nettle and burn-blossom.

'Okay *okay*. I'm doing it.'

Though the cups had a variety of different colours, some of them frothy, he recalled that they had all been as nasty as one another.

Under his breath he whispered 'Any ideas Alvorecer?'

'Just drink three at random.'

'Oh you're a *great help*.'

Nathan took three cups at random, drank them down then belched in protest.

'Don't you be sick on my floor again!' Xervren warned. 'Keep it in.'

'Okay.' The taste in his mouth was bitter.

'This ceremony would normally have taken place when you were much younger, but of course you were not here then...How does it feel to be grown up?'

'Like indigestion.'

Xervren motioned with her hand for the completion of the ceremony and the four maids stepped forward. Alvorecer also took its cue and suddenly slid away, leaving Nathan with his replica skirt and leather armour. The women never noticed the metamorph drain between the flagstones as the two maids emptied the contents of their baskets over him. Stepping away to allow the other two access, the flogging with fire-nettle and burn-blossom began.

Nathan experienced the bites, stings and burns as little more than irritating pinching and didn't collapse or even gag from the cups of poison. He accepted that this must have been necessary, insane as it seemed, for Alvorecer to leave him go through it.

The biting and stinging critters scuttled off his body under the flogging and were returned to their baskets. Then the flogging stopped.

'Nathan of Curumwal,' Xervren announced, 'you are now a *man*.'

There was no applause, which Nathan was thankful for. The ceremony had felt awkward enough. He did not offer any thanks.

'Go now and select your men then return with them in the morning and I shall show you, by prayer-circle, who the required boys are and where they live.'

Faces later, Nathan, Garowak, Purret and Camlod had retrieved all but one of the boys for prayer-circle training.

They had retrieved the eldest first. Selbani looked about eight years old to Nathan. He had been chosen to receive more training than the others. This was because Xervren wanted to teach him how to Minister prayer-circles.

This decision ran against expectations. Ministers on Krewlornia had always been women. Once again, Nathan had wondered whether his talks with his grandmother about his life on Earth were helping to open her mind to the benefits of equality.

Each boy began their training within a day of arrival at Curumwal. The order they were collected in related to the maturity of their talent. All villages had received messengers when Xervren had made her choice, so there were no surprises when Nathan and the other warriors turned up to escort the boys to the castle.

However, when Nathan arrived at Grenvek to collect the youngest boy, Nishtu, there was resistance. This boy's mother refused to let him go.

'I'm sorry Vashpor, but Queen Xervren has commanded us to escort Nishtu to Curumwal. She will not hear of any refusal.' The boy looked far too young for the long and difficult journey, never mind being away from home for any length of time. He looked about six.

'What can you *boys* possibly do about my refusal?...Nishtu is too young.'

Nathan tried to be tactful, building upon what he had told the other boys mothers. 'The Queen has chosen Nishtu for a reason. It is to be considered an honour that he has been chosen.'

To Nathan's mind some of the mothers had been all too ready to hand over their boys, but not Vashpor. Resistance would have been greater from these mothers had the chosen child been a girl, Nathan thought.

'You will see Nishtu again, as his talent develops. He will be taken good care of, better than other boys in fact. I promise you as the Grandson of Queen Xervren.'

Vashpor knew she had no choice. A refusal to comply with an order from the Queen would not bode well for the people of Grenvek. So, for the good of her village, it was with a heavy heart that Vashpor and her mate Ednil hugged their child goodbye. With tears in their eyes they both promised Nishtu he would be back soon enough. To encourage him to be brave they told him that he was going to have an exciting adventure, one which he would be able to tell them all about on his return.

Nathan took the young boy's hand and led him away. He knew as the going got tough he would be taking it in turns with his other warriors to take the boy on their backs, as they had done with a couple of the others.

As they got to the edge of Grenvek they turned, Nathan held Nishtu up for one last wave.

34

Once all of the chosen boys were settled in and progressing well with their training, as a complete prayer-circle, Nathan was sent for.

Purret and Camlod had returned to duties in their own villages and Nathan and Garowak had both been set to work tending the gibren. Nathan compared these to some sort of swamp kangaroo, farmed for meat and milk. Semi domesticated, these beasts knew they were to be milked every day yet were never in any hurry to be leaning over the milking bench.

It had seemed funny to Nathan when he was first taught how to milk a gibren. He was told off for attempting to milk the two small teats on their chest by hand as he might have done with a cow's udder.

Once shown what to do he had second thoughts about drinking any more gibren milk. The milk had to be sucked out and spat into a pot.

It was as he was suckling his tenth gibren of the morning that his remote-viewing sweeps picked up a royal guard approaching. Royal guards would only come out of the castle for one thing.

'The Queen wants to see you.'

'Okay. Tell Grandma I'll be along as soon as I'm done.'

'Now!'

'But I have to at least suckle this other breast before this gibren can be released.'

379

'Forget the beast.'

As Nathan got up from the bench the gibren turned and honked its disbelief, lifting a hand to indicate that her right breast was still full.

'Garowak!' Nathan shouted across the swamp to where he knew his colleague was though not in sight. 'You need to finish off this gibren. I have to go see Grandma!'

From the lakeside edge of the swamp they caught the waiting ferryboat across to the castle.

There were some fish-like creatures in many of Krewlornia's waterways. The lake in which Curumwal's castle sat had large Kontipp in it. These had two tails and bulging eyes on the top of their heads. As Nathan looked out from the ferry he counted the eyes to seven of these beasts. They were harmless, feeding on algal mats which grew so quickly it was nearly possible to watch them expand.

Nathan had secretly taken night swims in this lake. Alvorecer was able to extend flippers from his feet for added propulsion. And taking on rocks from the lakebed for ballast he was able to dive to the bottom of the deepest part of the lake where he discovered some eel-like animal living in the accumulated sludge there.

Curumwal had come to feel like a second home to Nathan over what must have amounted to well over an Earth year by now, if not two. This was not to say that he did not miss Earth, especially his father. Though he had tried many times to search with very slow focused sweeps of his remote-viewing he had never managed to find Earth.

Reaching the dock, Nathan and the guard strode on up to the throne-room. Nathan's footwear was leaving a trail of muddy footprints behind him just as they would have had the footwear not been Alvorecer's replicas. The metamorph could have avoided leaving prints, but the agreed rule remained to keep their partnership a secret.

Before the steps to the throne the guard turned away from Nathan, returning to her post.

'How are things in the swamp Nathan?'

'My feet never seem to dry out these days.' In truth his feet were always drier than Garowak's thanks to Alvorecer.

'Well you don't need to concern yourself with gibren any longer.'

'Oh?'

'I have decided to form an alliance with Tymbrenwal who we share our longest border with.'

'Right.' Nathan had no idea where his grandmother was going with this. She had never entered into any discussion with him before regarding politics.

'As you know, I have no heir to the throne of Curumwal.'

'What about *me*? Surely I…'

'You are a *man*. We can only have Queens ruling Queendoms. How ridiculous would it sound to have a man on the throne of a Queendom?'

'It would be King and Kingdom.'

'Don't waste my time with your nonsense words, Nathan. I have decided…You are to be mated with Princess Roshvik of Tymbrenwal.'

'*Mated*?' He didn't like the sound of arranged marriages but Xervren made it sound more like stud farming.

'Yes. I have agreed with Queen Taminil that if Roshvik has a girl child by you, the child will grow up to become Queen of Curumwal when I die.'

'And if I don't help provide a girl?'

'Then on my death Queen Taminil with join both our lands as one.'

'And I suppose if Queen Taminil dies before you then on your death Curumwal goes to Roshvik?'

'Exactly. Queen Taminil already has an heir to the throne of Tymbrenwal, with Princess Quella.'

'So what will become of *me*?'

'Whatever, Roshvik desires. It is the way of the world. You will be her property.'

'*Property*?'

'Do you *have* to keep repeating words that I'm sure you understand?'

'Don't I get any say in this, Grandma? What if I don't like this *Roshvik*?' He desperately began *remote-viewing* young women in Tymbrenwal castle, built high on a mountain top, attempting to identify Roshvik by lip-reading.

'You will do what you are required to do.'

'Once she has a girl can I come back?'

'No, no. You are not *listening*. Unless Roshvik decides to send you back, which I would find rather *insulting*, to spurn my gift, she will probably find you a herd of mountain Flek to tend.'

Nathan didn't know what to say.

'You are to leave today, so you need to get cleaned up. You will be given something more appropriate to wear, as her mate. You will also present to Roshvik a dowry, which includes a fine mating gown made for her by our best tailors.'

'I don't know what to say.'

'Thank you would be nice.'

'I mean, what do I say to someone I've never met, who I'm expected to have sex with? I've never been with a woman before.'

'I should hope not. You are being gifted as a virgin.'

This all felt very wrong, and was only to get worse.

By the time Nathan was washed and dressed in his new royal armour of multi-coloured scale-hide, from a Vamouror, he felt more the part of a groom.

However, as he returned to the throne-room for Xervren's approval, he noticed that she had one of her prayer-circles present. In the centre of the circle was a large square table with four baskets on it.

'Oh Nathan, what a sight you are, looking very royal in your Vamouror battle-dress. Roshvik should be well pleased with you,' said Xervren. 'Now climb onto the table and sit cross-legged on top of the dowry baskets.'

'Is this some sort of blessing ceremony, Grandma?'

'Your mating already has my blessing, Nathan. Otherwise I would not allow it. No, this is the *send-off*.'

Nathan frowned. 'Are you saying you are going to *teleport* me there?'

'Yes. I do not want to chance anything happening to you *or* the dowry on the way to Tymbrenwal castle, so you will indeed be teleported.'

'But I thought I had to be asleep for you to do that.'

'We certainly experienced less interference when you were asleep in bringing you here. A conscious mind, such as yours, with your remote-viewing, would seem to interfere with the destination prayer. It took a lot of practice to finally get you here. However, sending you across to Tymbrenwal will be fine, as long as you sit still and clear your mind.'

'And if I don't?'

'Well you could end up somewhere you don't want to be or just not get teleported anywhere at all.'

'So why could you not have brought the boys chosen for your new prayer-circle here by teleportation, instead of sending me to collect them?'

'Enough of your questions! Just sit still and clear your mind.'

As the chanting began Xervren focused on the task at hand.

Clearing his mind the best he could, Nathan made no effort to say goodbye to her.

This was the first that time Nathan was to experience teleporting whilst conscious of the process. It made him feel hyper-alert which was counter to the required clearing of his mind. Nevertheless, it was successful. Though it was an instant transition from one castle to the other, he arrived with a memory of the porting somehow taking a second or two. It had felt like he, along with Alvorecer, the dowry baskets and a circular chunk of table top, had all been shrunk to something smaller than a subatomic particle. This infinitely small package had then passed through a fold in space and then expanded back to normal size at the required destination.

It was a bit of a system shock but with a few blinks of his eyes Nathan recovered. He was in Queen Taminil's throne-room, still sitting on the baskets and the remains of the table.

His sudden appearance would have been more of a surprise had it not been on the agreed day, and sundial time.

Queen Taminil's throne-room was a different layout to Xervren's, and had been built using darker stone. The throne was on a balcony with stairs to either side. The Queen rose from the throne and stood at the edge. There was no guard rail and it seemed she might easily fall from there, especially since she looked much older than Xervren.

'Welcome to Tymbrenwal, Nathan.'

'Thank you, Queen Taminil.'

'Your Grandmother and I met a number of times while you were away collecting boys for her new project.'

'*Project*?...You mean prayer-circle.'

'Of course...Let me introduce you to my sister.'

Nathan turned to see an elderly lady move towards him from the side of the hall, and wondered when he would get to meet his bride.

'This is Roshvik.'

Nathan needed to say it was an honour to be chosen, as his grandmother had instructed him to, but he was speechless. Though younger in appearance than Taminil, Roshvik still had to be three times, if not four times, Nathans age. He didn't understand how this woman was still able to have children. No one had explained that Harlash women could give birth even when a hundred Earth years old.

'Ughh…Does Queen Xervren have no *other* grandson?' Princess Roshvik sounded very disappointed. 'This one has a deformed aura.'

Queen Taminil did not want to risk upsetting either Queen Xervren or her sister, so initially had Nathan sent to separate quarters. She then has her royal physician sent along to examine him.

Later, the physician reported to the throne-room, 'The deformed aura appears to be some sort of birth defect, creating an energy blockage within his braelic. Not any sort of psychic injury that I may have been able to heal with *my* talent. I apologise for this my Queen.'

'Would this deformity affect an offspring?'

'It *may* be hereditary yes, and yet it appears quite benign. Nathan is otherwise fit, if a little weaker than other young men. I hear it said that weakness of the less-useful sex can be quite *appealing* to some.'

'I doubt I will be able to convince Roshvik that this is an *appealing* trait. Nathan is to sire her child not simply fulfil bedding duties. She has a string of other young men for that.'

The physician thought for a moment then went on to say 'I have heard tell of an old woman called Hoscron, with a stronger talent than mine for correcting auras.'

'Then have her brought here immediately to treat Nathan.'

'Hoscron is not of Tymbrenwal or Curumwal even. She is from distant Pendorak, in the north, and if she still lives would be too frail for such a journey.'

'It is a shame that we do not have a teleportation prayer-circle as Queen Xervren possesses.'

'Indeed, my Queen.'

'This is all *extremely* frustrating, that Xervren should send us her damaged goods for me to fix. Nevertheless, the prize of getting control of Curumwal could still be worth it.'

Queen Taminil sent for ten of her best warriors to escort Nathan to Hoscron of Pendorak. Jewels were to be taken as payment, but only paid if Hoscron could heal Nathan's deformity.

Once Nathan had been removed from Xervren's throne-room and the remains of the table cleared away, the Queen called for her new prayer-circle.

It would take much practice for the boys to be fully prepared to carry out Xervren's plan; an act of retribution. This plan had been many *faces* in the making and Xervren knew that it had to work first time.

Even though the plan's success had been foretold, Xervren appreciated that it could not succeed if the circle was not fully trained. The prayer-circle would also need testing before

Xervren would engage the boys in their mission.

The boys soon filed into the throne-room and formed their circle with Selbani as trainee Minister.

Xervren had had the boys begin each session by meditating cross-legged with hands in laps, to clear their minds. Next they exercised in focusing their individual talents, standing and holding hands. Selbani, as ever, was there to gather the mix of powers and focus them on the set task.

Previously the task had involved lifting objects placed in the centre of the circle. This had progressed from empty baskets to baskets containing different weights. Then the day came when this exercise had had to be repeated all over again but without Selbani being a link in the ring.

Selbani found that not holding hands severely reduced his channelling of the powers at first. Nevertheless, with much practice he regained his sense of connection and focus. He began to lift the set objects in the circle before him.

The next stage in the training had been to tumble the basket. The challenge increased with the order to open the basket then remove the object inside. Each day filled the boys with excitement and a sense of achievement, building a confidence in them that they would one day be capable of doing so much more.

'Today,' Xervren announced, 'you will lift an empty basket, but this time you are to focus on breaking it apart.'

35

Nathan was glad to be travelling once more, even if the ten women were not as good company as the three lads had been. That wasn't to say that he would have refused any of them as a mate over Princess Roshvik. None of them looked much older than Nathan, and he was taller than all but three of them.

He wasn't looking forward to his eventual return to Tymbrenwal but intended to make the most of his journey to see Hoscron the Healer. He hoped they never found her, but searching ahead with his remote-viewing he thought he spotted her, not that he shared this fact with his escorts.

As they moved swiftly north by foot and at times by boat across inland seas, Nathan noted the temperature dropping slightly. He began to see animals he had only viewed previously.

His warrior escort knew what to watch out for though. They were hyper-vigilant, so it was clear to Nathan that none of these women had a talent for remote-viewing. Only two of the women could speak Curumwalish and they seemed easily irritated by his questions about the wildlife. He was sure their attitude would have been different had he been a woman.

One day as they crossed an expanse of savanna they were set upon by a mammoth cat-like creature. Four warriors made to scare it away with shouting and shaking of their spears but clearly the beast's only thought must have been *noisy food*. As it pressed its attack and took one woman in its mouth Nathan made to join in with his spear. However, two of the warriors held him back saying something in Tymbrenwalish which clearly must have meant *don't*.

Four more warriors joined the attack, throwing their spears into the beast's eyes and throat then drew their swords. Eventually the beast was beaten but not before it crushed another warrior under its heavy feet. There was nothing to be done for her and yet she would not die quickly. Sharalee, the lead warrior, crouched down, said a prayer then slit the fatally injured warrior's throat.

Though Nathan knew this was not really his fault, it did not stop him feeling in some way to blame for the two deaths. He was sure these women thought the same. If he had not been born with this deformity these women would not have been ordered to risk their lives.

Queen Xervren felt that the new prayer-circle was developing nicely. Recently she had had the boys make their first kill.

It had only been a zeshlec to start with, but this had been a turning point for Selbani and the other boys. The creature had been lifted from the basket, confused by the telekinesis, wriggling it suddenly went into spasm bleeding from its eyes, ears and every other orifice.

Watching the zeshlec go limp and lifeless Xervren applauded. However, she could see that some of the boys were shocked by what their prayer-circle had done, so Xervren immediately had them kill something bigger.

The next creature, a Hanmerel, was much larger. This one did not die so well. It squealed for some moments before both of its hearts gave out and it suddenly shed all of its scales. Nevertheless, this was not as much of a shock for the boys, as this was similar to the way its kind died in the kitchens when plunged into a cauldron of boiling water.

To wind the boys down at the end of each training session, Xervren began bringing in a second prayer-circle, mostly of women. They formed an outer circle around Selbani and the other boys. When Xervren then joined hands with this outer circle and began ministering the prayer, the boys were shown a view of a very brightly lit hall in the centre of their circle. This hall had an oddly curved floor, like a giant bowl, and suspended above it was an illuminated ceiling formed of tubes.

Every time the image was conjured up Xervren assured the boys they would one day have the honour of going there.

A couple of *faces* further north and Nathan's group reached the southern foot-hills of the Anlangra mountain range. There was not much further to travel now, as Hoscron the Healer lived in the northern foot-hills of this range.

The peaks of this range were shrouded in cloud and capped in snow and ice they looked like an impassable obstruction. Nevertheless, a pass was known to the party and examining the way ahead, Nathan had spotted this route too.

However, Nathan also spotted a number of people in that pass but not on the track. He had a bad feeling about their presence. They were mainly men, though a few boys were there too. Though they seemed reasonably well armed, with swords and spears, there was no sense of uniform about what they wore. They wore layers of clothes to cope with the cold, but the question was why did they choose to live at such harsh climbs?

Nathan tried to share his concerns, turning to Karolana one of the translators, 'I believe there will be an ambush near the crest of this pass.'

The warrior peered ahead as they ascended. 'I see no one.'

'Well I tell you they are there and they have spotted our approach now.'

'So *tell* me. How many warriors strong are they?'

'There must be four men on lookout and...'

'*Men* ha! You have *no* need to worry then.'

'But there are three times that many in a makeshift camp slightly further north. I think you need to pass on my warning to Sharalee.'

'Do you now? Well they just sound like runaways to me.'

'*Runaways*?'

'Masculists. Men who don't like to be treated like men but would rather be treated like women.'

Nathan frowned, 'Do you mean, treated like equals?'

'*You* are starting to sound like a *masculist* yourself Nathan. I would watch out with that. Princess Roshvik will not be well pleased with any such attitude from a mate.'

'Nevertheless, I'm telling you the men ahead of us look like bandits. Why else would they be up in a mountain pass, unless to rob? Queen Taminil surely won't be pleased to find out we lost the gems needed to pay Hoscron the Healer.'

'Well thank you for your *sage* advice *Nathan of Curumwal* but no man will survive long enough to even touch the gems that Sharalee carries. We are all well experienced warriors with a number of battles under our belts. So you need not concern yourself. Any attack will be met by a merciless death.'

Nathan did not bother trying to argue further. Karolana seemed insulted that he should think to suggest that these men might be any sort of threat.

Around mid-day the incline began to level out. The men were very close now, waiting among the rocks. All of the men were there and prepared for the ambush. Only the boys had remained at the makeshift camp.

Watching closely, Nathan could see that a couple of the men had a bow with a few arrows. So what were the others expecting to do? The boulder terrain was not safe to charge down from and none of the boulders looked prepared for being rolled down upon them.

As they came within range Nathan saw the men reach to the ground and to their belts but not for their swords.

'Slings!' Nathan shouted to Sharalee.

She heard his warning but like the rest of the women did not understand his English.

A well slung stone hit Sharalee right between the eyes with such force she fell dead instantly.

'Take cover!' Nathan warned in Curumwalish but the women seemed deaf in their arrogance.

With spears and shields in hand, the women tried to spot their stone slinging attackers. Nevertheless, they were struck again and again wherever was exposed.

Nathan held his shield up as protection, though knowing it was only an extension of Alvorecer, his original armour long gone. He ran for the pack that Sharalee had on her back.

A warrior bounding up into the rocks soon dispatched a man. As she removed the head just as Nathan had been taught in Curumwal he considered it must be standard practice.

Another warrior closed in on a man among the boulders but a stone from another in hiding hammered into her temple. She fell aside dead.

The men were not coming down to the track to fight with swords. With the availability of stones and the advantage of height, why would they.

The warriors, too proud and fearless to hide, were being picked off. Nathan however, with his remote-viewing sweeps was able to react and block all incoming stones aimed at him with his shield.

With the pack of gems in hand, slipping the strap over his neck and under one arm, Nathan called out in Curumwalish, 'Stop! Everyone *stop*! We can *pay* for passage!'

It was not clear whether any of the men could speak Curumwalish because the stoning continued. It didn't help that at that moment Karolana was stunned by a blow to the head then as she stumbled forward was killed by another strike. Now Nathan was left with no warrior translators.

'Would you like *me* to put an end to all this?' Alvorecer whispered in his ears.

'Yes.'

Another warrior collapsed dead, leaving only two. They continued trying to defend Nathan's position from attacks which ironically could not harm him whilst he had Alvorecer as his body-guard.

'Are you *sure*?'

'Yes *yes*!' he spluttered with no thought to ask what Alvorecer had in mind.

The outer surface of Alvorecer's shield on Nathan's left arm blistered. As each blister quickly burst, out flew a silver bug. The swarm flew in all directions, going over and between boulders and striking at necks.

These colony attack teams had been used before by metamorph Time-Slaves in many situations and in different ways. On hitting each neck they instantly reached round like necklaces then contracted like steel garrottes. The contraction did not stop until the metamorph had sliced through flesh and bone, fully decapitating their targets.

'Always remove the heads, *yes*?' Alvorecer remarked as its teams flew back to their colony.

Nathan was at first shocked beyond words, but when he could gather his thoughts it was to admonish Alvorecer, 'Why did you have to kill them? *And* you killed my last two warriors! They were on *our* side!!'

'Nathan...' Alvorecer stated simply, '*Nobody here*, but me, is on *your* side.'

Nathan stood there surrounded by the dead wondering what he should do now. The boys at the makeshift camp were unaware of what had happened at the pass.

Nathan cast his remote-view back to his grandmother. He realised there was little sense returning to her. She would only send him back to Tymbrenwal and then Queen Taminil would only send him out once more to seek treatment from Hascron the Healer.

As he watched what was going on in the throne-room he saw something very strange going on, not having been following her prayer-circle training. 'What *are* you up to Grandma?'

Xervren had Selbani standing in his prayer-circle, not joining hands but looking towards two gibren which had been brought into the throne-room. Around this prayer-circle of boys was an outer circle of older talents.

As Nathan watched the two gibren began to lift off the flagstones. Unnerved by going airborne the two animals began to struggle. Then suddenly they were clearly both in pain. He could not hear their honking. The struggles turned to panicked attempts to escape which soon became convulsions. Their flesh cracked and bled profusely. The blood pooled in globs, which defied gravity. Then the tearing flesh separated from the bones and the bones began to crack. It was like some sort of slow motion gravity defying disintegration.

'*Hell*!' Nathan gasped, 'That was gross!'

As he continued to watch, the remains of the beasts were dropped to the floor with a splash. Selbani stepped backwards to become part of the circle which he was ministering.

'And she complained about *me* making a mess on her floor!'

Nathan shook his head, still trying to comprehend what he was observing. It was only logical that prayer-circles could be used for purposes of good *or* evil. 'This cannot be good.'

Within the inner circle appeared a view of what looked to Nathan to be some bright chamber with a steeply curved floor like some skate-board park. He had never seen the like anywhere on Krewlornia, or Earth.

'Where *is* that Grandma?' he wondered aloud.

After some moments of watching and nothing more happening he grew impatient and his remote-viewing was turned instead to the old woman he thought could be Hoscron the Healer.

She was treating an unhappy looking young man who she had seated on a stool. The room was lined with shelves filled with pots which Nathan guessed contained herbal remedies.

Placing one hand on the crown of the young man's head and another between his shoulder blades, Hoscron bowed her head of long grey hair in concentration.

As Nathan watched, dust and leaves began to swirl up and around the two of them, caught up in some sort of draft. Hoscron's hair lifted up in the air current as if it were taking on a life of its own. After a few moments the swirling began to slow and Hoscron stepped away from the young man. He rose from the stool and turned towards her, clearly looking overjoyed. Whatever had troubled him was gone.

In that moment Nathan made his decision. 'We continue on to Hoscron the Healer,' he announced. 'Let's see now, what's the quickest way down?' It was a rhetorical question, not seeing anything quicker than the track he was on.

'You can go take a running jump,' said Alvorecer.

'Is that a refusal to continue?'

'No.'

Suddenly Nathan's metamorph suit took charge of his movement. He found himself take a running jump up from the track to a boulder. From that boulder he veered away from the track going quickly from one boulder to the next.

Looking ahead Nathan could see he was quickly approaching a very steep drop.

'Steady Alvorecer! I don't think this is a good route.' The metamorph kept him bounding headlong for the cliff edge ahead. 'Stop! I can see what is up ahead of us and there's no way down...*There's no way down*!...*What the hell do you think*...'

Together they leaped from the cliff. Nathan's shield and weapons contracted into the suit as it formed wings along his arms on down to his hips. At the same time a web-tail formed between his legs. It was like some advance form of sky-divers flying suit.

With the higher gravity he dropped much faster. Though the denser air and bigger wings compensated to a degree, it was going to be a messy landing unless Alvorecer was also good at parachute impressions.

'You need to look where we are going, Nathan, turning your head. *You're* the one with remote-viewing. *We're* just your wings.'

'Okay it's just over the brow of that hill there…we just past right over…there…down *there*…You've passed it!'

'Hey, *you're* the pilot.'

'Go back.'

Alvorecer banked round sharply and used their momentum to gain lift.

'The place in the trees there with the stone tiled roof.'

'Here you go.'

The tail and wings retracted then and from his shoulders Alvorecer spread a square chute above them.

Emily had never taken Nathan for any parachute practice but it had always been something he thought he would like to try some day. Luckily for him Alvorecer understood how to bring their companion in for a soft landing, immediately contracting back into the suit.

Alvorecer seemed to decide there was no need to recreate the Vamouror battle suit. It went instead for a matt black suit which appeared to finish at the neck but in actual fact transparently covered Nathan's head as it had been for a long time.

The change in appearance was not intended to fool Hoscron. However, it would not have fooled her anyway because Hoscron could clearly see Nathan's surrounding aura despite the layer of metamorph.

Before Nathan could introduce himself, Hoscron spoke knowingly. 'You are the *One.*'

'You speak Curumwalish.'

'I speak many languages of Krewlornia.'

'Why do you say that I am *the one*?'

'When the *One* comes down from the sky, it is *time.*'

'Time for what?'

'Come, child…Come into my home so that I may release the talents.'

'No I think you misunderstand. I have been sent here because I have a deformed aura.'

'Yes yes of course. Remove your bag and lie down on this table.'

'The bag contains a payment of gems for your service.'

'I will have no need of gems where I am going.'

Nathan was suddenly feeling less certain about this. The woman seemed a little *distracted*; in a world of her own. Nevertheless, he got onto the table as instructed.

'Just relax.' Hoscron placed one hand on Nathan's forehead the other on the centre of his chest.

'Princess Roshvik needs my aura *healed* so that I can become a suitable mate for her.' Nathan thought it best to brief her properly before she got started with anything.

'No no. Hush…The problem seems to be in the cells of your body. They are not fully *Harlash.*'

'Ah no…You see that's my metamorph.'

'Sshh!'

'I just want…'

'Sshh!!' Hoscron bowed her head. 'Your braelic is not fully formed so has been unable to initiate your talents.'

'Actually I have remote-viewing.'

'Well you certainly have no talent for doing as you are told, young man…Now be quiet. I must concentrate the energy if I am to bring alignment of the forces.'

Hoscron closed her eyes and focused.

The first thing Nathan noticed was the skitter of leaves off the floor and he began to wonder if this was all just some sort of telekinetic scam, whipping up the dust and making people believe their ills were then miraculously cured. However, he soon began to feel a heat throughout his body. It was not the pleasant warmth of a shot of alcohol. His skin began to crawl. This wasn't relaxing at all. He began to wonder if this was what it felt like to get microwaved.

'You know…I think I might pass…'

'Sshh.'

The discomfort became so intense, as the draft became a wind in the room Nathan decided to just get off the table. However, he found he could not. His muscles had been taken by a trembling paralysis.

'I think I'll just wait outside,' came Alvorecer's parting words as it poured away from the pain it was sharing, leaving Nathan naked on the table.

Nathan tried to respond but could not even speak now. The wind in the room became a roar, over which could be heard the sound of a crashing pot, then two more. The broken pots did not hit the floor but were taken around the room striking anything in their way. The debris filling air tore through the roof. The tiles and beams joined the smaller debris, as did the bag of gemstones.

Over Hoscron's home a great vortex grew, higher and higher into the sky, tearing the walls apart adding to the dust cloud of debris. It looked completely out of control to Alvorecer, now in girl form, stepping further and further away so as not to get swept up in it all.

The garden was lost with plants and paving slabs. Even trees were uprooted. They span through the air up and up before being dumped aside far away.

Nathan was no longer aware of the growing scene of destruction because he had fallen unconscious.

The sky grew dark. In all directions it now appeared to be revolving around what had been Hoscron's home. Alvorecer took shelter between two large boulders up the hillside a way. As an ex-Time-Slave, it knew that any attempt to intervene in this event would only be met with meta-interference. This was all exactly how it was meant to happen.

36

When Nathan regained consciousness, he did so as he had always done, keeping still, sensing his environment before opening his eyes or moving.

The most obvious thing of note was that he had survived Hoscron's treatment. The second most obvious point was that she had not. The old woman's lifeless form lay slumped over his chest.

Nathan began to notice a change to his vision. He could see his own aura. It looked amazing to him. Some extra spectral channel had been added to his remote-viewing. The colours and patterns swirled like some personal northern lights show that never ended.

He spotted other aura some way off. Some wary locals were now approaching the foot hills to investigate the storm now gone. He could see their auras, and they were different. He could also see the aura of Alvorecer emerging from shelter. This talent was like being able to view life energy. Poor Hoscron however had no aura.

Getting up from the undamaged table, Nathan lowered the woman's body to the ground. As he did this he became aware of something else new. It was as if he had developed an extension to his kinaesthetic sense of form. Not only did he have a keener sense of the extents of his own body, he could feel the extent of the dead woman too, and the table.

Stepping down to the floor and away from the table he lost his kinaesthetic connection with the table. Stepping away from the body he similarly disconnected from it. He felt this sense connecting and disconnecting with the floor as he walked across the ruins towards Alvorecer. He didn't like the connection with the ground, it felt like a distraction. However, he found with focus that he could disconnect by choice and limit what was included in his new talent for connectedness.

'She died, Alvorecer.'

'I know.' The metamorph offered its arms as if in comfort but the hug immediately covered Nathan's nakedness, becoming matt black from head to foot.

Nathan could sense the contact as he had done for so long now and took comfort from its closeness. However, now there was something else, as his extended kinaesthetic sense seemed to make Alvorecer more a part of him, bonding them like some duel entity.

'How do you feel, Nathan?'

'Like I'm part of you.'

'Good. We are together for always now.'

'Alvorecer…Did you know this would happen?'

'Yes.'

'That Hoscron would *die*?'

'Yes it was her time.'

'Was there no other way?'

'To succeed with your gene-therapy, no, but she knew what was coming. She had foreseen it a long time ago and accepted it. Our

404

approach from the sky was the sign that it was time to do what she had to do.'

'But why me?'

'Because now…*we* are the *One*.'

'What does that *even* mean?'

'We are the bringer of *death*.'

'*No*! I don't want us to be the responsible for anymore death. I want us to *help* people.'

'And so we shall.'

'I think we should bury Hoscron.'

'Bury? You know bodies are not wasted on Krewlornia. Locals are coming anyway. They will take care of her with a ritual feast in her honour.'

'That feels wrong.'

'Not to the Harlash.'

'Okay then…Let's get out of here.'

'Good idea. Where shall we go first?'

'Well I suppose we should head back to Tymbrenwal.'

'Why?'

'Princess Roshvik *expects* me to return.'

'Is that what *you* want?'

'Well no, of course not. What *I'd* like is for us to go home…To Earth.'

'Then there is little point wasting time with Tymbrenwal.'

'Agreed.'

Still with no plan for their near future together they made tracks up the mountainside to the pass.

By the time the locals reached the ruins of Hoscron's home there was no sign of Nathan and Alvorecer. They saw no explanation for the freak weather that had destroyed the old woman's home yet left her oddly uninjured, just dead.

Intrigued by his new kinaesthetic talent, Nathan occasionally picked things up along the way. Whatever he took hold of, plant or rock, could either be accepted as connected to him or disconnected. It was just not clear what use this talent could be. He could not view inside what he held or gain any further understanding of its nature with his probing mind.

He tried to talk to Alvorecer with his thoughts in case it was something which only worked when connected with conscious organisms but the metamorph did not respond.

Interestingly he seemed to notice something when he *wasn't* focusing on an object. The sensation was like an electrical charge. If he focused on the charge it began to build up like excitement. This *charge* came from within his braelic. Hoscron had healed some defect he had been unaware of. However, the building charge spread out from his braelic through his kinaesthetic connection to include Alvorecer.

'Ooo Nathan, what *are* you doing?'

'There is something else new about me. I'm trying to figure it out. Sorry if it disturbs you.'

'No it wasn't exactly *unpleasant*. It was sort of exciting…like preparing to take action.'

'Yes you're right…It's like some super-charged adrenaline buzz, of expectation. What do you think it could be?'

'We will find out when the time is right.'

Reaching the top of the pass the bandit boys had looted the dead bodies and carried one away. However, scared by the recent freak weather they remained hidden in a cave on the south-facing side of the mountain ridge.

Neither Nathan nor Alvorecer would be consuming any of the dead but both knew they would need food and water at some point.

They found a mountain stream to drink from and Alvorecer contained some for later.

Standing up from the stream, Nathan suggested, 'Fancy seeing how far we can glide?'

'Sure.'

Bounding up onto an outcrop of rock they ran across to the edge and then off, sprouting wings.

Hugging close to the mountainside, where thermals developed from the warmth of the sun, they gained some additional lift. However, as they began to bank further round, to the north, they broke away to head south again.

They flew some distance across savanna, passing over a herd of animals, before putting down with a change from wings to canopy.

By late afternoon they had both eaten some fruits from scrubland bushes they had passed. Then as the sun dropped, Nathan suggested they make camp.

'Since I haven't made my mind up what we should do yet, I think maybe I should sleep on it.'

'Sure. How about over there near those rocks.'

Alvorecer provided Nathan with a tent which from the outside looked just like a large rock in the ground. Inside the metamorph provided a bed which Nathan thought had to be the most comfortable one he had ever had to sleep on.

He fell asleep pondering over the purpose of his new powers. His remote-viewing still seemed to be his most useful talent. This train of thought led him to wonder what had really been achieved by his fateful visit to Hoscron? Many people would now miss the healer.

The next morning, with no waking epiphany, Nathan turned his mind instead to food using his remote-viewing to look for prey.

Breaking camp, Alvorecer pulled itself together, then joined with Nathan.

A little later they came upon a massive maggot-like creature called a plambac, basking in the morning sun. Nathan recognised it as something which travellers had occasionally brought to the castle to trade. Plambac tasted better than they looked though did need cooking.

Nathan had never tried to capture one before, however. As they drew close the big bug shuffled surprisingly quickly down its burrow.

'So much for that,' said Nathan.

'Allow me.' The suit extruded a tentacle from his left arm which shot down the burrow.

The tentacle immediately reappeared with the plambac quite dead and perfectly skewered on the barbed appendage.

'Neat. Now all I need to do is cook it.'

'*Really*? Not me.' The right arm extended a blade, chopped the plambac in half and before it had time to fall changed the blade to a bag to contain the loose half.

'I suppose you are going to digest that in front of me now.'

'No. This is *yours*,' Alvorecer lifted the bag then shifted it up Nathan's arm and round to his back before lifting the left hand. 'This is mine.'

Nathan watched the skewered half become smothered by a coating of black, glad he could not view what was happening inside. However, he could feel a fluid movement over his body as the morphocytes all took turns to share in the meal.

'Well I better look for something to make a fire with then.'

Nathan soon had kindling for a fire and with both hands free tried to create friction between a stick and a larger piece of dry plant material.

After only a couple of Nathan's failed attempts, having now digested most of its meal, Alvorecer said 'Let me help.'

Surrounding the stick in a loosely held fist the metamorph colony created a vortex around the shaft motorising the stick. The speed and pressure created on the plant material soon created an ember which ignited the kindling.

As Nathan and Alvorecer sat watching the plambac roast for his breakfast, Nathan said 'I wonder what Grandma is up to?'

Without even basic technology on Krewlornia, such as the written word, progress of the Harlash was limited and slow. They learned through songs and stories and relied upon prayer to give hope of control over their existence.

So it was little wonder that Queen Xervren had never quite managed to comprehend the concepts of time and space from her years of observations. Nevertheless, she had decided that today was *the day* of retribution.

From the moment that she had first viewed her daughter Xaviol on Earth, she had tasted the bitterness of frustration. Though she would not quit her practice with the prayer-circles, it only increased her bitterness that she failed to bring her home.

She tried to modify and improve the function of her prayer-circles with new and stronger talents but all in vain. She had been unable to communicate with Xaviol to tell her she loved her and needed her back, never mind affect a rescue by teleportation.

Each time Xervren felt she was close to succeeding in any meaningful way the mist, through which the remote-view portal formed would simply close back over. This was meta-interference; her attempt to interfere with what *Time* dictated.

She saw no reason, beyond coercion, why her daughter would work alongside the very demons who switched her at birth. However, time and again, as Xervren watched on, Xaviol was there with the male one and his portal.

Xervren had killed the female, posing as Ata the one more commonly called Dawn, and yet had seen this very demon again through the prayer-circle portal. Time-independence of the Apple planetoid, from whence the Time-Slaves came, was too difficult a concept for her to grasp.

From her throne Xervren commanded that the mission begin. It had been foretold that the boys would succeed with their mission. However, Xervren had learned not to trust her subordinates. Some would only tell her what they thought she wanted to hear.

Xervren had put to death a number of talents who had not met her expectations with their sooth-saying or time-tracking. So everyone was filled with some nervous energy on this critical day.

Selbani stood surrounded by all the boys he was soon to minister. They in turn were surrounded by the outer prayer-circle. Xervren descended the steps reaching out for hands to close the circle.

Everyone began to pray, the chanting rose to the ceiling and bounced off the walls. It all sounded more powerful that day than it ever had before, giving confidence to all involved.

Suddenly, almost too soon, the tight group of boys vanished with a *whumph*! The vacuum of their teleporting almost sucked the remaining prayer-circle into the bowl-like hole left behind in the flagstones. However, their chanting and Xervren's ministered prayers did not cease.

In place of the boys the mist thickened over the hole in the flagstones before parting from the centre. Then as the first sign of the coming success the remote-view within the prayer-circle was the sight through Selbani's eyes. This view was no longer directed by Xervern, and as such was dependent upon Selbani holding to the agreed plan. The Queen had never managed this before, at distance. She had coached Selbani in what he was to do upon arrival. She prayed that he would not fail her.

The first thing Selbani noticed was the lack of gravity. Turning to check the other boys he almost bounced. Nevertheless, it was clear that the boys were all present.

The second thing he noticed was that they were all imprisoned in a large cage containing other children. He did not panic however. This was just as Xervren had warned it would be.

Shortly, Xaviol appeared and opened the cage to free them, directing them to head down a tunnel.

As Selbani passed Xaviol he delivered his short message from the Queen. 'Your mother Xervren wants you to know she loves you very much and has tried everything in her power to bring you home.'

Xaviol smiled, but in that smile Selbani saw only failure. She had not understood her native tongue. If only Xervren had taken the interest in Nathan to learn English.

Xaviol had assumed the boy was just thanking her for saving them all from certain death in the Adrenochrome processing caves. She waved Selbani on up the tunnel.

Xervren lost sight of her for a while as Selbani move to where the male Time-Slave waited. Selbani stood behind a line of other children but behind him waited all of the Harlash boys.

Shortly, Xaviol came into view again and stood next to the Time-Slave. Then a magic door opened next to them. There was a look of routine to how Xaviol wave the first of them up to the portal.

As the first child approached, Selbani saw the door open onto a scene which made this child gasp with joy and dash through. The scene changed again for the next child and the next, but never their gasps of joy or the speed at which the children leaped to safety.

Soon it was Selbani's turn. Xaviol paid no attention as he reached her. She was deep in conversation with the Time-Slave, but then Selbani was concentrating fully on the door anyway.

The portal changed to the scene they had been praying for over many *faces*; the very bright room with the curved floor. Selbani leaped through.

The floor had slightly more gravity to it than Selbani had experienced with his short time on Earth. However, it felt different as he tried to walk up the curvature. Everywhere he stood felt like it was the bottom of the bowl.

The ceiling of glowing tubes was the source of the bright light, casting no clear shadows onto the curved floor. Selbani turned to look back at the portal and watched the last of the prayer-circle boys come through. Then the portal closed, to take the remaining children elsewhere.

Even though the portal connection to the Apple planetoid had closed, Xervern and her chanting circle in Curumwal could still see through Selbani's eyes. Xervren was pleased by this further step towards success.

Xervren had to control her emotions. She could not afford to lose this circle to circle link. She needed to see her retribution served.

The boys formed a circle around Selbani, joining hands and chanting. The acoustics of this chamber sounded nothing like the stone throne-room. Their voices somehow lacked power but each of them knew they must not waver.

Selbani started to lift off the floor and as he did so he reached up for a section of ceiling. Just as he made contact with a tube the female Time-Slave walked into view and stopped. She just stood there watching, in a suit of white armour, but saying nothing.

It was disturbing to be watched in this way, caught red handed. The silence seemed to hurt more than angry words. Selbani knew he had to concentrate. Knowing his Queen would see all through his eyes.

The ceiling felt soft and warm like a living thing. He had no idea it had a name and that if he spoke that name whatever he wished for would come true, *sometime*.

The door reappeared and the male came through, across from the female. Selbani noticed a nod between them. He was certain they were about to act, but with one final part of the prayer the Queen's retribution was served.

Selbani and the boys were terrified by what happened next, however neither Time-Slave were surprised. This was not what Queen Xervren had said would happen.

The ceiling certainly disintegrated just as intended but then everything else began collapsing and the boys chanting turned to cries of fear. Selbani lost his concentration and called out to Xervren to bring them home but it was too late.

Xervren lost the connection. Nevertheless, she was content in the knowledge that she had taken her revenge and the switchers of babies were no more.

What was not observed was the totality of the collapse. Some of the boys began crying out for their mothers, including Selbani. Dawn and Destiny did nothing to save the day, they couldn't. This was how it was always meant to end. It was like an implosion beyond anything imaginable. It was not just the destruction of reality engine *What-If*, the floor shook and fell upwards too, taking them all with it. The whole Apple planetoid collapsed into its core. Even that was not an end to the mayhem however.

The whole universe was collapsing, everything crushing and rushing beyond the speed of light to a gathering of black holes. This was where the multiverse singularity was brought about. Even the super-entity known to many as Imogen Powers could not stop this.

Oblivious to this distant end, Xervren dismissed her prayer-circle and turned to ascend the steps to her throne. She felt no remorse or guilt for what she had done with the children. She had never intended that the boys return. She considered them as expendable as any boys.

Nathan's remote-view of this activity in the throne-room put an end to any thought of breakfast. As the view through Selbani's eyes winked out and mist rolled in to cover the hole in the flagstones, anger ignited in Nathan.

'*No*!!'

That feeling of electric charge which Nathan had been wondering about spread out from his braelic in an instant. It was like a power-up to all that his kinaesthetic sense was connected.

Nathan and Alvorecer immediately shrunk to sub-atomic particle size, shifted through space, then came back to size. With barely a whisper in the air, they reappeared right in front of the throne, facing Xervren as she came up the steps, exactly where Nathan had been remote-viewing the unfolding scene from.

'Nathan. What are you doing here?!' Xervren couldn't believe he had just appeared. She thought he must have been there the whole time watching while she was busy ministering.

'Bring the boys back!'

'It cannot be done. They are dead,' she dismissed his demand and attempted to step up and around him to her throne.

However, Nathan blocked her way. 'I *promised* those boys, *and* their families, that they would return home!'

'More fool *you*. Never promise anyone anything Nathan. Promises are a nonsense which can never be guaranteed. Besides, I don't see what all the *fuss* is about. Though those children did me a great service, at the end of the day they were *only* boys.'

Alvorecer had monitored Nathan's brain activity long enough now, though his warrior training, to know he was imagining a blade in each hand.

'Wherever you sent them, it is *you* who have gone too far. *You* have crossed a line Grandma!'

With his kinaesthetic sense Nathan felt the blades grow in his hands. The rest was all second nature. The blades passed before him in a scissor action putting a stop to Xervren's rule. She tried to reach for her own blade in defence, but she was far too slow. Her body tumbled down the steps to come to rest in the bowl-like hole in the flagstones.

'Always remove the head unless required.'

Epilogue

Five Earth-years later.
Though Nathan never truly doubted that he had done the right thing that day, he never forgot the last look on his grandmother's face. It was not shock but pity.

There were certainly more difficult times and decisions ahead as Nathan declared himself King of Curumwal. Krewlornia had never had a land ruled by a King; a man with strange ideas yet so powerful that he feared no woman.

When Princess Roshvik heard what had become of her mate-to-be she wanted him all the more but he would not hear of it.

Queen Taminil sent a small army to bring Nathan to Tymbrenwal but he sent a warning back with these warriors. Teleporting about randomly among them, using his kinaesthetic connection, he removed their weapons and clothes. Unnerved by this magic they returned to Tymbrenwal shamed by their failure and nakedness.

This only angered Taminil because a man could not be seen to embarrass a woman especially not a Queen. So she sent in assassins. However, stealth was not possible against remote-viewing, and this time there was no warning. A swarm of bugs was seen to remove these women's heads, sending a firm message to all of Krewlornia of dark magic.

However, Nathan did not limit himself to the concerns of Curumwal, taking an interest the whole planet. When not dealing with situations across Krewlornia, Nathan's spare time was spent learning more about prayer-circles and how to minister them. He remained desperate to find a way of getting back the boys Xervren had sent on her suicide mission.

As he learned how different talents could be used to create specially purposed prayer-circles he began to try new combinations. When word of this got out, men with knowledge of Nathan's attitude towards equality came to offer advice. These men would never have considered offering such advice to a Queen. One such person explained that it was possible to track back through time. This was something Xervren had implied to Nathan was *not* possible. When Nathan asked his closest people, including Alvorecer, why he had not been told this before, they simply pointed out that he had never asked.

Nathan tried to be patient with his people. The sexist culture took a long time to improve, because the Harlash perceived *their* way of life as normal. He had offered Garowak a position within the castle but Garowak had turned him down, preferring to be tending his gibren in what he considered to be fresher air of the swamps.

Learning to perceive people's talents by their aura also took its time. Nathan used his remote-viewing and teleportation to bring together the best talents that Krewlornia had to offer.

Another commitment he made was to continue searching the stars in the hope of discovering where Earth was. None of Queen

Xervren's *distant planet* prayer-circle had known its whereabouts. Xervren had always kept *that* knowledge to herself.

Nevertheless, using the *distant planet* prayer-circle to search for the aura of life on other worlds, Nathan finally located Earth with its hundreds of Nathan clones. It had helped that Harlash auras were brighter than Human auras. Nathan made a mental note of which constellation Earth was within.

However, he was deeply disturbed by what he saw there. Needing to make sense of how life on Earth had got into such a state he brought his time-trackers into the prayer-circle.

His clones had been seen to escape from their Australian bunker by other Nathans with remote-viewing from other countries. This initiated a mass break-out from all of the bunkers across the world.

At first the humans did not seem to know what to make of hundreds of the same boy appearing everywhere. However, as all the Nathan's learned together by watching one another interact with the humans, the killing began. Anyone who posed any threat was set upon and killed by the Harlash.

The SOVs informed the security services around the world that one of Helga Sturmfeld's projects had developed a problem. They knew that police forces would not cope with these children. However, even joining forces with the military the SOVs were hard pushed to remove the Nathans. The worry was that ten years on it might be found that they could interbreed with humans.

The world had gone insane. Children had always been among the victims of wars but now these young Nathan's were the enemy. They used emotions to manipulate human sympathy in order to get their way. As long as they got whatever they wanted people were relatively safe. However, in their immaturity these youngsters didn't really know what they wanted and had never been socialised to value the life of others.

Watching this nightmare unfold from Krewlornia, Nathan was deeply disturbed by this turn of events snowballing out of control. He had to find a way of putting a stop to it all.

He was mature enough to know he couldn't just go with his first window of opportunity. This would have to be done right first time and that needed a great deal of observation and thought first.

He used his time-trackers to roll back to the cyclone where Xervren had taken him from the jail in Broome. He watched his father and himself being brought into the police station. He tracked forwards to what happened after he had Night-Ported away. He saw how upset his father was. He seemed totally traumatised.

In the following *faces* Nathan repeatedly used prayer-circles to exhaustion. Like with his teleporting there was little sense of physical exhaustion but the concentration required for extended use of his and their talents was mentally tiring.

Nevertheless, he used his circles to track his father and the others with him to the secret bunker. There he revisited the scene of his father's murder by the older clone which

Xervren had shown him so long ago. After that Nathan had everyone take a break for a couple of days. They all had to get their strength back and he had to remind himself that thanks to the time-tracking talents the urgency he felt for saving his father was not real.

Alvorecer also watched over what Nathan's prayers were ministering and warned him to be very careful. Meta-interference was to be expected to prevent him doing anything that was not meant to happen. So Nathan had to be prepared for failures.

Nevertheless, apparent success in changing the course of history would actually be the creation of a division in reality. This was where two universes went their different ways. Alvorecer explained that there would *always* be the one where his father died, but Nathan might create an alternative where he saved his father. He needed to consider what all of the consequences of that might be though, *before* he acted. Once an action was attempted it might not be possible to return to that point in time again, like muddying the water.

Taking this hint when Nathan reconvened his prayer-circle a few days later he continued to be more investigative.

He decided to check on what became of Stan during the cyclone. In the hospital at Bonney Downs, Stan and other patients had been moved to the centre of the ground floor for safety. This had been the right move by staff as the storm ripped the roof off and smashed the windows in with flying debris. They all survived with some minor injuries, doing better than others elsewhere in town who they also looked to help in the aftermath. Colt's car in the police pound, like others in the town, was wrecked. Nevertheless, when Stan was discharged from hospital he managed to get to the gold Nathan had hidden for him.

Nathan decided there was no need to tamper with time there he had not discovered any Harlash talents for weather control.

Nathan then tried to trace the Adrenochrome caves where Xervren had made her insertion of the boys. However, not having developed x-ray vision and not having seen enough of the cave system through Selbani's eyes, it continued to evade him.

While human men grew beards Nathan had never seen a harlash man with a beard, only grey hair. His hair was a long way off turning grey but he hoped he would find a way of saving the boys before it did.

Because his promise had been broken, there continued to be animosity towards Nathan as King. Despite all the good he tried to do across Krewlornia, he was not seen as a man to be trusted.

As the *faces* passed by, Nathan started to become disillusioned with what could be done using prayer. Again and again his time-tracking remote-viewing and actions were frustrated by meta-interference clouding the portal within his circles.

'Alvorecer, tell me honestly...Will I *ever* manage to save the boys?'

'No.'

'Could you not have told me this before now?'

'No.'

'Because of the meta-interference?'

'No. You had to know in your heart that you had done your best to put things right. Otherwise, had I told you this earlier and you had not tried, there would always have been some concern that you could have done more for the boys and their families.'

'I see...So does the same apply to saving Dad?'

'Not necessarily. However, it would still be problematic locating the right insertion point to create the correct *division event*.'

'I find it intensely frustrating that meta-interference prevents *you* from being part of my prayer-circles with what your remaining Time-Slave knowledge could add to the mix.'

'That is the way it is, Nathan. Even Xervren would not have been able to bring a Time-Slave into the mix.'

'What if I teleport a prayer-circle along with me to help sort out Earth?'

'Though Xervren had the power to teleport Selbani and his prayer-circle back to the Adrenochrome caves, you *do not*.'

'What do you mean? I'm *way* more powerful than Grandma *ever* was.'

'Not with everything...She was the only one in Harlash history to be able to bring someone here from a distant world. Even then she had to do that in stages. She *could* have teleported you back, just never would have. So the situation is this, once we are physically disconnected from your prayer-circle there will be no way for us to return here.'

'I'm not sure why we would ever *want* to come back here. However, won't I be strong enough, using kinaesthetic connection and teleporting, to one day be able to take my prayer-circle with me?'

'No. You will be limited in the mass you can successfully teleport. Those you could take with you, even with the amplifier talents in the circle, would still not be enough to get you back. Plus, of course, none of them would want to leave their families and friends to live on an alien world which is still struggling with women's rights.'

As time across the multiverse continued to bring about rights *and* wrongs as *division events*, other versions of the Apple planetoid ran in parallel with What-If at their core.

Destiny had brought about one such *division event* when he returned the rude girl, Sharon Steinstien, to the wrong time. Because of this event she never met private detective Dennis Damon Tandy, as a result of this he never ended up in space getting mind-wiped by the Star Cancer horde. The consequences of this were that the New Washington truck driver, Dawn Summers, never bumped into John Doe. As a result she never saved Earth from the metamorph invasion. Neither did she get to create Destiny with *What-If*.

The Earth was instead saved by a Russian gymnast who became infected, rather than digested, by a metamorph. This was Sonia Voronsova. It was Sonia who ended up a lone Time-Slave on the Apple planetoid, where on occasions she intervened in events involving

Juliz Starshooter and her team of Ochoba Space Spetsnaz.

In the secret bunker security control room Maeve had been asking 'What if we get out and just lock the clones in for a better supported team to sort out?'

The security man shook his head. 'The clones will work out how to get out before that could be organised. Their problem solving skills are through the roof, not to mention their ability to kill. It has been like being with a ticking time-bomb working in this facility. I told Miss Sturmfeld my concerns on a number of occasions. *She* should have listened. I cannot stress enough how unlike human seven year-olds they are, and the older one is even brighter.'

'The *older* one?'

'Yes. The one Miss Sturmfeld put in with Gavin. He is eleven.'

'Shit!' Emily didn't think much for Gavin's chances now. She looked to the screen where Gavin was seen lying on his bed watching the TV. A dark figure came into view, a heavy-set man. They touched Gavin on his right shoulder then both were gone. 'Has your clone learned how to teleport?'

'No. That wasn't the clone... *That's* the clone.'

The eleven year old came into view head tilted, remote-viewing for where Gavin could have gone, unable to understand what had just happened. Shortly the dark figure returned but only for an instant. Just long enough to remove the clone's head.

'What the *hell*?' Maeve couldn't believe it. It was like watching some special effects camera trick.

'I urr...' The security man had no idea what to say.

Ethan, Emily, Disney and the security staff looked to the bank of screens for answers. In one corridor they saw a swarm of large flies. On another screen were spotted the bodies of clones who had been decapitated. On another screen the dark figure reappeared, dispatched a lone clone and disappeared again, reappearing elsewhere.

'What is going on, Emily?' Ethan thought she might know.

'Never seen anything like it before,' there was a tone of admiration to her voice.

Gavin had reappeared on a bed. It was not his home. It would never be safe to return there. He thought he was just dreaming and would continue to think this for a while.

The dark figure's mask cleared. 'It's *me,* Dad. The *real* Nathan. I know I look a lot older than I did a few of your days ago, *and* sound different, but I've had to come from the future to save you all. You will be safe on this island which I have prepared for the three of us. I will be back shortly to explain more but my partner and I have to put things right first.'

Nathan vanished before Gavin could gather his still traumatised thoughts.

Watching the screens from the security control room the chaos and confusion only seemed to last a few minutes. This would be followed by surviving staff moving through the bunker also trying to figure out what had happened there.

'What *was* that?' asked Disney.

'Well, I *believe* what we are seeing here,' announced Maeve, with certainty and relief, 'is the return of *Fantasma da morte*.'